RIFT ZONE

RIFT ZONE

RAELYNN HILLHOUSE

A TOM DOHERTY ASSOCIATES BOOK
NEW YORK

This is a work of fiction. All the characters and events portrayed in this novel are either fictitious or are used fictitiously.

RIFT ZONE

This book is printed on acid-free paper.

A Forge Book
Published by Tom Doherty Associates, LLC
175 Fifth Avenue
New York, NY 10010

www.tor.com

Forge® is a registered trademark of Tom Doherty Associates, LLC.

Library of Congress Cataloging-in-Publication Data

Hillhouse, Raelynn.
Rift zone / Raelynn Hillhouse.—1st ed.
p. cm.
"A Tom Doherty Associates book."
ISBN 0-765-31013-9
EAN 978-0765-31013-2
1. Smugglers—Fiction. 2. Communists—Fiction. 3. Birthfathers—Fiction. 4. Europe, Eastern—Fiction. 5. Missing persons—Fiction. 6. Berlin (Germany)—Fiction. 7. Fathers and daughters—Fiction. 8. Americans—Europe, Eastern—Fiction. I. Title.

PS3608.I44R57 2004
813'.6—dc22

2003071102

First Edition: August 2004

Printed in the United States of America

0 9 8 7 6 5 4 3 2 1

To my mother, Donna Hillhouse, who refused to allow me to travel alone to the Soviet Union—so she went with me.
And to my father, Charles Hillhouse,
who was smart enough to stay home.

ACKNOWLEDGMENTS

Friends, family and colleagues have given of themselves beyond my wildest imagination and have made this novel take on dimensions that I could never have reached alone. I have them to thank for the strengths of this book.

Jim Froneberger, Lt. Cmdr. USN ret., my favorite bomb maker and storyteller, taught me more than I should ever know about explosives. Former Pan Am pilot, Bill "Flyboy" North once strayed into Soviet airspace as well as into my email box. Soviet MIGs didn't catch him, but I was lucky enough to snag him as a consultant, e-pen pal and virtual flying instructor. My dear friend, co-worker and fellow black operative, Michael Lukson, was a constant source of moral as well as tech support. Mike once told me that "real programmers don't do Web sites." Maybe not. But it's a truly special friend who learns two new computer languages to give someone such a phenomenal Web site as www.InternationalThrillers.com.

Gayle Lynds' steadfast confidence in my work gave me the assurance to take some particularly bold steps—and thanks to her wise counsel, they turned out to be just the right ones. Without her generous support, this novel would never have been published. Gayle is rightfully the godmother of this book. My agent, Bob Diforio, is a consummate professional and a delight to work with. He has been simply awesome. Thanks to Bob's tireless efforts, my first novel was not only published, but published well.

Sarah Wang's insightful critique, undying enthusiasm and perseverance through various stages of the manuscript have been invaluable. Former Finnair Moscow bureau chief and the only person I know who has ever smuggled himself out of the Soviet Union and back into it again on the same weekend, Timo Valtonen provided key Soviet airport and border details. I am also grateful to Captain Jerold Ogami-Van Camp of Aloha Airlines for letting me crawl around the floor of his flight deck. Many others contributed to the success of the project, including Maryann Palumbo, Daniel Siguara, Florence Jacobson, Jacqueline Deval and Danny Baror.

My warmest thanks go to Brian Callaghan for believing in me and championing the book. The staff at Tor, including Eric Raab, Nicole Kalian, Elena Stokes, Linda Quinton, Kathleen Fogarty and others behind the scenes, has done truly exceptional work. I am particularly in debt to Tom Doherty for once again challenging conventional wisdom in publishing—this time taking a chance on a Cold War thriller, some fifteen years after John le Carré declared them dead.

My family sacrificed countless evenings and weekends while I was absorbed with this project. I've often joked that I did it despite everyone—dogs barking, the Food Network blaring, chores demanding—but I could only follow my dream because they are my dream. My deepest love and gratitude belong to Cynthia Curatalo and my three furry muses, LynnDy, Jordan and Lily.

PROLOGUE

VNUKOVO AIRPORT, MOSCOW, USSR
1961

A Soviet border guard rummaged through the mother's battered suitcase, flinging clothes onto the floor of the customs hall while the toddler clutched her bear.

"We know." The official tapped the luggage. "Next time."

The mother plopped her two hundred pounds of hillbilly dignity onto the stone tiles and gathered their belongings as if sorting laundry on their front porch in Arkansas. The child studied a portrait of Khrushchev hanging on the beaten plaster wall and trembled until she noticed the bald man in the picture was smiling at her. She shyly smiled back and wondered if her daddy had looked like him.

Late that night, in a cemetery on the outskirts of the city, the girl and her mother met God's chosen and squeezed into an abandoned mausoleum for a secret meeting. "Come on, sweet pea," the mother said, "Jesus needs Teddy now." She yanked the animal from the child and plunged a dagger into the bear, sacrificing it to her god. Like entrails from a freshly butchered hog, stuffing burst from its belly. The believers shouted praises as she sank her hand into the gut, pulled out a New Testament and raised it toward the heavens.

No one noticed the terror in the little girl's eyes.

When the girl was old enough to understand that the Soviet state feared her mother, she realized she and the communists would share a lifelong bond.

PART 1

BETWEEN BERLINS

The Wall will stand another hundred years.
—ERICH HONECKER, BERLIN 1989

CHAPTER ONE

OLD JEWISH QUARTER, EAST BERLIN
TUESDAY, APRIL 18, 1989

The face of Stalin smirked at her from the bottom of a porcelain soup tureen as she bargained with an aging East German couple in the musty storage room of the Patschkes' millinery shop. A dozen mannequins peered from the shadows like faceless skinheads. She picked up a teacup by its awkward hammer-and-sickle–shaped handle. Before the communists, Dresden's master craftsmen had designed the world's finest china for European imperial courts. She cradled the cup and touched their humiliation. But it was a vintage piece, a testament to the pain of modern Germany and extremely marketable.

And Faith Whitney wanted it.

"You're a good customer, Frau Professor, so we'll make you a special offer. One thousand West mark. It's a complete service, immaculate condition, genuine Meissen." Herr Patschke's tiny round glasses slid to a stop on the hook of his nose.

Faith had only twenty-three minutes until a rendezvous, but reminded herself of Hakan's rule of negotiations: *Slow business is good business.* The

Patschkes admired efficiency almost as much as she did, so she forced herself to lean back in the wobbly chair and sip gritty East German coffee.

"Only two sets were commissioned for Marshal Stalin's seventieth birthday." Frau Patschke took the teacup from Faith and wiped her fingerprints from it. "It is pristine."

"And this is the only complete set in existence. One night at his dacha, Stalin hurled the other at his Politburo," Herr Patschke said without a smile and then leaned over and whispered, "Rumor has it this marked the beginning of more purges."

Herr Patschke nodded to his wife, his double chin swelling like a pigeon puffing its neck. Frau Patschke pulled a skeleton key from the pocket of her housedress and waddled to a chest. She removed a mahogany box and set it on the table. An eagle was carved into the lid; the bird of prey's talons clutched a swastika. Frau Patschke flicked open the gold latch. Inside the silk-lined box, crystal goblets sparkled even in the light of the single bare bulb.

A sudden chill was all Faith needed to authenticate the Nazi stemware as she picked one up with a tissue. A frosted engraving was identical to the emblem on the box. She hated contaminating her apartment with fascist trash, but this set merited sealed bids. "As usual, your taste is exquisite, but I'm in Leipzig soon and I have luck finding merchandise there more within my budget. If there's nothing more, I'll have to excuse myself." She spoke in unaccented German and stood, compelling herself to look away.

"Bohemian crystal, very lovely, very special. They were a gift to the Führer for the liberation of the Czech lands." Frau Patschke held a goblet in front of Faith's face and flicked her middle finger against it.

Nothing with a swastika should ring so clear.

"Tell you what. I'll give you one thousand for both the plates and the glasses."

The Patschkes squinted at each other while Faith rummaged through her oversized purse. She removed a camera and stole a glance at her watch.

Frau Patschke raised an eyebrow. "Is that one of those American models that make the instant photos?" Herr Patschke slipped his arm around his wife's sizeable waist, pressed his cheek against hers and grinned.

"A real Polaroid." Faith snapped the picture and the camera spit out the photo.

The Patschkes huddled together spellbound as the image materialized. He pointed to the snapshot. "Look, Hilda! Amazing. Simply amazing. Do you realize the private photos we could make with this?"

"Fritz!"

"If you include this camera—" Herr Patschke began.

"And plenty of film," Frau Patschke said.

"*Ja, ja.* Both for one thousand, five hundred West," Herr Patschke said.

Faith pursed her lips. "One thousand, three hundred."

"Wonderful." Herr Patschke shook her hand and snatched the Polaroid. "Smile, *Liebchen.*"

"I'd like you to use some special packing materials. Plus I need this to fit into three separate packages so it seems like I've got books. Bubble wrap, cardboard, then standard pink paper on the outside would be best." Faith placed a roll of imported bubble wrap onto the table.

Frau Patschke divided the Stalin service into two parcels while Herr Patschke measured a length of the coarse pink paper used in East German bookstores, but it ran out before he could finish the Nazi crystal. Frau Patschke handed him some newsprint with line drawings of vacuum tubes and slogans praising East German scientific advancements.

"Don't you have any more of the pink? I was counting on it." Faith fidgeted in her seat.

"I'm sorry. We are short right now."

Herr Patschke bound the two pink-wrapped boxes together and loaded all three onto a suitcase trolley Faith had brought with her. Like a child playing with a retractable tape measure, Herr Patschke stretched the bungee strap as far as he could, let go of it and then snickered as it snapped back.

He insisted on helping Faith with the packages. He pulled the cart through the labyrinth of their storerooms and removed the CLOSED sign from the front window. He paused with his hand on the doorknob and glanced back over his shoulder. "She didn't want me to say anything, but I believe you should know. Two men stopped by last week and inquired after you. They had no interest in what you buy—only in how you move things. Naturally, we told them nothing. Be cautious, Frau Doktor."

Privately run shops with brightly painted façades dotted the streets of the old Jewish quarter. A hunched woman with church-lady blue hair examined books in a display window of a Christian bookstore, one of the handful tolerated by the state. Her head moved as she watched Faith's reflection in the plate-glass window. Faith hurried away, invigorated by the sense of threat that permeated East Berlin like a foggy mist. Her blouse was damp from sweat and nerves.

She waited alongside two East German punks staring at the red pedestrian light and ignoring the empty street. Their purple hair stood straight up from their heads as though the hair itself were trying to escape their gaunt bodies. When she stepped from the sidewalk before the light turned green, they scowled at her. Not wanting to call attention to herself, she stepped back up and reassured herself she had three minutes before the window closed.

She dragged the heavy cart along the irregular cobblestones. The packages shifted off-center as it bounced along, making it difficult to maneuver, but she had no time to stop. She rushed past a long line of parked cars where a dirty Mercedes with red diplomatic plates stuck out among the tiny fiberglass Trabants.

One minute. Faith was watching the broken sidewalk ahead when she noticed a pair of legs. On cue, she stumbled. An African man tried to catch her, but she fell, raking her hand across the rough stones. She intentionally tipped the cart until the packages tumbled to the ground.

The man reached under her arm to steady her. The diamonds in his gold rings glistened. "So sorry, sister," he said in African-accented English. "You all right?"

"No major damage. Bruises add character."

"Let me have a look."

"Don't worry about it." She pulled her hand back. It burned so badly she hoped the muscle wasn't exposed, but only three scrapes crossed her palm.

In the commotion, another black man had climbed from the backseat of the Mercedes and stacked three pink packages back onto her cart.

"Hey, careful with those. They're extremely fragile."

"No worry. I do the job right." He winked at her.

Faith rolled her eyes.

Faith dashed into the Ministry of Education, worried her tardiness had blown her lunch engagement. She almost had the Assistant Minister of Education sold on sponsoring her as a visiting professor at Berlin's Humboldt University. The professorship came with a coveted multiple-entry visa that would allow her free passage between Berlins and throughout the GDR. Free of the restrictions of one-day visas that confined her within city limits, the entire country would be hers to plunder at will. She had worked on a scheme for months, creating a fictitious Ozark University and even getting it listed in a college guide. The time had now come to close the deal before Neumann upped his price or talked too much.

The porter called Neumann on the house phone and within a few minutes he arrived to escort her inside. The last time she saw him, Neumann had been balding. Now he sported a mane of jet-black hair that looked as if a mangy animal were humping his head. The way it was sewn gave it an almost avian quality she couldn't quite pin down. She couldn't keep her eyes off it as she tried to figure out the species.

Their footsteps echoed in the corridor as they passed red bulletin boards filled with the latest Party directives. Faith expected an elaborate dining hall for the government elite, but the canteen was humid and cramped. Neumann handed her a metal tray dripping with water and they waited in line. Steam gusted from the kitchen, depositing a sheen of grease on Faith's favorite silk blazer. *Definitely a schnitzel day.*

He led her to a corner table away from the other patrons where an orange salt and pepper set complemented the brown synthetic tablecloth. She cringed at the sight of reusable plastic toothpicks.

Neumann straightened the aluminum fork. "I'm impressed that you speak Russian, Frau Professor. Seldom for an American."

"How do you know I speak Russian?" Faith sought eye contact, but he looked away.

"Cabbage is tasty today," he said, his mouth full of red kraut.

"That's nice, but how do you know about my Russian?"

"I assumed. You're a professor and . . ."

"And I looked the type."

"Yes, yes. You do look brilliant. You're probably interested in Gorbachev's reforms and why our government has been so resistant to them. Wait until the old man Honecker's gone and you'll see change. I can introduce you to some others who feel this way, Party members who talk about social—" He interrupted himself and shielded his lips with his hand and whispered, "democracy."

She glanced at the oval Party pin on his lapel. That particular model dated his membership to the Stalinist period. Faith didn't believe in born-again anything, particularly communists and Nazis. "Herr Neumann, your dissidents don't interest me any more than your Party does. It's your household arts that intrigue me, which brings me to the topic of the professorship." She rustled through her purse without looking down and handed him a small paper bag under the table. Neumann peeped inside and then shoved it into his vinyl briefcase.

"Sponsor me for the visa and I'll be able to bring over fruit like that. It's almost kiwi season and I bet you'd love them. They taste a lot like strawberries, only better."

"Strawberries are my favorite."

The way he eyed Faith as if she were a juicy berry herself made her want to pummel him with rotten fruit, but she smiled instead. "If I get a chance, I'll bring you some."

"Only once is a tease."

"With the visa I could drop by every now and then with a few vegetables as a gesture of my gratitude for pushing the paperwork through within the week."

"You do know we have plenty of apples, onions, potatoes. And do not bring cabbage—we need no more cabbage here." He picked up the bowl and slurped lentil soup.

"So am I going to be a visiting art professor or not?"

"The outlook's improving."

"But I see we're not there yet. Did you get a chance to look over the Ozark U. literature I gave you last time?"

"Such a clean campus. I'd love to visit there sometime—maybe for a semester."

"And we'd love to have you. If this year goes well for me, I'm sure we can work something out. So what is the status of my visa?"

"Undecided, but there is one small thing. Our computer is broken. It's a Western model and no one here can repair it. You could transport it to the West for service. It would speed our work along. We can be of mutual assistance to one another."

"Sorry, but I'm already schlepping around too much today." She patted her packages as she eyed the exit.

"If it's not fixed soon, our visa backlog will continue to grow."

"I understand. Sometimes it can take Ozark U. forever to process paperwork for foreign exchange scholars."

"We can arrange for someone to help you carry it and your packages to the checkpoint. You could take a taxi once you're over there. We have West marks to reimburse you."

Red flag.

"I'm afraid I'd have problems on the border." *Like being arrested and coerced into spying.* She stood, debating with herself whether to abort or play things out as far as she dared. "I didn't declare a computer on my way in."

"I'll write a letter with an explanation of everything."

She stepped away, but her investment in the project stopped her and she paused. "I know a few things about computers. Let me have a look inside."

Neumann whisked Faith past his secretary. His private office was a memorial to all things Soviet. Framed posters exalted the Soviet chemical industry. On his desk was a stack of recent issues of *Izvestia*, *Pravda* and other Soviet newspapers she didn't recognize. Neumann hurried to plug in a model Sputnik rocket with blinking lights trailing behind it.

"Frau Muster mixes herself into everything. She doesn't approve of women, let alone foreign ones, in my office," Neumann said in a low voice. "She's an old-timer. When I tell her about some of the things that come out about Stalin, she warns me to burn the Russian papers before it's too late."

"Maybe she knows something you don't."

"She's seen a lot. Her husband was a prisoner of war who never came home from the SU. Her kids weren't allowed into the university. But she's right that Gorbachev threatens a lot of powerful people."

"Let me have a look at the computer." Faith knelt in front of the metal case and flipped it on its side. "You have a screwdriver?"

"I don't. You might as well go ahead and take it as is." He moved closer to her while she fished a Polish Army knife from her purse. "I love women with wide cheekbones. You look so Slavic." He brushed the back of his hand against her face.

She slid away from the touch. He acted as if nothing had happened and left the room. She sighed as she wondered if anything was worth putting up with such awkward passes. She popped open the antique computer and stared inside.

No dust.

She wiggled the cables to test if they were seated on the motherboard. They weren't. The floppy drive wasn't even connected to the power supply. It wasn't a computer, but a jumble of broken parts. Faith fumed at the insult of such an amateurish setup, but she wasn't sure whether to direct her anger toward Neumann or the Stasi. He deserved it, but her gut nagged her. The *Association*'s fingerprints were all over the machine.

Neumann returned, carrying a letter. "What are you doing?"

"This appears to be your problem." Faith picked a card at random and pivoted it until it released from its slot.

"Put it back and take the whole machine."

"The info I need is right here." She scrawled down numbers onto the back of a used U-Bahn ticket.

"Take it. I'll personally see your visa receives top priority."

"You have to work with me. I take the card or nothing. Your choice." She reached toward the desk to set down the part.

He grabbed her wrist. "The card. But the visa might be delayed."

Outside the air was stained from soft brown coal and it filtered all warmth from the sun's rays. A few blocks from the ministry, Faith boarded a streetcar. The filthy orange tram jerked into motion and her parcels slid a few inches, but she steadied them against her leg. She looked around for a place to sit. A mesh bag with shriveled carrots poking through it occupied the only empty seat. Its owner faced the window, but something about her seemed familiar.

The hair. The chemical-blue hair.

Faith tore off a ticket and stuck it in the machine and slammed the button with her fist. The teeth of the primitive contraption pressed holes into the ticket like a medieval torture instrument shoving spears into a heretic. The streetcar lurched forward. She grabbed a pole to steady herself. Her sweaty palm smeared the grime. Maybe she was being paranoid thinking the card was a setup for the Stasi to nail her on the border. Neumann could've insisted upon it only to save face after the failed pass. After all, the man was desperate.

The streetcar carried her past blackened façades cratered with bullet holes from the Second World War. Almost forty-five years later, the East Germans still couldn't afford to repair their capital. Aesthetics were not a communist priority. She looked away from the window and decided it was time to lure the Stasi out into the open. She aligned the wheels of her cart with the exit. At the next tram stop a man hobbled down the steep steps. Seconds before the automatic doors slammed shut, she bounded from the car.

The blue-haired woman forced the doors open and jumped to the street.

Faith walked down the avenue and the woman paced her along the other side. Faith stopped at a kiosk to buy a newspaper. The woman paused to look into a toystore window. Faith shoved the thin *Junge Welt* under her arm and continued down the sidewalk. The woman followed her. Faith had found a single tick crawling up her leg; now every little itch felt like the Stasi.

Abort.

Fifteen minutes later, Faith crossed under the railway trestle at Friedrichstrasse. Leaded exhaust fumes clouded the entrance. Each breath scorched her lungs and she tasted metal. She slipped the computer card and Neumann's letter into the newspaper and dropped it into the rubbish. In front of a bookstore a wizened man was hunched over a dented pail of mums. She dug into her pocket for the last remaining East German coins and selected a prop. *Flowers add innocence.*

The first wave of Western day tourists was pouring into the customs hall, returning from their own stale taste of the communist world. With each tourist, the odds tipped a little more in her favor. Faith adored Checkpoint Charlie's Cold War glamour, but no real professional would choose it over the crowds of the Friedrichstrasse. She plunged herself into the comforting masses. Her muscles struggled to compact her body into invisibility. She concentrated upon her breath and almost convinced herself her body was under her control. But she knew better.

"Good evening, Frau Whitney," the guard at the checkpoint entrance said before she could show him her passport. Protruding ears prevented his flat green hat from swallowing his head. He nodded for her to enter the restricted zone and then spoke her name into a microphone.

They were waiting.

She pressed her fingernails through the soggy newspaper and into the flower stems. It was too late to turn back, so she trudged ahead. Body odors wafted from the overheated crowd as she was herded down the steps past a monstrous X-ray machine with a small metal plaque, MADE IN BULGARIA. She could feel her cells mutate.

She flashed her American passport's blue cover to the customs inspector and turned it to the open page with her photo.

"Place the bag on the counter, please." The young man pointed to the stainless-steel table as he took her documents. He glanced into a security camera and nodded.

She set her purse on the counter. When she placed her hand back on the cart, a rush of terror coursed through her, a narcotic flooding her veins. Her body relaxed for a moment until she sensed someone approaching her from behind. She froze. The weight of the communist state closed in upon her.

CHAPTER TWO

We say the name of God,
but that is only habit.
—KHRUSHCHEV

NAGORNO-KARABAKH AUTONOMOUS OBLAST, AZERBAIJANI SSR

Children raced across the dirt yard of the orphanage to the dilapidated flatbed truck, frightening the herd of longhaired goats. That the Lend-Lease–era Studebaker had survived four days bouncing its way across high mountain passes from her Moscow orphanage was itself divine proof that Margaret Whitney was in God's will. The driver honked the horn and inched ahead, but the children encircled the vehicle, forcing it to a halt. Their plump expectant faces made Margaret forget her body's complaints. She was tickled with herself that she had once again hoodwinked the communists and she was about to deliver the contraband.

The orphanage director greeted her with a kiss on the cheek and walked with her arm-in-arm to an arbor of grapevines. A childcare worker in a clinical white uniform set dishes of roasted seeds and dried apricots onto linoleum nailed to a tabletop. A boy dressed in rags ran to bring bottles of carbonated water to the guest.

Margaret downed an entire glass of water and let out a long sigh. "We almost didn't make it this time," she said in English, then turned her head away, using her hand to shield a belch. "I can handle inspections from the

Soviet militia, but I wasn't ready for the Azerbaijani checkpoints. It took a whole pallet to convince them to let us pass into the enclave. They nearly tore the entire shipment to pieces looking for something."

"Weapons. They don't want us to defend ourselves," Yeva said, her English more fluent with each visit.

"I've ministered to this country nigh onto forty years, but I've never known locals to get away with setting up their own blockades. The communists don't usually play well with others."

"I always thought I'd be happy when the day came that Moscow lost its hold on us." Yeva shook her head and offered pumpkin and squash seeds to Margaret.

Margaret took a handful even though she believed they should've been planted in the ground where they belonged.

Oblivious to their patron, the children played, chasing goats. They laughed when the kids sprang straight up into the air. But one boy stood alone under a fig tree, his hands stuck in the pockets of his oversized breeches. He stared at the ground.

"That boy tugs at my heart." Yeva turned toward him, patted the bench beside her and shouted something in Armenian. He didn't move. Yeva walked over to him and put her arm around his slumped shoulders. She led him to the bench beside her. "They say he was like every other seven-year-old until the Azerbaijani tied up his family and slit their throats. His parents, grandmother, seven brothers and sisters—all dead. He was in the foothills with their herd at the time. He found them when he came back two days later." Yeva stroked his back. "Every day I pray for a miracle."

"I'll add mine." Margaret widened her eyes, raised her eyebrows and pursed her lips into a goofy face. The boy didn't respond.

"Three days ago in Askeran they massacred another family. They're now demanding all Armenians leave the territory. They're Turks—no one would put another genocide past them."

"I brought you Bibles and Sunday-school books in Armenian. You'll find them tucked between diapers."

"Maggie, your generosity's transformed this place, but we don't need any more Bibles. We need guns."

"Sister, trust in the Lord and He'll protect you." Margaret chomped on an apricot to get the seed taste out of her mouth.

"The Lord helps those who help themselves. And maybe that's why He sent you to us. You know how to move things like no one else can."

"Child, I'm a missionary, not an arms dealer."

"Look around and see the changes for yourself. We have no problem buying Bibles, Christian books—anything. Since Gorbachev, no one cares. Do not misunderstand. I admire your ministry and without you we'd never be able to take in so many, but the world doesn't need Bible smugglers anymore—neither does God."

"You're starting to sound just like my daughter." Margaret put her hands on her hips.

"We're not persecuted because we're Christians, but because we're *Armenian* Christians."

"My girl Faith turned her back on God. Don't you go and make the same mistake. God gave you both special gifts to use for His Glory, so don't you blaspheme Him by abusing your gifts to serve man. Jesus said, 'Blessed be the peacemakers for—' "

A military truck barreled down the drive of the orphanage like a tempest across the plains. Yeva sprang to her feet and shouted in Armenian, then Azeri. The children scrambled into the building as if it were a storm cellar. The truck screeched to a halt and six hooded men in Army fatigues jumped out and rushed toward them. The devil was in their eyes.

They waved old shotguns and shouted in heavily accented Russian, "Hands up. No moves."

Yeva wagged a defiant finger. "There are children here. Put those away."

"Bring me the Armenian bastards," the headman said, pointing his weapon at Yeva.

"Leave!" she said with the fervor of the pharaoh expelling the Israelites.

The man shrugged his shoulders and then strutted around the two women toward the children. Yeva sprinted past him and planted herself on the orphanage stoop.

"You will not take my children."

The man laughed as he knocked her aside. The others swarmed into the building and turned over tables. Dishes and bottles crashed to the floor. The children cried as they huddled together. The boy stood in the middle of the room, lost in the chaos. The leader fired his gun at a statue of Christ on the cross that hung on the wall. Fragments of Jesus pelted the hysterical children.

The man shouted, "You should've left Azerbaijan when you had the chance. Line them up against the wall."

"I take in all God's children—Azerbaijani and Armenian. You'll be killing your own babies," Yeva said.

"Line up the Armenians."

"No."

"You." He pointed with the butt of the shotgun to the boy whose parents had been murdered. "You look Armenian. Over there."

The child crossed his arms and rocked himself, but didn't move.

"Now!"

The child shuffled toward the wall. Yeva bolted toward him, but one of the gunmen grabbed her and threw her to the floor. She shouted to him in Azeri and Margaret prayed that the little Armenian would understand. The hand of God reached down and touched that boy's shoulder. He stopped and then turned back.

"Thank You, Jesus," Margaret said.

"Will you be such a hero with your people when they find out you massacred your own because you can't tell them apart?" Yeva pulled herself to her feet and placed her hand on the boy's shoulder.

"Don't move." The leader exchanged something in Azeri with the others and turned his gun toward Yeva. "We might not be able to pick out the Armenian children, but we know who you are."

Just as he pulled the trigger, the boy shouted and jumped in front of Yeva. In an instant, the child's face exploded into raw flesh and blood. Yeva opened her mouth, but no sound came out. She caught his small body and held him against her chest. Blood soaked her blouse. The leader nodded to a compatriot. He struck her with his elbow, pulled the child away and dropped the body onto the ground.

"Armenian harlot." He unzipped his trousers.

Beside the dying boy the men took turns with Yeva while the leader paced between the windows and the door. Margaret begged with the Lord for mercy, but He had none that day. The leader rushed back from peeking outside and shouted at the one having his way with Yeva. He kicked his hindquarters, but the Sodomite wouldn't get off her. He then motioned to others. They wrestled him off and then the headman aimed his gun at Yeva.

He shot her in the chest.

They ran away, vowing to return.

Margaret fell to her knees, the odor of sulfur, seed and blood sickening her. She ripped open Yeva's blouse and pressed against the torn flesh. With each heartbeat, warm blood pooled under her palms. She pushed until she thought her fingertips touched Yeva's heart. It beat twice and stopped.

Margaret scooped Yeva into her arms and bawled as if she had again lost her own daughter. *Why, Lord, why?* When the tears slowed, she beheld a picture of Jesus and ruminated. Then she made a promise to Him—one she knew He wouldn't like.

CHAPTER THREE

FRIEDRICHSTRASSE CHECKPOINT, EAST BERLIN

Faith listened to the crowd wedged into the customs hall and heard staccato whispers, shuffling feet and rapid breathing—the sound of fear. It echoed against the dingy yellow tile walls. The East German authorities carried no weapons. Like prison guards, they didn't have to. Every soul at the border was under their absolute control. They could confiscate anything, strip-search anyone or make anybody disappear. They allowed most to pass with a friendly smile.

But not Faith.

The officer stopped directly behind Faith, violating her zone. His silence crowded against her. She twitched and then tensed the wayward muscle into submission. Western tourists gawked at her as they shuffled by, but the occasional Easterners averted their eyes as if they might be implicated.

"Frau Whitney, come with me," the official said.

"I have nothing private with me. I've no problem with you inspecting my bags right here," Faith said without turning around.

"But I do. Come."

The officer took her passport and guided her into a restricted area. He helped her with her cart and she followed, staring at the three pink boxes loaded onto it. She knew she had left the Patschkes' with one gray and two pink packages, but it was too late to do anything about it right now. She felt as powerless as she had as a child, squeezing her violated toy with the contraband her mother had stashed inside. They could detain her for hours, even days, but no one would ever know. She longed for someone at home to worry about her, but she had only a roommate who probably wouldn't think much of her absence until weeks after the rent was due.

She remembered the subway ticket with the random numbers scrawled on it and feared it could be used to delay her. She slipped her fingers into the side pocket of her purse, her fingers bumping against keys as they searched for the U-Bahn ticket with the part numbers. Grit lodged under a fingernail, but she found the ticket, palmed it, then shoved it into her pocket.

They entered an overheated room where another officer and a female customs official awaited her. The woman's thin hair and frail frame indicated the poor nutrition she'd received growing up under the communists in the lean 1950s.

"Please." The woman reached out for her purse.

Faith handed her the purse, parked her trolley and sat down. The woman opened the handbag and spilled the contents onto the scarred table. She examined Faith's wallet, carefully removed the currency and fanned it out. Faith rested her hands on the table. The inspector paused and glared at Faith. "Hands away from the table."

"Sorry. I thought you would want them visible."

"Hands away from the table." The woman flicked the credit cards onto the tabletop as if dealing blackjack. She returned to the wallet and removed a yellowed piece of paper. The crease in it was almost torn through.

Faith moved forward in her seat. *No. Not that.* She had carried the note in her wallet most of her life and she read it religiously every day in memory of her father. It was the only thing she had from him, a few cryptic words written in old German script. *Please don't take it.*

The woman unfolded it.

"Careful. The paper's fragile."

"What does it mean?" The woman held it at arm's length and read, "We had no chance, but we made ourselves one."

"I have no idea. Just a piece of poetry my father read to me as a kid." She wished she had known her father so he could've read it to her. As a teenager she'd immersed herself in Goethe and Schiller, searching for those lines, for the message from her father. She never found it.

The woman carefully set aside the note and Faith let out a sigh of relief. She resumed her search. She examined the last fuzzy breath mint and patted the empty bag. "Please stand and hold out your arms." She frisked Faith, slowing down as she probed her breasts. She reached inside of Faith's pockets and found the U-Bahn ticket. Upon noticing the numbers scrawled on it, she presented the ticket to the officer.

"Would you like me to undertake a more intimate exam?" the woman said.

"That won't be necessary."

"The packages?"

"Not yet. You may go."

The younger officer read the numbers and dropped the U-Bahn ticket before Faith. "What does this mean?"

"It means you can go for a ride on the U-Bahn with one of these."

"The numbers."

"No idea. Looks like it's been living in the underworld of my purse forever."

"But we found it in your pocket. Maybe the number's a code."

"Maybe a direct number to the White House or a secret Swiss account at the Deutsche Bank? Or a—"

"Enough." The ranking officer held up his hand. "Frau Whitney, I have no interest in your purse trash. What you did today interests me."

"I had lunch with the Assistant Minister of Education." The air seemed thinner as she struggled to maintain the rhythm of her breath.

"You were in his office."

"He needed help with his computer. I opened it, tried to repair it, but couldn't. A part is broken."

"Where is the part?"

"I don't know. I showed him the one that was bad. Maybe he threw it away."

"You agreed to take it to the West for repair."

"I refuse to take state property of the GDR out of the country. I'm a law-abiding guest of the GDR. I'd never—"

"Frau Doktor Whitney, we know who you are and what you do."

"Apparently not," Faith said.

The officer snorted and turned to the younger man. "Get Frau Simmel back. We do have grounds for a body search, including all cavities. When Simmel is finished with her, I want to take a look in those packages."

Faith slumped over the table in the interrogation room, the now-wilted mums in front of her. She had been through several full physical searches before and had accepted them as an occupational hazard. Tonight was different because they weren't looking for anything; they knew her person was clean. They wanted to humiliate her.

They did.

The officers returned and Frau Simmel smiled at her, but Faith looked away.

"It's time to inspect those packages. Place them on the table and untie the bundles," the ranking officer said. "Frau Whitney, is there anything you would like to confess to first?"

Faith ignored him, unfastened the bungee cords and heaved the packages one by one onto the table. As she picked at the tight knot, the slick synthetic twine shredded into dozens of thin strands. She broke a fingernail and ripped off the jagged fragment. She finished and stepped aside.

The gangly officer folded back the wrapping paper. He opened a book and a cardboard bear sprang up. The corrupt Nigerian diplomats charged her a fortune to rent the diplomatic immunity of their Mercedes' trunk, but any price seemed worth it at the moment. The new method of hand-off needed some refinement, she thought, as she ran her finger over her scraped hand.

"What is that?" the officer said.

"Goldilocks and the Three Bears."

The senior officer pushed the other man aside and picked up a gray clothbound history of the Socialist Unity Party and flipped through the pages. "You expect me to believe you intend to read this, too?"

"I've had insomnia lately. Keep having nightmares the Stasi is out to get me."

He hissed. "Repack the bags and go." The officer looked her in the eyes. "Pleasant dreams, Frau Doktor."

The bastard could have released her beyond the final border control, but he didn't, so she still had to pass the final passport check. More than once she'd seen them release someone here only to return for them within minutes. Four of the fourteen Formica passport-control chutes were open. White metal signs designated lanes for different nationals, separating East from West, West Berliners from West Germans and GDR citizens from everyone else. Faith watched her arm tremble as she handed over her passport. The guard's head was motionless, but his eyes dashed between the photo and her face.

"Take off your glasses. Push your hair behind your left ear," he said in a monotone.

A purple light flashed from the computer scanning her passport. He straightened his tie as he waited for her file. He glanced into an angled mirror high on the booth opposite him as if it enabled him to read her thoughts. She emptied her exhausted mind. He turned page after page, studying her movements. He stamped it and then the lock on the door clicked.

She was almost in the West. Almost.

Faith dragged herself down the long corridor and up the concrete stairs on shaky legs, heaving the damn cart up one step at a time. The tourist rush was long past and only a handful of people waited for the train to the West. Sentries toting machine guns paced back and forth on the catwalk above the platform. Their wide, baggy pants were gathered into high black leather boots, casting an ominous shadow of an earlier Germany. She bought Swiss chocolate from a state-run kiosk peddling communist propaganda and duty-free Western luxuries. She devoured the candy, her excitement rising. She had almost beaten them again.

A commuter train rolled into the S-Bahn station. The blond wooden paneling and slatted seats had survived one, maybe two wars. She grabbed both metal handles and pulled open the heavy doors of the first car. Several minutes later, they crept from the station. High fences topped with barbed wire escorted the train the short distance through East German territory. Floodlights bathed the crumbling buildings, their windows bricked over to prevent their occupants from joining the handful of East Berliners who somehow scaled the Wall every month. She prayed tonight wouldn't be the night for another attempt.

Bright lights cast tall shadows from the dead strip between Berlins. Searchlights scratched the surface of the murky Spree. Spiked grates were invisible underneath the river's polluted waters, but visible in the mind of every Berliner.

Faith looked, just in case.

After the train rumbled across the bridge into the safety of the West, she smiled; a more buoyant celebration of her little victory went on in her mind. At the first station, flashy Joe Camel and Marlboro man ads greeted her to the West. Her brain needed a few seconds to adjust to the color onslaught.

A West Berlin engineer relieved his Eastern counterpart. The man glanced at Faith a little too long. When would these guys roll over and admit defeat? They couldn't do anything to her in the West, so she slumped in her seat, closed her eyes and promised herself a shower within the hour.

She couldn't drag the books another inch, so she decided to leave them on the train and take only the trolley and flowers. At the Tiergarten station she climbed off, anticipating the solitary walk along the Spree canal, gas lamps casting romantic shadows on the cobblestones. Tonight especially she needed the walk.

The stationmaster and two men in formalwear were the only ones on the platform. Faith quickly catalogued the young man's appearance: tall, blond, blue eyes, athletic—a Nazi dreamboat. The older gentleman seemed familiar, but she couldn't place him. His high forehead made his face long and kept his wide cheekbones from making it seem round. His silver-gray hair and goatee were meticulously trimmed, as if someone touched them up every day. He was striking now in his early sixties and Faith had the impression he'd been quite a ladies' man in his youth. Maybe she knew him from the movies.

The men did not board the train. They watched Faith.

Faith swung around toward the back exit, but it was cordoned off for repairs. The stationmaster blew her whistle. The draft of the train rustled the newspapers wrapped around Faith's flowers. She picked up her pace and veered behind the occupied bench. The men stood.

She walked faster, but they followed her.

"Frau Doktor Whitney. May I have a word with you?" The man with the goatee squeezed her arm. "Walk with me as if nothing's unexpected."

"Let me go!" Faith jerked away, dropping her mums, scattering them across stained concrete. "How do you know who I am?"

"You know." He held her firmly and forced her to walk with him. The Aryan squatted and gathered the flowers while the older one spoke. "We have a proposition for you, Frau Doktor."

"Sorry, I just got off work for the day. *Feier Abend.* We can talk tomorrow." How dare they violate the rules and come after her in the West. They'd played the game fairly for years, each time leaving off when she managed to get to West Berlin and resuming when she returned East. The Cold War depended upon honoring such clear rules of engagement. She sensed her commuter pass had just expired.

"I think these are yours." The younger man presented Faith with her mums.

The man with the goatee continued to hold her with one arm. "Be calm, Frau Doktor. We're here to apologize for our associates tonight. The cavity search was unauthorized. Henker is a crude man, usually effective, but crude. When I heard about it, I left my dinner to find you, but you'd already left pass control."

"I've never heard of anyone authorized to go West on a whim. Who the hell are you?"

"Someone in a position to assist you with a visa, among other things. You see, it seems you just paid your last visit to the GDR, unless we can come up with a mutually satisfying agreement, but I'm sure we can."

"What do you want?"

The older man looked at his watch before descending the stairs. It was Russian-made. "The cabaret hasn't begun yet. There's no reason for the entire evening to be ruined. Come along and we can discuss matters."

"Why should I?"

"You will enjoy it," he said as if issuing a command.

"I've been followed, set up, strip-searched and now you want to take me to dinner and a show? The Stasi has a lot to learn about dating."

"Actually only a show. We've missed dinner." A shiny Mercedes with West Berlin plates pulled up at the base of the stairs. "And you have no choice but to come as our guest."

CHAPTER FOUR

A ghost is haunting Europe—the ghost of communism.

—KARL MARX

WILDFANG RESTRICTED WILDERNESS AREA,
GERMAN DEMOCRATIC REPUBLIC
ONE DAY EARLIER, MONDAY, APRIL 17

Minister for State Security Erich Mielke aimed his shotgun at a quail. He wanted only one thing more than to blast the bird, but he knew he'd never get it if he violated the strict etiquette of a hunt with Erich Honecker and bagged more birds than the Party boss. His finger was on the trigger and he had a clear shot at the plump bird, but he still had to convince Honecker of his plan. Mielke bit his lip, shifted his aim slightly and fired. Leaves rustled as a covey of tasty quail fluttered away.

The day seemed unending as they walked from the meadow back into the forest of the private nature reserve. Hunting there was strictly forbidden, but rules never applied to the Party elite. The elderly leader Honecker stopped and raised his shotgun. Shaking, he followed a pheasant. It didn't matter that the bird wasn't in season, only that it was within his sights. He struggled to steady the firearm, but trembled even harder when he pulled the trigger. The recoil knocked him off balance and he stumbled. With a few frantic flaps of its large wings, the golden bird disappeared into the woods.

Honecker caught his balance and stomped the ground, smashing rotting leaves into the mud. “Drat! I should have had that one.”

“Next time, Erich. You’ve already shot more than I have.” Mielke patted his lifelong colleague on the back, disgusted that Honecker left him little choice but to leave their prey behind where they’d killed it. Just once he would like to eat their quarry, but Honecker couldn’t be cajoled to sample anything that came from the woods or water. Mielke hoped he could be persuaded into far more. Everything depended on it. “What do you say that we head back to the lodge for a nice thick *Kassler*?”

“Sorry, can’t hear you. Turned the thing down so I wouldn’t blast my eardrums.” Fumbling with his West German hearing aid, Honecker led his companion down the wood-chip-covered path. “I can’t get this morning’s briefing out of my head. What are the Hungarians thinking? Opening their border to the West is madness. They’re playing right into imperialist hands. Don’t they get what that’ll do to the socialist brotherhood? To us?”

Mielke said mildly, “My old friend, times have changed. I’m telling you, the day the Hungarians open their frontier to Austria, you’ll see our young people rush out of here faster than the Tsar left Petrograd.”

“You can’t know that for sure.” Honecker shrugged his narrow shoulders. “Our citizens love the GDR and they worship the Party.” His voice trailed off as he added, “And they adore me.”

“If there’s one thing my shop’s good at, it’s knowing what’s in the head of the GDR citizen. When someone takes a leak, we know. And I can tell you for certain that they’re pissing on us right now. You’ve trusted me for years, so trust me now: We’re looking at the end.”

Honecker stopped and held Mielke’s gaze for several seconds. He turned away and continued down the path, the butt of his favorite shotgun dragging along the ground behind. The younger Honecker wouldn’t have tolerated anyone abusing a firearm like that. The man was getting too old—they all were. But everything to which they had dedicated their lives was now falling apart and they somehow had to rally themselves for one last struggle.

Mielke walked behind the Party chief, studying the man for the right moment. “Our intelligence shows that Gorbachev himself signed off on the Hungarian plan. Unless we do something fast, it’s over.”

Honecker shook his head and muttered to himself as he ambled along.

Mielke’s chest tightened. He had to get through to the man. Not only was the Marxist-Leninist world at stake, but they themselves were in danger. As head of the Ministry for State Security, the MfS, the Stasi, Mielke had seen what they had done to their own people. Without the iron grip of the state security apparatus, he doubted they could survive forty years of repressed wrath. Even if they somehow escaped the vengeance of the GDR citizens, he knew they wouldn't make it past the West Germans. After the war, the communists had treated the former Nazis the way they deserved, but the West Germans had allowed them in their government and had promoted them within their judicial system. Mielke knew the old fascists were waiting on the benches of West German courts for their revenge. "Erich, comrade, do you hear what I'm saying? We might as well pack up right now and head down the beaten trail to South America."

Honecker kept going.

At the Land Rover, Honecker opened his firearm, removed the unused shells and then stopped. He stared into the setting sun until it disappeared. "You know the Soviet Union is my first love. My family and I celebrate New Year's Eve at midnight Moscow time—even though it's only ten here in Berlin. Still, Gorbachev has to be stopped before it's too late."

Mielke nodded. *Breakthrough at last.*

Honecker strolled to the passenger side and, on his second attempt, heaved himself into the high vehicle. "Did you get the last James Bond film for me? I want to review it before the new one comes out."

"We got it for you last month. You told me you didn't like the new guy because he didn't always wear a tux. You ordered the *Aerobisex Girls 2* and *Emmanuelle in Bangkok* for this week. My boys picked them up this morning in West Berlin."

Mielke had known Honecker most of his life and until that moment thought he could predict his every reaction. He studied his unyielding face and wondered if he really were growing senile. "Did I understand you correctly—that you want us to stop Gorbachev?"

"*Jawohl.* Under no circumstances are you to involve any factions of the KGB or Soviet Army. Our Russian friends are not to know. I want this to happen in two weeks—on the first of May—our gift to the workers of the world on their special day," Honecker said as he removed his horn-rimmed glasses and wiped them with a Tempo tissue. "You up for skat tonight? It's been a couple of weeks since we've had a good game of cards."

CHAPTER FIVE

Our GDR is a clean state.

—HONECKER

INVALIDENSTRASSE BORDER CROSSING, BERLIN
TUESDAY, APRIL 18, 1989

You are now leaving the British Sector.

The Royal Army soldier on duty in the guard shack read the *Daily Mirror*, oblivious to the kidnapping taking place during his watch. The Mercedes rolled past the Allied checkpoint into the Soviet sector and then serpentined through concrete barriers. Crossing into the East was like moving into a black and white movie. The bright colors of the West yielded to shades of gray and time seemed to shift backwards thirty years.

Faith pulled out her passport.

"Not necessary." The man with the goatee waved his hand.

"Last time I checked, you guys considered an American in East Berlin without an entry visa to be a capitalist spy," Faith said. "Gorbachev is bringing about a lot of—"

"Times are changing, but not here."

"Then for old time's sake, get me the proper visa." Her voice betrayed her unease.

"Don't worry, Frau Doktor. Everything's in order. Tonight you're a guest of the German Democratic Republic."

Faith hoped the GDR treated its guests well.

The driver handed the customs official four green West Berlin identity cards. He held out a five-mark piece and opened it, flashing a secret Stasi service badge. The guard returned the papers without peering into the car. She guessed the border routine was for anyone watching, but doubted the British soldier had exchanged his tabloid for a pair of binoculars.

The car approached the customs area, now out of sight of the Western guardpost. An official wheeled an angled mirror under a waiting car. The Mercedes driver pulled ahead of the others, again showed his service badge, and the customs official waved them through.

"Who are you, anyway?" Faith said.

"You can call me Schmidt."

She told herself it was Schmidt's poor choice in cologne that was making her queasy, but she knew otherwise. All her life she had dreaded this day. She knew she couldn't freelance forever, skirting union rules; the Cold War was a closed shop and it was time to pay the dues. So it was going to be the East Germans. They weren't a bad bunch to run errands for; the Stasi was efficient, professional and many considered it the best in the business. Not that the competition was fierce, save from the Czechs and Soviets. She could have done worse; she comforted herself as they drove through the last barrier. The bizarre blood rituals vowing allegiance to Ceausescu put the Romanian Securitate in the realm of the mystics rather than intelligence. The Bulgarians had proven they couldn't pluck the pope out of a crowd—even with his funky hat. And the Poles—one word: Solidarity.

But the Stasi didn't have Faith Whitney—not yet.

In the People's Own Cabaret, the black and gold compass-and-sickle state symbol of the GDR seemed to have been sewn onto the faded red stage curtain as an afterthought. Dressed in their Sunday best, middle-aged couples crowded around an arc of tables, each decorated with a solid plastic vase with a wilting carnation. A sign on an easel welcomed the MfS brigade to the cabaret; Faith was taken aback that the Stasi was so flagrant, but she assumed even repressive organizations had their own internal social functions. She rolled the admission ticket into a tiny cone, the cheap paper disintegrating in her sweaty hands.

Schmidt ushered her to a reserved table occupied by a plump woman in her late fifties.

"Where have you been? I had to finish dinner by myself. You missed the entire first half," the woman said.

"I think you'd like a drink at the bar now," Schmidt said.

"But you promised me the evening—"

"The bar. Now." Schmidt pointed to a bar that could have been a remnant from the original *Star Trek* set. Shiny chrome tubes connected a dozen spherical light fixtures with colored bulbs blinking in sequence. The woman gathered her purse and stomped away. Faith smiled with amusement, but stopped as soon as Schmidt glared at her. He summoned the waiter and ordered vodka for Faith and tonic water for himself. The waiter turned with military precision and left.

"You'll like cucumber after the vodka. Russian style," Schmidt said.

"I didn't think the Russians were in vogue around here anymore."

"There are always exceptions."

Faith looked her host over and tried to figure out who he was. He appeared to be someone who had once been in peak physical condition, but had since been softened by fatty German cuisine and a desk job. He was probably a former athlete, but something about him made her doubt he had ever played team sports.

"What does the Stasi want with me?" Faith said.

"Don't insult us with that Western designation. We're the Ministry for State Security—MfS."

"No offense intended. What does the *MfS* want with me?"

"Enjoy yourself tonight. The People's Own Cabaret is a special treat."

"I'm honored. But don't you think you've gone to too much trouble? Wouldn't a simple phone call and coffee and kuchen at the Grand Hotel have been easier?" She didn't want to admit it, but part of her relished the extravagance.

"From what I've read about you, you seem to like the world of cloak-and-dagger, but can't quite figure out how to get into the game. I understand you tried to enlist with the CIA once."

"Before I decided what to do with my life, I had a weak moment when I almost forgot my heritage of neutrality. And they didn't want me because of my mother and her escapades."

"That's what they told you? Their own records say your own extensive ties in the East made you too great a security risk."

"I liked it better when I could blame my mother."

The waiter arrived with their drinks. Faith threw back the shot of vodka in a single gulp and bit into the cucumber. The vodka sent a warm wave through her body, but she didn't dare relax. "I'm assuming you know what you're doing meeting me in public like this. I prefer it not to get around town I've ever spoken with you."

"Let's say I have a special working relationship with the management and the guests. Think of this place as a little Switzerland in downtown Berlin."

"A clean place for dirty business," Faith said. "Switzerland always gives me the willies."

"What would Europe be without Switzerland?"

"Flatter."

"Yes, I suppose it would be." Schmidt sipped his tonic water. "Suffice it to say, you've impressed some people. We've watched you for a long time. Some of us watched you grow up. As a matter of fact, as a young lieutenant, I used to be the case officer for your family."

"I didn't know we had a case manager."

"Case officer. You have your mother's radiant eyes, you know."

For a moment, Faith thought she saw his face soften. "Did you know my father?"

He nodded. Schmidt had her full attention and he seemed to know it. He paused for a painfully long time and then said, "A brilliant man."

"I never knew him. Do you know how he died? All she'd ever tell me was that he was following his calling when Jesus took him away from us."

"I can't help you." He motioned to the waiter for another round. "Back to the business at hand. We know what you're moving right now, but we have yet to ascertain how you're doing it. Impressive. My boys thought they had you nailed several times."

From the stage, the microphone squeaked as a small man with the stiff gestures of a marionette slurred his words. "*Meine Damen und Herren.* My ladies and gentlemen. Please welcome back the loveliest girls in our republic." The crowd clapped on command and a piano player's tired fingers tapped a staccato rendition of "Tea for Two." A buxom woman with legs covered by fishnet stockings pranced onto the stage twirling a cane, the tails of her tuxedo jacket flapping behind her. Her glittery red top hat emphasized high rouge-smeared cheekbones.

"You've done some impressive jobs. The KGB has yet to figure out how you moved that kidney for the Circassian millionaire from his brother in Abkhazia to Vienna in time for a successful transplant."

"There is a short window for transplants, isn't there? But who said that was my work?" Faith smiled, proud of her accomplishments. "And it was Kabardino-Balkaria. An extraction from Abkhazia would be something for amateurs—it's a straight shot across the Black Sea to Turkey. Not quite like crossing the Caucasus."

"You're considered among the best in your line of work," Schmidt said, ignoring the spectacle onstage.

"Should I be flattered?" She was, but she wanted more and she wanted to know the extent of the Stasi's knowledge of her dealings.

"Very well. You have a choice. You can assist us with a special project or you will never live or work or even think about traveling in this country again. Let's say it wouldn't be a safe place."

"No offense, but a lot of people live quite happily without the GDR." Faith glanced at the stage. A trombone belched "Chattanooga Choo-Choo" while a chorus line of drag queens kicked their way into the Stasi's icy heart.

"I said in this country. I picked you up in West Berlin tonight, didn't I? You know, you could easily have gone into the boot of the car."

She looked into his eyes and knew he meant it. A chill raced through her body. The game was over and she was entering into the unknown.

He removed a cigarette case engraved with a rifle and flag commemorating twenty years of the Ministry for State Security. "Cigarette?"

"I hate smoke."

Schmidt lit his cigarette anyway. "We'll provide you with the necessary details on a need-to-know basis. This is neither the time nor the place."

"I'm not working for the Stasi." Faith pushed herself back from the table and stood. "It's been interesting, Herr Schmidt. We'll have to do this again sometime."

He took a long drag from the cigarette and paused to hold the fumes in his lungs. He looked at her as if appraising the market value of her soul. "Need I remind you, you are in the GDR without a visa? You *are* aware of what we do with imperialist spies. Do I make myself clear?"

"Perfectly."

"You're making a scene. Sit." Schmidt smashed his cigarette into the ashtray. He stared at Faith.

She sat.

Outside, Herr Schmidt held the Mercedes' door open for Faith, leaving Frau Schmidt standing in the drizzle. "After you."

"I need a ride to West Berlin." Her voice was flat.

"Not possible. Most of the border crossings are closed, anyway."

"But some are open. You can rouse someone to open the others. And I suspect it wouldn't be the first time you've dragged someone out of bed in the middle of the night." *And then made them disappear.*

"I can take you anywhere you'd like here in democratic Berlin. I understand you keep your own safe houses."

"Obviously not anymore. And they're for storage."

"Agree to work for me and I can arrange for you to get back to the West tonight. You can even have the multiple-entry visa."

"Fuck you," she said in English. She turned and walked away, pulling her silk jacket tightly around her.

"You have my card. Call me in the morning with your decision. You know, Frau Doktor, I almost think you could get to the West on your own. But remember . . ." Schmidt's voice faded into the night.

Her jacket was useless against the heavy mist that seeped through her clothes. The colder she became, the less certain she was she had made the wiser choice.

The Mercedes pulled up beside her and paced her. She turned her head toward a shop window and hastened her tread. Heavy footsteps approached from behind as the mist thickened into rain.

"At least take my umbrella." Schmidt trotted alongside, getting drenched as he held his umbrella over her head. "Frau Doktor, it's one in the morning and I'm off work. *Feier Abend.* No more recruiting you tonight. Let me drive you home—to the flat in the Voigtstrasse. The rain's cold and our streets aren't as safe as they should be."

Faith slowed her gait and paused for a moment, looking straight ahead. "That's decent of you."

The blackened façade of her East Berlin flat was a leper, slowly shedding essential body parts. She had never imagined sleeping here even one night; the apartment was intended as a secret warehouse. She hesitated before walking in, but then decided the day the Stasi had cornered her would be an appropriate one for the balcony to crash down upon her—most everything else had.

Peeling plaster and a few broken ceramic tile fragments desperately clung to the walls of the front corridor. Many had already been pried off and found their way to West Berlin flea markets. Faith hurried through the first building and into the courtyard, where a few blades of grass struggled up through the broken concrete. She recalled how, during the day, the wings of the building eclipsed the right side of the house, condemning all but the top floors to perpetual shadows.

Her flat was one of the damned.

For a moment she wondered if she could outlast Schmidt, living as his hostage in the dark apartment, waiting for him to issue her an exit visa or escort her to the West. She entered her wing of the building and punched the glowing light switch with her elbow. The stairs creaked, threatening to drop her into the coal bin. She wiggled the flimsy aluminum key in the lock to her flat and dared it to bend. The lights went out. She grappled for the automatic timer, and grime embedded itself deep under her fingernails. If the last try didn't succeed, she would sprint down the road after Schmidt. The lock turned, but still she wanted to run after him. *Stockholm syndrome so soon?*

Years of cabbage soup had been steamed into the wallpaper. Her wet shoes nearly froze to the apartment's icy floor. When she had first struck the bargain with Dieter to sublease his studio apartment while he was away in Mongolia, she had been excited about the place's quaint tiled coal oven as a memorial to simpler days. Now she wished the coal bucket were sitting in a museum instead of her new bedroom. At the time she had ignored most of Dieter's meticulous instructions because a warehouse didn't require heat. Now his warning that the room would fill with black soot if she turned the damper the wrong direction haunted her.

Why didn't she just go along with Schmidt? She could be at home in West Berlin right now, eating cold leftovers. Her desperate stomach growled as she unwrapped the electric space heater that was her rental payment for the flat. She plugged it in. A burlap curtain partitioned off the closet where Dieter had squeezed in a mattress, converting it into his sleeping hutch. Unable to bring herself to stick her head inside, she shoved the heater's cardboard box into his chamber.

The tarnished mirror above the washbasin swallowed her reflection. How could Dieter live here without an indoor toilet, bathtub or shower? Who was she fooling? Outlast Schmidt? She'd never last a week bathing herself in a miniature basin like a condor in a birdbath.

The cold reached deeper and deeper into her body as she sat on the scratchy couch. Everything in this state was as stale as the air in the apartment. What did she need commie crap for anyway? There had to be a better way to make a living. *Just as easily gone into the boot of the car?*

Faith walked into the dark stairwell and felt her way down a half-flight of stairs to the communal water closet. Sitting on the toilet, she couldn't concentrate enough to read the cartoons about bodily functions plastered on the walls. A few moments later, she yanked on the chain, but the commode didn't stop running. The odor of overheated wiring wafted through the air. She rushed back into the apartment, jerked the heater's plug from the wall and crept back down to the toilet. With one last tug, the water stopped.

She returned to the apartment. She had been a conscripted pawn in the Cold War with her mother for far too long to enlist on one side or the other. Her life was about beating the system, not becoming a part of it. *Boot of the car?* The walls came nearer and nearer until the dank wallpaper stuck to her skin. She cocooned herself in a musty sheet, put her arm over her eyes and fell into a restless sleep.

In the morning, Faith stared at Alexanderplatz. A concrete tower skewering a colossal silver ball sprouted from the surreal landscape and a metal clock also defied the cobblestone desert. Although it displayed the time in Addis Ababa, Hanoi and Ulan Bator, the exact minute on Venus or on Alpha Centuri seemed more fitting here, less than a kilometer east of the Berlin Wall. Faith usually adored how East Germany managed to embody all of the tawdry grandiosity of old low-budget sci-fi movies. Today she'd give anything for stale popcorn and Scotty to beam her up out of this hellhole.

After a frustrating hour scrounging for breakfast, she resigned herself to queuing up for limp fries. Rancid grease coated the crisp spring air as she edged forward in line. When it was her turn, she bounced an aluminum coin across the counter. She stood at an outdoor table and tried not to think about the fries she was force-feeding herself.

Everything around her was gray—the high-rises, people's clothes, the sky—as if color had been banished as another capitalist decadence. She would never let herself blend in. Not in the East. Not in the West. She needed them both. She couldn't outlast Schmidt. She could probably get herself to West Berlin in the diplomatic immunity of the Nigerians' trunk, but she couldn't spend her life running from the Stasi. They had her trapped. They knew it. She knew it. The paprika-coated fries slid down her throat while the low Berlin sky pressed down upon her.

After throwing away half the potatoes, Faith called Schmidt to discuss the terms of her surrender. She followed his directions to a Stasi safe house in the old working-class district of Prenzlauer Berg. The door was ajar and the smell of bacon hung in the air. Before she could knock, Schmidt met her and directed her to the kitchen.

The safe house felt like a seedy motel, stained by the lowlifes who drifted through its doors. As a reminder that the building was constructed before the days of indoor plumbing, a glass shower stall was mounted in a corner near the stove. A Russian front-loading washing machine vibrated so hard that the chubby charwoman on the Fewa detergent box seemed to tremble in fear. Schmidt flipped a switch and the machine fell silent.

"The last one here left dirty towels. I'm reporting them to housekeeping." Schmidt picked up a fork and turned bacon pieces in an aluminum skillet. "I took the liberty of making you some breakfast. You didn't have dinner last night and I doubt you found anything proper this morning."

"You didn't need to."

"I know." Schmidt picked up a cracked ceramic bowl and whisked some eggs, using the top of a tiny refrigerator as a countertop. "Making breakfast in these places is a ritual I've missed ever since I left fieldwork. No matter where I was or what the situation, I tried to make myself a real American breakfast of bacon and eggs."

Faith wondered what kind of ritual he performed before ordering an execution, but decided not to ask. "So you've spent time in the States, or did you pick up the taste from an American expat?"

"I'm not at liberty to discuss it. Get me some spices from the basket—basil and anything that looks hot. I do miss your American pepper sauce—Tabasco, isn't it?"

Faith selected paper packets from the People's Own Spice Company in Gera. Schmidt poured the beaten egg onto the bacon chunks and then dumped a heap of paprika into the mixture. Faith sat and studied Schmidt, trying to remember where she'd seen him, now sure it wasn't in the movies. He dressed more like a Western business exec going casual than someone reliant upon the dowdy clothes selections in the East. Instead of an ill-fitting polyester suit and wide tie, he wore a neat polo shirt, khakis and Italian loafers. He no longer wore the Russian watch, but a Breitling. Either he was at the pinnacle of influence, not far removed from Honecker himself, or he had something lucrative on the side. Most communist countries thrived on corruption, but the GDR was Germany and they prided themselves on running a clean shop. She concluded Schmidt had to be one of the most powerful men in Germany, and what really unnerved her was that, in this part of Germany, power was unbridled.

"So why's an MfS general slumming with me?"

Schmidt chuckled. "Clever. What makes you think I'm a general?"

She smiled. "What do you want from me, *Herr General*?"

"Toast bread. Stick it in the toaster oven. There's orange juice in the cupboard, if you wish." Schmidt stirred the eggs. "Frau Doktor, I need you to do what you do best. Move some items for me."

Faith retrieved a can of juice and opened it. "There's something here I don't quite understand. The West isn't my turf. You have free rein in West Berlin and West Germany—and all of Western Europe, for that matter. I'm not the one to help you. My thing is Commieland. And don't get me wrong; I do mean 'commie' in the most affectionate, respectful sense of the term." She smiled.

"I need you to take some items between two socialist states."

"Come on. You know I don't do much in Asia outside of the SU. I'd be more lost in China than Nixon was."

"It's not China."

"Vietnam?"

Schmidt shook his head as he turned off the gas burner.

"Your African satellites are too corrupt for you to need me. A couple of bucks and a Pepsi can get anything in or out of those places. North Korea?"

"Europe."

"Albania? Want me to smuggle out a goat?"

He started to laugh, but stopped himself and let out a snort instead. "The SU." Schmidt placed two plates on the table. "Coffee?"

Faith nodded. "The Soviet Union? You're kidding. You have far better connections there than I do. Interflug flies there several times a day. You've got passenger, freight and military trains, not to mention diplomatic pouches. There are a billion ways that don't involve me."

"We require complete discretion."

"As in deniability? Can't you set up the Poles or Czechs? Make it look like they're doing something when it's really your guys? Moscow never trusted either of them after the Prague Spring."

"The Poles with good reason; though, I must say, the Czechs did get their house in order." Schmidt sat down at the table and scooped up a bite of eggs. "*Mahlzeit.*"

"*Guten Appetit*. Delivery or extraction?"

"Delivery."

Uncomfortable silence forced most people to talk more than they wanted. Faith waited for Schmidt to explain. She sipped the tart Cuban orange juice and was not comforted by the fact that Schmidt was important enough to rate such a scarce luxury item; she'd sampled it only once before, in the canteen of a cosmonaut training facility in a Soviet city closed to all foreigners. Schmidt stopped eating and stared at her. His smile told her he understood her tactic, so she broke her own silence. "I suppose you're not going to explain why you want to use me."

"It's in everyone's best interest not to question. You receive the goods in Berlin. I'll make it easier for you and arrange the hand-off for the West."

"Have there been any prior attempts?" She couldn't believe she was negotiating with him, but she was relieved to be back on familiar ground. "Do you have any reason to believe that Soviet authorities are aware of your intentions?"

"No to both."

"I need to know the contents."

"Knowledge can shorten a life considerably."

"It determines how I take it in."

"By the most reliable and expeditious route."

"What kind of weight and volume are we talking about?"

"Around five kilos and less than a tenth of a cubic meter in volume. And you have a forty-eight-hour window that begins upon receipt." He sipped his coffee.

"Negotiable?"

"Fixed."

"Forty-eight is tight even if everything runs perfectly."

"I found it rather generous. If the goods have not been delivered within forty-eight hours, we must assume you have either absconded with them or gone to the other side." Schmidt sopped up the egg remnants with a piece of toast. "Either way, we will kill you."

Faith pushed herself away from the table, knocking over the orange juice. She had to back out while she still had a chance. Staying in Germany wasn't worth risking her life. The time had come to move on. "Forget it. I'll find my own way back to West Berlin."

"Why are you making this difficult? You have the opportunity to learn much from me if you would only cooperate. I can guarantee you a magnificent career with the MfS—more exhilarating and rewarding than smuggling tchotchkes could ever be."

"I have no desire to be the Stasi's apprentice. Thank you for breakfast." She left the room.

Schmidt raised his voice, but remained sitting. "Frau Doktor, I know what happened to your father. And he's not dead."

CHAPTER SIX

To choose one's victims, to prepare one's plan minutely,
to slake an implacable vengeance and then to go to bed . . .
there is nothing sweeter in the world.

—STALIN

DEMOCRATIC BERLIN—MITTE
WEDNESDAY, APRIL 19

MfS General Gregor Kosyk hailed a cab on the former Stalinallee. Even though the recruitment of Whitney had taken longer than he had budgeted, he was now back on schedule. Taxis were rare, but a boxy green Wartburg stopped for him within minutes. He surveyed the street and jumped into the car.

"You should've been here on time," Kosyk said as he slammed the door shut. "Because of you I've been exposed on the street corner for two fucking minutes."

The cabdriver turned toward his fare. A tuft of hair peaked in the middle of each bushy white eyebrow. "It's a beautiful day for a drive to the countryside."

"Ivashko, haven't you known me long enough to dispense with this idiocy?"

He repeated the code phrase.

Kosyk sighed with irritation, then spoke with the mocking cadence of a schoolboy reciting a lesson. "Do you know if the Moskva restaurant serves solyanka on Wednesdays?"

"I make my own soup with ingredients from the Russian store on Andernacher Strasse."

"Many of our friends shop there, don't they? You feel like a real spook now, Ivashko?"

Ivashko dropped the flag on the meter and sped to the Soviet enclave in the Karlshorst district. The KGB residency there was the largest in the world, and, thanks to the Stasi's efforts, the most productive. Ivashko took a circuitous route through Lichtenberg, constantly glancing in his rearview mirror. Neither man spoke.

As the car bumped along the cobblestones of Köpenicker Allee heading southeast, Kosyk congratulated himself for his quick thinking during his meeting with Honecker and the other naïve conspirators. Taking personal control over the MfS surveillance of the Soviets was a stroke of brilliance. As Kosyk neared Karlshorst, the units assigned to the KGB residency were across town on a futile counterespionage mission following the chief resident to lunch. No one would ever learn of his secret meeting with the Russians or suspect him of betrayal.

The car turned into Rheinstrasse and immediately pulled up to a control point at the entrance to the KGB compound. Few efforts had been made to hide the purpose of the gray multistoried building that could have passed for regular barracks if it hadn't been for the roof: Antenna masts, cables and satellite dishes pointed to the truth.

A uniformed KGB officer waved the taxi into the residency and the driver parked in an underground garage that was large enough for only two cars. He escorted Kosyk through a private entrance to a conference room, drew hot water from an electric samovar and poured tea from a porcelain teapot into the hot water. Without querying Kosyk about his taste, he plopped two sugar cubes and a small silver spoon into each glass, both cradled by an ornate silver holder. He then slipped from the room, shutting the solid wood door.

Kosyk sipped his tea, regretting having allowed the sugar crystals to dissolve into the already-saccharine liquid. The longer he waited, the more he resented the KGB. The Stasi handed some of the best intel in the world over to the residency that it in turn transmitted to Moscow, claiming it as their own. Most of the KGB's intelligence on NATO and Western Europe was courtesy of the Stasi. Without the Stasi and its tens of thousands of operatives in the West and its advanced signal intercepts, the KGB would be nothing. How typical of the KGB to keep him waiting just like Honecker and the other fools in the Politburo. The arrogant bastards liked to remind everyone who the real bosses were.

He would show them soon enough.

A half-hour later, Lieutenant Colonel Bogdanov entered the room wearing the KGB service uniform with its royal-blue epaulets and trim. Her curly black hair, dark brown eyes and Mediterranean complexion made her look more Italian than Slavic. Kosyk guessed she had Tartar blood mixed with the Russian, and that would explain her guile. She shook Kosyk's hand and seated herself at the head of the conference table.

Kosyk spoke in German, although his Russian was flawless. "How's your father? So few ever make the leap from the Foreign Service to the Politburo. The news of his early retirement was a disappointment."

"For him, too," Bogdanov said in Russian, despite fluency in German.

Kosyk persisted in German. "So did he really step down for health reasons?"

"Comrade Kosyk, I don't know where you're leading with this, but I have no doubt you know Gorbachev removed him. You didn't request a clandestine meeting to chitchat about my pensioned father. Get on with it."

"You're certain this room is clean?"

"Absolutely. Only my assistant knows you're here and I even broke protocol and didn't inform the chief resident." Bogdanov sipped her tea. "Now what do you want?"

"Nothing said here today leaves this room without my consent. I need your word."

She nodded.

"In a way, I am here to talk about your father. What does he think about Gorbachev's reforms? About his decision to allow the Hungarians to dismantle the border to the West?"

"I haven't spoken with him about it, but it doesn't take a Gypsy to see the future on this one."

"True." Kosyk stroked his goatee. "And what you see pleases you?"

"I'm a loyal Party member. I believe in the progress of history toward communism, but I must say what I see right now is not progress."

"And I understand your career has also made little progress. Disappointing after your early meteoric rise. Your work impressed me. You had such promise."

"Politics haven't treated me well, but I got out of Pyongyang and back to Berlin. And I'm still in the foreign directorate."

"You used to be posted in capitalist states. It must be hard to go from plum assignments to here." Kosyk's left eye twitched.

"What's your point? I think you're going to have to get to it or leave." Bogdanov stood. "I've never liked you."

"I've never liked you, either," Kosyk said, reverting back to German. "But you're a highly effective operative, although I question some of your unorthodox methods. I also don't understand how anyone of your lifestyle can be tolerated in your position, especially now that your father is out of the picture."

"I suppose there is one advantage to glasnost, isn't there?" Colonel Bogdanov motioned toward the door.

"And because I don't like you, I trust you—fondness compromises objectivity. I know how we can avoid the impending chaos and move in the direction of progress—for both history and your career."

Bogdanov sat down and said in German, "Continue."

CHAPTER SEVEN

WEST BERLIN

Her roommate's study reeked of a photo lab, but today it was perfume to Faith. Negatives and prints cluttered a light table. Blown-up official seals from a dozen different governments were tacked to a wall above rows of homemade rubber stamps and an impressive collection of inks. When she walked in, Hakan turned down Wagner and squinted at her through the jeweler's visor. He flipped it up for a closer look. "What happened to you? You okay?"

"How can you listen to creepy Teutonic schmaltz like 'Ride of the Valkyries'?" She dropped her purse onto the floor.

"When you didn't come home, I thought you'd finally defected." Hakan grinned.

"You noticed? Your date must not have gone well," Faith said. German women seemed to adore Hakan. He had the perfectly proportioned features of an ancient Greek statue, but, because he was a Turk, Faith never dared tell him that. She picked up a piece of paper covered with round ink stamps of German eagles holding swastikas. She glanced it over and dropped it back onto the table. "I won't bore you with the details, but I'm now a Stasi secret agent woman."

"You're shitting me?"

"I wish."

"Congratulations, comrade. When's your first Party meeting?"

"Screw you," Faith said with a smile, content to settle into the comfort of their own faux Cold War. Over the last several hours she'd begun to harden herself to the idea of doing a Moscow run for the Stasi, but she was still stunned that her father might be alive.

"I didn't think you'd ever work for them. Thought you always said you couldn't bring yourself to choose sides just like you can't commit to a relationship." He pressed the stamp into an inkpad and firmly pushed it into the margin of that day's *Hürriyet*, flown in fresh from Istanbul. "What do they want from you? The Stasi starting up its own flea market?"

"I deal in antiques, not junk. They want me to transport something into the Soviet Union without the Sovs finding out."

"The commies always seemed weird to me, but I thought above everything else they stuck together like Jews." He lowered his visor and studied a proof. "Look at this! Another line break."

"Seems okay to me." Faith tossed it onto the table after a polite glance. "Yeah, spying on the enemy is one thing. It's embarrassing to get caught, but they have the routine down. Relations chill; the other side arrests known spooks, then they all meet on the Glienicke Bridge for a spy swap. There's even an East Berlin lawyer who specializes in arranging spy exchanges." Faith sipped her tea.

"I thought I caught everything when I touched up the neg. This isn't my day. Last time I pulled a proof, all the lines were too thin from overexposure. Can you hand me that stylus by your right hand?"

"This thing? I think my dentist stuck one of these in my mouth last checkup."

"This has to be perfect before I can do a run. You wouldn't believe what I went through to get the right paper, and I only found a couple of sheets."

"Give me a swatch and what you know about it—where it was produced, where it was used—and I'll see what I can do. I know a paper collector in Karl-Marx-Stadt. If it's old or from the East, either he's got it or knows where to find it. I hope this means you finished the job for me."

"Faith, I don't know if I'm ever going to finish it. It's not safe for you. Why don't you sit this one out? The big boys play for higher stakes than a couple of old dishes. It's not like you're dealing in something really valuable like jewels that might be worth some risk."

"Anyone can traffic stones. You have to make the documents for me in case I get trapped over there again."

Hakan used his palms to pick up a set of newly minted papers. He compared the fresh stamp to one in a worn booklet and then motioned for her to come closer.

"This is an Aryan pass? What the hell are you doing making Nazi documents?"

"It's a new product line. An Aryan pass can get you German citizenship. It did for me. The government accepts them as proof of enough German blood to qualify as a citizen. Fascist bastards. But I'm telling you, there's a huge untapped market in the Turkish community alone."

"Swell."

He carved on a rubber stamp, a tiny curl following the stylus blade. "Don't go back there."

"It doesn't matter. They're here, too." Faith detailed the interrogation and kidnapping.

"Faith, I don't want anything to happen to my best customer. It's got to stop before you get hurt. The cavalier way you were talking about it, it didn't seem like such a big deal."

"They said they knew what happened to my father." She paused for a deep breath to steady her composure, but tears streamed down her face. "They claim he's alive."

"Come here." Hakan helped her from the chair and into his arms. He held her tightly. She allowed her body to relax against him for an unguarded moment. She sat back down, but he remained at her side. "At least promise me you'll go to the Americans for help."

"Yeah, right. I'll march into the embassy. 'Hi, the Stasi is threatening my life and they just resurrected my dead father, so I thought I'd work for them, but I was wondering, would you like me to be a double agent or something? I know you didn't want to hire me before, but I think you can see that I've positioned myself well to serve your current interests.' "

"Just promise me you'll go to your embassy and ask for help." He rubbed her neck. "Promise?"

"Hakan."

"Faith, promise."

"Understand this is under protest. I promise I'll think about considering going."

"That's as good as I'm going to get, isn't it?"

"You know me. So does this mean you're going to do my papers?"

"I have to think about it."

"You still a student at the TU?"

"In my thirty-fifth semester and haven't gone to a single class yet. How else would I pay for health insurance?" He wiped fresh ink from the rubber stamp with a rag.

"Someday the Germans are going to catch on and start charging tuition. So you can still get jobs through the student employment office?"

"Haven't done it in a while, but it's not a bad way to pick up a few marks."

"Does Pan Am still use day laborers from there to clean the planes?"

"You'd think after Lockerbie—"

"I do my best not to think about airline security. I'm going to need you to be prepared to get something into Tegel for me. You don't even have to take it on the plane—just past security. Please, just do the groundwork now so we're ready to roll whenever they notify me. I'm dead if I don't get something to Moscow for my new friends. I also need those documents to stash away so I'm prepared for my next rainy day over there."

"At least think about quitting. Take a little time off—go to the States and visit some friends. By the way, I almost forgot to tell you, Summer called early this morning. It must have been really late his time."

"What did he say?"

"To tell you happy anniversary and you should give him a call sometime."

"Oh, no. I totally spaced it with everything that went on yesterday—not that I even could've called. This is the first time I've been living in the West that I didn't call him on our former anniversary."

"He'll get over it. It's you I'm concerned about."

"Hakan, please try to understand. I have to find out."

"They could be making up the whole thing about your father. Why don't you quit being so stubborn and ask your mother?"

"I don't even know what continent she's living on right now and she's not going to change her story. I've never even seen a picture of him. The only thing I have from him is a brief note Mama used to keep in her Bible and refused to show to me. I stole it when I was eight."

"Did it give you any kind of clue about who he was?"

"Only that he was a German with old-fashioned handwriting. I couldn't even decipher it until I was in high school. It wasn't signed, but the way

Mama acted about it, I knew it was from him." She reached down and gingerly removed the worn paper from her wallet. She read it again before she handed it to Hakan.

He pulled down the visor and examined it. "You're right about the handwriting, but the note's thirty years old and most adults would have written that way back then. The paper is interesting, though. You don't see such coarse paper in the West except in the immediate postwar period. I'd say it's from the East."

"It wouldn't surprise me. I do know they met in Berlin, but that's about all I know. I'm going to have to go along with them. It's the only way."

"So you're going back over there?"

"I finally got the multiple-entry visa and they want something from me so they're not going to arrest me before I do their job. That means I've got a window of opportunity right now to clean the place out and the Stasi will stand by and watch. I can't pass this one up—I'd never forgive myself for the missed opportunity or for letting their scare tactics get to me. The game's still afoot."

Hakan pulled a French passport from a drawer. "And I might not forgive myself, either, but you'll have the new documents by morning."

CHAPTER EIGHT

LUBYANKA (KGB HEADQUARTERS), MOSCOW
THURSDAY, APRIL 20

The director of the Counter Intelligence Service of the KGB's First Directorate, Colonel General Vladimir Vladimirovich Stukoi, lowered his head to each of the dozen telephones lined up on the table beside his desk. He picked one up and spoke, but the ringing continued. One by one he slammed each phone into the cradle with a curse and continued his search for the ringing one. Colonel Bogdanov looked away so as not to embarrass the general. On the fourth attempt, Stukoi was united with his caller.

Tired from the flight from Berlin, Bogdanov waited in the hard red leather chair, content to stare at a painting of Lenin inciting the crowds at the Finland Station to revolution. She didn't like how tempted she was by Kosyk's plan, but she was even more irritated that he knew it would get to her. If she went along with him, as the organizer of the Moscow side of the conspiracy, not only could she restore her father's honor, but she could position herself nicely in the new regime. Very nicely. She had the connections to pull it off. The future of the Soviet Union—her future—depended upon what she would report to Stukoi, if he ever got off the phone.

She absentmindedly straightened a lock of her short curly hair. She hated the curls. It was hard enough being taken seriously in the KGB as a woman without having curly hair, strikingly good looks and a taste for other women. At least she was tall, just shy of a hundred-eighty centimeters, and muscular. She trained and worked harder than any of her male colleagues because she had to be the best to have a shot at being equal. Restoring the old order would definitely assure her the respect she deserved—curls be damned.

The director slammed the receiver down. Bogdanov motioned toward his phone bank. "I'm surprised that they didn't put in the latest telephone-switching equipment when they built this new facility."

"My telephones are the most modern available."

"I mean the facilities to route multiple lines and numbers into one phone. It eliminates all but one of your phones and the need for a lot of operators. That would even save us on the copper wiring used for each individual line."

"We're a very rich country. We have copper." The general picked up a partially smoked cigar and champed on the end. "I must say I didn't expect to see you in Moscow for some time. I take it you're going to tell me who's selling our communications algorithms to the Brits?"

"We're narrowing it down to the residency, but we don't know yet."

"Then what's so important? Let me guess: Honecker's had an epiphany that his time is running out unless he gets with the program. The old fart's ready to do something desperate and invade West Berlin?"

"More like Moscow."

"Honie always was a cutup. I was at a get-together with him once out at Brezhnev's dacha. By looking at him, you'd never know the guy would turn out to be the life of the party. Every time Leonid left the room to take a leak, Honie would go into this great Brezhnev impression. I tell you, he had him down."

"He's serious, sir. He's plotting the assassination of Gorbachev."

"How the hell do you know that? You're supposed to be in counter-espionage, chasing after our own people. You screwing his daughter or something?"

"Major General Gregor Kosyk of the MfS—"

"I know Kosyk. Shifty little prick."

"Kosyk approached me on Honecker's behalf. They're convinced that the opening of the Hungarian border leads directly to the dissolution of the

GDR, the Warsaw Treaty Organization and eventually the Soviet Union itself. In their scenario, not even the People's Republic of Mongolia is left. Let's just say, if the Germans are right, the Chinese are going to be pretty damn lonely."

"They've got a point there." Stukoi waved his cigar.

"Sir?"

"Some of our analysts would concur; that's all I'm saying. Why did he approach you?"

"He's known my father for years and he believes I have reasons to be dissatisfied with Gorbachev."

"And they are . . . ?"

"Personal, professional and ideological."

"That about wraps it up. Are you? Are you dissatisfied with Gorbachev?"

Bogdanov shifted in her seat, searching Stukoi's face for the right response. "I believe you know the answer to that."

Stukoi pursed his lips and nodded his head. His large brown plastic glasses slid down his wide nose.

Bogdanov took out a cigarette and tapped the end on the table. "The bottom line is the MfS wants to lend its full support and cooperation to dissatisfied elements in the KGB to prevent the end of the Soviet era. Kosyk believes I'm cooperating with them and I've come to Moscow to recruit. He's hoping I'll even go outside the KGB and use my family's contacts to go after key military officers."

"Keep him thinking that. Tell him I'm in and I expect Gasporov to join us. We're going to let this one run its course, catch them in the act and then we'll clean house. And you're right not to trust regular communications; assume everything between here and Berlin is compromised. I'm putting a Yak-40 at your disposal. When you have something to report, do it in person. We'll let it leak that you've been reassigned to Internal Affairs. No one wants anything to do with Internal Affairs. Nothing you do will be questioned."

"I'm sure you're aware this jeopardizes my other investigation." Bogdanov lit the cigarette.

"A small sacrifice. Saving the General Secretary's life will give you your choice of postings. Who knows, your father might even get his full pension restored."

"What about Titov? The resident isn't going to like that I'm now reporting to you."

"You always have, anyway." Stukoi lit the cigar. "You afraid of Gennadi Titov?"

"All prudent officers at the residency are cautious, very cautious. Permission to speak freely, sir," Bogdanov said, aware no conversation was ever truly off the record. "Mikhail Skorik was one of the best officers I ever served with. I witnessed how Titov fabricated reports to get his position. Misha was the one who earned the Berlin slot, but instead he was sent to chase mujahedeen in Afghanistan. At the risk of saying so, I wouldn't be surprised if Titov would work with the Germans to eliminate Gorbachev if that would mean advancement."

"We nicknamed that devil years ago. You don't fuck with the Crocodile. People still call Titov that?"

"On occasion."

"I take it the Croc doesn't know you came to me directly. You ran a hell of a risk."

She took a drag from the cigarette. "It was my duty."

"You've got balls, Bogdanov. You did the right thing, but you've got balls."

"I'm going to need more than that. Like West marks and a staff free to travel between East and West Berlin, surveillance people. I understand Kosyk is attempting to acquire an American asset, and I don't intend to make things easy for him."

Stukoi cleared his throat. "Do not discuss this with anyone—and I mean anyone, including your father. You report to me and only to me. Do I make myself clear?"

"Yes, sir."

"Dismissed." The general turned toward a Robotron computer terminal on his desk.

Bogdanov noted the letters he pecked on the keyboard with his two index fingers: KUSNV and LATA33. She smiled and hurried out the door. The logon and password would grant access to the highly guarded SOUD system of joint acquisition of enemy data. Every Warsaw Treaty intelligence network fed data into the system, providing precise descriptions of enemy agents and their suspected contacts. KGB paranoia limited access to only the highest-ranking counterintelligence officers. Now Bogdanov was among the privileged.

CHAPTER NINE

The Party is always right. The Party. The Party. The Party.

—EAST GERMAN COMMUNIST SONG

GERMAN STATE LIBRARY, EAST BERLIN
FRIDAY, APRIL 21

Faith dashed into Jürgen's office, a room the East Germans called the "medicine cabinet" because it housed what the Party believed should be kept out of reach of its children. The walls were covered with books and a mezzanine sagged with the weight of thousands of censored tomes. The air was heavy with the scent of a used bookstore; Faith could smell the pages yellowing. Jürgen closed the door and cleared a stack of books from a chair for her. His eyes were red and Faith thought she smelled whiskey on his breath. He picked up a blue and white packet of Sprachlos cigarettes and lit one before she could object. He had recently gone through a rough divorce and it seemed to Faith he wasn't recovering very well.

"You might be interested that this morning I sent a protest letter on behalf of the library to the Party's Central Committee. Colleagues at all major libraries are also sending their objections about the recent censorship of Soviet periodicals. Right now I'm finishing up an appeal to Moscow for assistance."

"I thought you were the library's chief censor. What gives?"

"Read this over and see what you think." He pushed a piece of paper across the table. "You haven't heard, have you? They banned the last issue of *Sputnik* because of an article criticizing Stalin. *Sputnik*—not even a solid intellectual magazine, definitely telling of the cultural level of our Politburo. I've heard they'll decide day by day if they'll allow *Pravda* to be sold. Imagine our Party censoring the Organ of the Central Committee of the Communist Party of the SU. The world's coming to an end. It can't happen."

She picked up the letter and read it. It reminded the Soviet government of the clause in the GDR's constitution promising eternal friendship between the two countries and requested a symbolic intervention to pressure the East German government to follow Soviet reforms. Not once in the history of the Cold War had the East German communists defied the Soviets, and not since the worker uprising of 1953 had the passive East German public taken a stand against the government. Cold War melodrama didn't get better than this. Faith was almost hooked. In fact, she was inspired.

She saw a way out.

Jürgen picked up a coffee pot from a hotplate where it had spent the better part of the day, judging from the burnt-coffee smell. He poured her a cup. "I'm meeting a rep from the university library in a few minutes to jointly deliver the letter to the Soviet cultural attaché."

"Mind if I tag along? This could really turn out to be big—the beginning of a political thaw here. Besides, as a guest researcher, I have an interest in access to research materials." *And I have an interest in public contact with the Soviet government.*

"I don't know. But then, Americans don't seem to be the class enemy anymore, do they? In fact, word has it Honecker's doing his best to court your government for an invitation for a state visit to Washington." He wrapped a plaid scarf around his neck and put on a brown beret.

"I'd rather not carry this package with me to the embassy. Do you mind keeping it for me?" Faith pulled a small bundle from her bag.

"No problem. Give it here." He tossed it onto a stack of books on the floor. "I suppose this means you're coming along and you don't want the coffee."

Ten minutes later, they met Jürgen's colleague on Unter den Linden in front of the Bulgarian Cultural Center. The woman feigned interest in a display of an automated carpet loom, the Balkan state's latest contribution to the industrial revolution. He introduced Faith to her and they marched to the embassy.

The Soviet embassy was a granite cereal box built in the heyday of Stalinist architecture. Through the spiked wrought-iron gate, a bust of an angry Lenin snarled at passersby. He was no friendlier to Faith and her friends.

A sentry radioed their arrival and let them in. Both librarians remained silent while they waited in the cavernous lobby. A photograph of Gorbachev hung on the wall across from Faith. His bright eyes stood out as welcome contrast to the usual dullness of Honecker's. *Soviet Woman, Moscow News* and a pamphlet about the Autonomous Republic of Birobidzhan, the world's first modern Jewish state, were scattered on an end table. Faith leafed through the Birobidzhani propaganda documenting Soviet generosity toward its Jews. It included rare photos from the depressed Zionist outpost beyond Siberia.

The prospect of entering Soviet territory and meddling in East German affairs was precisely what had tempted Faith to go along. If the East Germans wanted her to smuggle something into the Soviet Union, they wouldn't tolerate any contact between her and the Soviet government. Getting caught in the middle of a petty international squabble over a youth magazine might compromise her beyond usefulness. She hoped.

A tall woman with short black hair in loose curls and wearing a smart tweed businesswoman's suit approached them. She introduced herself as Tatyana Mikhailovna Medvedev, the cultural attaché. Her youth astonished Faith. Faith was used to the pre-Gorbachev days, when embassy officials were somewhere between their late sixties and their state burial, not in their early thirties.

The attaché ushered them up a curved staircase to her second-story office. An enormous cherry desk dominated the airy room. Its marble floors were covered with hand-knotted Bokhara carpets. On the walls, paintings of Lenin proselytizing to the masses hung near a dusty photograph of Gorbachev joking with factory workers.

The librarians sat in front of the desk and Faith took a seat behind them. She twisted a loose thread on her sweater as she wondered how cold it really got in Siberia. The librarians explained their concerns to the official and handed her their letters.

"My government regrets the censorship, but we can't be of any assistance to you. An integral part of our new thinking is not to intervene in the domestic politics of our allies," Medvedev said in a clipped Berlin accent, and then threw up her hands in a very male gesture.

"Your position's clear. I suppose we shouldn't take up any more of your time." Jürgen's head drooped and he stood to leave.

The attaché walked with them to the door and then paused. "I spent most of my youth in the GDR. My stepfather was a diplomat here from fifty-three to sixty-eight. Off the record, I wish I could help. The GDR's a second home to me. In fifty-three my father sent in tanks when Ulbricht asked us to stop the workers' strikes. If I could, I'd send in troops again to atone for his sin."

Medvedev made direct eye contact with Faith and held her gaze.

"You're an American, my staff informs me."

"Professor Faith Whitney. I'm very interested in your government's reforms and the possibility of exploring a student exchange focusing on the change."

"Then let's meet to discuss it."

They made arrangements for the next afternoon. The way the attaché looked at her, Faith wasn't sure if she had just set up a business appointment or a date.

The small group left the embassy compound in silence. A northerly wind wrestled Faith for her breath. A few blocks away from the embassy, she heard the sound of footsteps on the wet sidewalk behind her. She hastened her pace. A man in a knee-length black leather coat surged ahead.

"Identification, please," he said.

He didn't flash a badge, but she knew where he was from. She avoided eye contact and stared at a poster in the window of the Aeroflot office promoting the Soviet Far East city of Khabarovsk. The librarians pulled out their blue personal-identity booklets. Faith slapped her passport into the man's stubby mitt. He motioned to his cohort and they stepped closer, a wall of leather closing in on her. She moved backward and teetered on the curb while the men examined the American passport. One spelled her name aloud into his lapel and then he pressed her passport between his fingers.

"What were you doing at the Soviet embassy, Frau Whitney?"

"I'm a professor and I'm exploring the possibility of an exchange program for my university. And, as a researcher here, I was also concerned with the availability of Soviet publications."

"Such a fuss over a child's reader." He handed her back her papers. The second man shoved the librarians into an unmarked car. Jürgen's bloodshot eyes pleaded for help, but Faith could only watch. "Frau Professor, you may go. But stay away from the Russians. We won't warn you again."

CHAPTER

TEN

NAGORNO-KARABAKH AUTONOMOUS OBLAST, AZERBAIJANI SSR

A chunk of plaster surrendered to gravity and crashed to the floor of the earthquake-damaged Armenian church. The battle-hardened militants didn't turn their heads and neither did the seasoned missionary. Men in tattered camouflage jackets guarded the entry to the clandestine meeting. Suspicion creased their faces as they eyed the outsider.

Margaret cleared her throat. "You Armenian Christians are Christ's soldiers on the frontline against the Antichrist. Satan seeks to rid you from your own house because, as the world's oldest Christian bastion, the house of Armenia has defied the Evil One for too long." She paused for the interpreter, but before she could continue, the leader interrupted.

"We know how your own freedom was at risk to bring us God's word when it was forbidden. For this you always have a place with us, but Bibles help us not when the Muslims drag us from our homes. You of all people should understand because you were there when they murdered Yeva and the boy."

"Don't dismiss me before you've heard me out. God's word saves." She patted her scuffed Bible. "It brought me here to witness the fulfillment of prophecy. We all know what the Mark of the Beast on Gorbachev's head signals—the final struggle has begun."

"We hear your words, but they alone won't protect us. Yesterday was the time to be emissaries for Christ, but today we're called to be His soldiers." The leader patted a crude homemade rifle.

"And that's why I came right back—not with the word of the Lord, but with His sword." She opened her Bible. The gold-bordered pages were glued together and a cavity was carved out. Between Genesis and Revelation was nestled a landmine.

CHAPTER ELEVEN

EAST BERLIN
SATURDAY, APRIL 22

A Chaika limousine with red diplomatic plates in Cyrillic lettering flaunted its diplomatic immunity in a no-parking zone at the busy intersection of Unter den Linden and Friedrichstrasse. Faith had rarely seen such an elegant Soviet-built car in East Berlin; she guessed the attaché had borrowed it from the embassy's motor pool to impress her. Still, it was hard to be impressed by a twenty-five-year-old Buick knockoff.

Delayed by heavy border traffic, Faith crossed against the light and hurried toward the limo. She strained to see if the woman were inside, but the windows were blackened. The driver emerged from the car as she approached. The man's eyebrows were the bushiest she'd ever seen. She hoped she wouldn't retain the image of the white clumps of hair sticking out of his ears. He opened the rear passenger door for her.

"*Dobryi den*'," Faith greeted the cultural attaché as she slid into the backseat.

"*Vy tozhe govorite po-russkii!*" the woman said, then switched from Russian to German and continued, "And I was already impressed that you spoke such flawless German." The attaché said to the driver, "Ivashko, take us to Treptower Park." She turned back to Faith, leaning her elbow against the black leather upholstery. "I thought we should be outside on such a lovely day. Yesterday I didn't think we'd ever see the sun again. Are you up for a walk?"

"Always. So how would you like me to address you? I'm afraid I don't know the correct title for a Soviet cultural attaché."

"Call me Tatyana."

Tatyana was undoubtedly from a colder climate. It was in the sixties, the first warm day of the spring, but it was too chilly for her snug sleeveless shirt. Her muscles had the definition of an athlete. The wiry woman was too fit for an embassy paper pusher. An image of Tatyana fresh after a workout popped into Faith's mind: Sweat glistened off every curve of those taut muscles; a soaked tank top clung to her small breasts and those wet curls. Faith never wanted to compete with this woman over a man. Judging from the way Tatyana was eyeing her, Faith felt she probably would never have to worry about that.

They arrived at the sprawling urban park some twenty minutes later and walked inside. Tatyana carried two pairs of binoculars.

A Red Army truck was parked near an overgrown flowerbed and a decrepit shack. A dozen conscripts stood nearby with rusting shovels in hand while a Berlin parks official pointed with a rolled-up blueprint. Half the soldiers began digging out the flowerbed; the other half ripped boards from the structure. Faith guessed the city official had illegally cut a deal with a local garrison so he could finish a project under budget—the free market at work. The women avoided them and walked on the far side of the path.

Tatyana led the way. Faith thought she was in good shape from her frequent dashes to catch trains, but she had to hustle to keep up.

"The golden oriole is rumored to be back from Africa for the summer. We might get lucky," Tatyana said. Suddenly she stopped and looked through her binoculars. "I think that's it! It just flew into that tree."

Faith watched the bird flutter into the tree and glanced at her watch. *Clearly the woman has been in East Berlin too long.*

"Survey the area and tell me if you notice anything unusual." Tatyana had the instincts of a spook and Faith prayed she wasn't one, even though she knew her prayers were never answered.

Tatyana hung a bulky pair of binoculars around Faith's neck. The clunky things weighed her down so that she was sure if she fell into a mud puddle she would be pulled straight to the bottom. "Standard Baltic Fleet issue," Faith said, impressed with herself.

The street noise faded as they went deeper into the park, passing a socialist-realist statue of a World War Two–era Red Army soldier with his arm around a German child, presumably protecting him from the Nazis. Faith hurried to keep up as Tatyana left the sidewalk to blaze her own trail through the urban wilderness. The attaché stopped and raised her binoculars, pointing them toward a flutter among the fresh leaves of spring.

Faith struggled to focus with the unfamiliar field glasses. Branches blurred and no bird came into sight.

Tatyana pointed. "Looks like we've got a Eurasian nuthatch working this linden tree. Right there, hanging upside down on the trunk. Let me help you." Tatyana slipped behind her and put her hands on each side of Faith's face. She pressed lightly against her cheeks, positioning her for best viewing. The softness of Tatyana's skin and the delicateness of her touch disarmed Faith, and she lost herself in the sensation. It had been far too long since she had melted into a sensual caress, but she wasn't sure what to think of it coming from another woman. Tatyana pulled her hands away so leisurely Faith didn't notice when they lost contact. Faith stopped herself short of savoring the dreamy moment.

Tatyana looked through her binoculars. "The trick to finding a target is to lock on it first with your eyes, then slowly raise the glasses up. It's tough without a good reference point when you're searching for something in trees or at sea. There's definitely an art to using them."

And an art to such a seductive touch. Standard KGB training?

"Okay, I've established a perimeter," Tatyana said. "The Stasi can't get anyone with a listening device close enough to monitor us without being noticed." Her words yanked Faith back into the Cold War. Tatyana continued, "There are a couple of trees we have to avoid. Follow my lead."

"Any Stasi squirrels we should be on the lookout for?"

"Trust me, they've bugged certain trees."

"And I swear I just saw a squirrel with an attaché case handcuffed to its paw."

"Only the Mossad rivals the Stasi in paranoia. You wouldn't believe the trivia they gather on people. Archival packrats, to misquote Stalin. They gather so much, they have nothing."

"So this bird fetish is a ruse to get them to give us some privacy?"

"It's a useful hobby. I actually love birding. I once traded in a lot of favors for a six-month stint in Cuba so I could see a hummingbird in the wild. The humidity is unbelievable, though I admit the Latins know how to enjoy life. I'll never forget the brilliant colors. Europe seemed so dull afterward." Tatyana began walking, her brown eyes vigilant.

Faith fell a few steps behind. Tatyana pointed out another feathered comrade, stretching her arm toward high branches. From an angle, Faith spotted a scar on her right shoulder. Definitely a scar from a bullet wound. What was she doing with this woman? Tatyana wasn't a KGB case officer, running agents from a cushy office like Faith had assumed. She was a field operative, someone from the frontline. She was danger.

"So is this business or pleasure?" Faith said.

"Both. We get far too little pleasure in this life."

"Thanks for not bullshitting me with the cultural attaché front." Faith wished she had.

Tatyana stopped and looked Faith in the eyes, holding her gaze for several seconds—several seconds beyond innocence. "We both know who I am and what I want."

Faith was sure of neither.

Tatyana stalked another spellbinding bird in the branches. "I was surprised to see you in my office yesterday. That morning I was working on how we were going to arrange a chance to chat with you. To be quite honest, I had no intention of working with you myself until I had the pleasure of meeting you in person."

"Let me be up-front with you. I have no intention of working for the KGB, GRU, CIA, KKK or any other three-lettered band of thugs. I'm not an agent. I'm a professor and a businesswoman."

"And one with good taste. I like some of the things I hear you're buying. I'd never thought about the artistic merit of our applied arts before. Our museums have never taken such interest." Tatyana noticed a large bird on the trunk of a tree and raised her binoculars.

"If you know anything about me, you know I'm fiercely neutral. I make the Swiss look partisan. As many times as you guys have approached me, I've never agreed to work with you, or anyone else, for that matter. Every shop in the business has come after me."

"Except the CIA," Tatyana said. "A typical case of them not recognizing homegrown talent." Tatyana tracked the woodpecker as he munched insects on his way up the tree. "The Stasi has plans for you. They've taken a lot of precautions to limit who knows what you're doing for them."

"Wrong. They never made it a secret. They even took me to some cheesy Stasi cabaret the other night."

Tatyana turned her binoculars on a man feeding pigeons, but looking away from the birds he was feeding. "They've given you some very public opportunities to turn them down—even in front of their own staff and a couple of our liaisons. We don't like it when they run black ops and don't let us in. Have you agreed to work for them yet?"

Faith remained silent. She raised her binoculars to her eyes to conceal her fear. What had she done? She had only wanted to be seen associating with the Soviets to make herself too risky for the Stasi to trust with a secret mission behind the Russians' backs. Now it was evident it was not only a stupid idea, but a fateful one. After a meeting with the KGB, she would be too much of a liability as long as she was alive. No one could ever survive playing the Stasi off against the KGB. No one had ever dared.

Tatyana continued, "Faith, I know they either have already or soon will threaten your life—and you will agree. Everyone does. And no one will blame you. Being a Stasi agent isn't a fate worse than death, though the career can abruptly end that way."

"I want to be left alone!" Faith surprised herself with her vehemence.

"You need to make a good show of rejecting me in a few minutes when we get to the park bench."

"I'm not working for you."

"You're trapped. I have substantial resources." Tatyana put her hand on her arm, but Faith pulled away and walked ahead of her.

"I can take care of it myself."

"One woman alone can't win against the entire state security organ of the GDR—not even the great Faith Whitney."

"At last count, I'm way ahead in the game. In Vegas, that's time to cash out and walk away."

"I've been to Vegas. High rollers like you can't walk away. I'd hate to see something happen to you. The Germans are a tidy people. They're not going to use an American smuggler to pull off something behind the KGB's back and then leave her around to boast about it. They need you now, but a time will come when they won't. Black ops agents don't have a long shelf life."

Faith stopped.

Tatyana didn't give up. "After this is over, we can help you in ways you've never imagined. Have you ever wanted an export-import business out of Moscow? We can arrange for you to have permission to scour our countryside for your treasures. Cooperate and we can expedite export formalities."

"You're a temptress, but a staid Moscow storefront doesn't sound very sporting," Faith lied. "I need something more—some information."

"Have you agreed to work for them?"

"They threatened my life."

"I know." Tatyana rested her hand on Faith's back as she pretended to point out a bird.

The solace felt genuine and Faith needed it at that moment. She gazed through the binoculars. "I don't know what they're up to. That's all the help I can give you. I don't want to be an agent, and I sure don't want to be a double agent."

"My dear Faith, you knew this day would come. Accept it gracefully. What kind of information do you require?"

"Everything the KGB knows about my father."

"That would mean going into the archives, but I'll see what I can do. Right now we're going to move over to that bench where our friends are listening. You're going to follow my lead and turn me down so they have no doubt that you're not working for me."

They approached a park bench. A young woman pushed a baby stroller nearby and the senior citizen continued to toss seeds to the pigeons, but he now appeared to be watching the birds instead of them. Tatyana sat down. "So, how did you find your first birding experience?"

"I never realized there were so many different ones here. I never paid much attention to anything other than gulls on the bridges and pigeons everywhere." Faith scratched a loose chip of paint from the bench. She was shaken and she hoped she was convincing enough. Everything depended upon it. If the Stasi believed she was talking to the KGB about them, they would kill her.

"Rock doves. Technically they're not pigeons, but rock doves. I think a summer exchange program focusing on the history of Soviet-GDR cooperation is a great idea, but I would have the students spend more time in Moscow than Berlin. We'll have to get the GDR's Education Ministry on board, and I can line things up on the Soviet side."

Tatyana turned her head toward Faith and lowered her voice. "You mentioned your interest in certain art objects. I have excellent connections. Is there anything special you're searching for?"

"Anything designed by Natalia Danko or Kandinsky from the Lomonosov Porcelain Factory in Leningrad."

"You have something particular in mind?"

"A chess set."

"I can get you any chess set you like in exchange for the right item."

"Probably not this one. 'The Reds and the Whites' from the early twenties. It's a masterpiece. The theme obviously is the Great October Revolution. The red figurines are modeled after the communists, the white the—"

"Imperialists."

"Including the Tsar's family. My favorites are the pawns. The reds are liberated reapers with sheathes and sickles and the whites are oppressed peasants, complete with chains."

"I can check around for you. If I find one, maybe you could find something for us in exchange."

"How about a Reagan coffee mug? Now the old geezer is finally out of office, they should start picking up in value. I'll even throw in an old 'Nixon Now' button."

"I think you know what I'm asking for. We always need help getting items on the List—fiber optics, computer chips."

"I can't help you. I agreed to meet you to work out a student exchange program, and I know you'll use it for some propaganda crap, and frankly I don't care. I like you, Tatyana, and maybe we can be friends. But understand this: If you ever try to recruit me again, that's the end. *Basta.*" Faith waved her finger in the air like a schoolteacher scolding a wayward pupil.

"I only thought it might be a mutually beneficial arrangement."

"Save your breath." Faith stood, raising her voice. She yanked the binoculars from around her neck and shoved them toward Tatyana. "Thank you for the interesting afternoon."

"I'm sorry. I won't mention it again. Allow me to take you home or wherever you want to go. It's the least I can do."

"For a few moments, I thought we might be friends without politics getting in the way."

"It is possible. Let me give you a ride back into town."

Faith crumpled into the seat, relieved the tinted windows shielded her from the Stasi's view. She wished she could hide from the KGB as well. "I'm serious—I don't want anything to do with this." Tatyana turned her torso toward

Faith and moved just beyond the boundary of her personal space. "I know you are, but the Stasi hasn't given you any choice. I'm offering help and asking nothing of you. If you should need to get in touch with me, don't call the embassy. Only contact me from the West." Tatyana gave Faith detailed instructions on how to signal her for a rendezvous in the other Berlin.

"And if I'm trapped in the East and need to meet you over here?"

"This is the Stasi's playground. Sorry."

Faith turned away and watched the green fade into urban gray.

"Faith, you don't get what I'm saying. If they saw us here together again doing anything outside of negotiating a cultural exchange with some of their officials present, they'd assume I'm running you and would liquidate you. You also can't go home and talk about this."

"Yeah, I know my phone's bugged."

"Did you know there's a camera in your kitchen? Hakan cooks you pancakes on weekends and sneaks vanilla into the batter when you're not looking."

"I assumed they kept one in the flat in the East, but in West Berlin? Are there bugs?"

"Only the kitchen, but my copy of your MfS dossier predates their current interest."

"Thanks for the heads-up. About the vanilla in the pancakes, I mean." Faith sighed and continued looking out the window as they passed rows of prefab high-rises.

"You're familiar with the Berolina Hotel?"

"Spooks from the Arab embassies hang out in the bar. Some real slimebags."

"It's watched more than average. We're almost there." She tapped on the driver's shoulder and spoke in Russian. "Ivashko, stomp on the brakes in front of the Berolina. Make a scene. Our guest is leaving us there." She switched back to German. "Jump out of the car screaming at me like you've just had a really bad date."

The Chaika drove away. Faith oriented herself by the television tower at Alexanderplatz. She headed toward the Friedrichstrasse border crossing. A Wartburg slowed and drove alongside her. Her heart raced and she quickened her pace. The car sped up. She ducked into a side street in near panic and the car screeched across several lanes of traffic to follow.

She pushed at the door of an apartment building, but it was locked. She smacked every button on the intercom. *Please be home.* She turned to run off just as a girl responded. She stopped.

"Post. Telegram," Faith said.

"Come up." The lock buzzed. Faith reached for the latch.

As she pulled, someone grabbed her from behind. She trembled and her knees started to buckle, but she caught herself.

"Frau Doktor, we must talk."

CHAPTER TWELVE

KGB SAFE HOUSE, DEMOCRATIC BERLIN–MARZAHN
SUNDAY, APRIL 23

The communist planned community of Marzahn was an architectural eugenics experiment gone awry. Bogdanov wound along the endless Ho-Chi-Minh Strasse searching for the back entrance to the KGB safe house, driving past clone after clone of prefabricated apartment buildings, grocery stores and restaurants. The recently constructed but already-decaying buildings reminded her of the inner-city tenements she had seen while on assignment in the States. She preferred the quaint old buildings and cobblestone streets of some of the older districts, such as Karlshorst and Köpenick, but the sprawling anonymity of Marzahn made it much easier to run a safe house and conceal it—even from the Stasi. The Wartburg's brakes squeaked as the colonel parked it in a row of Trabis, Skodas and Ladas.

Bogdanov arrived a half-hour before Kosyk was expected. She was surprised that someone had actually cared enough to add pleasant little touches to the place. Instead of the usual wilted mums in algae-filled water, fresh Gerber daisies decorated the coffee table. A dish of candy sat atop a hand-crocheted doily. She wished she could get this fussy housekeeper reassigned to her office at the embassy before her cleaning crew allowed the dust to cover her pictures entirely. She drew the living-room curtains and poured two shot glasses, one with water, the other with vodka. Kosyk never drank on duty and was known for his irritation with anyone who did. She wanted him in just the right mood.

Kosyk arrived early, even for a German. He slammed his fist onto the table directly in front of Bogdanov, knocking over a vase of flowers and sloshing liquid from the shot glasses. "Who are you to recruit my asset? You're compromising the entire operation."

"You're making a mess. How un-German of you." Bogdanov held herself back from righting the vase and sopping up the water. She instead crossed her legs, leaned back in the green plaid armchair and watched the puddle expand toward the edge. "I think you should calm down, lower your voice and tell me what you're babbling about. You also might want to remember with whom you're speaking. Regardless of any cooperation on this special project, the MfS does not give orders to the KGB."

"You know what I mean—the American. Whitney."

"The professor?"

Kosyk snorted.

"Herr Kosyk, you need to control your agents. And I'm surprised with you. The first rule in this business is never to reveal the identity of your agents—even to a friend like me. I think we're both talking about the one I've designated FedEx."

"FedEx?" Kosyk laughed. "You like the Americans, don't you?"

"Their government's the enemy, not the people. But I want to make it very clear I was not the one who initiated contact. FedEx approached me on an unrelated matter with two of your citizens. They were all hot and bothered because you censored one of our magazines—sort of sweet, actually. I'm surprised you didn't know about it, because I heard you picked up the librarians."

"Stay away from her."

"Not an issue."

"You met with her a second time."

Bogdanov took a piece of Russian hard candy from a glass dish and unwrapped it. "I thought her skills might be useful in acquiring some materials we've been looking for. I had no idea you were interested in her." *Or how interested I would be.*

"You took her to a park."

"It's a much more effective technique to befriend potential assets rather than to coerce them into cooperation—which I understand is your preferred style."

"It's a question of effectiveness." Kosyk's left eye jerked to the side; the right one remained fixed on Bogdanov.

"What are you planning with FedEx?"

Kosyk stood to leave. "We agreed you'd handle recruitment in Moscow and arrange on-site logistics. We handle all disinformation and we deliver you the means to strike the target. Upon receipt in Moscow, the KGB takes control. Beyond this, I see no grounds to share operational details."

"Very well." Bogdanov twisted the waxed candy wrapper as the water from the spilled vase dripped onto the new carpet. "Then I see no need to go into additional details unless you want to have a seat and remind yourself we're working toward the same goal." Bogdanov pointed to an armchair.

Kosyk continued to stand, his arms crossed. "I'm listening."

"Suit yourself." *Arrogant little bastard.* Bogdanov refused to look up to him and instead stared at him as if he were sitting down, but, unfortunately, his crotch was eye level. "Good news from Moscow. We have strong initial support from Gasporov. Our own Spetsnaz unit is with us. Let's drink to early success." She pushed the shot glass of vodka across the table to him and picked up the water-filled glass.

Kosyk shook his head. "Too early and I'm working."

"You're more German than the Germans. But you're a Sorb, aren't you? Your High German's too pure, too practiced. You grew up speaking *sorbski,* didn't you? Tell me, Gregor, did you grow up as *Yurij?*"

"That's of no consequence," he said with force.

"Isn't it? The thought of native Slavs in their *Deutschland* never sat well with our German friends. They've never seemed to like the Sorb minority in their midst, have they? But then, I guess they're not too keen on minorities in general. They've spent the last thousand years trying to assimilate or eliminate our little West Slavic brothers, among others. With you I'd say they succeeded." Bogdanov drank the shot of water. "I wonder if Markus Wolf would've gotten such a sweet retirement deal from the MfS if he'd grown up an ethnic Sorb in Hoyerswerda."

"Wolf deserved nothing." Kosyk's face turned red and his voice quivered with anger. "He was a politician, not a real spook. Good staff, a lot of politics and *Der Spiegel* blew his reputation out of proportion. If he were a Sorb, he never would've advanced beyond major."

"But I hear he's not really retired. He's a major behind-the-scenes player."

"He's nothing. He doesn't even know—" Kosyk interrupted himself and studied Bogdanov. "You're not extracting information from me. Crude, Bogdanov."

"A question of effectiveness."

"Stay away from FedEx. Understand me: If I believe my asset is compromised, I will eliminate her."

CHAPTER THIRTEEN

To learn from the Soviet Union is to learn victory!
—EAST GERMAN COMMUNIST SLOGAN

MFS CENTRAL DETENTION CENTER, [EAST] BERLIN–HOHENSCHÖNHAUSEN

Chipping gray naval paint and smears of blood and feces covered the cinder-block walls of the Stasi prison. The room contained only a table and chair for the interrogator, a stool bolted to the floor, and a slop pail in the corner. Recessed fluorescent lights glowed overhead day and night in the windowless cell. Her side ached from when she fell off the stool and they'd kicked her awake. At this point she would have welcomed a smelly mattress or even a few moments of peace on the grimy floor. Her thoughts were jumbled, but she was certain of one thing: No one ever left this wretched room the same person she went in—except the Stasi interrogators. They never changed. They had no history, no future and probably no present.

The interrogator slapped her, nearly knocking her to the floor. "What does the KGB want with you?"

"I told you. I refused." Faith ran her fingers over her stinging cheek.

"How long have you known Tatyana Medvedev?" The voice was flat, as if the interrogator were bored with the repetition.

"Since Friday."

"Why did you go to the Soviet embassy?"

Faith closed her eyes and turned away. Her mind was numb from fear and exhaustion. She didn't think she could hold out much longer, but she had to. If they believed she'd even talked to the Russians about them, it was over.

"Frau Whitney, answer my question."

"Over and over, I have." Faith sighed and glanced over toward a picture mirror. They had taken away her eyeglasses and everything was a blur, but she knew Schmidt was there, studying her. "Get Schmidt."

"How often did you meet Frau Medvedev?"

Faith turned toward the two-way mirror. "Schmidt," she said and paused for a breath. "Stop, please. I'm not working for them. You've got to believe me. It's the truth."

"Pay attention. How often did you meet Frau Bogdanov?"

"Twice. Wait—Bogdanov?"

"So you do know Bogdanov. When do you meet her next?"

"I don't know Bogdanov. I'm tired. I can't think straight."

"You admit you met Bogdanov twice. How do you contact her?"

"I don't know Bogdanov."

"When did you first meet Zara Antonovna Bogdanov, lieutenant colonel in the KGB?"

"Medvedev's Bogdanov?"

"How do you contact Bogdanov, your KGB handler?"

"I don't know." She pressed her cracking lips together to spread whatever moisture remained and stared at the clear bottle of seltzer water on the table four feet away. "I'm thirsty. Please."

"How do you contact her?" The interrogator looked at Faith with the dissociated gaze of an executioner.

"I don't know."

"What did they offer you?"

"A chess set."

"Why that?"

"I collect."

"Were you interested in their offer?"

"No. May I have water?" Faith yawned. She struggled to concentrate. Small variations could mean hours more of questioning. Or worse.

"So you were interested."

"I'll never work for the KGB." Her words were halting.

"And why should we believe that you would work for the MfS and not the KGB?"

"You know about my father." She fought back tears, but they streamed down her face anyway.

"Did you tell her you're doing a job for us?"

"Absolutely not."

"What did they want?"

"Fiber optics."

"Did you tell them we've approached you?"

"No."

"And why would you work for us and not them?"

"I want to find Daddy." Her voice cracked. "Water, please?"

"Very well."

The interrogator popped the rusty cap from the bottle of seltzer water and poured it into a glass.

"Thank you." Faith reached for the glass. The interrogator jerked it away, threw it into Faith's face and left the room. Faith rushed to the bottle and gulped the remains. She crawled onto the filthy floor, drew her legs tightly against her body to fight away the cold. At least they hadn't taken away her clothes. She fell asleep to the acrid odor of stale urine and dreamed of her father valiantly rescuing her.

Sharp pain awakened her. She grabbed her side just before the interrogator's boot smacked into it again.

"On the stool. I told you never to get off that stool unless I give you permission. What does the KGB want with you?"

"Technology from the List." She clutched her side and had no idea if she had been asleep for seconds or hours.

"Did you tell them you're working for us?"

"No."

"What did you agree to do?"

"Nothing."

"When did you first meet Colonel Bogdanov?"

Faith once again gave the same answer she had every time, but this time the interrogator suddenly left the room. Faith sat on the stool, waiting, but no one came back. She wanted nothing more than to crawl onto the floor and rest. Still, she waited on the stool, wobbling from side to side as she started to fall asleep. She hoped someone knew where she was. Tatyana, or rather Colonel Bogdanov, might know, but she wouldn't help her in East

Berlin. *Dean Reed.* Faith's thoughts kept returning to the American folk singer who defected to the Soviets during the Vietnam War. Soviet youth flocked to his concerts; the more savvy East Germans laughed at their Soviet counterparts, who believed Reed was an American pop icon. Dean Reed couldn't settle into bleak Soviet conditions, so he chose the GDR as his home. He lived peacefully outside East Berlin until he fell out of favor with the regime a few years back. When his body floated face-down in an East German lake, the communists insisted it was suicide. *Dean Reed.* Face-down in the lonely water.

Faith had been in the cell for days, but, without any clues from the outside world, she had no idea how many. Hunger and fatigue stretched the time.

She yawned as she forced her thoughts back to the puzzle. What would happen if they found out the KGB knew the Stasi had successfully recruited her? *Dean Reed.* She had to keep up the lie. Whatever they wanted her for, they didn't want the Russians to know. It made no sense. The Soviets and East Germans were on the same side. East German loyalty had never wavered. Not in fifty-three, when they ordered their own troops to shoot their own workers. Not in sixty-one, when they divided Berlin with a wall. Not in sixty-eight, when their tanks quashed the Prague Spring. The East Germans were Soviet lapdogs. Why would they suddenly want to keep their masters in the dark? Geopolitics aside, what did she have to do with a rift among communists? All Faith wanted was to find out about her father, but she knew she was caught in the rift zone.

And Faith sat on the stool, waiting.

The interrogator kicked her awake from where she had fallen to the floor. She awoke from one nightmare into another.

"What are you doing for the KGB?"

"Nothing." Pain doubled her over as she held on to the stool and tried to pull herself up.

"On your feet. We've had enough." The interrogator yanked her hair.

Her scalp burned. The interrogator pulled a blindfold from a pocket and bound it around her head. Fingers sank into her arm. The interrogator led her from the cell, deliberately running her into the hated stool.

Light seeped under her blindfold. *Artificial. Night, or a windowless hallway?* She sensed someone behind her. She turned her head.

"Walk." The interrogator shoved her.

Damp cool air rose toward her. She tripped on a step, but someone caught her. She smelled the aftershave. *Schmidt. The fucker was here all along.*

The interrogator pushed her into a car and climbed in beside her. The other door opened and Schmidt wedged himself into the backseat. The car seemed smaller than the Mercedes that had picked her up in West Berlin. She doubted he was taking her home. They still needed her, she thought—she hoped.

The car sped down a long, straight road. *Karl-Marx-Allee? Frankfurter Allee? Leipziger Strasse?* She didn't hear many other cars. The bursts of streetlight under the blindfold grew farther apart, then only darkness. The steady swish of the windshield wipers counted down the minutes of her life.

The car stopped.

"Out!" The interrogator pulled her from the car and dragged her several yards into shallow water.

Faith was shoved onto her knees and she sank into the deep cold mud.

The interrogator grabbed her hair and pushed her down. Faith inhaled just before her face smacked the water. It stung all the way up her nose and the burn radiated through her sinuses. She coughed, inhaling more. She fought, but sank deeper. Terror.

The interrogator jerked Faith's head from the water. Faith gasped for air. She couldn't hold on much longer, but she knew her life depended upon it.

"For the last time, when did you first meet Colonel Bogdanov?"

"Friday." She sputtered.

"How do you contact her?"

"I don't."

"What did she want from you?"

"Technology." *Dean Reed.*

"Did you tell her you're working for us?"

"No! No! No!" She was falling into hysteria. "No!"

The interrogator shoved her back under the water. Faith held her breath. Her head throbbed with pressure. Suddenly her lungs contracted. She inhaled, sucking in water. She coughed. She gasped.

Then she was back to the surface.

"What did you tell them about us?"

Faith heaved, her body convulsing. She knew she was going to drown the next time. She had to give them what they wanted. She opened her mouth to tell them the KGB knew.

Before she could speak, the interrogator forced her back under the lonely water.

Dean Reed.

CHAPTER FOURTEEN

If people don't like Marxism,
they should blame the British Museum.
—GORBACHEV

PERGAMON MUSEUM, EAST BERLIN
EARLIER THAT DAY

Margaret prepared to break her vow to God for the second time in some thirty years as she rushed past the Altar of Zeus with its sinful carvings of Greeks exposing their privates to the world. She was taking a shortcut to do His will and she hoped Jesus would forgive her because she wouldn't forgive herself if she took too long to help and more innocent folks were massacred in Armenia. Yurij had proposed the meeting place even though he knew that as a good Christian lady she'd never go near a pagan altar. He always did have a charmingly ironic sense of setting.

She slowed down as she passed under the towering Gate of Ishtar and spotted him pretending to admire the mosaics of scrawny lions on the walls of Babylon. Yurij was an agent of the devil assigned to tempt her away from the Lord and once he almost succeeded in his mission, but this time she had the wisdom of age on her side. He stole a glance and from the way he looked at her she knew he still saw her as the vibrant missionary reaching out to East Berliners before the Wall. She didn't want to let herself see the urbane young gentleman who had duped her into believing that she had led him from Lenin to Jesus. She eyed Yurij and wished he weren't as eye-grabbing as the first day they met.

They stood beside each other, studying some critter made out of glazed brick from the lascivious city of Babylon. Desire tugged at her to reach out and touch him, but she respected protocol. She tapped on a tape recorder borrowed from the museum for a self-guided tour and shrugged her shoulders as if she couldn't get it to work. She pretended to ask Yurij for help.

"Maggie, too many years have wedged between us for me to believe this is a casual visit."

"I think we share a common interest," she said.

"We always have." He took the recorder from her, removed the tape and tightened it. His hair had gone from blond to distinguished platinum.

"I know you people don't like what Gorbachev is up to. And, to tell it to you outright, I don't, either. What's the point in being a Bible smuggler when Bibles are everywhere, but no one's reading them? I can't imagine the spy business is too rewarding nowadays, either. If Gorbachev keeps doing what he's doing, we'll both be victims of history."

"Then there won't be anything more to keep us apart, will there?" Yurij said with a smile.

"Only God and your wife—and I know the one you fear," Margaret said. "But I don't have the right connections to round up enough of what I need. I need you to bend a few rules."

"I don't bend rules."

"I recollect you're more apt to break them." Margaret gestured toward a dragon figure, carefully watching Yurij out of the corner of her eye. He was as fit as always, though he'd added a few pounds to his butt. She still remembered what it was like to squeeze those tight buns.

He randomly pushed buttons on the recorder. "What do you want?"

"Landmines. Lots of them."

"Impossible. What would you do with anti-personnel mines?" Yurij's left eye twitched.

"Military types call it 'territorial denial.' I call it protecting some innocent folks from genocide."

"You'd be better off giving them assault rifles."

"I'd never forgive myself for giving someone offensive weapons they could hurt someone with. I want something purely defensive so I can sleep at night."

"What the devil are you doing?" He put on her headset as if testing the equipment. "You're not getting mixed up with the Caucasus, are you? It's worse there than the Balkans ever were. At least the Serbs feel some guilt when they slit your throats—the Tartars feel only pleasure."

"I've got to try to save them. Children are dying and it's not right. God had to take a very special lady from me to get me to listen to Him. Right before she died in my arms, she delivered a message from the Lord." Tears pooled in Margaret's eyes. "That girl was just like my daughter."

Yurij gingerly pushed back her hair and placed the earphones on her head. "I've seen your daughter. She has her mother's beauty and her wiles."

"You stay away from my girl."

"You two haven't talked in years."

"She's still my baby. Look me in the eyes and promise me you'll leave her be." She faked a smile for anyone watching.

"I'll arrange the Moscow contacts you need to acquire the mines. I don't have the funds to underwrite you, so you'll have to finance them yourself."

"Promise me?" Margaret said.

He shook hands with her to maintain the façade of two strangers and slipped her a hotel key. "You know I can never resist you, Maggie. Meet me there in a half-hour. I've waited on you for so long."

Jesus forgive me, but my flesh is weak. Margaret wrestled with the guilt of rapture as she formulated her prayers for forgiveness.

CHAPTER FIFTEEN

A single death is a tragedy,
a million deaths a statistic.
—STALIN

EAST BERLIN
1:17 A.M. TUESDAY, APRIL 25

Faith knelt in the muddy shallows, coughing and gasping for life. She ripped off the blindfold and stumbled to the riverbank. She lay on the ground, hacking, purging the water from her lungs. With each cough, white pain shot through her side.

She crossed her arms and pressed them against her shivering body to preserve heat. Wet hair clung to her face. They had her glasses, but they would have been useless in the pounding rain and darkness. She looked around, but could make out only shadows. The sky glowed in one direction. West Berlin. *Thank God for capitalist decadence*. She pushed herself up and dragged herself toward the light, toward the West—even though she had no way of crossing the Wall.

She wandered through the woods for what seemed like hours. She stepped into a hole, jarring her entire body. Curling up and sleeping was all she wanted to think about, but she pushed on. The rain pelted her and melted the forest floor into mud. Her foot sank several inches into the muck, but her next step met resistance. *A sidewalk.* She cried tears of relief as her foot tapped against the concrete. She followed it with renewed determination when she saw lights flickering through the trees.

Even without her glasses, she could recognize a familiar figure, a titanic Red Army soldier protecting the child. At that moment she wanted to take the child's place. She told herself she'd be okay and, for the first time in days, she believed it. She knew where she was—Treptower Park. Back on familiar ground, her thoughts were free to move beyond survival. She realized she'd done it—she'd convinced them she had nothing to do with the KGB. Faith Whitney had beaten the Stasi—at least in this round. The rush energized her and she picked up her pace.

The rain slacked off as she reached the S-Bahn station. It was deserted except for several stray cats. No suspicious cars were parked nearby. She collapsed onto a bench and waited for a train. Her tormentors were probably at home, sleeping off their fun. She'd never truly desired to kill before, but she wanted them dead. Most of all, she wanted to get Schmidt. Maybe he was the one who took her father from her. He was old enough to have been there. She craved revenge for herself and for her father as she stretched out on the hard bench and quivered with rage, chill and pain.

Faith had no visa, no passport and no money, but she hoped she had a friend. She clung to the shadows as she darted into Jürgen's apartment building. She removed her shoes so she didn't leave a muddy trail for the Stasi to follow. She knocked on the door, too depleted to worry about his reaction. No answer. When she couldn't wait any longer, she pounded. A light switched on.

"Faith, it's three in the morning." Jürgen slurred his words. A hasty knot held his bathrobe barely closed. "Come in before the neighbors—"

"Thank you." Her voice was raspy, her throat raw. A test pattern flickered on the black and white television. Cigarette ashes floated in a glass beside an empty whiskey bottle. Jürgen rustled through a stack of old newspapers and spread a *Neues Deutschland* on the floor for her shoes.

"Sorry about the hour. I need help."

"I see that. Don't worry about it. I haven't gone to bed yet." He rubbed his glassy eyes.

"Hakan and I had a fight."

"You here to talk about it? I'm the last person you want to talk about relationships with."

"Any signs after the embassy visit that the Stasi's been here?" Each word was an effort.

"Come to think of it, Friday, when I came home, the place didn't feel right. I haven't thought any more about it, but it struck me at the time that some things were a little off, a chair in the kitchen, some papers on my desk. What's going on?"

"You checked for cameras or bugs?" She steadied herself on the back of a chair and lied to herself that she was safe. Her ribs ached with each breath.

"Faith, are you all right?" Jürgen reached out and steadied her, then helped ease her down into an armchair. "Hakan didn't beat you up, did he?"

"Hakan, never." Faith shook her head. "They hide them in light fixtures. Any electric plugs go bad lately?"

"Yeah, now that you mention it, one in the kitchen went out late last week. I should get you to a doctor. You look really bad."

"Check it."

Faith wanted to soak longer in the tub, but was afraid she'd fall asleep and slip under the warm bathwater. The bruises on her rib cage had turned a deep purple. She forced herself to palpate them. Some had to be cracked. She carefully pulled on a bathrobe and shuffled into the kitchen.

Frayed wires hung from the wall and a tiny camera and microphone were proudly displayed on the table. She sat down and Jürgen draped a wool blanket around her shoulders. She downed two spoonfuls of honey immediately in hopes of quickly raising her blood sugar. Jürgen poured coffee into a chipped mug. "You take cream, don't you?"

Faith nodded, conscious of the weight of her head. She slopped butter onto dark whole-kernel bread, slapped a piece of cheese on top and downed it in a few hasty bites. "I can't thank you enough."

"Looks like you could use a friend right now. Want to tell me what's going on? Why are they watching me?"

The food revived her. "You went to the Soviet embassy. They're allergic to anything related to Gorbachev." She bought herself time to think with a mouthful of cheese. She wanted to trust him, but he was a Party member and a man with problems. The Stasi specialized in people like him. "Hakan and

I had it out—but he didn't touch me. I should get my own place. It's stupid, but it always is. I had to get away, so I came East and went for a stroll in Treptower Park. I forgot how few streetlights there are here. It got dark fast. I fell into the mud and lost my glasses. I got turned around."

Jürgen studied her face with the care of a palmist reading every line. "You don't act like this is the first meal you've missed. Your eyes are bloodshot like from lack of sleep, not swollen like you've been crying. When women fight, they cry. Believe me, I know. So, how badly do you want me to believe this bull?"

"Enough not to want to involve you."

"You know I stand up for what's right, but you have to be straight with me."

Faith took a breath, opened her mouth, then hesitated. Jürgen once wrote a dissertation that his adviser called brilliant, but refused to accept until three politically inappropriate footnotes were removed. He refused and left the doctoral program rather than compromise his principles. Faith supposed she could trust him. She had to. She had to connect with someone and let out a little of the terror.

"I can't go into details, but I spent time with the *Association.*"

"Jesus Christ."

"What day is today?"

"Tuesday."

"Almost three days. I thought four or five." She devoured another slice of bread with cheese. "They thought I had something going on with the Russians. They kept asking me about our trip to the embassy, implying I was working for the KGB."

"Are you?"

"No." She finished the coffee and held out her cup for more. "They dumped me. It's wretched out there tonight." Memories of her struggle for breath were too raw to touch. She coughed and it hurt.

"Yeah, it's been months since we've had so much rain."

"They kept everything, including my passport."

"So you refused them."

Faith spread black currant jam on the bread. "I'm sure they're trapping me here for another crack at me, but I'm not giving it to them. I'll scale the Wall first." She sipped the coffee, ignoring the grit.

Jürgen stared at her. "I saw a report on West Berlin TV the other day. A dozen people make it over every month."

"I was joking. I've heard the shots at night. I am getting out of here and then I'm leaving Germany for good. The stakes are too high. Please understand that if you tell anyone I'm here, your words could translate into my death."

"They talk to me from time to time, you know. I don't like it, but what can you do?"

"Try not to talk to them until after I'm gone. Please."

"You know how it is." He bowed his head, paused and then pushed himself back from the table. "I'll make you up a bed on the divan. Stay as long as you like. I have a friend I trust who's a doctor. If you want—"

"Thanks. Some ribs are cracked, maybe broken, but there's not much anyone can do for that."

"You're very pale."

"I can't risk it."

"I'll get you a sports bandage and something for the pain. It'll help you sleep, too."

"That package I left with you before we went to the embassy. I need it."

"It's somewhere in my office. The library's closed at this hour, but I could get it if you really need it."

"Get it to me right after work—five at the latest should give me enough time. I know a call to the West is out of the question, so could you send a telegram to Hakan?" She picked up a pen and scrawled on the back of an envelope.

Happy Birthday. Weather bad here. Hope your day is clear. Love MP.

She shoved it across the table to Jürgen and hoped Hakan hadn't again disappeared on another wild date.

CHAPTER SIXTEEN

Sometimes . . . when you stand face-to-face with someone, you cannot see his face.

—GORBACHEV

LUBYANKA (KGB HEADQUARTERS), MOSCOW

Colonel Bogdanov entered the new KGB building through the main entrance on Dzerzhinsky Square, masking her true emotions as she had learned to do in Party meeting after Party meeting. The palatial entrance with its towering marble columns, crystal chandeliers, plush red oriental carpets and mahogany paneling was too reminiscent of the opulence of tsarist and Stalinist designs for her taste. The illusion of grandeur only reinforced the feelings of omnipotence among the petty bureaucrats working within those walls. And she had seen too many suffer at their hands.

A few minutes later, she entered Stukoi's outer office. The warm greeting from his secretary indicated she was anticipating another gift from Germany. *Good.*

"Pyatiletka, every time I see you, you look younger," Bogdanov said. In truth, every time she saw her, she not only had aged, but had also added to her babushka physique.

"Did you get my cheese? The one with the peppercorns?" Pyatiletka said.

Bogdanov sat in the chair beside her desk and suddenly found herself looking up at the stumpy woman. She was certain Pyatiletka had sawed off a few inches from the chair legs so that she could tower over any visitors. "Any news for me?"

Pyatiletka took a deep breath, leaned closer to Bogdanov and spoke in hushed tones. "I hear that General Titov isn't happy about your being reassigned away from his direct command. He threw quite a fit here a few days ago. I'd watch my back around him, if you know what I mean. He has family in high places. Remember what he did to Skorik."

"How is he?"

"He was here a few weeks ago. He left Afghanistan, but it hasn't left him. Sometimes I wonder what the point of this place is. What is the point? Everyone's scurrying around, recruiting agents, stealing enemy documents. We're all up to here in information." The fat of her upper arm sloshed back and forth when she held her hand above her head. "And despite all of it, we only write reports of what our leaders want to hear. Now I was talking to a girl in the typing pool—I can't say who—I think you understand. She says it happens to her all the time. She types up a report from one of our boys and it goes to his supervisor. Three days later the supervisor makes her retype it, only this time, things are all rosy: Socialism is on the march and the imperialists are cowering in fear. And that's always the report with the distribution list for people at the top. I don't know how anyone can know what's really going on in the world from the whitewash that comes out of here."

"That's why Gorbachev has been trying—"

"Don't get me started on Gorbachev." Pyatiletka made a spitting sound. "You can't buy anything right now on my salary. Speculators everywhere steal goods that are supposed to go to state stores and sell them for too much. They've siphoned everything away from the stores. In Stalin's day, none of this would happen." She wagged her plump finger.

Bogdanov dropped a package wrapped in white butcher's paper onto her desk. She motioned with her head toward Stukoi's office. "So, what's the big boy up to lately?"

Pyatiletka shoved the German cheese into her drawer. "Do you think you could get me some bratwurst next trip?"

Bogdanov nodded.

Pyatiletka's eyes darted back and forth and she made an exaggerated check for eavesdroppers. She lowered her voice to a whisper. "Ever since you were here last, he's been leaving at odd times. He won't tell me what he's up to. At first I thought he had swapped mistresses again, but I asked the other girls. Now, you didn't hear this from me, but Zolotov, Karlov and Gasporov have all been unaccounted for at the same times."

"I thought Stukoi despised Karlov."

"And Titov hasn't spoken to Gasporov in over ten years—until this week. But remember, you didn't hear it from me."

When Bogdanov entered Stukoi's office, he greeted her, ignoring the ringing bank of telephones beside his desk. He motioned toward the sofa and walked over to join her. Bogdanov was surprised at the uncharacteristic engagement of her former mentor, who was famous for endless telephone conversations in the middle of scheduled meetings. Even when he was attentive, he was skimming field reports.

He wants something.

Whatever it was, she wouldn't give him FedEx—not yet. All assets were disposable to him, and she didn't want him making any decisions that might put the woman at further risk. Kosyk endangered her enough.

"You've generated significant interest around here." A cigar dangled from his mouth as he spoke.

"I thought we were going to keep this very quiet." Bogdanov studied his face, but couldn't read him. He was too professional to let any hint slip that might confirm Pyatiletka's suspicions.

"Tell me what our Germans are up to."

"They're attempting to use an American agent I've designated FedEx to move goods from here to Moscow. My working assumption is it's some type of weapon, most likely American-built. What I'm not so sure about is why they're using a courier unless it's part of a scheme to blame the Americans. I wouldn't be surprised if they plan on burning the agent to expose CIA involvement."

Stukoi took a long drag from the cigar. "Assumptions, speculations. What do you *know*?"

"The Germans are going to run into difficulties controlling FedEx. She's got a mind of her own and knows how to use it."

"Sounds like some of the problems we've had controlling our agents—don't get me started about problems with some of our immigrants to Israel. We help the goddamn Zionists get there and then, once they're there, they thumb their big noses at us." He tapped the cigar on the edge of the crystal ashtray.

"Kosyk didn't exactly approach her with a soft touch. After she met with me, he had a long talk with her—at least a day long and counting. I'm assuming they wanted to know what we wanted with her."

"You fool! And you're speculating again. Don't you know anything? How could you be so sloppy as to let them know we've approached FedEx?" He banged his fist on the coffee table and ashes toppled from his cigar. "Why did you have to screw it up?"

"I salvaged the situation. FedEx came to me in the embassy on an unrelated matter and requested a follow-up meeting. At that point, I knew they would assume I was running her. I chose a very public place for her to refuse to cooperate with us."

"You took a big risk. Too big."

"I trust my judgment. And now we have them convinced we're not a threat."

"Or at least that you didn't turn their stubborn agent. You idiot, Bogdanov. Stupid moves like this are why you'll never make full colonel."

"FedEx is mine," she blurted out and immediately regretted it. "I turned her."

"Interesting. Get back to Berlin immediately and find FedEx after they let her go and make damn well sure she's cooperating with them—and us. When you meet with Kosyk, tell him General Karlov sends his greetings. His Moscow garrisons will not be coming out in defense of Mr. Gorbachev."

CHAPTER SEVENTEEN

EAST BERLIN

Faith slept until noon, awoke long enough to stumble into the bathroom and then went back to bed. It hurt too much to breathe deeply, so she settled for short, shallow breaths. The stabbing pain was now intermittent. Mostly she ached.

She tossed and turned for hours, worried that Jürgen had gone to the Stasi. When her fear became strong enough to force her awake, she got up and dressed in his ex-wife's clothes. At least now she had the costume to pass for an East German while she wandered the streets trying to devise a better escape plan. Then she heard Jürgen walk into the apartment. She checked outside the window for a fire escape, but the building's architects didn't plan on a fire. She took a deep breath and went into the living room.

He carried flowers and an assortment of groceries she recognized from Delikat, the state-run chain selling Western and high-quality Eastern goods at inflated prices. She smiled and helped him carry the bundles into the kitchen.

Faith sat at the table and sipped a Vita-Cola. Over her years in the East, she had grown fond of the East German Coca-Cola imitation. She swished it in her mouth, savoring the full-bodied kola-nut flavor as her short fingernails plucked at the chartreuse label, working their way toward the bear logo. Jürgen tossed a parcel onto the table. She caught it before it slid into the squat bottle. Its seal was still intact.

"Thought I wasn't going to find your stuff for a minute. I didn't realize I collect so much in a day or two."

"Thanks. So I take it no one came around asking about me." Her throat had quickly recovered and it no longer hurt to talk.

"I have to disappoint." Jürgen rifled through a cabinet, clanking pots. "Come to think of it, the cultural attaché, Medvedev, did call just as I was walking out the door. She wanted to follow up on our visit. She asked about you, if I'd seen you lately or knew how to reach you."

She feigned indifference, although she wanted nothing more than Bogdanov's help to get out of the East.

"I told her you always seemed to pop up at odd times." Jürgen pulled a pot from the cabinet, reached inside and retrieved a roll of West German marks. He held his forbidden life savings in his left hand. "Maybe this can help you get out of here."

"That's so sweet of you, but you already brought me everything I need." She patted the package.

Jürgen nodded and bent down to return his stash to its hiding place. "Medvedev is interested in arranging an exchange for me with my counterpart at the Lenin Library in Moscow. It'd be interesting to review how the new access criteria are formulated now under glasnost."

"You mean how they make up new censorship guidelines? Fascinating." Faith tuned out Jürgen's discourse on censorship criteria while she mulled over Bogdanov's intent. She had made it clear that she couldn't help her in East Berlin, so why did she try to get information about her? Faith finally interrupted the monologue. "I don't mean to be rude, but there are a few things I need to take care of before I can be on my way. I have an appointment in a couple of hours."

"Anything I can do to help?"

"The less you know, the better off you are. Give me some time in private."

"You need anything?"

"A flat surface, your brightest lamp and a magnifying glass, if you have one."

"I've got one with my stamp collection. I'd offer you my desk, but I haven't seen the surface in recent memory. Kitchen table okay? I'll see what else I can find."

Jürgen delivered a desk lamp and a scratched magnifying glass, then excused himself. She ripped into the package. It had seemed excessive when she assembled it, but now as she sat in East Berlin without her passport, it seemed minimal: a dog-eared French paperback, a plastic bag from Galeries Lafayette, an oversized European wallet, three train tickets, a blank East German transit visa and a cardboard box. She opened the wallet and counted the banknotes—five hundred dollars, fifteen hundred marks and three thousand francs. She hoped it would be enough.

She removed her new passport, *République Française.* Hakan had done a flawless job replacing Marie-Pièrre Charbonnier's picture with hers. Madame Charbonnier was a few years older, but, given her recent experiences, she was certain she could pass.

The Berlin border guards would be on alert for her and several knew her by sight. It seemed ridiculous to take a roundabout route to get to the other side of town, but this was Berlin and the two parts of the city were worlds apart. She fanned out the Reichsbahn tickets purchased in the West: *Hamburg*, *Praha* and *Warszawa*. The frontier to West Germany was almost as tight as to West Berlin, and they would expect her to head West, so the Hanseatic city was out.

Security between Eastern Bloc countries was high, but not as severe as between East and West. She had considered Prague, then making her way to West Germany, but the Czechs were more Prussian than the East Germans and might cause trouble for her on their side.

On the Polish-German frontier, the focus was on political and economic smuggling, the emphasis shifting with the direction of the border traffic. Guards scrutinized arrivals from the East for any Solidarity or glasnost contaminants. Eastbound travelers to Poland were searched for East German consumer goods; chronic shortages of basic necessities in Poland ensured a thriving black market between the two countries. No one would expect her to head farther east to flee to the West. She selected the one-way ticket to Warsaw and shoved the rest aside for disposal.

The ticket, passport and money were useless without the appropriate East German visa and corresponding entry stamp. Hakan had already taken care of the Polish document—a business visa valid for the next three months. Faith wished he could have done the same with the East German one, but GDR transit visas were only issued on the day they were valid and they were only good for the expected length of the journey. The East Germans had high standards.

Hakan had assembled everything she needed to issue herself a visa into a cigar box. She prayed that the years of watching his meticulous work were enough. If only she had paid more attention to his tedious instructions.

She calculated her fictitious time of entry. The evening train would leave Bahnhof Zoo in West Berlin at 9:45 and in about ten minutes it would enter a secured area of the Friedrichstrasse station, where border guards processed the transit visas for travelers to Poland and beyond. Her entry time into the GDR would be twenty-two hundred hours—two hours away. She picked up the rubber stamp and studied it, admiring Hakan's carving skill. The state seal of the GDR was in the upper left corner, an electric-train icon in the other. Faith needed to insert the date and hour into the middle of the rectangular stamp. She opened the box, unfolded a tissue paper packet marked TIME, and squinted to make out the rubber numbers he had sculpted for her.

The rubber-cement vial had glued itself shut. On the way to the sink she managed to twist it open. She scraped a toothpick against the brush to collect a small drop and dabbed it into the middle of the stamp. She turned the toothpick around and removed the excess. Pain zinged through her rib cage and she jumped. Holding her breath, she picked up the tiny number, flipped it backwards, and teased it into place. As she had seen Hakan do countless times, she held the stamp at eye level and checked the alignment. She shook each bottle of ink and twisted off the caps. She dipped a toothpick into the blue ink, smeared it on the lower third of the stamp and then repeated the process with red on the upper portion. She checked her fingers for splatters and stamped the passport, then the visa form.

With a flick of the razor blade, she scraped away the face of the rubber stamp, then dumped the shavings and the extra numbers into an ashtray. The flame of Jürgen's lighter melted the evidence. Faith rolled it between her palms into a ball. She wished she could show it to Hakan, even though she knew her handiwork wouldn't pass the master's inspection. Fortunately he wasn't a border guard working at a lonely outpost on the graveyard shift. She'd done a damn good job, under the circumstances.

The train rumbled into the East Berlin Hauptbahnhof just as Faith dashed up the concrete stairs as fast as she could, given her shooting pain. The wide green Soviet cars rolled by her, each displaying the state seal of the USSR. Destination signs hung on each one: PARIS, BERLIN, WARSZAWA, MOSKVA. Next came the Polish cars, but she waited for the more comfortable and cleaner Reichsbahn wagons. She held a second-class ticket, but would bribe her way into a first-class sleeper once in Poland. She climbed onto the train, favoring her right side, and searched for a seat.

The conductor blew his whistle and the train lurched forward. She steadied herself with the rail as she walked along. She passed by a cabin filled with Arab students. The odds were good they would be closely scrutinized and she didn't want to risk any guilt by association. Two Polish women sat in the next cabin along with a young man reading a French travel guide to Krakow. A conversation in her weathered French was something to be avoided, so she went on until she found what she was looking for. In the next compartment a couple sat together on the side facing the direction of travel. From their clothes, hairstyles and demeanor, she knew she'd found what she was waiting for: a staid East German couple probably off to visit relatives who got stuck in Poland when the German border was shoved west after the war. She went inside and settled into the window seat, facing west as the train carried her deeper into the East.

A little before midnight, the train rolled into Frankfurt an der Oder—the *other* Frankfurt. Faith placed the French paperback on her lap. She took her passport from the plastic bag and crumpled the bag on the seat next to her with the French logo visible. She was Marie-Pièrre Charbonnier, a French national, on her way to see Warsaw. Nurturing her anger at the fictitious thieves who stole her purse and luggage in West Berlin, she sank further into character.

"Passport control." A guard slid the door open. A metal case hung around his neck by a wide leather strap. A small shelf folded down from it like the display case of a 1950s cigarette girl.

"Passports, please."

Faith handed him her documents.

He glanced at her picture and flipped through the pages until he found her handiwork. The officer pulled out his stamp, aligned it with the edge and pressed it against the passport. He unfolded the visa, stamped it and filed it in his case.

"Please." He held the passport out to Faith.

"Merci." She smiled but didn't exhale. She wasn't in Poland yet.

A second official entered the cabin. "Customs control. Your customs declaration, please."

Merde.

CHAPTER EIGHTEEN

EMBASSY OF THE USSR, DEMOCRATIC BERLIN

The KGB technical support staff moved the antenna up and down along the walls of the cultural attaché's office as if washing a window with a squeegee. Bogdanov noticed him pausing for a moment near a picture of Gorbachev joking with assembly-line workers. For months the cleaning crew had ignored the coat of filth along the frame, but in the few hours that Bogdanov was away in Moscow that morning, someone had been inspired to dust. The technician finished the wall and removed his headphones.

"The room's clean."

"Would you mind leaving your equipment behind? I'll have it sent to you shortly," Bogdanov said.

"I can't. I'm responsible for it."

"Since when is anyone around here responsible for anything? That's an order."

He set the device on the table. "I should stay in case you have any questions about how it functions."

"Dismissed."

The lieutenant left the room.

"What's this all about?" Bogdanov's assistant, Major Alexander Ivashko, tapped his pen on the cherry-wood desk.

Bogdanov held a finger in front of her lips and put on the earphones. She walked over to the print and moved the dial to the highest sensitivity setting, noting the low setting where the tech had left it. She waved the antenna over the corner of the frame. It shrieked. She yanked the earphones off and rubbed her ears. Even with the low sensitivity level the tech had used, the tone was unmistakable.

She removed the picture and found a tiny slit cut into the brown-paper backing. She ripped away the paper, furious someone was checking up on her. A transmitter was lodged in the corner of the frame. She plucked it out. Both the MfS and KGB used the Soviet-designed remote-listening device in their arsenals of tricks, but, with German perfectionism, the MfS had its own improved production line. She recognized its origins immediately.

Made in the USSR.

She dropped it into a cup, splashing stale coffee onto the desk. Without bothering to wipe up the spill, she donned the headphones again and swept the entire room. After her search yielded no additional eavesdroppers, she sat down in an armchair across from the major.

"Us or them?" Ivashko said.

"Who would ever have thought 'us or them' would mean KGB or MfS?"

"I heard Titov was throwing bottles across the room when he found out you're reporting directly to Moscow instead of to him. How'd you know the tech was lying?"

"Some of my dust was missing. And the tech jerked his head a little when he got the hit."

"You think it's Titov?"

"Probably, but I don't want to get caught up in residency politics." And she didn't want to speculate with Ivashko that Stukoi might even be behind it. From now on, she'd trust no one. "Moscow wants us to find FedEx, fast. She can't go directly to West Berlin from the East. She's a known quantity. She'll somehow get to West Germany and fly to West Berlin. We'll catch up with her there. I want the officers assigned to both Tegel and Tempelhof to be on the lookout for her. Have them check the arrival manifests for the last couple days. Get them her photo, known aliases. And check with every hotel in West Berlin. Put your best surveillance team on the Turk she lives with. She'll contact him and the Turk will take us to her."

CHAPTER NINETEEN

A lie told often enough becomes the truth.

—LENIN

EAST GERMAN–POLISH BORDER
12:03 A.M., WEDNESDAY, APRIL 26

Faith sat on the bench in the stuffy train compartment staring at the seat numbers, feeling trapped. She hated herself for being so careless as to forget the customs-declaration form. The Berlin border guards never bothered with it and their complacency had lulled her into her own.

The customs official stood before her and repeated his request for her form.

Charbonnier. Je suis Madame Charbonnier. But the real Charbonnier wouldn't understand the seriousness of her faux pas. So from that second on, neither did Faith.

"*Rien à déclarer,*" Faith said as she studied the hammer-and-compass state seal on his uniform's aluminum buttons.

"This one," the East German customs official said in heavily accented French and held up a declaration form.

"I have none."

"You fill one out when you arrive in the GDR."

"No, no. I have nothing like that. I filled out a card and paid five marks.

The officer in Berlin gave me the visa. That was all." She shook her head with stereotypical French indignity.

"Wait here." The officer stepped into the hall and called his supervisor.

"So what do we have here?" the supervisor said in German.

"The Frenchwoman. She has no customs declaration."

"What does she have with her?"

"I don't know. She doesn't have the form."

"Find out what's she's got."

The official turned to Faith and asked for her luggage in broken French.

"This is all." She waved her hand over her plastic bag. "My valise and purse were stolen at Bahnhof Zoo in West Berlin. You can contact your colleagues there. I made a police report. There was no time to buy anything or I would have missed my train."

The officer translated for the supervisor. The older man shook his head. "Tell her she should have gone shopping in the West when she had the chance."

Exactly twenty-four hours after Faith had left Jürgen's apartment, she arrived at the Hotel InterContinental in West Berlin—ten kilometers from where she started. She showered and crawled into bed. CNN International repeated a story about the environmental impact of last month's Exxon Valdez oil spill, but she was too groggy to care yet too wired to sleep. Sometime the next morning, a persistent knock jarred her into consciousness. Every muscle in her body complained of its miserable existence as she jumped from the bed and fumbled with the hotel robe. She rushed across the room and pressed her ear against the door.

"Hey, it's me. Open up," Hakan said.

She unbolted the door and shielded herself from view behind it. Hakan squeezed through the crack in the doorway and then she locked the door. She slid her arms around him and didn't let go even after she noticed her robe soaking up moisture from his drenched trenchcoat. She squeezed too tightly and sharp pain radiated from her ribs.

"You okay?" Hakan said.

"I'm going back to the States." Her voice was weak.

"I've called the Interconti nonstop since the telegram. I haven't been able to get any of my work done except your backlog. You know, I even considered going East to try to find you."

"Really? You'd break your vow for me?"

"I said 'considered.' " He flashed a smile, but she didn't return it.

"I would have given anything to have had you there a couple days ago. Your junior-counterfeiter's kit was a lifesaver."

"What can I say? You trained with the best. I do have some ideas about things I'll add next time . . . if there is a next time." Hakan placed his wet umbrella in the wastepaper basket beside the writing table and set a small suitcase on the floor. "How serious was it?"

She turned away from him and walked to the window. She pushed back the heavy drapes and peeked out. Sheets of rain nearly hid the bombed-out shell of the Gedenknis Kirche. She jerked the curtains shut before anyone could see her. "It's over."

"No way."

"The goddamn Cold War's gone hot on me, too hot. I can't do it anymore. I'm getting out," she said in a monotone.

"I never thought you'd come to your senses and, honestly, I don't believe it. You can't let go that easily. You're an addict."

"I just overdosed. I'm leaving Berlin and getting out of Germany and I don't give a crap if I ever set foot on this screwed-up continent again."

"I'll never understand what you see in the whole communist mystique, but it's what you do, who you are. It's what you grew up with, for Christ's sake—and I mean that literally and figuratively."

"Then I'll just have to join a twelve-step group to get over it. 'Hi. My name's Faith. I'm a spy-a-holic. It's been nine days since my last strip-search.' "

"This isn't like you."

"And it's not like you to encourage me to stay in the game."

"If I told you to get out, you'd jump right back in. I've had a lot of time to think since the telegram. At first I thought I should do whatever it took to get you to get out, but then I realized it would be a tragedy. You wouldn't be you anymore. I've seen it before when people abandon their loves. It's not pretty. Granted, I think it's strange what you do, but it gives you life. Regular jobs drain it from you. You know what it's like to have a zeal for your work and you won't settle for less, but less is pretty much what's out there." He turned on a lamp beside the bed. "You also can't stay in the dark like this."

Faith squinted as she adjusted to the light. "I'm not as pathetic as it looks, holed up in a dark hotel room. I really was sleeping before you got here." Faith ran her hand along the base of the desk lamp, gathering dust as her fingers searched for a switch.

Hakan disappeared into the bathroom and returned with a towel. "What would you do? You're not the nine-to-five type."

"I have a real doctorate from Michigan. I could become a real professor."

"I can't see you grading freshman papers and dreaming of the upcoming alumni tour you get to lead down the Ohio. Maybe during your lecture you'd get to drop a story or two about your last secret-police encounter—the big one that put you on the sidelines and sent you downriver with a bunch of geriatric donors."

"The price is too high to stay in the game. They've threatened my life if I don't cooperate and do a run to Moscow."

"That's old news." He mopped the beads of water from the valise, turning the towel brown as he wiped through strata of dirt.

"The KGB thinks the Stasi's likely to kill me even if I do cooperate. They offered to help, but it's all too much."

"Not for the Faith Whitney I know. That's enough to pique her interest." He leaned into the bathroom doorway and threw the soiled towel onto the floor. "What did they do to you?"

"Held me for days of questioning and dumped me in a park—without my glasses or my passport."

"That should have been enough to get you hot and bothered. So why aren't you plotting the overthrow of communism or some other way to pull their pants down? They did something else to you, didn't they? Look at me and tell me nothing else happened."

Faith returned to the window and glanced outside. She closed the dusty curtains, but held on to them in silence. After a minute she spoke. "I can't go up against the entire Stasi alone."

"You have before. And I thought you said it seemed like only a small group or cell or gaggle or whatever they're called."

"It's a handful at best. They definitely want to keep it contained."

"So it's you up against a couple of secret agents and the KGB volunteered to help. If it weren't against my religion, I'd put my money on you."

"That's sweet of you, but it's time to roll up shop for a while. Set me up with American papers, someone not very well traveled, no Middle East, no communist stamps. I want to go through US customs without anyone looking at me twice. If I need to get a message to you, I'll go through Bahadir. Just make sure he knows not to tell you anything over the phone."

"He knows your standard procedure—gets quite a charge out of it."

"You're going to have to take me seriously on this one." She peeked out the window. She didn't recognize anyone or anything suspicious, but the rain blurred everything. "I'm not paranoid. It might interest you to know the Stasi has a camera in our kitchen. And you were almost ready to commit me when I first insisted the phone was tapped."

"What right do they have to spy on me? I'm calling the Verfassungsschutz."

"And tell them that the Stasi is observing you eat your Rice Krispies? Snap, crackle, pop."

"They can't do that. This is *West* Berlin—not their Berlin."

"It's all their Berlin. I've got to get out of here."

"What the hell do they want with our kitchen?"

"Forget about the kitchen. What I'm worried about is your study. I don't want them to see what you're doing for me. Look around and even check the smoke detectors I brought over from the States, though I doubt the installers ever stray from their usual tricks."

Hakan opened the suitcase. Usually he was an exacting packer, but the clothes were wadded and shoved together. Faith could tell he had left the flat immediately when he knew she was back in town. She felt his concern in every wrinkle.

"I have a new identity for you—Jutta Menning. Oh, I nearly forgot; this arrived on the doorstep for you yesterday evening." Hakan dropped a small package onto the crumpled bedspread. The distinctive coarse gray paper bound with twine screamed "Made in the GDR."

"They won't leave me alone." She tugged at the string. Hakan pulled a knife from his pocket and sliced it open. A glass case was accompanied by an envelope with her name typed on it. She flipped the case over and read the gold inscription: MADE FOR KARL-ZEISS-JENA. She slid the glasses onto her face. "The Stasi interrogates me for days, threatens my life, dumps me in a bog in the middle of the night, but goes to the trouble of finding a glass case and a nice one at that. Go figure." She pulled her glasses off and held them up to the lamp for inspection. "They even cleaned the lenses."

"They might be commies, but they're still Germans."

"After this, I'm going back to my contacts. Did you bring them?"

"In your cosmetic bag. Faith, look at me and tell me what they did to you."

She glanced at him and then turned away, shaking her head. He put his hand on her shoulder. She slowly turned her head back to him. *Dean Reed.* "They held me under the Spree."

"That could make you really ill. You didn't swallow any, did you?"

"I never swallow."

"I wouldn't know." Hakan smiled, exposing his mouth full of gold fillings.

"I didn't think they were going to drown me at first because they need me, but when the water got into my lungs, I thought it was over." Her affect was flat. "I just went through Warsaw and both Frankfurts to go a couple of blocks across this schizophrenic city."

"I'm not responsible for your poor sense of direction." Hakan paused while he studied her eyes. "Come on, laugh for me. You're starting to scare me, and I'm not talking about the Stasi stuff."

"Nothing like a near-wrongful-death experience to shake you up a bit," Faith said.

"I could handle it if you were agitated, but if we hooked you up to a heart monitor right now, we'd see a flatline. When did you start feeling this way?" Hakan hoisted a suitcase onto the bed. The leather trim was worn to a slick, shiny finish.

"Don't go crawling into my head," Faith said, then paused to think. "I guess I kind of shut down when I made the decision to quit."

"Think the two are related?"

"Back off, Sigmund." She opened her mouth to say something, then closed it. She looked him in the eyes for the first time that morning. "You might be on to something. Before the decision I was angry and terrified, but I felt alive, very alive. You can't imagine the thrill of facing death and beating it, beating them. I realize it sounds warped."

"At least you're aware how sick it is."

"Thanks. I was in the Lufthansa office in Warsaw when I came to terms with the fact that it was time to move on; things had become too dangerous. Since then I've felt as empty as the dead zone between Berlins."

"I'm going to hate myself for pointing this out, but you're quitting before you get your payoff. You passed their initiation test—whatever it was about."

"They had to believe I wasn't working for the KGB."

"And you convinced them of that now?"

"Undoubtedly."

"Have you thought of any other way to find your father?"

"Even if I could bring myself to ask my mother and if she'd tell me everything she knows—both highly unlikely—she'd never know how to find him now, not thirty years later. Cooperating with Schmidt is the only way unless the KGB comes through for me, but they'll only help me if I work with Schmidt." She sighed.

"All you have to do for him is a Moscow run?"

"Yeah."

"Can you?"

"You know I've done it all my life."

"Then do it. Find out about your father and don't ever mess with them again." Hakan watched her and after a pause he spoke. "So, how are you going to do it?"

"I was thinking about using the Estonian mafia through the Gulf of Finland as a backup plan."

"I thought you were retiring from the business."

"It's not a business—it's a calling." Faith smiled.

"More like an obsession. Welcome back."

Someone knocked at the door. Faith jumped. She glanced at Hakan, who shrugged. He stood to answer it. Faith fled into the bathroom.

"For Frau Charbonnier."

"Go ahead and put them on the desk." A pause. "It's okay. You can come out now."

"What was that all about?" Faith walked over to the bundle on the desk. She folded back the paper. Roses. A dozen long-stemmed red roses. How could he have been so careless to call attention to her—especially now? Hakan had never given her flowers before, and it had been too long since someone else had sent her any. The damage was done, so she might as well feign appreciation. As she picked them up, a pink envelope fluttered to the worn carpet. Hakan sprang from the bed to retrieve it and handed it to her.

"They're lovely. Thank you."

"You'd kill me if I did something that reckless—not that I even thought about it."

"Then who the hell knows Marie-Pièrre Charbonnier?" She threw the roses onto the desk and ripped open the envelope. "It's in French." She translated it for Hakan:

My dearest Marie-Pièrre!

Welcome home! I tried to send birds of paradise, but they only had roses.

A friend of your father.

"What's this all about?" Hakan walked over to the desk and studied the note over Faith's shoulder.

"If the KGB knows, the Stasi might know, too," Faith said.

"I don't get it."

"Bird of paradise—birds—I went bird-watching with a KGB agent on Saturday in East Berlin. That's what ticked off the Stasi, but I'll spare you the long story."

"What's that about a friend of your father?"

"There's got to be something else here, some kind of message. Maybe they have something for me about Daddy." She held the note up to the light, but couldn't see anything.

"You're not looking for some kind of invisible ink, are you?"

"They really do that kind of stuff—microdots hidden behind stamps on letters, secret radio transmissions, dead-letter drops. The East Germans sometimes mark passports with secret stamps that you can only read under a UV light. We'll find a message if we can get it under a blacklight. You followed all the precautions coming here?"

"I swear. I thought it was wacko at the time, but I'm sure no one knows I'm here. And with this rain you can't see more than a couple of meters ahead, anyway." Hakan handed her the envelope from the Stasi. "Don't forget this."

Faith ripped it open and shook it until her American passport fell onto the bed. "I'm not sure when it'll be safe enough to travel on it again." She flipped through it. "Here's my entry stamp from the day I last went over." Faith lowered herself onto the hard bed, staring agape at the document.

"What's wrong?

Faith pressed the passport shut and shook her head, engaged in an internal dialogue.

"They put an exit stamp in it: Frankfurt an der Oder, 25 April. They knew. I've got to get out of this hotel before they find me."

"You got through, so don't beat yourself up."

"Could be they didn't realize it at the time, but did later when they reviewed the logs. I forgot the customs declaration. I'm too sloppy, Hakan."

"Where are you going now?"

"Hotel Hamburg. And do try to extract that message for me as soon as possible."

"Why does it matter? You're really sure you're not calling it quits?"

"I have to find out about my father. What if he really is still alive? I need to know what the KGB's trying to tell me."

"Long-stemmed red roses are a clear enough message."

"I thought they were just a cover."

"He could have sent up dry cleaning or something—not long-stemmed red roses. Faith, don't go get yourself in trouble."

"Hakan, are you jealous?"

"I'm quite happy with our friendship, as is. We both know that when it comes to relationships you're like throwing a match into gasoline."

"That's not fair. I was engaged for years and I still care for him. I admit that, after him, it's been rocky. And, for your information, the KGB agent isn't a he. It's a she."

"Is that enough to stop you?"

"You *are* jealous." She stepped toward him, but he held up his hand.

"It's nothing. I'll contact you this afternoon when I figure out the message."

"Thanks; I couldn't do it without you."

"That's what I'm afraid of." Hakan closed the suitcase.

Faith picked up the envelope that her glasses and passport had arrived in. She started to throw it away, but first checked inside. A small piece of paper had escaped earlier notice. It was the right size. Her heart raced. *Please be the note from Daddy.* She tipped the envelope toward the light and sighed. It wasn't *her* note. They'd kept her wallet with it inside. The Stasi had taken her only connection to her father. She closed her eyes for a moment and remembered the bold strokes. Her father was definitely a self-assured gentleman.

She removed the piece of paper, read the message and looked up at Hakan. "The Stasi's scheduled the hand-off for tomorrow. Says here I can cooperate or they'll hunt me down. You know, the KGB's notes are a lot classier." She folded it, running her fingernail along the crease. "I think it's time to call an old friend and ask for help."

CHAPTER TWENTY

Who would believe I've read Marx?
—BREZHNEV

MFS HEADQUARTERS, DEMOCRATIC BERLIN–LICHTENBERG
THURSDAY, APRIL 27

Rather than use the cramped elevator, Kosyk climbed to the second floor of the imposing gray monolith on Normannenstrasse, preparing his progress report for Mielke. The MfS chief had initially wanted no contact except a signal before the mission went down. Now he demanded a face-to-face meeting. How typical of him to pry where he didn't belong. He left the stairway and marched into Mielke's office.

The secretary showed Kosyk into the MfS chief's office suite and instructed him to wait in the trophy room. The walnut-paneled room was stuffed with the secret police chief's treasures. Scattered throughout were dozens of figurines of Lenin in every imaginable position: Lenin shaking his fist; Lenin wagging his finger; Lenin pointing into the air. The older Karl Marx was more sedate, preferring to sit at a desk or stand with arms at his side. Kosyk knew that Mielke kept an even larger number of Stalin figurines hidden from public scrutiny. *He's a boy playing with dolls.*

Overshadowing the toys in quantity and originality were scores of gifts from friendly secret-police organizations. The Jamahariya Security Organization had commissioned a portrait of Colonel Qaddafi crafted from tiles looted from a mosaic in an ancient Roman villa near Tripoli. A jeweled sword right out of the Arabian Nights hung on the wall in honor of the close ties between the MfS and Saddam's Mukhabarat. A more modest hand-hammered copper plate with Arabic inscriptions from the South Yemeni Ministry for State Security thanked the MfS for its extensive technical assistance. Kosyk seethed. The plate should rightfully hang in his office. He was the one who engineered the transformation of that remote half-nation teetering on the edge of the Arabian Peninsula into the world's foremost training ground for international terrorists.

After an indignant half-hour wait inside the manifestation of Mielke's ego, the secretary reappeared and took him deeper into the suite. He was surprised to find not only Mielke, but Honecker and several of his most trusted allies. When he entered the room, all discussion stopped. Willi Stoph smashed his cigar into the nearest ashtray.

Kosyk knew he was superior to the most powerful men in his country, but they neglected to recognize it with a Politburo seat. If they wouldn't reward his genius, someday they would be forced to acknowledge his power. He had access to their every dirty little secret. He knew that Honecker wore only garments from the West and had GDR seamstresses replace the imperialist tags with MADE IN GDR labels. He knew about Erika the masseuse. He knew which of Honecker's trusted colleagues had made a secret play to oust him, but had failed to gain Soviet backing. He knew that Mielke popped amphetamines to get himself going, then barbiturates to bring himself back down. Kosyk shook each Politburo member's hand and smiled, not out of social grace, but because he knew.

But he didn't know enough—not yet.

Kosyk took a seat in one of the high-backed, royal-blue chairs. Honecker looked up at him. "Well, report."

"Operation Friendship is progressing well. I've recruited assets trained by the American special forces. They'll be inserted into Moscow as tourists. I'm in the process of arranging for the transfer of the armaments."

"And our friends?"

"They suspect nothing. The bulk of the residency here is occupied with some new information I arranged to be shared with the First Chief Division about members of the Second Division clandestinely meeting with Turkish intelligence. I've also arranged for one of the Second Division's informants to give them additional information about suspected ties between the

Russian mafia in West Berlin and some members of the First Division. If I understand my internal KGB politics correctly, which I do, the chase after one another is now their highest priority. They're too occupied to concern themselves with my shop."

"Keep it that way. Is it running on time? Will we have something to celebrate on International Workers' Day?"

"Naturally. It is my project, isn't it?"

"Plans have developed since we last spoke. We're undertaking an operation in Berlin designed to coincide with the Soviet leadership vacuum. The West won't intervene because of upheaval in Moscow, since they'll understand that the Soviets didn't have the intent to begin the next world war the same day their leader was assassinated. They'll perceive that the action was ours alone, but they won't move against us because they understand an attack upon us is the same as one upon the entire Warsaw Treaty Organization. Before our friends have a chance to stop us, we will have united our capital."

"*Jawohl!*" the chair of the Council of Ministers Willi Stoph said.

All heads turned to Stoph, unaccustomed to spontaneity in a group whose advanced age and boredom with running a Soviet satellite had long ago sedated their meetings. Kosyk was more astonished with Honecker's leadership, since he usually ran meetings like a disinterested chairman of the board, counting the days until he stepped down into retirement or until senility eased the tedium.

"May I speak openly?"

"No. It has already been decided at the highest levels. In less than four days, Greater Berlin will be ours."

And the GDR will be mine.

CHAPTER TWENTY-ONE

I am not a Marxist.
—KARL MARX

WEST BERLIN

Faith emerged from the U-Bahn at Nollendorfplatz later that evening and zipped around puddles on the sidewalk, unsure that she should be accepting the woman's invitation for a drink. Hakan had exposed the paper to ultraviolet light and extracted a message from Tatyana—Bogdanov, or whatever her name was. She warned that Faith's cover identity had been blown and it would only be a short matter of time before the Stasi found her at the hotel. The note also included the place and time for them to rendezvous, but gave no specific directions. Hakan knew the Berlin club scene well enough to get Faith to the correct neighborhood, and a cabdriver directed her to the right doorway and buzzer. Like many chic clubs in Berlin, no sign marked Cornuta's entrance. She doubted that would make it any harder for the Stasi to find her there *in flagrante delicto* with the KGB.

A bouncer cracked open the door, frisked her with her eyes and let her in. Faith's vision slowly adjusted to the muted light in the achromatic club. Whereas East Berlin shunned color for variants of gray, West Berlin abandoned it altogether. Everyone was dressed in black. A woman in a sequined evening dress played a baby grand piano and sang classic cabaret songs from the twenties. A cloud of smoke churned, wending its way around the patrons until its fingers encircled Faith, coating her freshly bathed skin. Stares of women touched her every curve as if sketching a contour drawing. As a non-smoker, she preferred the stares.

She needed to keep a low profile, but knew everyone was studying her, wondering why she was walking among them. They could tell she wasn't one of them. She turned toward the exit and spotted her. The woman sat at the end of the bar, smoking a cigarillo and laughing with the bartender. With her deliberate gestures she projected a sexy air of confidence. She wore a sleek short jacket without a lapel, a silk V-neck with a plunging neckline, and tight slacks.

As Faith neared the door, the cool evening air brushed her cheeks and she remembered the fingers caressing her face when she had steadied the binoculars. Faith looked back over her shoulder at her. What if Bogdanov really did know something about her father? Faith spun around, navigated the crowd and walked up behind the KGB agent. Faith shouted a greeting over the loud music and ordered vodka, neat. Both women watched silently as the bartender poured the drink. Faith picked up the shot glass, nodded to her and mouthed, "*Na zdorove.*" Faith slid a five-mark coin onto the bar and they moved to a more private corner.

For several minutes the two women sat, staring at each other until Faith broke the silence. "I don't know if I should trust you, Colonel Bogdanov."

"Why don't you call me Zara? Sorry about the Tatyana cover."

"Is Zara your real name?"

"It's as real as any."

"It's not a Russian name, is it?"

"Actually, it comes from the Arabic for 'flower.' But in my case it's Italian. My great-grandmother was Swiss-Italian. She met my great-grandfather when he was living in exile in Zurich before the revolution."

"Nice legend." Faith smiled. "Back to business, Zara. I don't know if I can trust you."

"It seems to me that you've already made that decision or you wouldn't be here. Now why did you decide to come?"

Faith held her gaze and flirted, hoping she could hide the intensity of her interest in her father. As a trader, Faith knew the price always went up when the other party sensed desire. "I followed my passion for all things unique, exceptional."

"So you decided you do want the chess set? I have located the one you're looking for," Zara said.

" 'The Reds and the Whites?' You really do know how to turn a girl on."

An anorexic waitress interrupted them to take their drink orders. She sported a studded leather collar that would have made a pit bull proud. They ordered drinks.

"To be quite honest," Faith lied, "up until some roses arrived in my hotel room, I was on my way back to the States—ready to walk away from the East."

"You're not now?"

"I don't know. For the last several days, all I've thought about is getting away from the whole East-West mess. Do you know what I've been through? I've been kidnapped, held for days of questioning. Have you ever been tortured—held underwater and then yanked up just before you drown, only to answer the same goddamn questions they've been asking for days? I was dumped over there without any papers. I needed your help then."

"No, you didn't. You got out on your own. If they'd found out I'd helped you, they would have liquidated you."

"Believe me, I know." Faith stared at the steel chains around the waitress' neck as she slid the two brandy snifters onto the small round table and placed a glass of mineral water in front of Faith.

"If it means anything to you, I didn't sleep for days. I knew they had picked you up and I knew it was because we had been seen together. I could only guess what they were doing to you."

"Come on. This is business for you. You don't think twice whenever some agent you're running gets picked up for questioning. You probably even knew they were going to do that."

"Faith, rest assured, you're very personal for me. Remember, I chose to work with you myself after you came to my office. I usually don't work the field. You can't imagine how relieved I was when our Warsaw office reported a probable sighting of you boarding a Lufthansa plane to Frankfurt."

"So why'd you send the roses?" Faith sniffed the cognac, then took a sip and savored it in her mouth.

"To lure you here. I wanted to see you again."

"Did you expense them?"

"That's not a fair question."

"Yes, it is. Who paid for the flowers—you or the KGB?" Faith set the glass down.

"I'm a Soviet official posted in East Berlin, paid in worthless rubles. How would I ever get the hard currency on my own to send someone flowers in the West? Everything I do in the West has to go on my expense account and has to be written up as if it's official state business—regardless of whether it is or not. That's how the system works. And I don't think it's all that different from capitalist businesses."

"It wasn't a polite question. Access to Western currency is an uncomfortable subject, but I wanted to know."

"I want to know how you felt when you saw them."

"Irritated. I thought they were from Hakan, and I couldn't believe he would be so sloppy."

"And when you realized they were from me?"

"Maybe I felt a little less perturbed." Faith grinned and tilted her head. "Thank you. They were lovely. And the note warning me to leave the hotel was appreciated. After I got your flowers, I was suspicious they'd find me. So I moved before we deciphered the message."

"Suspicion is one of your biggest allies right now. You're going to have to trust your instincts."

"If I rely on instincts around you, I'll get myself in big trouble." The alcohol eased Faith into the mood of the club, and she liked it more than she wanted to. She missed flirting and decided she needed to treat herself to it more often. The practice couldn't hurt, even if it was with a woman.

"You're in big trouble right now."

"I know."

They looked into each other's eyes. Zara leaned forward, but Faith turned away at the last minute. Zara's lips met her cheek.

"So, you want to tell me about it? What have I gotten myself into?" Faith said.

"Right now, they're not going to do anything to you, unless they know you're in contact with me. They're searching for you and we believe it's because they're ready for you to transport."

"It's going down tomorrow."

"So they do know you're here."

"They took a guess. They dropped off a package with my glasses and passport at the apartment in care of Hakan. The bastards kept my purse, but a note was stuck in my passport."

"Do you know what they want?"

"More or less."

"And you're not going to tell me?"

Faith pushed her hair back out of her face. "I don't know how it would help me at this point. I don't even know if I'm going to do it. Like I said, until those roses showed up, I was on my way to the States." Faith tinkered with the time line.

"A few flowers were enough to prevent you from leaving?"

"They were enough to get my attention. To make me think about what makes me feel alive—about where my passions lie."

"And where is that?"

"You tell me. You've studied me."

"Let me see." Zara rested her head on her hands. Loose curls fell across her forehead, as if her hair were relaxing along with her. "Faith Whitney, the passionate smuggler. She delights in risk—that is, risk she believes she has some control over. She doesn't like feeling out of control. But she gets an incredible high playing on the edge between control and chaos. Now, in her personal relationships, it's a little different. As long as the risk is there, she enjoys it. When things start to settle down and become predictable, under control, she gets bored and moves on. So are you really going to abandon the one fulfilling relationship in your life?"

"Don't you think you're coming on a bit too strong? I hardly know you. And I don't know what kind of intel you have on me, but I'm not a lesbian. I have impeccable heterosexual credentials. So you're not exactly the one fulfilling relationship in my life."

"I meant with the East, not me."

"I wouldn't say it's the one fulfilling relationship in my life. I've had others." Faith picked up her glass and pressed it against her lips.

"And I understand you abandoned that one."

"We're still close. I just couldn't see myself trapped in a traditional marriage at the time." Faith sipped the cognac. "I love what I do and I need my freedom. I don't want to give it up, but I don't want to die, either."

"What would you do if you quit smuggling?"

"If I couldn't play with the East, I'd find other playmates. There are a lot of markets in the world and even more governments that restrict free trade."

Zara signaled the waitress for another drink. "Seriously, what would you do?"

"Like I said, there are a lot of opportunities for those willing to take the risk, but I wouldn't touch most of them. What can I say? I'm too ethical for my own good. I'd never trade arms, and even so I understand it's a tough market to break into. Drugs are out of the question. I'd probably go for antiquities. The thrill of the hunt would still be there, even if Third World governments aren't as fun to mess around with as you guys."

"I have a difficult time seeing you get excited over Greek vases."

"I was thinking more like Khmer ankle bracelets, but your point's well taken. I'd die of boredom." Faith sipped her drink. The cognac took the edge off her surroundings. "The East is where I belong. I've flirted with the Stasi and KGB all my life. It's a love-hate relationship, but, as you pointed out, it's maybe the best relationship I've got."

"So you're telling me you're in."

"Depends. What have you got for me?"

"Your mother's file covering the year and a half before your birth is sealed."

"What the hell does that mean?"

"Whatever happened back then must still matter to someone with the authority to block access. I also tried to look at our copies of the MfS files from that period, but it was the same thing. I'm working back channels, but I can't make any promises other than to do my best."

"I think we can come to a mutually agreeable arrangement."

"How far I can go with the Moscow storefront depends upon what you can offer. Right now we know the MfS is running a black op and taking great care to conceal it from us, but that's about it. That's not worth much more than assurances we'll help you out as much as possible."

"What happened to the import-export business in Moscow, permission to scour the countryside for antiques and all of that?"

"It's possible, but the compensation depends upon the value of the project. And that depends upon the Germans."

"I'm not comfortable entering into an agreement without first nailing down the terms, but I usually know what I'm peddling."

Zara patted Faith's hand. "You're going to have to trust me. I promise you I'll do my best to secure you the maximum honorarium."

"I don't doubt you will." Faith rolled her hand from under Zara's and ran her index finger along its back, exploring the ridges and valleys of her knuckles. She was aware the alcohol was helping her blunder in a dangerous direction, but permitted herself the sensuality of the moment.

"Before you distract me too much, you need to tell me everything you know about what they're planning," Zara said.

Faith sensed something feline about Zara. She suspected she could be purring on her lap one minute, scratching her the next. Faith prided herself on being able to pet neurotic cats, knowing just when to jerk away to avoid the claws. Faith moved her hand away from Zara, revoking her sensual liberties. "They want me to move something from Berlin to Moscow and they want it done quietly."

"To Moscow? Your price went up."

"Substantially."

"Do you know what it is?"

"All I know is they want it done quickly—there's a forty-eight-hour window before they start hunting me down if I don't deliver. I'll bargain for more time when I receive the item, but I don't have the impression they're too flexible. I also got the sense it's an important piece of a bigger puzzle they don't want associated with the GDR."

"When's the hand-off?"

"Tomorrow—somewhere between Checkpoint Charlie and the Reichstag. Now I've given you something. I expect something in return." Faith forced down several gulps of water to dilute the alcohol.

"We don't know what they're planning, but it gets our attention anytime the man you know as Schmidt gets involved in a project. You do know who he is?"

Faith shook her head.

"Kosyk, Major General Gregor Kosyk of the MfS."

"Sorry."

"You know of Markus Wolf?"

"The spymaster who was behind infiltrating Willy Brandt's cabinet and stuff like that."

"Kosyk is more dangerous. Wolf is a traditional spy. He runs agents who use proven methods—usually sex—to place informants in high governmental positions in the West. Kosyk—your Schmidt—is from the dark side of the business. He believes the future of espionage isn't with cloak-and-dagger, but terror. He made his name in seventy-two in Munich. He arranged contacts for Black September to get the weapons into the Olympic Village. There were two additional terrorists in that mission the West Germans never knew about, and Kosyk got them out through the GDR. He's fostered the Red Army Faction in West Germany—sort of adopted them once Baader and Meinhof were apprehended. Remember when they blew up the Lufthansa jumbo and the other planes in the desert? He helped with the training in Yemen. He's behind the GDR's support for Carlos the Jackal,

Abu Daoud, Abu Nidal, among others. Recently, he worked with the Libyans on the bombing of La Belle."

"The Americans haven't been able to definitively pin that on anyone, have they?"

"Reagan bombed Tripoli over it, but they haven't been able to hold anyone legally responsible. Your government loves those show trials in The Hague—a legacy of Nuremberg, I suppose. Anyway, Kosyk reports directly to Mielke and has his own small group of operatives. It appears only a few in the Politburo know what's going on."

"I don't like the sound of that."

"It gets worse. Kosyk's funds do come from the Stasi, and all the Stasi's resources are at his disposal, but for practical purposes Kosyk controls his own black organization."

"A boutique spy shop?" Faith said.

"You should feel honored."

"I get the impression Kosyk isn't well respected in the business."

"I'm from the old school, where you use only as much muscle as necessary and you don't associate with terrorists. In my book, Kosyk is a terrorist."

"You make me feel better and better every minute, girl."

"That's my intention." Zara slipped her hand behind Faith's head and caressed her hair.

"I warned you, I've flirted with the KGB all my life, but I won't go all the way."

"You're hardly a virgin. And I'd say you just got knocked up by the Stasi."

"It was forced. And I'm not easy."

"Nothing about Faith Whitney is easy."

"Zara, I think we could be friends, but not like you want, especially not now." Faith moved away. She threw her head back with the last gulp of cognac. "Now I've had a few drinks, I admit that I'm flattered, even a little turned on, and very scared—and I don't mean scared because of the lesbian stuff. But I am disappointed in you. A honey pot to lure an agent into service is the oldest trick in the book."

"You're alone against the resources of the entire intelligence apparatus of the GDR. They'll kill you unless you do what they want, and they'll probably dispose of you even if you cooperate. The KGB has offered help and protection, and all we ask is to be kept informed about what the MfS is up to."

CHAPTER TWENTY-TWO

STUMP NECK, MARYLAND, USA

Max Summer molded enough plastic explosive to bring down an airliner into the shell of a Sony radio. His thumb sunk a blasting cap into the doughy substance and then he twisted its wires into a receiver. He taped the receiver to the radio and then tossed it to the young Arab.

The Arab slipped it between a faded pair of jeans and a University of Oklahoma sweatshirt. Faded USDA inspection stickers and airline-security markers from international flights were the only clues to its owner's identity. He closed the suitcase and shoved it inside a Pan Am 747 cargo container. It blended into the Samsonites and American Touristers.

The young man secured the cargo container and signaled to clear the area. They drove a short distance away. "Fire in the hole." Summer flipped a switch on a radio transmitter.

An intense flash and the container was gone. A loud clap roared through the Maryland woods and the ground trembled. Toothbrushes, clothes and twisted metal rained down while a high-speed camera snapped pictures at five hundred frames per second. Lieutenant Commander Max Summer and Special Agent Maria Fuentes strolled toward the debris.

"C packs a wallop, doesn't it?" Summer said. "I'd say it was enough to bring down Pan Am 103."

"Who says these tests have anything to do with *Maid of the Seas*?" the FBI agent said.

"Doesn't take a special agent to figure out what's going on when the FBI sends me a semi with Pan Am cargo containers and wants me to blow them up." Summer turned to the half-dozen enlisted men assisting the R & D department of the Naval Explosive Ordnance Disposal Technology Center. "I want everything picked up and put into this bin. You've got ten minutes. Make me happy in five. Go to it." He turned back toward the FBI agent. "You need to keep in mind this shows how much damage a given amount of C-4 can do to a filled cargo container. My understanding is that it isn't that easy to come by for international terrorists. If it was C-4, you should've picked up some microscopic markers called taggant that'll show you what production line it came from. But I'm betting they used Semtex."

"The *New York Times* ran a story that both our analysis and Scotland Yard's came out positive for Semtex," Fuentes said.

"Before you came down here this morning, I checked with a buddy in Defense Intelligence who knows a little more about Semtex. Both it and C are made of pretty much the same stuff—PETN and RDX—but the yield is really going to depend on the formulas. He couldn't give me any blast-yield conversions, but he said it varies a lot with Semtex. He wasn't sure if it was because of the usual slipshod commie quality control or because they have different types for different purposes, but—"

"They do have different types. Semtex-H is a terrorist favorite. The Libyans bought a ton and a half of it from the Czechs a couple of years ago. That story's also been in the *Times*."

"My point being, just because we're able to demonstrate eight ounces of C-4 were enough to do the job doesn't mean that eight ounces of Semtex-H —or whatever designation—would do the same amount of damage. Unless this is taken into account, we've just wasted our time. Not that blowing things up is ever really a waste of time." He smiled, revealing his perfectly straight white teeth. "Don't get me wrong, I'm happy you brought us the containers. Blowing up luggage is a nice change of pace from old ordnance."

"I want a few more tests with four, six and ten ounces."

"You got it."

A Dodge Ram screeched to a halt in front of the commander and a yeoman jumped out. "Sir, I received a phone call for you about five minutes ago.

It was a civilian. She said it was a family emergency. She'd call back in an hour."

"She say who she was?"

"No, sir, we got cut off. One thing, though, the connection was bad. There was kind of a delay, the kind like I used to get when I was stationed at Subic Bay and I'd talk to my wife stateside."

"I'll be along shortly."

The yeoman sped off, leaving a dust cloud behind.

"You should also note another difference that really shouldn't have much bearing on your investigation, but it's worth mentioning," Summer said.

"If you have to go, I understand."

"I will in a minute, but let's finish up here. My chief can supervise any additional tests you need. But as I was saying, you might also note we're using a simple radio detonation device to set it off. Unless it was some kind of a wacko suicide bomber, they wouldn't have done that. They'd probably use a delayed arming timer and a barometric triggering device set to explode when the air pressure dropped to a designated level. That way they could've sent it on some other flight to London, where it was transferred onto 103."

"We know. We think they used at least two of them and sent the bag from Malta to Frankfurt, where it was loaded onto 103."

"I bet that was in the *Times*."

"No, the *Frankfurter Allgemeine*."

Chief Rashid approached them. "We've completed removal of the container fragments. What would you like us to do with the, uh, collateral debris? A lot of it's not hurt. I saw a rather nice leather jacket, some Ray•Bans, Nikes. The men were asking . . ."

"You need this stuff for additional analysis?" Lieutenant Commander Summer said.

"The pictures are enough."

"Anything that's not part of the radio or container, they can dispose of at their individual discretion. I have some other matters to attend to. You're now in charge. Assist Special Agent Fuentes with anything she needs. Tell the boys happy hunting." He turned toward the FBI agent. "It's been nice catching up on the papers with you. But I do want to know one thing. Where did you find all this luggage?"

"The airlines. They have tons of lost baggage. I can get you some to practice with, if you want."

CHAPTER TWENTY-THREE

CHECKPOINT CHARLIE, WEST BERLIN
FRIDAY, APRIL 28

You are now leaving the American Sector. Faith read the multilingual sign at Checkpoint Charlie a couple of dozen times while waiting as the Stasi's note had instructed. Per their request, she set a leather satchel at her feet each time she stopped for precisely seven minutes at one of the viewing platforms along the Wall. She ignored the stream of tourists climbing the wooden stand to sneak a glimpse of Berlin beyond the Wall and spent seven long minutes thinking about her father. Who would still want to cover up whatever happened to him thirty years ago?

A border guard raised the red and white striped metal barrier and allowed a tiny East German Trabant to exit to the West. The Trabi wound its way through the maze of concrete barriers. The gray hair of the driver suggested another retiree had come to enjoy his thirty allotted days in the West, but the East German guards took no chances. They followed the grandpa with their binoculars, guns at their sides.

She glanced at her watch. It was 10:15 in the morning and time to move on, as the note had instructed. Why did the Stasi want to deliver the package in one of the most highly watched areas of Berlin? They must want someone in the East to see her receive the drop in the West. Any less touristy section might have drawn attention. She climbed down the viewing platform. Each step jarred her sore rib cage. Two American soldiers sat in a white guard shack, studying her more than the Trabi as it rolled toward the West.

She intentionally walked two feet to the right of the white line painted on the cobblestones marking the beginning of GDR territory, where not too long ago President Reagan had taunted communist authorities by sticking his foot across the line and through the Iron Curtain. She strolled along the Wall, pacing herself as she pretended to admire the graffiti on the ugly cement structure. Kurdish and Albanian political slogans were scrawled beside an elaborate painting of a view into the East as if the Wall had been knocked away. She glanced back toward the checkpoint. Nothing.

A few hundred yards later, she stopped and looked down into collapsing ceramic tiled chambers dug into the ground. They were filled with water from the recent rains. When she recognized them as the recently unearthed basement of Gestapo headquarters, her breath became shallow. She felt numb with pain, but wasn't sure if it were her own. She had read about the recent discovery, but had avoided going to see it. Even before the torture chambers were located, she had always hastened her pace along this section of the Wall. Faith had no doubt Berlin was haunted, but she refused to believe in ghosts. She zipped up her leather jacket. She blinked back tears when she peered in the torture chambers. She took a deep breath and for an instant felt water fill her lungs. She coughed. Tourists gawked at her. A camera clicked.

The rubble screamed at her. Unable to tune out the cries, she marched along the Wall two minutes ahead of schedule. With each step into the soft earth, she pushed down her fears and concentrated on the job.

An overgrown lot was fenced off from the public. Rusting signs on it warned it was GDR territory and hadn't yet been cleared of ordnance. They needed a good explosives guy; she knew she did. She had no doubt the package would be booby trapped. She looked at her watch and adjusted her pace. When she came upon another platform a few feet from the Wall, she climbed it and set the attaché case at her feet.

Seagulls flew into the no-man's-land of Potsdamer Platz, the former bustling downtown square, now a vacant field surrounded by the Wall and high steel fencing. The emptiness swallowed her.

A concrete East German guard tower stood within a hundred yards. She wondered how the soldiers coped, all by themselves, day after day, watching over this desolate strip of cobblestones and weeds between two worlds. Two figures stood in the tower. One looked familiar. She squinted and could make out a uniformed border guard and someone in civilian clothes. The guard slid the reflective window closed.

But she knew who was there.

As she watched doves fly about the demarcation zone, she heard a loud group of Americans approaching. She glanced around and saw a dozen college students. The platform shook from the weight as they scrambled up the stairs. A young man wearing a Drury College sweatshirt maneuvered in the crowd and pushed in beside her. He set a leather bag down onto the platform next to the one she had carried, just as the Stasi instructions had described. Faith leaned over to him and whispered the code phrase in English, "Berlin wasn't founded by the Romans like Vienna."

"Huh? I guess so, but do you know where Hitler's bunker is? I heard it's supposed to be out there somewhere," the young man said with an upper Midwest accent, pronouncing "out" as if he were from Northern Michigan or Canada.

Faith waved her arm toward the left of the no-man's-land. "Over there. I've heard it rumored there are some really creepy murals from the SS still intact down there."

"This is going to sound weird, but a woman around the corner gave me a hundred marks to bring this bag to you. Said I'm supposed to swap it with the one you've got. Said I get to keep it. That okay? I'm also not supposed to talk to you except to say something corny like 'the clock's ticking.' And she made it really clear I shouldn't open it."

Faith pointed to Potsdamer Platz as if they were still discussing the bunker. "You ever hear of RIAS radio station and the announcer Jo Eager?"

The young man nodded. Faith was certain he had never heard of that American institution in Berlin.

She smiled. "I could lose because I'm telling you this, but this is part of their annual 'Spy versus Spy' contest. I'm a finalist and I've got ten thousand marks riding on this. Just quietly take the bag next to my feet and walk away as if nothing unusual is going on."

"Got it. Good luck." He whispered from the corner of his fever-blistered mouth and picked up the empty bag.

Faith glanced at her watch and knew Schmidt was looking at his. It was 10:54 A.M. The package had to be somewhere in Moscow by Sunday morning—in forty-eight hours. Her ribs hurt with each step as she climbed from the platform.

She walked on. Small white crosses behind the Reichstag marked where East Germans had been killed while scaling the Wall. She reached into the satchel's side pocket and removed a slip of paper with a Moscow telephone number. A few feet west of the Wall, a faded white line traced the legal East-West demarcation. She intentionally crossed the line into the East and stood on the worn cobblestones between the line and the Wall.

"Here is the Border Patrol of the German Democratic Republic!" a guard said through a megaphone. "You are trespassing on the territory of the GDR. You are ordered to leave at once."

The guard watched her through binoculars. Faith glared at him. He watched her. So did the shadowy figure behind his left shoulder. She stared; they watched.

Then Faith waved her middle finger at Kosyk.

CHAPTER TWENTY-FOUR

DEMOCRATIC BERLIN—KARLSHORST, KGB RESIDENCY

Major General Gennadi F. Titov, the KGB's chief resident in the GDR, slammed the solid birch office door shut and stomped to his desk, muttering obscenities to himself. Lieutenant Colonel Bogdanov breathed deeply as she walked to a corner seat. Titov stared at the colonel for several minutes, his pockmarked face reddening with each passing moment. Bogdanov struggled not to blink, hoping the general's blood pressure would reach critical mass and he would have a heart attack before beginning the meeting. She needed to assess whether the general was a threat to the operation.

"Is there anything you want to tell me, colonel?"

Your fly's unzipped, sir. Colonel Bogdanov decided someone else could break that news to him later in the day. "Nothing that I'm cleared to discuss, sir."

"Don't you ever cut me out of the loop again. I don't care how valuable they think you are in all of this. After this is over, I know you're counting on a cushy position in the West. Mark my words, I'll find a way to send you to Kabul, where the mujahedeen will be constantly chasing that pretty little ass of yours." He grinned, slipping the tip of his tongue from his mouth to slowly lick his thin upper lip.

"Sir, we pulled out of Afghanistan a couple of months ago."

"That doesn't mean I can't get you sent there. Bet it would be even more fun now." Titov stuck his thumb in his ear and twisted it. He pulled it out and sniffed it. "You made a fool of me in Moscow. And I don't forget. Friends told me someone stationed here in my very own residency was putting together a coup. It didn't take long to find out who it was. Stukoi told me everything. Operation Druzhba, huh? You wanted me cut off from the action, didn't you? Save it all for yourself. If you weren't on the right side of this little event, you'd be getting it from me right now. I know it's what you really want and we all know you need it, you pervert."

"I report directly to Colonel General Stukoi. I suggest if you have any questions or complaints about my work, you direct them to him."

"And I don't like that one bit. Suddenly a group of my staff is reassigned to some 'Internal Affairs' op reporting to Stukoi. That's a crock of shit. So what's your little internal-affairs group up to?"

"Contact the general. I understand that I'm supposed to be enjoying your full cooperation."

"And you'll have it—until the second this is over, then I'm going to fuck you, real good and hard."

Vasily Resnick sprinted up the residency stairs to his chief's office. Titov was not a man to be kept waiting, and Resnick wanted nothing more than to curry his patron's favor. Before entering, he checked his posture in a mirror and admired his Olympian physique and Nordic features. He marched into the KGB general's office and stood at attention in a manner that would've made a Prussian proud. "Comrade General."

"The idiot Stukoi chose Bogdanov to do a man's job." Titov bit off the end of a cigar and champed down on it. He shoved a file across his desk. It was marked FEDEX—TOP SECRET. "Follow FedEx. She has a delivery to make to our friends in Moscow. Make sure Bogdanov doesn't fuck it up and get in her way."

"When do you expect movement?"

"Now. And whatever you do, don't involve any of our German friends—not even Kosyk. Keep this compartmentalized. Remember Comrade Lenin's advice."

"Whoever is not for us, is against us." Resnick recited his mentor's favorite phrase from the founder of the Soviet state.

"Do not forget that it's also true for the KGB. Anyone outside of Operation Druzhba is your enemy. Treat them accordingly."

Titov's secretary slinked into the office with a message and the men stopped talking. Titov rustled through the papers piled on his desk, cursing under his breath. His secretary picked up a copy of Sun Tzu's *The Art of War* and removed the general's round reading glasses from the book. He snatched them away from her with a snarl. "Dismissed." He skimmed the document. "Putin spotted FedEx in Tiergarten carrying a leather satchel. The fool lost her somewhere in Kreuzberg. She's got the package and could leave the city anytime."

"Do I understand correctly that I'm to escort this American to Moscow? Wouldn't it make sense for me to dispose of her and take the item myself?"

"It must be FedEx. Everything is prepared to link her to the CIA to take the blame for the incident. Resnick, I'm counting on you to make sure FedEx makes an on-time delivery."

CHAPTER TWENTY-FIVE

WEST BERLIN

Faith waited in the borrowed apartment in Kreuzberg with the leather bag the Stasi had passed to her less than six hours before. Every creak in the hall sounded like them checking up on her even through she was certain she had ditched her shadows. Shortly after the hand-off, a dozen of Hakan's friends had met her with similar satchels. Everyone took off at once, overwhelming the small surveillance team. By the time Faith left, no one was around to follow her. Or at least no one from the Stasi.

Heavy footsteps came up the stairs and stopped in front of the door, then a loud knock, a familiar rhythm. She opened the door and pulled Max Summer inside and into her arms. He hugged her tightly and she winced.

"Not too tight. I'm a little fragile right now," she said.

Tears welled up as she pressed her head against his hard chest. He dropped his gear. She didn't realize how frightened she was until she noticed herself trembling. She let him hold her for the first time since they were to have married nearly thirteen years ago. The safety of his embrace made her crave more, but she knew better than to indulge herself. She blinked as hard as she could to push the last tears from her eyes and discreetly wiped away the traces before she moved away.

"You're favoring your side. What happened to you?"

"I fell down."

"You sure jumped high when I squeezed you for just falling down."

"I fell a lot."

"Right." The Arkansawyer shook his head and looked her in the eyes. "Show me what you've got, missy."

"You know better than to call me missy," Faith said, waving her finger at him.

"Careful where you point that thing. Liable to go off." He wrapped his calloused hand around her finger. "And you know how I hate explosions."

"Like a hog hates mud." She freed her finger and slipped her arms around him again. She felt only firm muscles. The man was in incredible condition. She immediately let go of him when she caught herself wondering how that would translate into bed. "Summer, I can't tell you how good it is to have you here. I can't believe it was just yesterday I called you."

"I had the time difference going for me, and I would've been here faster if TWA had its act together. I don't hear from you as much as I'd like and I've never known the invincible Faith Whitney to ask for my help. Soon as I hung up with you, I told my CO I'm outta here." His light Ozark twang sounded like home. Being with Summer felt like home.

"What the hell happened to your hair?" She rubbed her hand over his bald pate.

"Hair's a hygiene issue."

"I admit you do look sexier this way, but I'm not sure about cleaner." She never understood why, but bald men were an incredible turn-on. Summer wasn't making things any easier. Faith started to drag his duffel bag into the other room, but the pain in her side stopped her. She led him into the combination living room–bedroom. He followed closely, moving into her personal space, but she didn't mind. "Now, you promise whatever you see or discuss here stays between us."

"Faith, have I ever let you down?"

"Never. I wish I could say the same."

"Guess you had to do what you had to do. Now show me what you've got."

"Actually, I was hoping you could tell me what it is, or at least get it open for me so I can figure it out. I think we can count on it being booby trapped."

"Sure enough. If we didn't assume that, I think you would've opened it on your own and I'd still be stateside. Now you're gonna have to tell me everything you know about it."

"I don't want to drag you into this." They walked into the tight galley kitchen.

"You drag me here all the way from the States and you don't want to drag me into something? I'd say I've already been dragged. Talk to me." His green eyes invited her.

"You really don't want to know."

"Probably, but I have to if I'm going to help you."

"I got it from the Stasi."

"Holy moly. There goes my security clearance."

"I didn't even think of that. I never would've called you if I'd real—"

"I was playing with you. Don't worry about me. You need me right now and I'm happy to help you. Always am. Now let's get down to work." He set a dented aluminum case on the narrow kitchen table and flipped open the locks.

"I was warned not to open it. I have a forty-eight-hour window to deliver whatever's inside, and the clock started running about six hours ago."

"Doubt if there's a timer if they gave you that long, but that doesn't mean you're necessarily free and clear. Since the only way out of West Berlin without going through East Germany is to fly, it's a safe guess you'll be taking this on a plane."

"Definitely," Faith said as she poured two glasses of sparkling water and added shots of a Turkish fruit syrup she found in the cupboard.

"They could've rigged it to blow with a barometric triggering device."

"Wouldn't it have to be extremely sensitive, since airplanes are pressurized?" Faith said.

"Even when a plane's pressurized, there's a measurable pressure change. You know how when you're flying and you open those little creamers for your coffee and they spurt all over everywhere?" Summer inspected the bubbling purple liquid and raised an eyebrow. He took a guarded sip. "I'm not making any guesses and I don't know what's in there or what the East Germans are up to, but I know they've been involved in more than one terrorist bombing. And I wouldn't trust a commie as far as I could throw 'em. You're the one who follows politics, so you can make more educated guesses than I can."

"The East Germans don't always hang out with the best crowd," Faith said. "They have a strong relationship with the Libyans, pretty good ties with Iraq and they've been buddying up with North Korea lately, since they're so pissed at the Sovs over Gorbachev's reforms."

"There you go. And they're always after the West Germans. Now all I'm saying is targeting a plane is a possibility we shouldn't rule out."

Faith downed the soda. "All Allied flag carriers have to fly at a max of ten thousand feet through the air corridor over East Germany, and they climb as soon as they get over West German airspace. Guess it would be simple to set something to go off then."

"Faith, blowing up anything is easy long as you know what you're doing. Most people don't. No sense in speculating until we know what's inside. It's not as easy to bring down a plane as you'd think. It's like any demolition job. You have to know exactly where to plant it so the blast wave does optimal damage. I've read in the *Times* the FBI thinks the terrorists got lucky with 103 because the blast wasn't that strong. The suitcase with the bomb happened to get in a container loaded at just the right point in the airframe. If a baggage handler had thrown it into a different container or had loaded the containers in a different order, it would've still ripped a hole in the plane, but probably wouldn't have resulted in catastrophic structural failure. So the East Germans would be kind of stupid and careless to depend on wherever your suitcase got packed. From what you've told me, they have direct access to West Berlin and could mount a bomb wherever they wanted. I only brought it up to mention one of the things we're going to look out for. We're also going to check if there's a light sensor or motion sensor that would set it off when we open it. So I need to know what you think we're dealing with."

"My best guess, some sophisticated electronic device booby trapped with plastic explosives, or it could be just Semtex booby trapped with more Semtex."

"Faith, what the hell are you doing with that stuff? Tell me you're not selling it."

"Summer, you have my word."

"If you're not selling it—you're not thinking about blowing something up yourself, are you?"

Faith took a drink, leaving lipstick on the glass. She would never admit it, but the makeup was for Summer's benefit. "I want to put a hole in the Wall to get some friends out and I need your help."

"Faith, don't you go messing around with me. You know there's nothing I'd like better than to go out and blow up that damn Wall, but not until I get orders to do it." He smiled at her.

"Sorry, I was joking. I'm not about to blow anything up or help anyone blow something up, for that matter."

"But that doesn't tell me what you're doing with this stuff."

Faith shook her head. "Don't concern yourself with that."

"I'm here and I'm concerned. Now, if you want my help, you're going to have to level with me. Tell me everything and I'll be as nonjudgmental as I can."

"Okay, but remember, you wanted to know. The Stasi kidnapped me last weekend, tortured me for several days and then nearly drowned me in a swamp early Tuesday morning. They kept my passport, but I managed to get out by sneaking across the Polish border and flying back here through West Germany. They want me to help with some kind of black op."

"That's a good one. So what are you really up to?"

Faith pulled up her shirt. She wasn't wearing a bra, but Summer wasn't looking at her breasts. Bruises covered her midriff with overlapping splotches of deep purples, browns and yellows. Her right side seemed in the worst shape.

"My God, honey." He caressed her so lightly she felt only his affection. "Who did this to you?"

"The Stasi."

"That's it. You're going back to the States with me. I won't stand for someone beating you up like this."

"I can't."

"Are you out of your frickin' mind? I know you like to play cat-and-mouse with the commies over your toys. I don't approve of that, but I always figured you came by it naturally, with your mama a Bible smuggler and your grandpa a bootlegger. But your genes aren't going to help you with this one—you're outta your league. You need professional help."

"That's why you're here."

"I mean like someone from Langley."

"No way. They'll kill me if I don't cooperate."

"Sure they won't even if you do what they want?"

"Summer, please. It might not bother you, but we have a bomb on the kitchen table. I really think it ought to take priority. We can talk over a nice warm German beer after it's defused."

"Fair enough. Has it been moved?"

"It's got a few miles on it. It's had quite a tour over here while I ditched the Stasi. Why?"

"'Cause if it hadn't been moved, I wouldn't mess with it. Some bombs are rigged to blow from motion. We'd have to shoot it with a water cannon right here."

"A water cannon? And how would you propose getting a water cannon into this apartment?"

"You told me to bring what I need." He held his hands a couple feet apart. "It's only yay big. I've got one packed with my gear. I'm pretty sure you saw one that time you visited me in Virginia Beach and I showed you how we'd handle a bomb in a suitcase."

"Oh, yeah, that metal tube thing you put the sandbags behind because of the recoil."

"That's it. A high-powered burst of water disrupts the electrical circuit every time, but since you've lugged this all over creation, it's safe to handle. We're going to need to X-ray this puppy so we know if we can go in."

"I don't know how we'd ever get access to an X-ray machine. Maybe I could pay my dentist to let us take a couple of pictures."

"You think I'm going to dig into a bomb using teeny-tiny dental X-rays? You always did have a good sense of humor. Now, see if you can find us some better light while I get my toys." He sauntered over to his luggage, retrieved a metal box marked Golden Portable X-ray.

"I knew you were in a mobile EOP unit, but I guess I never really understood exactly how mobile you were."

"EOD—Explosive Ordnance Disposal." He opened a panel and pulled out the electric cord. He held out three electric plugs and she pointed to the one with two long round prongs set about an inch apart. "Now if we can get a good picture, we can hand-enter."

"And if you can't?"

"I'd be glad this isn't my apartment."

Faith stared at him, her eyebrows knit.

"I'm kidding. We'd use the water cannon in the woods somewhere—less problems with the neighbors if it blows." He built a platform with the books and balanced the X-ray machine on it. He aimed the lens at the top of the case, handed a rectangular film frame to Faith, then clasped his hands over hers and repositioned her. "Find a way to get something to hold this right about here."

Faith went into the bedroom and returned with a coat hanger. She bent it and placed the film cartridge inside.

Squinting his eyes, Summer traced the line from the lens aperture through the top of the case to the film. "Can you come down about an inch?"

"Doesn't this thing come with a lead apron or something?"

"I forgot how cute you are when you're all fussy. Looks good. Step out of the way." He pressed the remote and the machine clicked and then he handed her another frame. "I want to get a couple of side shots of the locks while we're at it. It's harder to wire it up to detonate when you turn the lock, but the government over there gives everybody a job, so who knows what they piddle around doing." He attached a film frame to a box and then turned a crank. Like with the first Polaroid cameras, he ran each film through the developer, waited three minutes and studied the X-rays against the light. "They definitely didn't want you opening it up and snooping inside."

"What's this little thing?" Faith pointed.

"I'd say it's a C battery—the electricity source to set off a blasting cap." He studied the next X-ray. "And I'd say this thing with the wires running off it is an alligator clip. We're gonna find it's pinching a little strip of something nonconductive."

"You're losing me."

He lightly pinched the tip of her index finger between his thumb and middle finger. "Now your finger is that little strip keeping my fingers from making contact. My fingers are the alligator clips. My thumb is wired to the battery and my finger to the cap. When I pull away from you and my fingers touch, it completes the circuit so electricity flows to the cap and detonates the Semtex. Now that little strip is pinched by an alligator clip and is attached to the top of the case so it's pulled out of the clip when the lid is opened." He pulled his fingers away from her until they made contact.

"I get it. Boom."

He examined each X-ray. "I'm guessing they stuffed some Semtex in a can and the cap's inside. Seems pretty straightforward. Doesn't look like there are any extra electronics, but you've got a few slabs of Semtex in there, though guess it could always be a couple bricks of heroin or something." He pointed to fuzzy white forms on the film.

"The CIA is the one who works with drug dealers. I've never heard of the commies getting messed up with that."

He picked up a scalpel. "We're going to hand-enter."

"You're sure it won't explode if you puncture the Semtex?"

"Faith, I do this every day and I still have all ten fingers. Plastic explosives are so stable I've nailed them to a wall before. You could whomp it with a sledgehammer and it wouldn't go off." He plunged the scalpel into the satchel, sliced away a half-moon window and then peeled the leather back. "Holy moly. This isn't Semtex. Where'd you say you got this stuff?"

CHAPTER TWENTY-SIX

BONN-BAD GODESBERG, KGB RESIDENCY

Even in his cover identity as Second Secretary of the Soviet embassy, the chief resident of the KGB in West Germany rarely received Western visitors, let alone American ones. The residency in the West German capital was a KGB backwater. The most important intel on NATO and the West was extracted in Bonn—not by the KGB, but by the Stasi. The Stasi had penetrated Bonn from the train station toilets to the Chancellor's office, and it freely handed the flood of information over to the KGB. To the Berlin-Karlshorst residency. The Bonn residency was in the center of Warsaw Treaty Organization intelligence activity in Western Europe, but was cut out of the loop. At least tonight the Americans remembered that they were still in the game.

Aleksei Voronin straightened his tie, wondering why the CIA station had been so bold as to tap into his secret direct line and to demand an immediate meeting on a Friday evening. He gulped down the contents of his glass and dropped his half-empty bottle of vodka into a drawer. As he waited for his assistant to escort the American cultural attaché to his office, he began talking to himself in English: "I am very pleased to meet you. To which do I owe the honour?"

The American pranced into his office. The striking woman had fine, delicate features that were rare among the hearty Slavs. Her petite body was poured into evening attire, a French designer dress with a plunging neckline. Her supple breasts begged to be touched. Voronin was pleased they'd sent a woman, and he hoped the CIA had sent her to seduce him. He would have to play along—anything for the Motherland. He didn't bother to force his eyes away from her chest when he took her hand and kissed it. Stumbling over the English words, he said, "It is very pleased to meet you."

"I can see that." She glanced down, then rolled her eyes.

"To which do I owe the honour? You like a drink with me?" Her perfume intoxicated.

"I've only got a minute. Obviously there's somewhere else I'd rather be—and will you please quit staring at my boobs?"

"I was looking at your necklace. It's charoite from Russia, is it not?" He jerked his eyes away, but stepped closer to her and fingered the deep purple beads of her necklace.

She swatted his hand. "I don't have time for bullshit, and you sure don't. I know who you are and you know who I am, so let's cut the introductory crap. Your government's in danger."

He pulled out a chair for her. "Please sit."

She ignored him. "We've picked up chatter—a lot of it. Someone is planning a terrorist attack against your government."

"Terrorists are going to attack the embassy?"

"Are you crazy? Do you think I'd be here with you? There's some kind of plot against Gorbachev." She walked over to his desk and fished a piece of hard candy from a crystal bowl. "All I can tell you is that we're reasonably confident the terrorists and their weapons are being channeled through West Germany."

Voronin swallowed hard. "The CIA warns me that terrorists soon attack the Soviet government?" He backed toward his desk chair, staring into space as he lowered himself into his seat and reached for a drawer. Without looking at what he was doing, he pulled out a bottle of vodka and dumped it into his glass, spilling some. He downed it and poured more. "You want?" He raised his eyebrows and tipped the glass toward the American.

She shook her head as she slowly pulled on the ends of the candy wrapper.

"Who are they? Where are intercepts come from?"

She shrugged her shoulders. "Even if I could tell you that, I don't know. You know as well as I do that we can't reveal sources."

"We know you listen."

"You have no idea. A drunk can't call his mother from a pay phone in Pinsk without us on the other end." She was careful to keep the candy from touching her ruby lipstick as she popped it into her mouth.

"Tell me more. When is it happening?"

"All we know is that a terrorist or terrorists are attempting to move some kind of weapon from here to Moscow. We don't know what it is, but we believe it's highly mobile—most likely no larger than a suitcase."

"Suitcase? You saying an American suitcase atomic weapon is missing and terrorists are taking it to Moscow?"

"I honestly don't know. But today the chatter spiked. Our analysts believe that it's going down within the next twenty-four hours. And I'll give you a tip, Aleksei. Don't trust the Germans—either flavor." She turned to leave, her stilettos clicking on the hardwood floor. She stopped and looked back at him. "And I wouldn't be so sure about everyone in your home office either, if you get my drift."

Major Natalia Nariskii slammed down the phone, dropped the stolen copy of *The Detonator* magazine onto the bed and quickly dressed. Voronin had slurred his words on the phone. He was plastered again, but he wasn't going to get away with it this time. Just like before, it was Friday night. And, just like before, he demanded she come to his office at once without notifying anyone. She stopped to slip her prized Chechen dagger into her pocket. *Fool me once, shame on you. Try to fool me twice, you lose your balls.*

She dragged herself into the chief resident's office. Voronin sat at his desk in a stupor. He looked up at her, his eyes bloodshot and glassy. She would've sworn he'd been up all night on a binge, but it was only ten-thirty. "Reporting to duty as ordered, sir."

"Sit, major."

She preferred not to restrict her movements. "I prefer to stand, sir."

"No, you won't." He shoved the bottle away. "I've had a visit from the CIA. About half an hour ago. Sometime within the next twenty-four hours a terrorist is taking a nuclear suitcase from the FRG to Moscow. The plan is to take out our leadership. The agent wouldn't come right out and say it, but she implied that the Germans are working with some of our people."

Nariskii pulled out a chair and sat down. "What are you saying?"

"I'm saying the CIA is telling me there's a German-KGB conspiracy to assassinate Gorbachev."

"Disinformation."

"I think not."

"Which Germans?"

"Does it matter? They're all Nazis. I remember the day when they rolled through my village." He poured more vodka, but only drops came out. He tossed the bottle into the wastepaper basket and glass clinked, betraying the other empty bottles. Voronin stood and stumbled over to his bookshelves and reached behind a row of the blue and red volumes of the collected works of V. I. Lenin. He pulled out a fresh bottle. It wasn't dusty. The stash definitely had high turnover.

"Sir, with all due respect, you shouldn't be drinking." She walked over to him and grabbed his arm. "Not now."

Voronin slumped over his glass. "There is no better time. I'm facing the greatest crisis of my career and I don't know what to do or who to trust."

"If it's imminent, Moscow couldn't help anyway. Cut them out. I'd like West German assistance, but I don't trust them. I'll leak a story to a leftist reporter for the *TAZ* who we use from time to time. I'll tell him the Americans are trying to cover up the loss of a nuclear suitcase and that the Russian mafia is trying to get it out of Germany. As soon as it's on the wires, the BKA and BND will be screening everything moving East. If it's their op, it's blown. I'll activate every network we have—even sleepers—but I'll avoid any shared assets."

He inhaled deeply. "You're a good officer, Nariskii."

"I serve the Motherland." *And I regret that it sometimes means saving your ass.* "I assume I'm authorized to use any force necessary."

"Do what you must." He shoved aside the bottle. "Nariskii, if you were tying to get a nuclear suitcase from here to Moscow, how would you do it?"

"A boat if I had no hurry. Trains cross too many frontiers." She glanced over at the calendar hanging on Voronin's wall. Although it was almost May, the page was still turned to March. *Almost May. May Day.* "Monday is the first of May—International Workers' Day."

"Most of the Politburo will be atop Lenin's tomb for the parade."

"They're in a hurry. They have to have it in position before Monday morning."

Voronin stood, but wobbled. "They'll do it by air."

"I'd go through Frankfurt. It's the busiest airport on the continent—too busy to carefully screen anything. Aeroflot, Lufthansa and Pan Am—they all fly nonstop to Sheremetyevo."

Voronin cleared his throat. "Concentrate your people there. Once you activate the networks, I want you in Frankfurt. Take what you need to stop them. Whatever you need."

As soon as Nariskii left, Voronin returned the vodka to its cache behind the Lenin library. He felt a rush like back in the old days, before alcohol and the boredom of a small town in Germany had taken such a toll on his career. Voronin was now heading the effort to stop a nuclear terrorist threat to Gorbachev. For the next twenty-four hours, he would be the most important man in the KGB. But no one could be trusted with that knowledge. He swallowed the last gulp of vodka that he'd be having for a while and felt the juices of youth warming his veins. The one person to whom he'd really like to boast wasn't even in Moscow. Voronin convinced himself his old classmate from the Dzerzhinsky Higher School had to be far enough removed from Lubyanka as not to be involved with the conspirators—if there were any KGB conspirators. What if the CIA were lying?

A call to an old rival wouldn't hurt. He reached for the phone to dial the Berlin residency. It had been years since Aleksei Voronin had been able to gloat about his importance to his successful comrade. And working to stop a nuclear threat to Gorbachev was indeed reason to rub it in to Gennadi Titov.

CHAPTER TWENTY-SEVEN

Catch a man a fish and you can sell it to him.
Teach a man to fish and
you ruin a wonderful business opportunity.
—KARL MARX

WEST BERLIN

Summer and Faith looked through the half-moon slit in the leather satchel. Four rows of white rectangular bricks stacked two high, each one wrapped in clear plastic. Summer pulled out a package of something that looked like Play-Doh. "You really got this from the East Germans?"

"What is it?" Faith said.

"C."

"What the hell are the East Germans doing with American explosives? Are you sure that's what it is?"

"I've never actually seen Semtex, but it's supposed to look a lot like C-3, kinda yellowish, but not as brownish. More orange. But I'd recognize C-4 anywhere, and this is it. They could've stolen it from the military or a private firm. We use it all the time—all the EOD units do. Our allies—the Brits, Australians—they all use it. Even civilians with the proper ATF licenses can order it. I think it comes from a place in Texas."

"And there's a black market for everything," Faith said.

"You oughtta know. Whatever this is about, I'd say someone wants it to look like it's an American job."

"Can you really tell whether it was Semtex or C-4 after something's blown up? I thought they were chemically about the same."

"They both use the same stuff, but lab boys can tell them apart. About ten years ago, the government started encouraging manufacturers to include something called taggant—microscopic chips coded so you can tell where and when it was manufactured. Now I think this was mainly for the stuff they sell to civilians. I'm sure it's not in what we use in the field in SpecWar—SEALs don't always want to leave a calling card."

"Would the East Germans know about taggant?"

"It's not highly classified." He dropped the explosive onto the table. "You owe me an explanation, and I don't think this can wait until a beer."

"Promise me you won't get mad and you won't even think about trying to get involved."

"At this point, Faith, I can't promise you much."

"I'm sorry, then I can't tell you much, but I do have a craft project I need to tackle after we're done with this. I'm going to need you to buy some Play-Doh for me in the PX or Exchange or whatever it's called."

Summer began packing his tools.

"What are you doing?"

"Pulling my things together because, as much as I care for you, I can't do this for you unless you're up-front with me. And I'm going to have to confiscate this and take it to a base to disarm and dispose of it."

"You can't do this to me."

"Or you me."

Faith sighed. "They'll kill me if I don't deliver it on time. I've been blackmailed into transporting it."

"Where? Can't you do better than that? I'm a naval officer, and that means I can't stay on the sidelines if this is going to terrorists that might hit a US or allied target."

"It's going to an East Bloc capital."

"Moscow? The East Germans are using you to smuggle C into Russia? You've gotta be kidding."

"I didn't say Moscow."

"Well, hell, where else would they bother with? The Germans think they're better than everyone else, so you don't think they'd go to such lengths to blow up some frickin' Romanian, do you? You're in over your head—and I don't mean just a couple of inches. I've got contacts in the DIA—"

"Don't even think about Defense Intelligence. The Stasi would think I'd turned on them. They'd kill me if they knew I was meeting with you, personal history aside." Faith brushed her hair from her face and felt sweat gathering on her forehead.

"So then why did you risk meeting me?"

"They wouldn't tell me what I was dealing with, and for all I knew they could have been setting me up to carry a bomb on a plane. They made it clear it was booby trapped, but I knew nothing was tamper-proof with you—you proved that when I was sixteen." She flashed him a smile.

"So why are you going along with them?"

"I told you, they threatened me." She forced herself to make eye contact with him, but couldn't; she looked away.

"That's not good enough. You could get away from here or get help from the government. Why, Faith?"

"I didn't want to tell you because it's so far-fetched, but I've received information from the Stasi about Daddy. You know how Mama would never say anything about him or about how he passed away?" She blinked rapidly, fighting back tears.

He nodded as he turned a chair around and sat in it backward.

"They claim he's still alive, and if I cooperate, they'll help me find him. I'm guessing he's been held in a gulag or in one of their special psychiatric hospitals, like the dissident physicist Sakharov."

Summer removed a pair of scissors from the kit and snipped away the leather flap, widening the hole, gradually exposing a metal cylinder wrapped in duct tape. The end of the soup-can-sized container was recessed like the bottom of a wine bottle and its top was cut away. It was stuffed with C-4.

He set down the scissors. Four colored wires disappeared into the plastique; a third set linked everything together. His eyes followed each wire as if he were searching for hidden patterns, decrypting a secret code. "Not good."

Faith held her breath, afraid to speak. Summer snatched up a handful of X-rays. His eyes darted between the X-ray and the case. He held up one after another to light, all the while shaking his head. He tossed them on the table with enough force that they slid off the other side. Faith crawled under the table and retrieved the film, blowing away the dust.

"Son of a buck." He traced an ellipse on the X-ray with his index finger. "See this shadow at the bottom of the battery? It's got to be a capacitor. I missed it before because of the angles of the pictures. Too many wires and they're so tightly twisted together I thought they were singles."

"I still don't get it."

"They really didn't want you messing with this. If it was only single wires, it would be a matter of snipping any one of them to prevent the circuit from closing. You know how in the movies you see two wires going into the bomb and the hero has to decide which one to clip—one will stop the timer; the other will blow 'em to kingdom come?"

"I've seen that flick a couple times."

"It's a bunch of horse hockey. If you only have two wires, it doesn't matter which one you cut because either one will keep it from getting a current and setting off the cap. But now we're facing a different story. We don't know which wire is which. The extra wires and the capacitor muck up everything. Let me take you for a tour." He pointed at the small cylinder cocooned in duct tape. "This is the battery and this swatch of furnace tape—"

"I haven't heard anyone call duct tape furnace tape since I left the Ozarks," Faith said.

"As I was saying, this swatch of *duck* tape on the top hides the alligator clip with the two sides you don't want to touch each other, like I demonstrated earlier. I'm not sure how it's stuck under there so that the spacer would get pulled out, but it doesn't really matter to us right now. The blasting cap is buried in the C in the can. Now the shape of the can at the bottom makes it kind of nasty. They've made a shaped charge to increase effectiveness. When the detonation wave hits it, basically the indented part is going to separate from the sides, collapse on itself and form a little slug that'll come flying out the end with enough force to go through three or four inches of steel."

"Glad I didn't think they were bluffing and open the case."

"Amen. I'd say it could take out a good chunk of this building if I'm not careful. But don't worry. I'm always careful."

"Maybe we shouldn't be doing this."

He grinned. "You're not going to take this away from me now when it's starting to get fun. Leave me be."

"You do this for the rush, don't you?"

"And let me tell you, it's a damn good one—probably about like what you get from playing hide-and-seek with your KGB friends."

"Summer, listen to me. I don't want to blow up this apartment—it's on loan from one of Hakan's friends who's visiting family in Antalya. Actually, it's not even borrowed. Another friend is supposed to be watering the plants and he gave us the key." Faith shuffled the X-rays as she stared at the satchel. "And there is this little matter about our own safety."

"Let's get one thing straight. If I thought for a second I couldn't beat this thing, we'd be blasting it with the water cannon. I won't do jobs if I'm not confident I'm going to win, and I sure as hell wouldn't put you in danger."

"Have you ever been in the middle of a job and not been so confident you were going to be able to defuse it?"

"In the middle, of course, but, like I said, I've never started a job I wasn't sure I could finish safely." He winked at Faith, then turned toward the case, reached into it and grabbed a package of C-4 with both hands. Bending it, he extracted it through the incision.

"Think fast." He tossed the C-4 to Faith.

She dropped the X-ray and fumbled to catch the explosive and then glared at him. "Am I supposed to think that's funny? What the hell do I do with this?"

"Whatever you want. I told you it was extremely stable."

"You made your point. Don't do it again."

"If you're going to be dealing with this stuff, you have to learn its parameters. Now calm yourself down. I've played with explosives every day for well over a decade, if you only credit my military time. We won't count the times when I used to use dynamite to blow stumps out at the farm for my dad." He pulled out another C-4 package and handed it to Faith.

"Seems like I remember you blowing up the water main to the whole river valley once." Faith stacked the plastique on the table beside the other slab.

"If Possum had been a better water witch, I never would've touched that stump."

"Yeah, yeah. And you can spare me the story of using dynamite to blast a basement under your grandma's house."

"Didn't hurt that house one bit. And she loved her new basement." He extracted another package and handed it to Faith.

"I'm assuming you're unpacking this to minimize any possible explosions."

"Mainly to get more room to work inside this thing. I wouldn't expect the packages to go off even if the can high-ordered. It could blow, but I'd be surprised."

"So I take it then it doesn't really matter if I stack them on the table or across the room."

"Wherever they don't get in the way. When you're done there, see if you can find a can opener in one of the drawers." He turned the cylinder stuffed with plastique so that the bottom faced upright. "I need you to hold this very steady for me while I cut it open. You've got to be careful not to pull it too high or move it too much because we don't want to yank any of the wires apart."

Summer sank the blade of the can opener into the metal and turned the rusty crank, moving it around the cylinder. The metal seemed thicker than an ordinary can and Faith marveled at the strength in his fingers. She missed those fingers.

She contorted her body, ducking under his arms as the can opener worked its way around the cylinder. One small fragment of metal held the conical lid to the rest of the cylinder. Setting the opener aside, he twisted the lid until the metal snapped. He sailed the lid into the trash like a jagged metal Frisbee. He held the metal container and pressed the C-4 through the newly opened hole. It popped out like the orange ice cream push-ups they shared as kids. He held the plastique with the wires running away from him and then pushed both thumbs into the substance.

"There. I feel it." Summer molded the C-4, kneading it and pulling it out toward the edges, as if shaping clay into a pot. It grayed with dirt as he handled it. He picked away at the C-4 until he exposed the blasting cap. A red and a yellow wire led directly into it. "A number-eight cap. They're using all American hardware."

Faith wished she hadn't noticed small beads of sweat forming on his forehead.

"Hand me the small wire cutters and take a look. Which one do you think we should cut?"

"Don't ask me. You're the expert. I thought you'd know."

"It's gotta be one or the other. What do you think, red?" He slipped the blades of the wire clippers around the red wire.

Faith didn't move. She held her breath. "No, don't. The yellow."

He removed the wire from the clippers and put the yellow wire between the blades.

"No, don't listen to me. I don't know."

"Yes, you do." He snipped the yellow wire. "I told you, when it's just two wires going in, you can cut either one. We're done. The dummy wires were tucked into the C, but not wired to the cap. It's all over." Summer stood up, examining the explosive embedded under his nails.

Faith punched him in the stomach, doubling him over. "You son of a bitch."

"It was a test and you didn't do too well, honey. You've got a lot to learn if you think I'm going to leave you alone with explosives."

CHAPTER TWENTY-EIGHT

In the Soviet Army,
it takes more courage to retreat than advance.
—STALIN

SCHÖNEFELD AIRPORT, GERMAN DEMOCRATIC REPUBLIC

Colonel Bogdanov hurried through the separate Soviet-controlled terminal, fresh from her final meeting with Kosyk. She had already given her assistant instructions to signal Moscow that the countdown had begun. FedEx had made her pickup. From her discussion with Kosyk, she now knew the details of the operation and was on her way to Moscow to relay the final plans. The drab terminal was nearly empty, save for a few boisterous Soviet Army officers drinking vodka and munching on salami sandwiches at the snack bar. She carried her KGB uniform in a garment bag to change into once in the privacy of the airplane. The small three-engine Yak-40 waited for her at the gate; it sported the blue Aeroflot livery.

Just as she was about to walk out onto the tarmac to board her aircraft, someone shouted after her.

"Zara Antonovna." General Ivanovski, Supreme Commander of Soviet Forces in Germany, called her by her patronymic. The bear of a man waddled to catch up with her, the gold stars of two Hero of the Soviet Union medals swinging back and forth on his chest. His four aides followed.

"Uncle Yuri! How are you?" She greeted him, exchanging small talk about their families. The aides stood a few respectful meters back.

"My little Zar! I have wanted to speak to you privately, and I have a few unexpected minutes now. My staff informs me a mechanical repair is needed on my personal aeroplane."

"I'm in a bit of a hurry. And depending upon how private, that could be difficult here."

"As the little spy of the family, you should know those things." He laughed, swelling his already puffy double chin. "I take it you are going to Moscow. I will fly with you. My plane can follow with my staff whenever they're finished taping it up. I only need to take along my communications officer so that I stay in touch in case . . . you understand why. This way we can talk under four eyes."

Colonel Bogdanov guessed that they had crossed the Polish border about the time the plane leveled off at cruising altitude. She sat with the general in the first-class section at a table with four seats facing one another. Her back was toward the cockpit, allowing the general to sit facing the direction of travel. The uniformed Aeroflot flight attendant served the general vodka. Bogdanov chose Armenian cognac in hopes she wouldn't be expected to keep pace with her uncle, a robust drinker even by Slavic standards.

The flight attendant covered the table with a linen cloth and fanned out a stack of napkins embossed with the signature winged hammer-and-sickle. After arranging silverware, she set a basket filled with black bread on the edge of the table along with crystal dishes mounded over with butter and caviar. She brought out a silver tray of white cheese and hard salami slices before fetching the drinks.

"Bring us the bottles and go in the back. We will call you when we need you." He lifted his glass in a toast. "*Na zdorove.*" He downed the vodka.

The colonel sipped her cognac.

He splashed more vodka into his glass. "To the future, may it return past glories." He drank it and let out a sigh. "I understand you're the genius behind Operation Druzhba."

Zara froze for a moment, staring at her uncle. She then threw the remaining cognac into the back of her throat. "You flatter me. I can't take all the credit. I'm only a liaison."

"That's not what I've been told. You always were too modest." He reached for bread and smeared it with a thick layer of butter. He dipped the same knife into the caviar, leaving butter traces in the precious roe.

"What are they saying about me and who's saying it?"

"I thought the first rule of your trade was to protect your sources."

"Of my trade, not yours. So what are they saying?"

"That you are working to restore order from the chaos and shame Gorbachev has leveled upon us. And that you're doing it for the Motherland, for Marxism-Leninism and for my brother-in-law—your father." The general popped the bread into his mouth and chewed as he spoke.

She now understood. They had used her. They had set her up. Operation Druzhba wasn't intended to avert Gorbachev's assassination and the overthrow of his government. It was to ensure it.

"Child, are you all right? You're suddenly pale. I'll have the pilot turn up the oxygen." The general's belly hit the table as he pulled himself to his feet. Vodka and cognac sloshed from their glasses.

High above the Polish capital, Zara Bogdanov realized she was trapped. And she had trapped Faith Whitney. She knew it was her duty to prevent the coup, but she didn't know whom to trust. Her stomach churned as she recognized it was in her personal best interest for the putsch to succeed. If it failed, she'd be convicted before a secret military tribunal and executed within hours. If it succeeded, she'd enter the Soviet pantheon as one of its greatest heroes, the restorer of the lost order. With the elevated status, she'd enjoy all of the perks of unbridled power and her father would be rehabilitated. Either way, Faith would be killed.

Her choice was deceptively elegant in its simplicity: duty or power. She could either attempt to stop the coup single-handedly in a futile heroic effort or do her damnedest to make it succeed and save herself. Both were a gamble, but she knew the odds favored the coup—and the payoff was significantly higher. She pressed her face against the cold round window, looked down on the dying forests of the Polish countryside and hoped Faith had broken her word and was headed back to the States.

PART 2

THE RIFT ZONE

History punishes the one who comes too late.

—GORBACHEV, BERLIN 1989

CHAPTER TWENTY-NINE

TEGEL AIRPORT, WEST BERLIN
SATURDAY, APRIL 29

Faith handed the crumpled papers to the German flight attendant and boarded the Pan Am flight to Frankfurt, hoping that the Teutonic obsession with order would make the woman pay more attention to the crinkles than to the forged interline document. The flight attendant held the paper against the bulkhead and ironed the wrinkles from it with her hands. Faith ignored her, praying she didn't get too picky with the documents. She eyed the last passenger to board, a gorgeous blond, probably some Scandinavian hockey star.

The flight attendant returned the papers to Faith. "The passengers are all seated. Take any seat you can find."

Faith walked past her toward the open door of the cockpit.

"Hey, where do you think you're going?"

Faith ignored her and went onto the flight deck. "Permission to come aboard, Captain Ian?" She gave the captain a mock salute.

"Granted, my dear! Granted. I was starting to fear I'd have to leave without you. Take the jump seat." Ian's London accent was as strong as ever.

Faith could never figure out how or why he became an American citizen, particularly since she didn't think he'd ever lived in the States. He gestured toward the man in the right-hand seat. "Art Kivisto's my first officer today. Frosty McGuire's my flight engineer, best in the business. Gentlemen, this is—"

"Candace Adler. Pleased to meet you." Faith bowed her head quickly.

Frosty shook Faith's hand and spoke with a heavy southern drawl. "Heard a lot about you over the years. Listening to this guy, you're almost a legend. Here, let me stow these for you." Frosty wedged her plastic cooler and carry-on bag between his feet and a bulkhead.

Faith squeezed into the cramped jump seat behind the captain. She fumbled with the heavy shoulder straps of the seatbelt. The belts were wider and the metal clasp larger than those used for passengers. She fastened herself in and then released it to reassure herself she could get out. Time and painkillers had taken the edge off most of the ache, unless she moved in just the right way to send stabbing pain through her side. She wasn't going to take any chances with the shoulder harness pressing too firmly on the wrong spot, so she loosened the belts. "Thanks for letting me join you up here. I always love the bird's-eye view."

"Think nothing of it, *Candace*." Ian's bad breath wafted over to her when he leaned toward her.

"With all due respect, sir, it's a violation of FAA regs to have non-airline personnel traveling on the flight deck during operations," the first officer said.

"Is that so? The tradition's always been captain's discretion with another pilot. She's a Pan Am alum. Now flies interisland in Hawaii."

Please, Ian, don't do this to me again. "Somebody has to man the hardship outposts of the world," Faith said.

"Art just rated on the 727. He's been flying the little buggers for years for Pan Am Express."

"So, you fly in Paradise? You weren't the lady pilot who brought in that convertible Boeing, were you?" Kivisto said.

"As a matter of fact, she's the very one." Ian smiled, revealing his yellowed front teeth.

"You know I don't like to talk about it." Faith forced a smile when she really wanted to snarl at Ian.

"That's not what Ian's told me," Frosty said with a conspiratorial grin.

The flight attendant stuck her head into the cockpit, much to Faith's relief. “The final count is seventy-two and eighteen.” She glared at Faith. “And one non-revenue.”

“Almost a full house,” Ian said. “Let’s finish the checklist so we can get this bird in the air.”

“Bugs?” Frosty drew out the word, emphasizing his southern drawl.

“One-four-one and one-fifty-three,” the first officer said. He moved markers on one of the many indicators.

Ian repeated the settings.

“Pitot heat?” Frosty said.

“Pitot heat on.” First Officer Kivisto flipped two switches on the far right of the overhead panel.

They finished the checklist routine and within minutes the plane pushed back and taxied toward the runway. Ahead of them, an Air France Airbus lifted effortlessly into the sky. Faith noted that the first officer was flying the plane today. She would’ve preferred Ian and his years of experience. She was fascinated by aviation, but an uneasy passenger. She’d studied the numbers and she knew the odds were that she could fly every day for nineteen thousand years before being in a crash. Statistics aside, ever since she was a child, she’d known in her gut that it wasn’t going to take her that long to meet fate.

“Roger that. Clipper six-three-niner cleared for rolling takeoff eight-Romeo.” Ian repeated into his headset and then called out the increasing speed.

The first officer pulled back on the control column. Immediately after becoming airborne, the craft banked right and crossed the Wall into the East. Faith smiled at the West’s Cold War doggedness as the Pan Am Clipper asserted American rights to the skies over all of Berlin. An Allied flagship once again gave the Russians the bird as the jet banked high above the silver television tower at Alex. The plane climbed into the air corridor to cross the GDR to West Germany. Faith struggled to make out the last signs of the division, but the two Berlins blended into one.

“Berlin Centre, Clipper six-three-niner is out of nine thousand for ten,” Ian said into his headset.

The plane soon leveled out to cruising altitude for the corridor, and the first officer turned back toward Faith. “So tell me about that famous flight, Candace. It’s always fascinated me how someone could land that plane, the shape it was in.”

“That’s a beautiful dog.” Faith pointed to the picture of a chocolate Labrador stuck to the right of Frosty’s control panel.

"That's old Clipper. He's my best bud. I'd even take him over old Ian here—and that says a lot."

"That was a 737-300 that lost its top, wasn't it?" The first officer persisted.

You'll pay for this, Ian. Faith racked her brains for everything she ever knew about the ill-fated flight. The photo of the open air cabin had etched itself into her mind and flashed into her consciousness every time she flew on an older plane, but the picture was about all she could remember. It happened last year, when she was in Burkina Faso, and the local media hadn't given it much coverage. She looked at the flight engineer, her eyes pleading for help. He scribbled on his notepad and tipped it toward her. She strained to read the number. "No, it was a . . . 737-200." She mouthed a thank-you to Frosty.

"What was your altitude when the decompression occurred?"

"Higher than I would've liked. Whoa!" The plane dropped several feet. Her stomach flipped, but she was grateful for the interruption. She stared at three vertical rows of five instruments each. The needles in each row moved in tandem with one another, but she had no idea what they meant. Everyone seemed calm, so she guessed they weren't going down—yet.

"Sorry. Didn't see the bump," Ian said. "I'm afraid it's going to be a bit choppy today through the corridor. You might want to keep yourself strapped in until we get to Western airspace and can climb out of it. Ten thousand feet doesn't make sense now with pressurized cabins. The war's been over for more than forty years. One would think they would have renegotiated a higher ceiling by now."

"Come on, room to maneuver when we go over the Hartz mountains would take the sport out of it," Frosty said.

Ian turned back toward Faith. "So, what's your mother up to nowadays?" Ian exchanged his services as a Bible courier to Moscow for priceless icons Faith's mother salvaged from rotting Soviet churches. Because Ian's motivation was less than spiritual, Mama Whitney only used him as a last resort; she even suspected he might be Anglican.

"I have no idea what continent she's weighing down at the moment. I haven't had contact with her in years. You know better than to ask."

"But I always do. She is your mother. She's in Moscow arranging adoptions of orphans by Americans. I took in some CARE packages for the little ones a few days ago. Adorable little things—you want to take them all home with you."

"I wonder what she's really up to. She hates kids—believe me."

"I don't understand whatever happened between you."

"Let's just say it was one too many exorcisms for me—for her, one too few."

"If we could only find a happy medium. If you do decide to look her up, it was Nadezhda orphanage somewhere near the Arbat. She's been running that place for years. You know, there was one curious thing, now that you mention it. I'd always heard about how few caretakers the children have in Russian orphanages, but in your mother's place there were almost more adults than children. And as I think about it, they all seemed Levantine to me—definitely not Russian."

"As in one of the Turkic tribes in Central Asia, or do you mean they were Semite?"

"One of those."

"She's definitely up to something. So what did she really have you bring in?"

Ian turned to the first officer. "Art, Candace and I are old flames. Would you mind giving us a few minutes alone? Frosty here has heard everything. Don't mind if he stays."

"Oh, oh, so sorry. I didn't realize it. Of course, of course. I'll go back and talk to the stewardesses. I was hoping to get a chance to go over emergency evacuation procedures with the redhead." He unfolded himself from the chair and left the cockpit.

"Old flames? Ian, you old dog. Dream on."

"It brought us some privacy, didn't it, *Candace*? And I was friendly with a Candace once, for that matter."

Frosty swiveled his seat around and extended his hand. "And you must be Faith—the resourceful lady I've heard so much about." He shook her hand again, this time with more vigor.

Ian reported their position and altitude to air traffic control, then returned to the conversation. "I knew you were incognito when I reviewed the manifest and couldn't find you. Don't worry about Frosty here. We go all the way back to my Royal Navy days, when I was on a training exchange at White Sands. Now, what is it we're moving today that warrants an anonymous trip?"

Faith placed her finger in front of her lips and whispered, "Cockpit voice recorder."

"A cockpit voice recorder? You want to take a CVR to Moscow?"

"No. We're being recorded."

"Jeez," Frosty said as he put a headset over one ear. "Ian wasn't joking that you've spent too long behind the Iron Curtain—the rust is rubbing off."

"Hey, paranoia's a lifestyle for me," Faith said.

"And for me," Ian said. "Don't mind the CVR. There are privacy workarounds. Not particularly legal, but effective nonetheless."

Frosty grinned. "I call it the Bill North maneuver, after the guy who taught it to me back when I was flying out of Miami. The 727s have an erase button that only works when you're on the ground with the parking brake set. But pull the parking brake latch lever in the air and the plane thinks it's at the terminal. Push the erase button at the same time, and presto. Butt is covered." Frosty chuckled.

"So what's so hush-hush? Stasi making an arse of itself again?" Ian said.

"Like you wouldn't believe."

"You know, I once had a mechanical in Bucharest and had to overnight. Everywhere I went it was the same thing. Two men in the most horrendous leisure suits were attached to us like limpets." Ian glanced at the instrument panels.

Faith ignored Ian and turned to Frosty. "All the spooks monitor who's booked in and out of Berlin. The master here has taught me they don't pay much attention to the comings and goings of airline personnel, so I used interline travel papers or whatever they're called to get out of Dodge with as little of a trail as possible."

"Why all of the cloak-and-dagger, my dear?" Ian said.

"I need you to do a rush delivery for me. It's critical."

"I gathered that when you rang me up yesterday. You were so out of breath, you sounded like you'd run a marathon. We both know that would never happen, now don't we? So where are you headed?"

"I've been dreaming of a few days of R and R in Amsterdam." She closed her eyes briefly and found herself admiring Van Gogh's sunflowers, dodging bicycles, and gorging herself on *nasi goreng*.

"You had to slip out of Berlin posing as airline staff and you expect me to believe you did it to go on holiday?" Ian said.

"It's never easy to get away, is it?"

Frosty spoke into his headset, "Roger that on the bogie, Berlin. Range twelve miles." He turned toward the captain. "We got traffic, Ian. Five o'clock westbound. Coming up on our tail."

"Take the right-hand seat and have a peek. I'm disengaging the autopilot. We won't do anything unexpected. We'll let him avoid us. He only wants to give us a cheap thrill—I hope." Ian flipped a switch on the control yoke with his thumb.

Frosty slid into the co-pilot's seat and leaned back to search the sky over the right wing while Ian searched port. "Got him. A MIG's hanging off the starboard wing. Right at three o'clock."

"Jesus." Faith grabbed the seat and braced herself for a collision. No one spoke. A minute passed.

"Here he comes."

A plump snubnosed fighter cut in front of them, rolled and flew straight up.

"Now let's all wave at the commie." Frosty gestured toward the window.

"I'd estimate the Faggot was within five hundred feet."

"That was an awful close five hundred feet. I'd swear that guy needed a shave." Frosty chuckled to himself.

"A faggot?" Faith eased herself back against the hard seat. Her palms were sweaty.

"MIG-15," Ian said. "Faggot's the NATO designation, I swear. I saw these all the time in Korea when I was flying the blockade. Dreadful buggers. We were in Sea Furies, piston-engine craft, and those jets would scream out of nowhere. Haven't seen one of those in years. They must have taken it out of the mothballs for me."

"This isn't going to be like the Korean Air Lines over Sakhalin?"

"Nah, they're just yanking our chain," Frosty said.

"They're not supposed to be in the corridors, but they do this all the time," Ian said.

Suddenly the MIG reappeared ahead of them and flew a parallel course, slightly to their left. Faith guessed it was less than a thousand feet away. She strained to see over Ian's shoulder. "Is it Russian?"

"Actually, I think that's a Jerry. Can you tell, Frosty?"

"You know them commies all look the same to me." He winked at Faith.

"The fifties, sixties, that's when it was fun to fly this stretch of air. You never knew what was going to happen next. I was flying for BEA in those days—BAC one-elevens. A splendid plane. One time a MIG flew in front of me and all at once the sky filled with chaff and—"

"Isn't this kind of dangerous?" Faith gasped as the MIG soared across their path to their starboard.

"Yes, extremely hazardous. As I was saying, I suppose the Russians were trying to block whatever dirty work they thought we were up to. They released the chaff and the entire sky filled with this glitter sparkling in the sun. Quite lovely, actually. Anyway, I radioed in to control, 'Berlin Centre, Bealine six-eight-five—I can see the Iron Curtain!' "

"Aren't you worried about a midair?"

"Keenly. But without proper missiles, there isn't much I can do, is there? Unless you prefer me hiding in the clouds. I'll do that if he fires on us and misses, but until then I prefer we all stay in plain sight, where there's less chance of bumping into one another. And the clouds only work if he hasn't been retrofitted with modern equipment. Did I ever tell you the story about the Air France pilot flying the corridor in the fifties who really did have to take to the clouds after a MIG fired on him? Landed at Tempelhof with eighty-nine bullet holes in the fuselage."

Faith was sure the gap between the two planes was narrowing.

In the main cabin, Vasily Resnick flipped through *Clipper* magazine, pausing to study an ad for Pan Am's WorldPass frequent flyer program. He was pleased with himself that he figured out what FedEx was up to just in time to hop the same flight out of Berlin. He had contacted Titov from the gate. The general warned him that the Bonn residency knew about the shipment and was trying to find FedEx. Thus far he'd seen no signs of meddling from his former Bonn colleagues. The only unusual development was that FedEx had something going on with the cockpit crew. She hadn't left there since she boarded. At least he knew whatever she was carrying was either checked in the belly of the plane or safely with her up front.

He set down the magazine and took the blue plastic sandwich box from the stewardess. From the way her gaze fondled him, he knew she wanted him. Too bad he was on assignment. He pulled the rubber band off the boxed meal. Salad, sandwich, water and cake. The Americans sure knew how to treat passengers well. Aeroflot could learn from them. He squirted mayonnaise and mustard on the ham and bit into the sandwich.

Then he saw him.

The Bonn residency did have someone on board. Resnick immediately turned his head away and reached for an imaginary object on the floor. He stayed bent over until the agent passed. Resnick glanced back to check for any sign the man had noticed him. Kivisto stood in the back, oblivious to anything other than the redheaded stewardess he was hitting on.

Art Kivisto. Artur Kivisto—son of Estonian immigrants. His grandmother was an easily intimidated Soviet citizen still residing in Tallinn. Back before Titov had rescued Resnick from the incompetence of the drunk Voronin at the Bonn residency, Resnick had recruited Kivisto as an informant. An informant for the *Bonn* residency's network. He had come from the cockpit, where FedEx was. Kivisto was the type of snitch who would pass along any information he thought he had a remote chance of getting paid for. He had undoubtedly seen enough out of the ordinary to file a report with the residency as soon as he got to Frankfurt.

The Bonn residency couldn't be allowed to learn that FedEx was on this flight. The greedy fool Kivisto was probably already adding up his new bank balance. Resnick fingered the fountain pen in his shirt pocket, pleased that his escort duty was turning into an interesting trip.

Sunlight streamed through the many flight deck windows and Faith wished she'd brought along sunglasses. The sun gleamed off the shiny MIG hanging in the air just ahead of them. She held up her hand to block the glare and squinted. The Faggot rocked its wings from side to side.

"No way, buddy," Frosty said.

"What does he want?" she said.

"To play follow-the-leader."

"Distance to West German airspace?" Ian said, watching the intercept.

"Seventy miles."

"He'll stand down soon. I'm not about to follow him out of the corridor. Faith, just try to relax and enjoy the flight."

"Right." Faith stared at the console's dials. They didn't seem to be moving much. Everything about the plane seemed normal and safe, save for the fighter off its nose—the fighter whose instructions they were ignoring. The sky had cleared and she no longer had hope of hiding in the clouds. She had to block out the MIG and focus on her objective. "You know Svetlana?"

"A most delightful soul. Don't you remember? You introduced us two, three years ago. She keeps promising to take me on a tour of the Crimea, but the paperwork to travel privately is horrendous. I'm assigned to the Moscow run right now, but my crew visa is good for Moscow only. How strict are they?"

"The Sovs? Very. They even restrict movement of official visitors from other commie countries. I mean, you can sneak around if you blend in. I might have done it once or twice, but I usually cover myself with the right papers, dress the part and my Russian's passable."

"Are you implying I might not blend in?" Ian said.

"Buddy, she's saying we might as well start forwarding your mail to Siberia." Frosty returned to the engineer's station and slipped off his shoes.

Faith pointed to her cooler. "This is a birthday surprise I have to get to her by tonight. A small gift and some Häagen-Dazs to mark the occasion." Faith heard the tension in her own voice and struggled to sound more lively. "You know how Russians love ice cream. I'm betting she's never even imagined chocolate cheesecake and chocolate raspberry tort flavors. All I've ever had there is . . ." Her voice trailed off. The MIG was again rocking its wings from side to side. "Vanilla."

"I had no idea it was her birthday. I'm taking her out to dinner tonight and I suppose now we'll make it a celebration. That might make the evening even better for me, if you know what I mean." Ian smiled to himself.

"So will you take her my gifts?"

"Have you found anything interesting for me lately?"

"She's holding some amazing Armenian glass icons for me. I've never seen such intricate work. They're waiting until I can move them out."

"These birds have all kinds of hiding places the authorities never think to look in."

"The hitch is Soviet customs." Faith was always fishing for new contacts and Ian had them. The man knew every corrupt or corruptible airport employee between Karachi and Sofia, but he rationed his contacts, doling them out one at a time. "Frosty, you want to hand me that cooler? I know how Ian always wants to do a visual on whatever he's taking in for me."

"Not that I don't trust you. I do have a responsibility for my passengers' safety and we all know I'm not taking something into Russia if I don't know what it is. I don't know how to put this delicately, but I find it difficult to believe that you're sending a mere present."

"Come on. My mother smuggles things in. I'm the one who takes them out. That way we both stay out of each other's way. It works for us." She opened the lid and tilted it so he could look inside. She glanced ahead. The MIG was still there, waving away.

"Frosty, would you be so kind and inventory the container?"

"Sure thing, boss."

Frosty removed the lid and pulled out packets of dry ice, then the ice cream, two cartons of each flavor. "Whoa, there's enough here for a little party right now."

"Trust me, I didn't overbuy. There's always some shrinkage on the border."

Frosty picked up a large brown dinner plate with crude blue, yellow and red flowers painted on it. He displayed it to Ian.

"Ghastly."

"What can I say? Sveta wanted genuine Mexican hand-painted dinnerware. Guess you can't get lovely plates like that in Moscow."

"I should hope not." Ian turned back to the instruments.

The MIG suddenly broke away to the left in a steep ninety-plus-degree turn. Ian responded by rocking the 727 from side to side, just as the MIG had done earlier. "He's signaling me that we may proceed. I'm telling him I'll comply this time."

Frosty tilted his head as if listening to something in his headset; then he laughed. "The MIG just broke into the emergency frequency and wished us a safe flight. Didn't know the Reds had a sense of humor."

"Thank God he's gone," Faith said.

"I thought you played chicken with the commies all the time. You going yellow on us?" Frosty slipped his hand into the cooler beside the plates for a perfunctory check. "Just a Leatherman. Those things are great—beat the socks off a Swiss Army knife." Frosty repacked the cooler and closed it. "Looks like you can trust the little lady."

Faith was silent while Ian thanked the Berlin air controller and changed radio frequencies in the hand-off to the West Germans. He confirmed their position and the new flight level, then pulled back on the yoke and began the climb. Faith cleared her throat. "So you'll have this to Sveta by tonight? I owe her big time and absolutely have to make sure she gets this on her birthday." Without the delivery, Faith doubted she would ever leave the Soviet Union alive.

"As I told you when you rang me up, both Frosty and I are scheduled for the Frankfurt–Moscow run this afternoon. We're only doing the Internal German Service twice a week. You got lucky today." Ian flipped an overhead switch.

"Actually, I'm stepping out on you, buddy. I need the cash. I'm doing the IGS milk runs without you in a couple of days." He turned to Faith. "The IGS is a bit short-handed this month and they're letting a few of us sub for old time's sake."

"You don't take this same plane to Moscow today, do you?"

"No, no. We have an equipment change in Frankfurt. IGS has its own fleet."

"I take it the German flight attendants stay with the plane and don't go on to Moscow?"

"We pick up a fresh crew in Frankfurt. Anything else you want to know, my dear?"

"Not at the moment."

Ian turned back toward Faith and smiled. "It was cash."

"Excuse me?"

"Cash. The shipment for your mother was cash. I haven't a clue what she's doing with it, but two days ago I ferried in—"

The cockpit door pushed open and First Officer Art Kivisto squeezed onto the cramped flight deck. His gaze paused for a second too long on the Moscow-bound cooler; then he intentionally averted his eyes away from Faith. *He couldn't be*, she chided herself. *Spooks don't hang out on flight decks.* Faith usually trusted her instincts, but maybe she really had spent too much time playing with the communists and was getting paranoid.

Kivisto slid into the co-pilot's seat, strapped himself in and checked his radio. "Sorry, guys. Didn't want you to think I'd bailed on you. Anything interesting happen?"

"Not a thing," Ian said. "As I was saying, the shipment included over one hundred thousand quid and I don't want to know what else—"

"How much longer until Frankfurt?" She flipped the back of his hairy neck.

He swung around and looked at her, knitting his eyebrows. "Not your typical Moscow CARE package."

Faith made eye contact with Ian. As soon as she had his attention, she looked toward Kivisto, then the cooler.

Frosty shook his head and giggled to himself. "Slick."

Ian reached to the center of the overhead panel and pressed a button while he slipped his other hand down to the rear of the power pedestal. He turned back toward Faith and whispered, "Rest assured, my dear, this conversation never happened."

CHAPTER THIRTY

LUBYANKA (KGB HEADQUARTERS), MOSCOW

Colonel Bogdanov marched past Stukoi's secretary and entered his office with only a cursory knock. Stukoi studied the urgency in her face and concluded his telephone call.

Mustering every ounce of discipline, Colonel Bogdanov shoved aside her anger and said firmly, "You didn't trust me. I'm very disappointed."

"We were working on a need-to-know basis, and you didn't need to know."

"You used me." Her voice grew louder, slipping from her control.

"I saw to it you're getting credit for your role." He took a drag from his cigar.

"You set me up so I have little choice but to help this succeed."

Stukoi opened an envelope, unfolded a letter and began reading it. "It wouldn't be in your best interest for it to fail, now, would it?"

"Clearly not. Half the KGB and Soviet Army seems to know what's going on. They believe I'm the lynchpin to all of it."

"Do you have the final operational details from Kosyk?" He didn't look up from the letter.

"Yes, but I don't think his plan is going to work. He says we should expect to receive six kilos of the American plastic explosive C-4 containing microscopic markers linking it back to the American government. We're to use the explosive to kill Gorbachev. The MfS plan is that we couple the forensic evidence with the fact that FedEx smuggled it into the Soviet Union to blame the Americans and justify political crackdowns here and in Eastern Europe. It might work, but it's not a plan I want to risk my life on."

Stukoi looked up from his mail. His glasses slid down to the end of his nose.

Bogdanov continued. "Would you buy it? We know the Americans never will. Kosyk's aiming for public sentiment in Western Europe. He wants to split NATO enough to keep them from destabilizing the new regime, but I don't think anyone will believe the Americans are behind it when the only body we can link is an expatriate smuggler. Europe will be outraged, and I think we can expect everyone will work against us to subvert our new regime."

"Suggestions?"

"Yes, but I'll have to return to Berlin at once. If all goes well, I'll bring back a member of the US military's elite special forces. He's cross-trained as a Navy SEAL and an explosives expert. I've given him the designation Otter to protect our interest in him, even though he's not an agent at this time. We have some surveillance pictures linking Otter and FedEx in West Berlin. We can make it look like he carried out the mission after receiving the explosives from the CIA operative FedEx. We'll apprehend him trying to escape Moscow after murdering Gorbachev. He's FedEx's ex and our phone taps indicate he's still smitten. We can use FedEx against him: her life for his confession. Then we have a swift show trial and you know the rest."

"Excellent. Someday we're going to have to have a talk about your choice in code names. We can always tell which agents are yours. Too much flair."

"My style works for me," Bogdanov said.

Stukoi shoved his glasses up and returned to reading his mail. "I'd feel more comfortable if you'd stick around in Moscow and have your staff pick up Otter and ship him here."

"Too risky. I have to be the one to approach him personally. I know enough about his old girlfriend to enlist his cooperation initially. The last thing we want right now is problems with the Americans for the botched kidnapping of a Navy officer."

CHAPTER THIRTY-ONE

Death solves all problems. No man, no problem.

—STALIN

FRANKFURT AM MAIN AIRPORT, WEST GERMANY

Resnick stood in front of the center seat in the coach cabin of the Pan Am 727, watching and waiting for the cockpit door to open. As the other passengers crowded the aisle, he smiled and motioned for them to go ahead of him. He was helping a grandmother remove her old-fashioned overnight case from the overhead compartment when he saw light coming from the front of the plane. "I carry it for you. Very heavy," he said in accented German, certain this was the quickest way to move her along so she wouldn't slow him down.

"That's very sweet of you, young man. Is this your first time in Frankfurt?"

"No, ma'am. I'm a guest worker. Since fifteen years." Resnick slowed as he entered the first-class cabin and saw his mark step from the flight deck. He kept his head and upper body bowed as he chatted with the woman.

"Where are you from, young man?"

"Poland—Krakow. Same as the pope." Resnick followed the flight crew down the jetway. As soon as they were at the gate, he presented the woman with her case. He kissed her hand as he wished her a pleasant stay, allowing the flight crew to get a few more meters ahead of him.

The huge arrivals and departures board clicked and growled as the letters and numbers flipped around, updating the information. Resnick stalked the crew through the bustling Frankfurt airport, always careful to remain anonymous. One of the crew juggled FedEx's cooler along with his own case. He noted that Kivisto's head turned each time they passed a telephone. The snitch was probably repeating the contact number that Resnick himself had given him five years before.

The group stopped at the inconspicuous door to the Pan Am airport operations center. Resnick fell back. He spotted a newspaper on a bank of chairs, grabbed it and took up a position across from the entrance to the ops center. He pretended to read the *Frankfurter Allgemeine Zeitung*.

One of the crew punched in a code for the door. Seven, two, seven, three—Resnick made a mental note. FedEx hugged and kissed two of the crew members good-bye, then nodded to Kivisto. She walked away, leaving the cooler in care of the crewman with the peppery white hair. The crew disappeared behind the security door into the restricted operations center and FedEx ducked into the ladies' room. With tradecraft like that, no wonder Titov thought she needed a chaperone.

Resnick turned the page of the newspaper. He had run Kivisto for a year and hundreds of others like him over the last fifteen years. He knew his rats. Any moment Kivisto would tell his crewmates he needed to buy a present for a niece or go for a walk and he'd dash to the nearest pay phone to cash in on his information.

Before Resnick could finish reading about Bayer Leverkusen's injured goalie, Kivisto emerged from the door. His rat was beginning to run the maze. Kivisto hurried to the first shop he passed, a pharmacy, and went inside, probably to get change for a phone call. The shops along that corridor had no other public exits, and Kivisto was not one to dare push his way into the back room to find a service exit. Trusting his mark would reappear, Resnick continued reading the soccer article, all the while monitoring the concourse. Then he saw something unexpected.

A Pan Am stewardess walked out of the WC. In all the time he had been sitting there, an attendant from Lufthansa and two from British Airways had gone inside, but no one from Pan Am. He studied her as she wheeled her flight bag in front of him. He raised his newspaper, but not before he saw the jolt of recognition in her eyes. She approached the Pan Am operations door and entered the security code. So FedEx's tradecraft was better than he'd thought.

Resnick didn't think the same of Kivisto. The target stepped from the pharmacy, counting his change. The first officer looked both ways, then darted to the nearest phone booth and went inside.

Resnick dropped the newspaper as he got up. He removed his fountain pen from his pocket and took off the cap, revealing the razor-sharp tip, ready to write Kivisto's epitaph with its poisonous ink. As Resnick reached for the door of the phone booth, he felt a gentle tug on his arm. He swung around, prepared to strike.

The old lady from the plane jumped back. "Oh, my goodness. I didn't mean to startle you. While you're waiting for the phone, would you mind taking my picture with the planes in the background so I can show my grandson? He loves airplanes."

Resnick glanced at the phone booth. Kivisto picked up the receiver and held it against his shoulder. He dropped a coin into the slot, but the phone didn't register any value.

"It would mean so much, young man."

Kivisto opened the change return, took out the mark piece and tried again.

The phone call could not be allowed, but Resnick didn't want to take out the grandma in the middle of the concourse if he didn't have to. Thanks to Kivisto's incompetence, he had a few moments to spare. Resnick shoved the cap back on his pen and snatched the Instamatic from the lady. "Quickly. Stand here by the booth so I can get the planes in the background." His German was now perfect and without accent. He nearly picked up the woman and planted her at the side of the phone booth. Kivisto had now given up on the bad coin and was trying to stuff the phone with a handful of change to get his call through to Bonn.

"Smile." Resnick framed the picture so as to cut the woman out of it so that there would be no image of Kivisto for any authorities to pore over after they found his body. The snitch was now dialing.

"Have a nice stay in Frankfurt." Resnick shoved the camera at the woman and put his large hand on her back and pointed her down the concourse. "Now go on to your family. They'll be worried about you."

Kivisto dropped the mark into the phone and dreamed of buying his own plane and retiring in the Med. Art Kivisto usually had shit for luck, but today was his lucky day—the big payday he'd been waiting for. The KGB was desperate for any information about an unusual package going to Moscow. Last night was the first time his handler had ever insisted on a rendezvous in the middle of the night. Now he had information Moscow craved. He didn't fear betraying his country or anyone else, only that he might unknowingly do it for too low a price. The mark clinked as it plopped into the coin return. *Damn! Nothing's ever easy.* He scooped it from the coin return and dropped it in again. And it fell through again.

He reached in his pocket and noticed a man outside the booth taking a picture of his elderly mother. Kivisto fiddled with his coins and jammed every German coin he had into the slot, and then dialed the number.

New Life Ministries answered, and he identified himself according to established protocol. "I found the lost dog you're looking for." He heard a click and thought they either transferred him or put him on hold. "You still there? I said I have the information about the lost dog, but first we have to talk money." Kivisto watched the man return the camera to the old woman.

"How much do you want?"

"I was thinking twenty-five grand, then I realized you must want this really bad to wake a little fish like me up in the middle of the night, so let's just double that." Kivisto smiled and leaned against the side of the booth. *Art, you are the man.*

"Fine."

"That was fast. Clearly I sold myself short; let's double down again." *Art, the man. Double-0-727.* Kivisto recognized something about the man with the old lady. Maybe he'd seen him in the movies or sports pages.

Resnick squeezed the shoulder of the grandmother. "Go to your family, now!"

She didn't budge. "I was hoping you'd have coffee and kuchen with me. You're the sweetest person I've talked to in days."

Resnick saw the meter on the phone begin to count down Kivisto's remaining money. The rat was now connected. Resnick reached for the pen and took off the cap with the same hand. "You don't really have a family waiting on you, do you?"

"No. I'm all alone."

He gingerly patted her on the arm. "Well, then, I'll have kuchen with you and I'll be your family now."

Her eyes widened with joy. Then Resnick poked her with his pen. The cobra-venom derivative acted with only a few seconds' delay. He gently lowered her to the ground and shouted, "Help! Call an ambulance! My mother's having a stroke!"

Kivisto watched the younger man take a few steps with the elderly woman as he listened for the KGB's response to his hundred-thousand-dollar proposition. He was lousy with faces, but he definitely knew that man from somewhere. His handler came back on the line. "Agreed. But no more. Now the details."

"It's going in on PA1072 today." Kivisto witnessed the man quickly stabbing the old lady's forearm with something; then she fell to the ground. "What the hell?"

"What's coming in? Who's behind it?" the handler screamed into the phone.

Then Kivisto recognized him. the man he once knew as Sasha.

"You've double-crossed me! You bastards!" he shouted into the phone, then reached for the door.

Resnick bolted for the phone booth, shouting in German, "I need to call an ambulance. My mother's dying!" Resnick yanked open the door just as Kivisto scrambled to get out. Resnick plunged the deadly writing tip into the first officer's neck.

CHAPTER THIRTY-TWO

HOTEL HUGENOTTENHOF, FRANKFURT AM MAIN AIRPORT

Major Natalia Nariskii sat crammed into an airport hotel room with two other operatives and cases of equipment, temporarily coordinating all efforts of the Bonn KGB residency at the Frankfurt airport. Despite the importance of the operation, Voronin wouldn't spring for a suite. She looked at the digital clock. Eleven-thirty in the morning. She and twenty-six operatives and informants on the ground at the Frankfurt airport had worked through the night and into the morning. Not a single good lead had been turned up. The CIA said it was going down within the next twenty-four hours—and that was thirteen hours ago. Time was running out.

The secure line rang and the communications officer answered. He cupped his hand over the receiver. "Major, it's General Voronin."

Nariskii picked up the phone. "Listening."

"We've got it. Pan Am 1072 today."

Nariskii pointed at a blue flight schedule and motioned for the assistant to toss it to her. She cupped her hand over the phone. "Not that one. Pan Am. Right there. It says 'New daily nonstops between Chicago and Frankfurt.' "

He found it and tossed it to her. She caught it and flipped through the pages as she continued to speak with Voronin. "Anything else to work with?"

"No, the informant started shouting something about being double-crossed. We heard a commotion, then nothing."

She ran her polished nail down the column of the flight schedule. "Not good. PA1072 is scheduled for a noon departure. That's in half an hour. Do you at least know what we're looking for?"

"A nuclear suitcase is a suitcase. Figure it out."

"There's no time to go through all checked luggage and cargo even if I could come up with a way to do it. I suppose we could call in a bomb threat."

"No. If the Germans are behind it, they'll let it pass through. Even if they aren't and they find it, the terrorists will still be out there. There's only one way."

"I don't like it. It's a civilian craft."

"Just make sure it happens over our territory so we can sanitize the crash site."

Nariskii turned to her communications officer. "Get me Gudiashvili immediately!"

Moments later, the com officer handed her a two-way radio. She hated unsecured communications, but was pleased with herself she had the foresight to give all of the Moscow flights of the day a special designation and assign codes to various contingency plans. "I understand there is a problem with the plumbing. Do your best to take care of it until help arrives. I need forty-five minutes to an hour. Afterward, I'm taking everyone out to eat."

"Understood. Problems with the plumbing and we're going out to eat."

Nariskii put down the radio and turned it off. "Belenko, get the car. We're leaving in ten minutes. Have the insertion team ready to meet me and get me onto that plane."

Nariskii hoisted a weathered leather suitcase onto the bed. She prayed she had tossed everything she needed into the case when she packed last night. She opened it and inventoried the contents: a jumble of wires, batteries, tools, an alarm clock and a slab of Semtex. The soldering iron would need a few minutes to heat up, so she grabbed it first and searched for an outlet where she could plug it in. The cord of the lamp on the nightstand disappeared behind the bed. Following its trail, she shoved the mattress away from the wall and then reached behind the bed until she found the plug. She tugged, yanking it from the wall. Then she plugged in the soldering iron and set it on the nightstand.

She arranged a battery, an electric blasting cap and wire on the bed and sketched out a diagram in her mind, opting for a basic time-bomb design, simple but reliable. She waved her hand over the soldering iron and felt the heat rising. Time to get to work.

Careful to make sure she had a solid contact between the back of the clock and the copper wire, she soldered one end of the wire to the clock and the other end to the battery. Now she needed a screw. She ran her hand through the suitcase, but found nothing. "Get me a short screw! But with no paint on it. Try taking one off the toilet paper holder."

She removed a drill from the suitcase and tossed it to her com officer. "Plug this in somewhere—just don't mess with my soldering iron."

"I thought you wanted the screw."

"What! You don't have the screw yet? Plug this in and find me a screw now!"

She picked up her shiny metal travel alarm. As long as she kept it wound, it had served her well. Saving her government was a good cause for its donation, but she'd miss its little face waking her everywhere from Havana to Vladivostok. And she wished she had a more professional device, like her favorite MST-13 timer. MEBO's Swiss timers were almost as accurate as an atomic clock and the precise day and hour could be programmed into them, but she hadn't seen equipment like that in ages. She knew she should count her blessings that support services at the Bonn residency actually had a slab of Semtex and a blasting cap left over from an aborted mission years ago. No one could even remember what the operation had been, only that there was surplus Semtex. The lack of collective memory surprised her, since Bonn saw real action so rarely. Black operations for the Bonn residency usually meant sending a whore to seduce a foreign dignitary and doing the photographic work. West Germany was the Stasi's turf, and they ran it well. And it was the Berlin KGB residency that ran the Stasi, so Bonn was a backwater and Nariskii was stuck using screws from toilet paper holders and her own travel alarm to save the Politburo.

"Where's my screw? I need it now!" She selected a fine bit and drilled a starter hole in the clear plastic face of the clock.

The officer handed her two screws.

"I asked for one. Do you have a flashbulb or a bulb like from a penlight? I want to test this circuit."

"I have, but I fear there is no time. It is better if you do it right and do not test."

Nariskii glanced at her watch. Eleven forty-two. It was too late for testing. She had to do it right the first time. Her hand shook from stress as she threaded the screw through the plastic face above the Roman numeral twelve. The screw reached just far enough to make contact with the metal hands. "Hold this." She picked up the blasting cap, spread its wires apart and soldered one wire to the battery. "It's hot now. Whatever you do, don't let the loose lead touch the clock or the battery. And turn that damn radio off before you blow us up!" Nariskii popped the plastic face from her alarm and snapped off the minute hand. "Sorry, old friend." She took a knife and scraped off the luminescence from the side of the hour hand to ensure a good contact. "Help me here. It's a three-hour flight to Moscow and we want to make sure it's over our territory. I'm guessing two hours after takeoff would be safe. Problem is calculating how long it takes us to plant it and for them to get in the air."

"Last time I flew out of Frankfurt, we taxied thirty, forty-five minutes before takeoff."

"If I only had a barometer, we could start the timer when the cabin pressurized."

"Hurry. Gudiashvili is good, but he cannot delay it forever."

"How quickly did he say they'd get me onto the ramp?" Nariskii put her finger on the hour hand and pressed lightly.

"Ten to fifteen minutes."

"He always underestimates. Half-hour to the plane, another fifteen minutes to plant it and for them to close the door. A lot of charters leave midday on a weekend, so I'll add forty-five for taxi, then two hours into the flight. And I always add an extra ten minutes for the bombmaker. I'll set it for three hours and forty-five minutes from now. It's eleven forty-five, so it should go off at five-thirty, Moscow time." She moved the hand to a quarter past the numeral eight. Her hands trembled as she took the lead from the blasting cap, vigilant not to allow it to touch the metal casing of the clock. She paused for a second to study the wiring before she dared complete what she hoped was a broken circuit—broken until it closed at five-thirty Moscow time. Nariskii soldered the lead to the screw.

The com officer held the bomb while Nariskii set aside the soldering iron and jerked the cord from the wall. She picked up the brick of Semtex and weighed it in her hand. Four hundred grams, she guessed—a little more than their Libyan friends had used on Pan Am 103. It would suffice. She shoved a pencil deep inside the orange, claylike substance, pushed the blasting cap into the hole and then bundled the parts together with electrical tape. Not her finest work, but probably her most important. She wrapped it in a hand towel to ensure it wouldn't make contact with the metal container in which she was going to stow it.

"Let's go. We've got a plane to catch."

CHAPTER THIRTY-THREE

FRANKFURT AM MAIN AIRPORT

The passengers were boarding the Clipper Pocahontas for Pan American World Airways flight 1072 from Frankfurt to Moscow when Faith scurried down the jetway. Airline identification tags flapped against her chest. Her blue jacket was a size too small and the gold buttons were poised to pop off if she breathed too deeply. She was pleased to have found a new crew tag for her bag. The paper things wore out so fast, even from her infrequent usage, that she didn't understand why they didn't switch to something laminated. She wheeled her carry-on bag across the foot of a businessman. "Sorry. My first Moscow run and I'm late. I'm so nervous. I've never been behind the Iron Curtain before."

"Please." The man stepped aside and motioned for her to pass. He leaned over to his colleague and spoke in German. "Lufthansa's first class was booked. At least it's not Aeroflot."

The thirty-something purser stood in the doorway, glaring at Faith as he watched her scattered approach. If he booted her off the plane, it would spoil the run, and she didn't want to think about what the Stasi would do to her if she didn't deliver. She greeted the purser and shoved the wadded papers into his hand. "I'm so sorry I missed the preflight. I'll never do it again." She unclipped the identification badge from her jacket and shoved it into her small black purse.

He glared at her.

"I couldn't help it. Let's just say, unexpected female problems."

"Step inside the galley and wait for me. You're blocking the passengers." He waved for a flight attendant in the coach cabin to come to the front. He held his hand up to halt the German businessman. "One moment, sir. I do apologize for the delay." He went into the galley and jerked the blue curtain closed with such force that Faith feared he might pull it off the metal hooks. "You will never do that to me again. Do you understand?"

"Yes, sir." She looked down in deference. A coffee stirrer was stuck to the floor under a stowed galley cart. *Definitely not Lufthansa.*

"You're not on the crew manifest, Reeves."

"I was just assigned. I gave you the addendum."

"I've never known of a last-minute assignment on a Moscow haul. The Russians require too much paper—"

"I was supposed to start Moscow service next month." She opened her purse and removed her thick business-size passport with a light brown folded paper inside. She held Hakan's forgeries out to him and almost didn't recognize her own hand with its fake press-on nails hastily polished in crimson surprise.

"Why would they add someone at the last minute?"

"I don't know. I just work here and do what I'm told. Maybe because of a heavy load or something?"

"We're only expecting forty-seven and six."

"Maybe the return's heavy out of Moscow."

Someone tapped on the galley service door from the outside. The purser looked through the porthole, then glanced down to make sure the emergency slide was not already armed. He opened the door. Three LSG Sky Chefs caterers stood on the elevated platform on the back of their truck.

Two men immediately jumped aboard and pushed their way in. The purser and Faith stepped back. They started to remove the metal bins with the hot in-flight meals, but the purser stepped in front of them and blocked their way. "What in the world are you doing? We just got those meal inserts."

The swarthy supervisor crowded into the galley. "I apologize, sir. But these are the wrong meals. My staff brought you only low-sodium meals, and you know how bland those are. Pan Am passengers deserve the best and we can't have our reputation for excellent cuisine damaged, either. We'll have you a new set of meals here in no time."

"You can't swap them out right now?" the purser said.

"No, sir. But, rest assured, they're being freshly prepared and we'll have them here in no time." He nodded to his crew to remove the metal bins.

The purser threw up his arms. "You are not taking these. Just give me some extra salt packets."

The supervisor leaned over to the purser. "Sir, I didn't want to have to tell you this. The truth is these meals are designated MM."

"I'm losing my patience here. I want an on-time pushback. Is everyone here conspiring to hold up this plane?" He threw his arms into the air. "Get me the salt and get out of here."

"Sir, I don't think you understand. MM is short for Mickey Mouse."

"I don't care if it's Donald Duck à l'orange in there. I want an on-time departure."

The supervisor whispered, "This is a delicate matter. It's a Mickey Mouse problem. As in mouse. As in rats got into the food. As in rat spit. Rat pellets. Get it?"

The purser crinkled his face. "That's just gross. Get those out of here. How long will it be?"

"Just a few minutes, sir."

The caterers left, promising to return in ten minutes. The purser turned back to Faith. "This is not a good day. Give me your passport. It's in order, but you didn't report for the preflight and you caused a bit of a stir with the first-class passengers blundering down the jetway. I'm not able to allow you—"

A shout in Russian interrupted him.

"Ma'am, you can't take this aboard the aircraft." A flight attendant raised her voice.

The purser pushed back the galley curtain. A robust Russian woman hoisted a boxed Sanyo television onto a first-class seat. She dragged an overstuffed red, white and blue striped burlap bag behind her. It was larger than the television box. Her travel companion wedged two other bags into the cabin exit. The purser rushed through first class to the forward exit.

"We have to check these or you'll have to disembark from the aircraft."

The purser held up both hands with outstretched palms as if he were pushing her back off the plane with each word.

The woman barked something in Russian, first wagging her finger at the purser, then pointing at the TV. He repeated his instructions in French, speaking more loudly in case it helped the woman better understand. She screeched at them. The German businessmen shook their heads and whispered to each other. Passengers filled the jetway, craning their necks to watch.

Faith tapped the purser on the shoulder. "Let me see what I can do." He switched places with her. Faith transformed from flustered innocence into the tough-love charm of a jaded Aeroflot stewardess. She spoke in flawless Russian. "Look, lady, this isn't the train to Nizhniy-Novgorod. You can't bring aboard everything you can manage to pack onto your tree-stump legs. This is an American airline, and you're violating American law."

As she spoke with the woman, Faith glanced at the crowd in the jetway. And she recognized someone. The man with the newspaper in the concourse. He was the blond on the plane from Berlin. And now he was tailing her to Moscow. She pretended not to notice him and continued, "You have a choice, babushka: You can keep throwing a fit and we'll toss you off the aircraft right now and turn you over to German authorities—and I'm sure they'll notify Moscow—or you can cooperate with this nice woman and let her check your plunder. If you're lucky, we won't take anything for our troubles. Understand?"

"*Da.*" The woman lowered her head in submission.

Faith turned to the purser and said, "I explained how the FAA regs don't allow such large carry-ons. She completely understands and agreed to cooperate fully. She'll hand her things over for a gate check." Faith then switched back into Russian. "Don't think you just scammed your way into a couple hundred pounds of free excess baggage without us knowing what you're up to. I'm letting you get away with it this one time, but if you cause me any problems on this flight, I'm personally informing Soviet customs you're trafficking in Western goods. You might be able to bribe your way through alone, but they can't turn a blind eye if an American airline reports you. Next time, take the train."

"What'd you say?"

"I told her I know she has a choice when she flies and I hope next time she again chooses Pan American."

"You're on. Take the jump seat up front with me. Now, where are those damn caterers?"

Twenty minutes after the scheduled departure time, Nariskii arrived wearing an LSG Sky Chefs uniform. She was nearly out of breath, but she'd made it. Gudiashvili apologized to the purser for the longer-than-expected delay as he returned the same meal inserts his crew had earlier removed. Nariskii slid in a specially prepared bin, sealed in case anyone tried to open it within the next three hours.

At five-thirty Moscow time, the meal insert would open itself.

CHAPTER THIRTY-FOUR

KGB SAFE HOUSE, BERLIN-WEST, DAHLEM DISTRICT

Colonel Bogdanov kicked off her East German penny loafers and pulled off her Soviet-tailored ladies' suit and exchanged them for a black silk blouse, black Benetton slacks and a matching blazer. She picked up the ugliest piece of jewelry she'd ever seen, an avant-garde brooch with twisted silver icicles dripping from a polished oval of lapis. She flipped it over; a miniature microphone transmitter was mounted on the reverse. She set it on the dresser. After a few brushes of mascara, she put on a pair of blue designer frames with nonprescription glass lenses. As a finishing touch, she rolled up her right pant leg and strapped on her nine-millimeter Makarov service pistol.

Bogdanov walked into the living room. Her assistant, Ivashko, spoke into a radio, holding the receiver against his hairy ear. Did Ivashko believe he was working to save or assassinate Gorbachev? Was he working for her? Titov? Stukoi? She had been on several operations with him over the last decade, but she still didn't know the man. In Pyongyang while evaluating North Korean nuclear capacities, he had praised the Stalinist regime's tight social order. On a mission in Cuba, he couldn't say enough negative things about Castro's iron-fisted regime. The only thing she was certain about the man was that he resented any physical movement.

Ivashko twitched his bushy white eyebrows when he spoke. "Good. I want you to follow him wherever he goes, and that includes the john. If he starts to leave, figure out a way to stall him. I don't care what you do—order him a round of beers, fake a heart attack—I don't care. Whatever you do, prevent him from going onto a US base. If he goes there, it's over. We can't touch him." Ivashko paused. "Think. Cause a minor traffic accident. If he's on foot, stage an attack on one of our female crew. He's a good boy. He'd stop to help her. You think you can handle it now? Good. Report back any change in status." He set the microphone beside him on the sofa but continued to wear the earpiece. He looked up at Bogdanov. "That was a fast trip to Moscow. I thought we'd wrapped up the Berlin side of things and were done with Otter when FedEx left town this morning."

"It was decided we need to tie up a few extra loose ends. I can't say more. Any developments?"

"He just bought a third round of beers for the table. That is, the third round that we know about. They were already drinking when we caught up with them."

"Any idea who his friends are? How many? Are they armed?"

"We know very little, only what we've picked up from surveillance. A major and a Negro captain—both US Army. They don't seem to be carrying firearms."

"Do you have papers for me in case something goes awry?" Bogdanov said.

"Already in your new purse. You're now a subject of the Queen, complete with British driver's license and a few assorted pound notes."

"I told you I wanted to go as an American. Americans innately trust other Americans more than they do Europeans."

"I had problems getting the papers together. I got the blank passports and collateral documents you requested, but we didn't have time to create new ones for you. We had to use papers from an existing legend. I didn't have the manpower to spare to search your embassy office for one of your American passports, but the residency did have this on file along with a Canadian set."

"I told you not to use the residency." Bogdanov raised her voice.

"The last orders I had from you were to use any means at my disposal to pull this off. You required some very specific things. The residency was the only way."

She removed the British passport and skimmed through it. "Doesn't look like Veronica gets around much except to Spain and Malta."

"You're a nurse from Brighton here visiting a German friend, Beate Hirschbein of Krumme Strasse eleven. You met her while vacationing last October on Majorca. Hirschbein's a sleeper we'll reactivate and brief if you're held for questioning."

"I don't anticipate it. I expect he'll come along with me willingly, particularly if I use that Canadian cover. Americans don't consider Canadians foreigners—they're not really sure what to think of them, but they're definitely family. I want everything possible going for me. It's also fast for Berlin authorities to get a check on a British national through the British occupying forces here. After three years at the San Francisco residency, my American is much better than my British, so I'm Canadian tonight." She returned the British passport and driver's license to Ivashko. Each time she worked with him, it became clearer to her why he had never advanced beyond the rank of major despite his three decades with the KGB.

Ivashko opened his scratched plastic briefcase and removed a manila envelope. He tore it open and let the Canadian documents drop out onto the ratty sofa. Bogdanov thumbed through them, committing the pertinent information to memory.

"I'm now a nurse from Toronto. Otherwise, the same legend." The colonel slipped the passport and driver's license into the purse and flicked the gold latch shut.

"I arranged for Kolvich and Valov to accompany Otter as guards on the flight with you to Moscow, unless you want someone else."

"They're adequate for the job, but I don't need anyone," Bogdanov said.

"Otter is a strong guy, well trained in hand-to-hand combat."

"He'll be cuffed and on a plane."

"Violate protocol if you wish," Ivashko said.

"Okay, I'll take the muscle."

"They'll be waiting for you at the airport. We have two taxis on surveillance. Both are set up for you. You have to make sure he's the one who touches the backseat's door-handle—passenger side. It's the one inside that you have to worry about. It has sharp edges coated with a chemical that should knock him out in two or three minutes. If he tries to get in on the other side, the driver knows to tell him the door's broken and he needs to go around. If you absolutely have to get out through that door, roll the window down and use the outside latch."

"Fast work."

"I think it's clear to you now that I had to get help from the residency."

"No, it's not. My standing orders were to avoid contact. And I have one last order—do not injure Otter. Make sure everyone understands that. The more bruises he has on him, the harder time I'll have getting FedEx to cooperate. So when they transfer him to the trunk of my car for the ride East, I want them to be civil. I've seen what they do and I don't want a lot of marks, and definitely no injuries."

"Understood. The other items you requested will be loaded on your Yak by the time you're there. Looks like you forgot the wire. It's on the back of the silver pin in the bedroom. Given how cobbled together this operation is, I figured we'd better be listening in just in case something doesn't go as planned."

"Things will go as planned. No self-respecting Canadian would wear that piece of trash. I don't want it."

"You never know what's going to happen." Ivashko leaned forward in his chair, coaxing an extra boost from the inertia of his body. "I'll get it for you."

CHAPTER THIRTY-FIVE

Bombs do not choose. They will hit everything.

—KHRUSHCHEV

IVANSKOE AIR CORRIDOR, MOSCOW ATC REGION
5:27 P.M., MOSCOW TIME

Faith picked up the last food tray, stowed it in her trolley and headed back to the galley. Serving meals and apologizing for a shortage of blankets and pillows was not her idea of a good time. At least the flight was going well. She'd been worried that they'd hit turbulence and her fear would give her away. No one seemed to suspect that she wasn't a regular flight attendant.

The passengers were a typical mix of Russian expatriates and West European businessmen with an occasional Western student thrown in. Only one passenger intrigued her—the striking Nordic-looking operative whom she couldn't place. When she delivered him the meal, she spoke with him in German and he sounded straight out of Saxony. They chitchatted in Russian when she picked up his empty tray. This time he commanded a perfect Leningrad accent. With her mind on the mystery agent, she wheeled the cart into the first-class cabin before she realized it. She rolled the awkward contraption backward and bumped into someone.

The purser shielded his mouth with one hand. "Let me through. Fast. Mickey Mouse." He disappeared into the forward lavatory.

She wrestled the cart into the galley. Four flight attendants huddled inside, finishing up their meals. Faith rammed the cart into its dock and locked it into position.

An Asian flight attendant looked up at her. Her name tag read "Mae." "Help yourself to lunch. From the looks of Jeff, I wouldn't recommend the stuffed tennis balls today."

"I need a drink." Faith rummaged through the drawers of the beverage cart, searching for a tiny airline bottle of booze. She was sure Ian had a duty-free bottle in his briefcase on the flight deck, but she hoped to make it to Moscow before he realized she was a stowaway.

"This is a Moscow flight. They wiped us out."

"Guess I'll eat something after all." Faith tugged at the small aluminum handle of the meal insert, but the door didn't budge.

"It's jammed. We haven't been able to get it open. Good thing it's a light load today." Mae pointed at the bin.

"Forget it." She wasn't that hungry and she didn't want to hang with the attendants and give them a chance to realize she wasn't really one of them, so she decided to go back and chat with secret agent man. What difference would it make? Her cover was blown with him. His cover was blown with her. And she was very, very bored. She took two spoons and an extra dessert from the presidential-class service and then entered the coach cabin. She glanced at her watch—five twenty-nine, local time. Not much longer.

The operative took up his space in 19A. The armrests of the two empty seats beside him were pushed up and magazines were spread out. Faith decided industry protocol didn't matter a hell of a lot at that point in her short-lived Pan Am career. She approached him with the chocolate mousse and leaned over the empty 19C. "Compliments of the house. It's part of our new World Spook Class service. Thought you might share it with me while we get—"

A brilliant flash. A thunderous clap. The plane lurched to port and shook violently.

Lockerbie.

The first row of coach passengers vanished. Faith dived onto the seats beside the agent. Her hand landed on a seatbelt. She grabbed onto the strap. A tornado engulfed what was left of the cabin, whipping purses, swizzle sticks and insulation into anything in its path. Overhead luggage compartments sprang open, their contents flying toward the open sky. She fought to hold on, but the force tore at her, pulling her away. She was being sucked into the air. She strained to hold on, but the strap slipped through her hands.

Frosty was ready to be on the ground and stretch his legs. *It's going to be Georgian food tonight*, he decided. *Shashlik. With lots of fresh cilantro.* He could taste the chunks of marinated lamb as he glanced at his engineering console and the picture of his pooch. Everything was running beautifully and ol' Clipper was happy as ever. At least they'd managed to pick up some time; they'd be starting their initial descent in about twenty minutes. He decided to go to the galley and see if he could find a snack to tide him over.

He reached to unfasten his seatbelt. An earsplitting explosion went off like a shotgun blast beside his ear. Dirt, charts, loose insulation and Clipper's picture were sucked backward toward the passenger cabin. The force jerked Frosty's head toward the door.

Lockerbie.

He snatched up his oxygen mask and donned his headset. The air fogged, then quickly cleared.

"Frosty, Jackson, you with me? Initiating emergency descent," Ian said, his voice steady but barely audible through the mask mike.

"Affirmative. Initiating rapid decompression checklist." Frosty's ears popped like firecrackers and hurt like hell. Within seconds he confirmed that the air-bleed switches were open and that the pack switch was on. He closed the cargo heat outflow and attempted to restore cabin pressure manually, even though he knew it was hopeless. His stomach sank along with the plane.

He visualized the blue and white shell of the *Maid of the Seas* on the Scottish Highlands.

Lockerbie.

Faith fought to hold on, but the belt slipped through her fingers. She felt her body fly into the air. Then someone grabbed on to her. The operative wrapped his arm around hers. And he squeezed. She struggled to hang on.

Suddenly the sucking force subsided. A mist filled the air and then settled on everything. The roar of the wind and the engines filled the cabin. She could almost feel the sound hitting her body. Her ears throbbed with sharp pain. She moved her jaw back and forth to try to equalize the pressure, but the ringing in her ears wouldn't stop. She breathed hard, gasping for the thin air.

The yellow oxygen masks dangled above some of the seats, but the ones above her failed to open. She stood and pried at it with her fingernails, feeling dizzier by the second. The operative whisked out a pocketknife and popped the panel open. They both grabbed the masks and inhaled deeply. The front of the plane pitched downward and they began rapidly losing altitude. Someone ahead of her began shrieking. Others joined in. And she wanted to cry out, too.

An icy gale battered her, but she could now stand. The plane's interior panels had been ripped off and sucked away. A chunk of the ceiling was gone and she stared at the bare green skin of the plane. Overhead bins were open and one bank of them was missing. She looked toward the galley where all the flight attendants had been eating.

Blue sky. Nothing but blue sky.

Frosty flipped on the no-smoking and fasten-seatbelt signs. He felt vibrations and scanned his panel. The EPR on the number-three engine went to hell and the exhaust temp was plummeting. "Ian, number three has low EPR and EGT and no N_1 indication. Ate something it didn't like."

"Initiate emergency shut—"

The engine-fire warning bell went off, drowning everything out. *I should've taken that early retirement. What was I thinking?* The flight engineer's console blinked like he'd won the jackpot in Vegas. But Frosty McGuire was never one to walk away with money in his pocket. Like water seeking its own level, he always stuck with something until his luck turned bad. Frosty silenced the bell, then began shutting down the number-three engine. He prayed the other two hadn't also ingested more debris than they could handle.

Faith stared at the blue sky. An invisible force pulled her toward the hole. She grabbed the back of a seat. She knew she was going to slide out if she took a step and she also knew her fear was taking over. She was probably the only flight attendant on board—or at least the only one wearing the uniform. The galley was gone and the cabin crew with it. Already passengers were beginning to look toward her, their faces expectant. She had to pull herself together and do something. She sat down and took three deep breaths of oxygen. It was just like smuggling across a border, she told herself. *Stay in character. You're Sandy Reeves, Pan Am flight attendant, trained for emergencies.* She fingered the wings on her uniform.

Sandy Reeves stood, blocking out Faith's fears. She knew what she had to do. The first rule of triage: life support. She snatched the pocketknife from the operative and took a deep breath from her oxygen mask. She moved quickly to the next row of passengers, where masks hadn't deployed. With a twist of the knife, the panel opened and the masks dropped down. Before the passengers could put them on, she tugged on one and took a couple of deep breaths. She worked her way from row to row, hanging on to the backs of seats as she went.

The plane continued to sink.

The closer Faith got to the former galley, the more the floor sagged. Broken electrical wires hung from the ceiling, buzzing and arcing as they whipped around. She couldn't hold her breath any longer. She filled her lungs with the thin cabin air. It was icy cold, but breathable. They'd lost a hell of a lot of altitude. Thank God the Russian countryside was flat. She hoped it was flat enough.

Frosty pulled the fire bottle for the number-three engine for the second time as he listened in on the first officer's exchange with the ground.

"Moscow Centre, this is Clipper ten-seventy-two; we are declaring an emergency," First Officer Jackson said.

"Here is Moscow Centre. Is that Clipper ten-seventeen on emergency?" the controller said with a heavy Russian accent.

"Clipper ten-seventy-two, ten-seven-two, declaring an emergency."

"Moscow Centre, Clipper ten-seventy-two, on emergency."

"Moscow Centre, Clipper ten-seventy-two, descending out of—" Jackson ran his finger down the metric conversion chart "—seven-five hundred meters for . . . four-two hundred meters. Request clearance to nearest airport."

The controller struggled with the foreign words. "Clipper ten-seventy-two, this is Moscow Centre. Negative on request. Nearest airport is with military restriction. Proceed to Sheremetyevo."

"Moscow Centre, Clipper ten-seventy-two, we're experiencing emergency depressurization and failure on number-three engine. Repeat request for emergency clearance to nearest airfield."

"Clipper ten-seventy-two, here is Moscow Centre. Repeat. Negative on request. Negative on request."

"Captain," Jackson said.

Ian visibly struggled with the sluggish controls. "I copied. Distance to Sheremetyevo?"

"One hundred eight nautical miles," Frosty said. "Real neighborly folks, those Rooskies."

CHAPTER THIRTY-SIX

WEST BERLIN, AMERICAN SECTOR

The Papagei Pub catering to GIs was packed with its usual crowd of servicemen, their German girlfriends and young working-class Berliners looking for American dates. The men at the bar watched a time-delayed broadcast of a baseball game on the Armed Forces Network. Each time a loud cheer shook the room, the mascot macaw perched at the end of the bar squawked, "Touchdown! Touchdown!" The bird then settled back into its routine of plucking out the feathers around its mangy neck.

The blues, pinks and greens of the blinking neon parrot in the pub's window reflected on Summer's face. Socializing with his old Army classmates from the joint-services Explosive Ordnance Disposal School was fun, but hardly distracted him from the nagging sense that he should have stopped Faith—even if her fury had meant the end of their friendship. He absentmindedly lifted his beer with his buddies in a toast to younger days and sipped the pilsner through the foam head.

Captain Leroy Walters reached for a handful of popcorn and threw a kernel into his mouth. "Man, I don't know what's with the Germans, why they don't have good finger food. You'd think any people who know how to make beer this good would've come up with something to snack on while you're drinking it. You know, this place only started serving popcorn a couple of months ago."

"That right?" Summer said automatically.

"Come on, Summer, you ready to tell us now what you're doing, coming all the way over here on a moment's notice?"

"I told you, I was on a rescue mission for a damsel in distress." He picked up a stack of cardboard beer coasters advertising Warsteiner Pilsner and shuffled them. He didn't like the feeling lodged in his gut: Faith was in trouble.

"I'm sure you did the right thing."

"She never would let me do that." He dropped the coasters one by one from one hand into the other. He should've stopped her this morning, but she was so damn headstrong.

"What kind of trouble she in? You can get into a lot of trouble in this city."

"The kind you don't want to know about."

"Well, that narrows it down to female troubles or problems with the communists."

Summer stared at the neon bird.

"Oh, shit, man. You gotta be real careful in this town. You know, I used to use that same Turkish car mechanic—*der Meister,* we called him. He was the one they busted for helping that guy with the 513th carry all those documents to East Berlin."

"You don't say?" Summer said. His thoughts were eight hundred miles east.

"Yeah, I used to take Francine's Pontiac into his shop. All the guys used *der Meister*. He could fix anything. The nicest guy you'd ever meet. No one could believe he was a spy. They say he took microfilm to East Berlin through a hole in the fence the KGB showed him. You know, we do get them coming over here, taking pictures of what we're doing. You can always spot 'em. It's always one or two little guys in cheap suits. They pretend to walk dogs by you and they'd be taking your picture all the while. They won't use the same guy twice because we'd be too suspicious, but they never thought to change the damn dog! I tell you, I can spot a KGB agent every time." He turned his head toward a tall woman walking by. She had closely cropped dark curls that reminded him of an old girlfriend. She slowed her pace as she neared the pub. "Oh, she's nice looking. Out for a night on the town. You boys might have to excuse me."

The men turned their heads and watched the sexy woman pass the window. She wore the ugliest brooch Summer had ever seen. She glanced at him and then looked away.

"Her step's too deliberate," Summer said. "You might always be able to spot a KGB agent, but I can always tell when a lady is too complicated to mess with. That woman has a mind of her own. Trust me, you don't want to get involved with that one."

"Sounds like she reminds you of someone. Your damsel in distress, maybe?" Meriwether finally spoke.

The woman entered the pub and stood near the doorway, surveying the room. When her gaze fell upon their table, Walters smiled at her and motioned for her to join them.

"Control yourself, Leroy," Summer said. "Don't let your dick go busting up our reunion."

"She looks like she's looking for someone, and maybe I'm her man."

"I'm sorry to bother you, guys," she said in an American accent. "But I'm checking out all the military hangouts for a friend of a friend. I know this sounds pretty weird, but it's real important for my friend Faith that I find him."

Summer jerked his head up and stopped playing with the coasters. "You know Faith? Faith Whitney?"

"Yeah. I'm trying to find a guy named Max Summer."

"She all right? What's happened to her?"

"You're Max? Thank God I found you. She got word to Hakan she needs you as soon as possible. He's out looking for you, too."

"She say anything else?"

"It didn't mean much to us, but she said it has something to do with a package you helped her with."

"Where is she?"

"Do you know Berlin?" the woman said.

"Barely."

"I do," Meriwether said.

"At an apartment in Steglitz. I can take you to her."

"Let's go." Summer stood, reaching for his wallet.

"I got it, man." Walters threw a blue hundred-mark bill onto the table.

"By the way, I'm Kathy," she said as they left the bar. Kathy raised her arm in the air to hail a taxi. A tan Mercedes taxi turned its lights on and pulled up to the curb.

"You don't need a cab," Leroy said. "We can drive you wherever you need to go. I've got my wife's Pontiac tonight. We can all pile in the cruiser." He pointed at a blue Grand LeMans with Virginia license plates.

"The plates kind of give you away as a US serviceman. It could be dangerous for Faith. I think we'd better go for the cab," Kathy said.

"Thanks again, but she's got a point," Summer said as he opened the door for Kathy. "We'll follow you to the base to get my stuff. No telling what she needs help with. Wait at the gate for me and I'll ride in with you. She can stay with the taxi."

She slid across the leather seat, making room for Summer. He closed the door behind her and she rolled down the window. "Hey, aren't you getting in?"

He pulled on the handle of the front passenger door and leaned over to the back window. "I'm kinda funny about riding in the back of cabs—particularly in foreign countries and New York City." He hopped into the front seat and put on his seatbelt. He greeted the driver with a nod. "Wait a second, then follow that Pontiac."

The driver shrugged his shoulders. "No English."

"I'll take care of it." Kathy translated for the cabbie. He shook his head at first and then after a few more words seemed to understand. The driver waited for the Pontiac.

"Was that some weird dialect of German you were speaking with him? It sounded kind of funny," Summer said as he took note of the off-duty cab behind them.

"Oh, I speak Swiss German. I was an exchange student in Zurich for a year. Swiss German is really different from what the Germans here speak. You know, when West German TV shows movies from Switzerland in Swiss German, they use subtitles because it's so hard for Germans to understand. I keep wanting to learn High German, as they call it, and I'd hoped to pick it up in Berlin."

"He seemed to understand you without subtitles. It sounded like you switched languages or something all of a sudden."

"I think he's an *Ausländer*, a foreigner. They usually only know Low German because that's what the Germans speak with them when they work in the factories and stuff. But you did hear a shift. I switched from my stab at High German to my regular Swiss German, which is a sort of Low German. At least I got my point across."

The cab sped up. Summer jerked his head around. "Hey, where'd they go?"

"I think they're ahead of us. He's speeding up to catch them."

"They must've turned. Tell the cabbie to turn around."

Kathy spoke to the driver, then to Summer. "He says he knows a shortcut to the base."

How does he know which base we're headed to? "How did you say you knew Faith?"

"She's my nephew's professor at Ozark U."

"Ozark U., is that right?" *A professor? Ozark U.? Bullshit.* Summer discreetly unbuckled his seatbelt and reached for the door handle.

Before he could jump out, Kathy pushed a gun against the back of his head.

"Put your hands on the dashboard. Now!" Kathy said, then immediately shouted orders in another language.

Now Summer recognized it. *Roosky.*

He wished he hadn't had so much beer as he placed his hands on the dashboard and surveyed the front of the cab for potential weapons. Not even a stray pencil lay on the floorboard. A professional must have gone over the car. The taxi raced through the empty residential streets. It felt as if they were going south, but he knew that, in West Berlin, every direction led East.

"What do you want with me?"

"I told you, you're going to help your friend."

"Bullshit. You don't need to kidnap me for that. You know the Allies will stop you before you can get me through the Iron Curtain."

"Didn't Faith explain to you that all of Berlin is behind the so-called Iron Curtain? No one checks cars leaving West Berlin. The cavalry isn't going to come over the hill and save you, cowboy. You were on our turf as soon as you set foot here. The East Germans aren't particularly keen on it, but it's quite a convenient arrangement for us."

"I'm happy for you. Would you mind not pushing that thing against my skull? I'm not giving you any resistance, and I'd sure hate for it to go off next time we bounce over a pothole." In the rearview mirror Summer saw the Pontiac run the other taxi into a fire hydrant and speed past it. *Come on, Leroy.*

"Sorry, commander. I know about your training."

The Pontiac was gaining on them. *Punch it, Leroy!* The driver turned onto a wide boulevard. Floodlights. Barbed wire. Watchtowers. *I'm fucked.*

Leroy's car was closing the gap. Fifty feet. Thirty feet. Twenty feet. Five feet. The border was seconds away.

Now, Leroy!

The Pontiac rammed the Mercedes. Tires squealed. The car spun and the gun moved away from his head. He shoved the door open and sprang from the vehicle. Spotlights blinded him.

"*Hände hoch!*" A sentry butted a Kalashnikov against his chest.

Summer stared at the white line across the cobblestones. *Ten feet. Ten fucking feet behind the Curtain.* He threw up his arms.

Guards swarmed around the taxi and the Pontiac, weapons drawn. Steam poured from under the hood of the Pontiac. The engine growled, but wouldn't turn over. *Come on, start, damn it. Start.* The engine let out another pathetic growl, but wouldn't fire. *You son of a bitch.* The Pontiac straddled the boundary, the front half clearly in the East, the trunk in the Free World. Guards yanked the doors open and dragged Walters and Meriwether from the car. Soldiers poured from a bunker, firearms drawn.

A black Mercedes with red Cyrillic license plates sped across the border and screeched to a halt. At the same time, the driver and Kathy jumped from the taxi. The East Germans drew their weapons. Kathy shouted at them in German, then Russian. She grasped the handle of her weapon with two fingers and held it into the air. A guard stepped forward and snatched the weapon from her. Summer understood her when she cursed him in German.

"*Oberst Bogdanov der KGB, du Arschloch.* Don't point your weapons at me." She repeated herself in Russian, her voice rising in tandem with her anger as she struggled to salvage the botched operation. She gritted her teeth and shook her head as she watched the chaos unfold around her. *Where was German order when you needed it?* She looked in the eyes of the teenage sentry and saw fear. *Not good.* His rifle barrel trembled. So did his finger on the trigger. For more than a minute spotlights had been shining on her black operation. Anytime now the West Berlin and Allied military police would be there, photographing the melee. "Get your captain over here at once if you don't want a tour of Siberia with me. *Mach schnell!*"

"Captain Holtzer, you'd better get over here. She says she's a KGB colonel," the kid shouted.

The captain strutted toward the colonel with slow Prussian arrogance. She yelled at him in German with a heavy Russian accent, hoping it would expedite the situation. "Colonel Bogdanov, KGB. I'm taking charge of the situation. Ivashko in the black Mercedes has my identification. You can verify it when we're all safely away from Western eyes. Order your men at once to get these cars out of sight. If they're not concealed within one minute, you fly with me to Lubyanka tonight. *Davai! Davai!*"

The captain barked orders to his troops. Three guards tossed their weapons over their shoulders and pushed Leroy's car completely across the divide onto the sovereign territory of the German Democratic Republic.

CHAPTER THIRTY-SEVEN

LUBYANKA (KGB HEADQUARTERS), MOSCOW

One of General Stukoi's twelve phones began ringing. He moved his head over the phone bank and touched the third phone. He felt the vibrations of the ringer and picked it up with confidence. "Listening."

"We're fucked." General Titov from the Berlin residency didn't bother introducing himself. "That drunk, Voronin, just called me from Bonn. His people got a bomb onto the plane they believed FedEx was on."

"Goddamn it! We've got to get that plane on the ground." He yelled for his secretary without bothering to put his hand over the receiver. "Pyatiletka, get me the supervisor at Moscow Air Traffic Control at once." He spoke into the phone. "Gennadi, what flight did you say your man followed FedEx onto?"

"I just had that fucking number in front of me," Titov said, then continued to swear as Stukoi listened to him rustle through papers. "Wait a minute. Here it is: Pan Am 1072."

Another phone rang. Stukoi dropped the one with Titov onto his desk and could hear him ranting. Pyatiletka introduced the new caller as the senior supervisor of Aeroflot's Area Control Center.

"There might be a problem with an inbound Pan American flight," Stukoi said.

"We're working it right now."

"Is it still in the air?"

"It's up, proceeding to Sheremetyevo."

"How long until it's there?"

"Fifteen, twenty minutes—if it makes it."

"Make sure you get it there." Stukoi hung up. "Or I'll have your ass."

Titov was still carrying on about the incompetence of the Bonn residency and hadn't noticed Stukoi's absence. Stukoi grabbed the other phone. "It's all going to hell!" He threw down the receiver and shouted to Pyatiletka, "Get my car. Now!"

CHAPTER THIRTY-EIGHT

108 NAUTICAL MILES FROM SHEREMETYEVO

Faith worked her way toward the hole, not sure what to do next and hoping that the sagging floor held. She shivered. It had to be well below zero. Several passengers were bloody from the flying debris. The purser, who had apparently been in the lavatory, throwing his guts up during the explosion, sat, strapped into a jump seat, making the sign of the cross. Over and over. The two men seated behind the galley's bulkhead were missing. So was their entire bank of seats. In the next row two women sat with their feet dangling over open air. One was screaming, the other staring straight ahead as if engrossed in an in-flight movie.

Faith turned toward the rear of the plane and pointed at the operative. She motioned for him to come. He got up and hurried to her, his gaze fixed on the hole.

She shouted into his ear. "*Deutsch? Russkii?*"

"*Russkii.*"

"Name?"

"Call me Igor."

Faith screamed in Russian and pointed to the two women. "The floor's collapsing. I'm not sure how long it'll support the weight. Can you help me get them out?"

He nodded. Faith moved the passengers from row twelve to the rear of the plane. She and the operative slid into the row behind the women. Faith yelled to the one in the former window seat, first in English, then in German and Russian, "We're getting you out. When we get a firm grip, I'll tap you on the shoulder. That's your signal to unbuckle the seatbelt."

Igor slipped his powerful arms underneath those of the woman. Faith tapped her shoulder. The woman sat there frozen, staring straight ahead. Her face and left arm were bleeding. Faith hung over the seat, almost dizzy from the view to the ground. She reached to unbuckle the woman. The woman slapped her away. Faith tried again. The woman slugged her.

"This is nonsense," Igor said.

He struck the woman on the back of her head, stunning her. He grabbed her under the arms while Faith unclasped the seatbelt. In a single movement, he hoisted her over the seats and plopped her down on the row behind them. The second woman stopped screaming and latched on to Igor's arms. He and Faith hauled her over the seat. They walked the women down the aisle to the last row.

"You strap them in. I'll be back."

Faith went into the lavatory and grabbed a handful of paper towels. She returned to the injured woman. Blood streaked from her eyebrow to her chin. Faith wiped the blood from her face, but didn't see a wound. She felt a wave of nausea when she realized what had happened. The blood must have spurted on the woman as an injured passenger was sucked from the plane.

The other woman's arm was bleeding. Faith pressed the towels onto the wound. "Keep pressure on it until it stops." She repeated herself in the two other languages. She turned to Igor and shouted into his ear, "You just got a field commission. You're part of the crew now. I know the KGB's trained you in first aid. Treat the worst first. Check the overheads. One should have a first-aid kit. Go."

The plane was in stable flight at fourteen thousand feet, and the two remaining engines were hanging in there—for the moment. Frosty couldn't raise the cabin crew on the intercom. The captain ordered him to go back and survey the damage. Ian had throttled back a little, so the sound had dropped a few decibels along with the airspeed. He took off his oxygen mask and was greeted by a lot of fresh air. He stepped from the flight deck, expecting a mess, but wasn't prepared for what awaited him. The galley was missing—along with the last starboard row of first class and the first row of coach. The armrest of 10C was twisted so that he feared they'd lost at least one passenger on the port side as well. Mountings for a bank of overhead lockers were visible underneath the stringers and tattered insulation. He could see the fuselage frame, but didn't like the distorted floor panels and support beams. Catastrophic structural failure wasn't far away.

As he inched past the chasm, he felt the floor buckle a little under his weight. *Not good.* A stewardess was ripping a blanket into strips, he guessed for bandages. She seemed very familiar. Too familiar. He hoped to God he hadn't slept with her.

"Frosty!" Faith turned around and hugged him.

"Alooo-ha." The wind whipped around them. He stood close to Faith's ear as he spoke over the din. He pointed to the galley. "What'd you do to my plane?"

"It was a bomb. I saw the flash." She didn't smile. "We lost at least two passengers and three are unconscious. Several have pretty bad lacerations."

"The crew?"

"Eating in the galley when it happened. All except him." She pointed to the purser. He sat in a jump seat, moving his lips and crossing himself. "You're looking at your crew: me and KGB Igor over there." She used her head to point out the operative.

"I don't want to know." He held up his hand. "I'm just glad you're here. We're limping toward Moscow. The paranoid SOBs won't let us land anywhere else. We're about eighty miles out. We'll start the descent when I get back up front." He rested his hand on her shoulder. "Can you get everyone ready for landing? I don't like the looks of it over there. I could feel the floor move as I walked over it. Reseat anyone within three rows of the hull breach, including those to port. Spread them out. This isn't the time to mess with our center of gravity."

"Are we going to make it?"

"You betcha. You're flying with the dynamic duo." Frosty winked at her. "I don't know about the landing. Get them prepared for a rough one. When we come to a full stop, evacuate them. Do you know what to do?"

"In theory. I always prep my covers."

"There's a megaphone stowed in an overhead up front. When it's time, take the front jump seat by the Holy Father and pray along with him." He hugged her. "You'll do great."

Back on the flight deck, Frosty reported the situation to Ian, but omitted the identity of the remaining crew. "I'd say you've got one shot to land it. I wouldn't like to see the stress on the airframe from a go-around. If the floor collapses, God knows what might fly out and into those engines."

The seasoned professionals concentrated on their landing preparations. Sheremetyevo reported visibility at six miles, a cloud ceiling of two thousand meters and a wind out of the north gusting up to twenty-five knots. Ian adjusted the heading to compensate for the crosswind. "Gear down."

"You've got it. Gear down," First Officer Jackson said. "I've got green on the main, but the nose isn't budging."

"Extend manually," Ian said.

"I'm on it." Frosty flipped a switch to depressurize the gear's hydraulics.

"Landing gear lever off," Jackson said.

"Ian, can you drop speed? I need two-seventy or lower." Frosty grabbed the red crank mounted on the rear bulkhead beside the fire ax. He climbed onto the floor near his station. The metal ring that served as a handle on the access panel was missing, but he got it open. He inserted the shaft and cranked it clockwise three times, hoping the doors opened. Sweat beaded on his forehead and he wiped it with his forearm. He turned the crank three times counterclockwise. For good luck, he visualized the latch moving back and allowing the gear to go into a freefall. Frosty prayed his last three clockwise turns had locked the gear down.

He glanced over to the instrument panel in front of the first officer, but didn't see the green light he wanted. Squinting, he looked through the view hole, but couldn't see the red reference stripes. Oil and dirt caked the viewer. He slammed the panel shut. *Those jerkoffs in maintenance.*

"Ian, I can't get a green light and shit's smeared all over the view hole. I hope it's not oil from hydraulics. Given the state of the back end, recommend we proceed with a couple of Hail Marys."

"Jackson, advise the tower we don't have a safe nosegear-down indication, but we're coming in anyway. Make sure they have the equipment ready. Everything they've got."

Ian aligned the craft with runway 25L. The first officer set the flaps to fifteen degrees and the aircraft slowed. Frosty noticed it yawing heavily to the right and rolling side-to-side. "Is it easier to control with the flaps up?"

"Put them back to five," Ian said. "Engineer, give me a V speed for a flap-five landing."

Frosty flipped through the flight manual and read, "V_{ref} forty plus thirty for flaps one through fifteen."

"English, please, sir," Ian said.

"Uh, V_{ref} forty is one-two-two knots . . . no, one-fifty-two knots."

They broke through the clouds and Frosty could see the flashing lights of fire trucks racing to meet them. As Ian reduced the speed, the plane rocked and rolled. Ian struggled with the yoke.

Frosty was confident he could read Ian's mind. He pulled out the let-down chart. "I just checked. The runway's over twelve thousand feet—enough room to take it in at warp speed."

"Then warp speed it is." Ian pushed the power levers forward and the rocking decreased. *Just let the gear be down and locked.*

From the altitude and angle of attack, Faith knew the landing was only moments away. She had prepared the passengers to assume crash position at her signal. As the plane slowed, it began to toss like a boat in high seas. Then she felt the increase of speed. *Please don't do a go-around.* The ground got closer and closer. She picked up the microphone and squeezed the button. "Brace, brace, brace."

CHAPTER THIRTY-NINE

SHEREMETYEVO AIRPORT, MOSCOW

Man, I had a dreadful flight. I'm back in the USSR.

The plane kissed the tarmac in one of the gentlest landings Faith had ever experienced. Fast but smooth. Ian was good. Damn good. She looked through the opening. A fire engine on the parallel access road was speeding to catch up with them. As the craft rolled to a stop, some passengers applauded and cheered wildly. Others just sat there, staring straight ahead.

Faith sprang up, swung the lever on the emergency exit counterclockwise and pushed the door open. The yellow emergency slide inflated, a giant tongue hanging from the exhausted plane. KGB Igor stood, awaiting her instructions.

"Go to the bottom and help them as they come down." Faith smelled jet exhaust, but didn't notice any smoke. The engines seemed finally to be quieting down. She picked up the megaphone. "Proceed to your nearest exit. Don't take anything with you. Go!" Passengers mobbed the front of the craft. "Jump. Jump. Don't take anything with you." She wrestled a package from the babushka with all the plunder and shoved her down the slide. "Jump. Jump. Don't take anything with you."

After the last passenger was evacuated, Igor caught Faith at the bottom of the slide and helped her onto the tarmac. He held Faith's hand in a firm grasp and walked her away from the crowd. Ian, Frosty and the first officer were left to take care of their own escape.

"Thanks for the help," Faith said. Hair wisped across her face. She didn't bother to push it away. "Am I correct to assume it wasn't your bomb? It sure as hell wasn't mine."

"You were a hero." The operative continued to shake her hand. "You have my word that, if I have to kill you, it will be merciful."

"Swell. Guess it's back to our game. I can't do this right. I've been through enough for today. Give me a second to regroup, will you?" She retracted her hand and stepped away, turning her back toward him. Ian was tallying passengers.

Igor followed her. "Did the package make it? My orders were to ensure that it did."

"Those were your orders, huh?" Faith whirled around. "I tend to believe you. I don't think you'd plant a bomb on board, then go along for the joyride. Who wants to stop delivery?"

"KGB politics are deadly. Do not concern yourself. Did the package make it?"

"You saw all that crap flying around up there." She shrugged her shoulders. "All I can guarantee is that it's definitely in Moscow oblast—either in that plane, on a debris field or it arrived last night through Helsinki." She smiled. "You were my guardian angel in there, but pardon me if I don't completely trust you."

"The devil had angels, too, didn't he?"

The glint in his eyes was chilling. Faith looked away and saw five gray GAZ jeeps speeding down the now-closed runway ahead of two fire engines and an ambulance. She knew the jeeps could only belong to the KPP—Soviet-style airport security and a directorate of the Committee for State Security.

The first wave of the KGB had arrived.

Faith watched the operative walk toward a jeep from the airport militia. How the hell was she going to get the C off a plane surrounded by the KGB? She looked up to the cockpit. It was a good two stories above her and there were no stairs. Then she sensed someone approaching her from behind. "I'd like to commend you for your gallant work, miss." Faith recognized Ian's voice and swung around.

"Faith?" Ian said. "Bloody Christ, what are you doing here?"

"Before you say anything, it wasn't my bomb. I swear." She put her hand over her heart. "This is an international emergency. Lives are at stake, including mine."

His face turned bright red. "Young lady, you have gone too far."

"Ian, I'm not doing anything you haven't taught me."

Frosty came running up to them. "Skipper! Hold on! If it hadn't been for Faith, you wouldn't have had a cabin crew. We're damn lucky she was on board. She performed like a vet while our chief steward was strapped in, giving himself last rites. Faith's a hero. You owe her, buddy."

Ian exhaled slowly. "I'm sorry. I didn't realize—"

"That's all right. Just help me get that cooler off the plane and to Svetlana's before morning."

Frosty shook his head. "No can do, honey. That puppy's a crime scene. No way will they let us back on there."

"You've got to find a way. Ian, did I forget to tell you the rarest of the Armenian icon shipment at Svetlana's are from the Nagorno region? They're yours upon delivery to her."

"Nagorno? How in heaven did you ever locate them? I've tried for years." He placed his hand on her back. "Faith, I'm sorry. There's no way."

"There has to be. Convince them it was metal fatigue. Everyone saw what happened to that Aloha plane last year."

"One look at it and a child would know it was a bomb."

Frosty pointed at Faith as he spoke. "Maybe she's on to something. They did think at first that United flight out of Honolulu was a bomb. Turned out the cargo-door latch blew."

"No. There's no way I can get you back in there."

"You have to. That cooler on your flight deck." Faith paused. "It's packed with plastic explosives."

"Did you take leave of your senses?" His face flushed.

"I had no choice. They'll kill me if I don't deliver it. I couldn't bring it myself. They're expecting me."

"You're telling me when the KGB starts to search for who planted the bomb, they're going to find explosives on my flight deck? I'll lose my license."

"License, hell, I don't want to be some commie's bitch in a Siberian gulag. We've got to get that sucker off the plane."

"I need my bag, too. I think it made it. It was stowed in the last overheard locker, port side," Faith said.

"Anything else, my dear?" Ian said.

"I was kind of hoping one of you would be willing to let me use your hotel room to change and crash for the evening—no pun intended."

"You know you can bunk with me anytime." Frosty winked at her. "Even in Siberia."

"Now we'd better find a way to get back on that plane, *Candace*."

"And, by the way, Candace stayed in Frankfurt. I'm Sandy, Sandy Reeves." She pointed to the name tag on her blue uniform jacket.

He squeezed her shoulder hard. "I sincerely hope the KGB doesn't harm you, my dear, because after this is all over, I will kill you."

Dazed passengers wandered around the tarmac in circles. Others sat on the runway in a stupor. Medics treated the injured, but no one seemed in a hurry to evacuate them. The KGB now stood guard over everything, Kalashnikovs in hand. Ian, Frosty and Faith approached a group of officials talking to one another, their long gray-green coats flapping in the wind. Igor spoke with a man in an ill-fitting suit near a group of airport personnel. Ian selected an airport militia officer whose uniform had the most fruit salad and started to speak: "Sir—"

Faith tapped him on the arm and whispered, "Wrong guy. You want the highest-ranking KGB officer and I'd say that's him talking to Igor, your flight attendant."

As soon as the Pan Am crew approached, Igor and the other man halted their conversation.

"Do you speak English?" Ian said.

"Little," the plainclothes KGB officer said.

"How long are you going to leave my passengers here? Why aren't the injured being taken to the hospital?"

"Not possible. They must pass immigration."

"Station a guard on them if you have to, but get them to a hospital. A good one."

"Not so simple."

"And when can I get back on my plane? I want to go aboard and inspect it."

"Cannot. It is crime scene."

"Don't be silly. It's clearly metal fatigue. It happens all the time. Don't you read the papers? Remember those planes in Hawaii?"

A shiny Zil limousine barreled down the tarmac. It was the type of government car Faith had seen crossing Red Square and driving through the gates of the Kremlin. It screeched to a halt. The driver climbed out, but before he could open the door for his passenger, a uniformed KGB general jumped out and stamped over to Igor. They moved out of earshot and talked briefly; then the general ignored the Pan Am crew and spoke to the airport KGB officer in Russian. Faith listened in.

"I want you to get the luggage off the plane as if nothing's happened. Allow the crew to return on board and retrieve their personal belongings. These people have gone through enough. And take those injured to an infirmary."

"But sir, this is a crime scene. It can't be disturbed. The evidence—"

"There has been no crime. Take one look at it and any idiot can see that the plane came apart. Capitalist maintenance."

"But, sir—"

"That's an order, captain. Get that plane off the tarmac and out of sight in a hangar immediately. Also, see to it that one of your people escorts the captain and his crew to the front of the immigration line. No need for interviews today. They will be with us for a while."

The general turned toward Ian and asked, "*Vy kapitan?*"

Ian nodded. The general flashed him a thumbs-up. He turned and walked back to his car. As Igor climbed into the staff car, he nodded to Faith.

As they drove off the tarmac, General Stukoi picked up his car phone and called Titov at the residency in Berlin. "We're back on track, thanks to your man Resnick. Contact Voronin and get Bonn to stand down. Tell him I personally arrested the terrorists and we have his nuclear suitcase under our control. He'll get the Medal for Irreproachable Service as long as he keeps this to himself. Tell him whatever you want. Just make sure he believes there's no longer a threat to the leadership. I don't want any more interference."

An Aeroflot movable stairway was brought to the plane and the crew was allowed aboard just long enough to grab their personal belongings. Somehow most of their things survived the chaos. In the Aeroflot bus to the terminal, Faith saw Frosty grin as he looked at the salvaged snapshot of his dog. He stuffed it into his wallet.

Ian whispered to her, "It's not really in the cooler, is it?"

"No. Forgive me, but I had to motivate you. I have the cargo." She made eye contact with him and then looked at her carry-on.

"Did you understand what that general was saying? Why did he countermand the other chap's orders and permit us on board?"

"KGB politics are deadly. Let it go."

A Pan Am employee and a uniformed KGB lieutenant greeted the bus and escorted them to the crew passport-control line. He ordered the official to process them even though they lacked the requisite crew manifest. The border guard examined each passport and then stamped a separate loose document. Hakan's handiwork on the document that Zara had provided passed scrutiny. She thanked the official in English and joined the others at customs.

A squat man with the cheeks of a chipmunk stopped the purser and asked him to open his bag. The official removed a Grundig shortwave radio and said something in Russian. The purser shrugged and looked toward Faith for help. She ignored him. As far as the Soviets were concerned, all American citizens were suspected spies and Americans fluent in Russian *were* spies. The first officer elbowed Faith and relayed the message. She moved ahead in line, guarding her ribs from any accidental bumps. "What's up?"

"Something with my radio." The purser was still pale and withdrawn.

"Says it's radio," Faith said in broken Russian with a heavy American accent. "BBC. Radio Moscow, you know."

The guard handed the purser a customs-declaration form.

"What's he saying?"

"I don't know, but I think you have to declare it along with your currency and make damn well sure you export it when you go. Whatever you do, don't leave with any extra cash beyond what you declare." She maneuvered back to her place in line.

The purser whispered to Frosty, "What's with her? In Frankfurt she was fluent—"

"Keep it quiet, son. Do your patriotic duty and play along."

While waiting for him to complete the declaration form, the inspector motioned for Ian to place the cooler on the counter. The official removed the dry ice and ogled the ice cream, then took out one of the hand-painted plates. He ran his hands around the side of the cooler and paused at the Leatherman. He folded it back so that it became a pair of pliers and proceeded to pull out each blade. "Not bad," he said to himself in Russian. He tried to fold it back, but the last knife blade wouldn't move.

Ian took it and pushed, but the blade was locked into place.

"Gimme," Frosty said. "Takes an engineer." He closed all the tools. "Safety mechanism. You guys wouldn't know about those." He handed it back to the customs officer.

The official made eye contact with Ian, glanced at the Häagen-Dazs and then looked back at Ian. "I'm sorry. You cannot take weapons into the Soviet Union."

"The tool? I can assure you, it's no weapon. I'm certain we can arrive at some understanding." Ian slowly reached for the plate and returned it to the cooler. Without breaking eye contact, he stowed two containers of ice cream, put back the dry ice package and closed the lid. Two cartons of Häagen-Dazs were left behind on the counter.

"I suppose it is but a pocketknife." The Russian smiled, his eyes now making love to the chocolate-cheesecake ice cream. In a single swoop, he returned the Leatherman and whisked away his booty. "You may go."

The inspector motioned for a subordinate to replace him and he disappeared into a restricted area with the ice cream. The crew shuffled on. Faith followed them in tight formation.

"*Devushka!* Girl! Not so fast. Let me have a look," the subordinate officer said.

Faith stopped, placed her Travelpro on the low counter and unzipped the bulging main compartment. The inspector removed a leather attaché and a neatly folded brown leather jacket. He pulled a ballpoint pen from the bottom and read the advertising embossed on it promoting Froneberger Reisen, a Berlin travel bureau. Faith prayed he wouldn't unscrew it to find a few inches of time fuse.

He dropped the pen back into the case and set the jacket aside. He patted down the clothing, stopping when he came to her underwear. At that moment, she wished she had packed some chocolate to speed things along.

He carefully lifted the clothes from the bag and stacked them on the brown leather jacket. He glared at her. "What is this?"

The entire bottom was filled with rows of small yellow canisters. He pulled out a Play-Doh can that she had coaxed Summer to purchase for her at the Army PX in Berlin. He opened it and pinched off a small portion of the doughy white substance.

CHAPTER FORTY

SHEREMETYEVO AIRPORT, MOSCOW

The customs inspector wore the uniform of the KPP, the KGB border guards: greenish-gray with hunter green piping. He motioned for assistance. His supervisor came over and opened a Play-Doh can. Faith steeled herself for a long delay. *Please, not a chemical analysis.*

Faith faked broken Russian. "Play-Doh. Gift for children without mama and papa. For orphanage."

The supervisor sank his fingers into the Play-Doh and felt for contraband stashed inside. He ordered the inspector to do the same. They poked and prodded. By the third can, the supervisor crafted a crude bowl, momentarily losing himself as his fingers worked to even the sides. When he noticed his subordinate watching his handiwork, he smashed it. He shoved the doughy substance back into the can and probed the next one.

Faith shifted her weight and thought she felt the wire of a blasting cap through the insole of her shoe. Thank goodness Play-Doh and C-4 looked exactly alike. She reached over and plucked off a small portion, rolled it into a ball and took a small bite. She swallowed and hoped the nasty stuff wasn't as toxic as it tasted. She switched to English. "It's harmless. Won't hurt the kids one bit if they eat it." Faith stifled a gag.

The supervisor sniffed the Play-Doh and replaced the lid, running his fingers around the edges to make sure it was closed. "Kids prefer ice cream," he said with a sigh.

A few hours later in downtown Moscow, Faith used a public phone and received drop instructions from Kosyk's man. As agreed, she called Zara from another phone to pass along the information so that her KGB backup would be in place.

No answer.

She dialed again.

The phone rang. Faith wasn't sure she was doing the right thing. *Who the hell had planted that bomb?* What if Zara was involved and had set her up? Kosyk had the real information about her father. Maybe she should cut out the KGB and deal directly with him. Just then the phone clicked as if the call were being rerouted. Someone picked up.

"Listening."

Faith recognized Zara's voice, but didn't speak.

"Hello? Faith? Faith?"

Faith hung up the phone.

Five minutes later, in the cramped Intourist hotel room, Faith molded the white Play-Doh into a brick and wrapped it in cellophane. Frosty helped her.

"This really is Play-Doh, isn't it?" Frosty said.

Faith nodded.

"That means inside the cooler?"

She nodded again. They finished the craft project and Faith lowered the last one into the leather attaché case. The Play-Doh bricks could pass for C-4. She didn't know what she was going to do, but she was confident that as soon as she handed over the C-4, they wouldn't need her anymore and she doubted they would want to keep her around. She had to leverage the whereabouts of the plastic explosives to keep herself alive.

"I don't know what that phone call was about, but ever since then you don't look too hot," Frosty said. "I hate to say this, but you looked better when you got off that crippled plane."

"Not here." Faith held her index finger in front of her mouth.

"I don't mess with other people's business, but at least let me walk you to the Metro, *Sandy*."

Frosty insisted upon carrying the attaché case with the faux plastique. She hated sexist chivalry, but she had a soft spot for Frosty's old-fashioned manners. She inventoried the faces on the sidewalk, but no one seemed to be following them. "Frosty, you're a sweetheart, but this is too dangerous."

"I'm a friend. At least tell me what's eating you about that phone call. You don't have to go into details, or even make sense."

"I got the drop site, but it's sloppy. It's in a KGB-controlled hotel bar and the guy I'm doing business with knows better."

"A setup."

"Afraid so. And I think my backup might have been the one who arranged for the bomb."

"I always was a sucker for a gal in deep kimchee."

An hour later, Faith walked down the long, raised concrete drive of the Hotel Cosmos—without the satchel packed with the imitation C-4. The hotel was so imposing that Faith suspected those who designed it for the 1980 Olympics secretly had created another memorial to Stalin. Sputtering Intourist buses from the state-run travel monopoly were dwarfed alongside the shiny behemoth. The glass structure reflected the nearby memorial to the first Sputnik satellite, its grooved-metal exhaust fumes shimmering in the setting sun, as if sparks were trailing the plump rocket.

A man wearing Levi's rushed toward her and walked alongside her. The last thing she needed right now was a black marketeer preying upon her and drawing undue attention to her as if she were another Western tourist looking for a cheap souvenir.

"What country are you from? Do you have anything you want to buy, sell or trade?" The bug-eyed man spoke in English.

"Not now." She didn't look at him and walked straight ahead.

"I have whatever you want—*matrioshki*, lacquer boxes, *znachki*."

She ignored him.

"True Red Army *Kommandirskie* watch. Only sixty dollars American."

He rolled up his sleeve and stuck his wrist in front of her face, too close for her to focus.

Faith pushed his arm back. The clunky timepiece's metallic face had a large red star and a parachute with two jet fighters zooming away from it. A cameo of the Soviet cosmonaut Yuri Gagarin decorated the leather band. "Thank you, Frosty" was written all over it. It would be a perfect token of her appreciation for his impromptu assistance, and buying the thing would be the most expedient way to get rid of a persistent black marketeer.

"I saw your eyes. You want," the man said.

"My eyes say get lost, militia everywhere," she said in Russian.

"No worry. I paid this week. You speak Russian. Then for you, special price. Thirty dollars."

She reached in her pocket and rolled a twenty into her sweaty palm and flashed it to him. "You have two seconds. Decide now."

He pressed the watch into her hand, snatched the bill and disappeared.

Faith dropped it into her pocket as she walked past a militiaman slumped against the glass lobby window. She never could figure out if the militia was the same as the local police, but their military uniforms were much more ominous than any other local police she had ever encountered.

A doorman stopped every Russian attempting to enter, but didn't ask Faith for identification. She pushed the heavy revolving door, went inside and climbed to the mezzanine, where the hard-currency bar was located.

She paid far too many dollars for a Carlsbad and took a position on one of the bar's gaudy couches. Five women with heavy makeup and expensive Western dresses sat alone on various sofas, each sipping a glass of water. Any one of them could have been a Paris model. Faith guessed that, in their profession, they might be asked to model from time to time. Alongside them Faith felt particularly dowdy; her sweater matched the carpet and a third of the paisley swirls in the sofa. Someone might mistake her as part of the furniture—not as a call girl from the KGB's stable, even though she was whoring for them all the same.

She sipped the Danish beer. Her tastebuds already missed Germany.

A man with a trimmed beard and mustache sprinted up the stairs. As he approached her, he removed his aviator glasses and made eye contact. She assumed he was another European businessman looking for a good time. He ordered a martini from the bar and took a seat across from her.

When he opened his mouth, Faith expected a stale pickup line, but instead he said in German, "Although the apple is a Central Asian native, the pomegranate—"

"Shove it. I don't have the item with me. Meet me in the small park in front of the Bolshoi during tonight's intermission." She dashed from the hotel to the metro.

No one tailed her to the columned rotunda of the VDNH metro station entrance, but a large crew could be assigned to her and could be passing her off along the way. She took a five-kopek piece from her pocket and shoved it in the turnstile. Four sets of escalators disappeared down a steep tunnel, running at an intimidating clip. She studied their rhythm and jumped on, clutching the rubber guide rail. Several dozen Soviets rode the escalator. She examined them, but couldn't place any at the Cosmos. A metro veteran directly behind her read Pushkin as the long escalator ride carried him deep underground.

Air gusted up the long tunnel. A train was on its way. She walked down the escalator, weaving between people. When she stepped off onto the granite floor, inertia hurled her forward. She caught herself, then bounded onto the car as the recorded female voice blared on the loudspeaker.

She rode five stops and switched lines. When the train arrived at the Prospekt Marksa station, Faith remained in her seat. The automated voice announced, "Danger. Doors are closing . . ." She bolted out, twisting sideways to escape the guillotine of the doors. She turned back around and looked into the car. The man reading Pushkin leaped from his seat and slammed his body into the closed doors. He mouthed something. It wasn't polite.

She navigated the underground passages, grateful for her year at Moscow State, when she learned her way around the labyrinth. She emerged from the metro beside the red brick Lenin history museum abutting Red Square. The fairy-tale onion domes of St. Basil's glowed in front of her. Spotlights bathed the gaudy cupolas, towers and spires. The crowd of Soviet and Western tourists that she was counting on had already assembled for the hourly changing of the guard. She was late.

With military precision, the three honor guards goosestepped toward the red granite mausoleum. Each pointed his rifle straight up, the polished bayonet glistening in the camera flashes. Faith quickened her pace, racing them toward the tomb. Tonight several hundred people waited. She slipped into the crowd, but didn't see Frosty with the leather case and Play-Doh bricks she needed for the hand-off at the Bolshoi. The sharp click of the guards' heels against the brick came closer. Where was he? The guards approached the mausoleum. Two took their places on the inside of the ones they were relieving; the third stood in the center. Faith had only seconds until the clock sounded the hour.

Then she spotted him.

Frosty had positioned himself near the front, several dozen people away from her. She shoved her way to him, contorting her body between tourists. She pushed up against him. They didn't acknowledge each other. All eyes were fixed upon the honor guards. The clock on the Kremlin tower struck. The guards swiftly maneuvered around one another with perfect choreography and Frosty fumbled the leather briefcase as he handed it to Faith. She dropped the watch in his pocket by way of a thank-you. The clock played the familiar chimes and then the crowd dispersed.

Faith was already gone.

She walked at a fast clip down the dusty back streets to the Bolshoi. She reached into the side pouch of the satchel. Frosty had come through as promised. She glanced at the Bolshoi ticket and shoved it in her jacket pocket. He had even managed to get her a decent seat—too bad she wouldn't get a chance to enjoy it. She'd make the drop and weave through the intermission crowd to the theater. Ticket in hand, she could go inside and hide in the ladies' room until the performance was over and then exit in the collective safety of the masses.

From the shadows of a doorway across the street, she surveyed the popular small plaza in front of the theater. Like wrinkled toothless bulldogs, two babushkas staked out their territories on separate benches, balancing their squat frames on the few intact slats. Several men wore sweaters tied around their shoulders and a few clutched keys in their hands as they paraded around the dry concrete fountain. A handful of women in low-cut cotton dresses intermingled with the sparse crowd. A black Volga sedan was parked on the far side of the square in a no-parking zone.

A company car.

The doors to the Bolshoi opened. Well-dressed Soviet couples and underdressed Western tourists poured out between the white columns. The man from the bar stepped out of the waiting Volga and strolled toward the fountain. When he turned back toward the Bolshoi to scan the crowd, Faith crossed the street. She approached him from behind and handed him the satchel.

He swung around and grabbed her arm. His other arm took away the case.

She swirled around, using her weight to try to break free. Pain radiated from her shoulder as it twisted, but he hardly moved. His fingers coiled so tightly around her wrist that she could feel the bones shift.

The man forced her toward the Volga, shouting in Russian, "If I ever catch you with another man again, you'll pay for it."

The Russians turned away from her, not wanting to get involved in a domestic dispute. The Westerners watched.

"Help! I'm not—" Faith shouted before he slapped his hand over her mouth. She bit him until she tasted blood. She kicked and squirmed. She bent over, then straightened up and slammed against him as hard as she could. Her ribs throbbed, but he laughed into her ear. She fell limp, but her weight meant nothing to him; he dragged her across the broken concrete.

"Let her go!" Frosty said as he pushed through the crowd and ran toward her. Frosty punched the kidnapper's face, but someone took hold of his arm.

The kidnapper shouted in Russian, "My wife's not your whore, you capitalist bastard!"

Frosty threw off his assailant and jumped the kidnapper. The man dropped Faith. Sharp pain slowed her as she pushed herself up to see two more pile out of the Volga. They seized her arms and hauled her into the car.

"Frosty, get out of here! Go!" she shouted just before they slammed the door.

CHAPTER FORTY-ONE

It is true that liberty is precious;
so precious that it must be carefully rationed.
—LENIN

LYSENKO RESEARCH FACILITY, MOSCOW
SUNDAY, APRIL 30

Faith didn't know if she had passed out from a blow or from fear. Either way, her head throbbed from the scuffle, the pain reaching down her neck until it met the twinge coming up from her ribs. She didn't know how long she'd been out. She gagged from the stench; the room reeked of a high school biology lab. She was alone—at least they didn't get Frosty. But she was alone. And scared.

As she pushed herself up from the cold tile floor, pain shot through her ribs and right shoulder. She stood in the dark room and slowly shuffled her feet as they blindly explored her confines. A band of light emanated from the bottom of a door. She inched her way to it and pawed for the latch. She pushed it, but knew it was locked.

Plaster fell off into her hands as she patted her way around the room. Then she hit something, a flat surface. *A shelf.* Grit coated her fingertips. She reached above it and found another. Floor-to-ceiling shelves were built into the wall. The back of her hand hit a smooth, cool cylinder. *A glass jar.* She ran her hand along it and estimated it held over a gallon. The entire shelf was filled with the containers; hundreds of them lined the walls. The strong chemical odor guarded them from the curious.

When they apprehended her, they had no way of knowing she had brought them Play-Doh. So if the Stasi thought they got what they wanted, why were they holding her? Shouldn't she be free or dead? And where was Zara, along with her promised KGB assistance? KGB headquarters was close enough to the Bolshoi that they could've walked over to help her. Frosty had defied her instructions and had come to the theater to help her.

An electric hum came from overhead. Faith squinted as fluorescent lights glowed. No one appeared. A hunk of wrinkled flesh floated in each jar. *Brains. Human brains.* And she had almost reached inside one.

Each brain was labeled with initials, a last name and a reference number. She'd heard rumors that Hitler's brain was pickled somewhere in Moscow. The Soviets did keep brains of gifted luminaries for research into the origins of their intelligence. For the last fifty years, their scientists had sliced away and stained brain specimens of their leading citizens in their quest to perfect the New Soviet Man. She recognized the names of a geneticist, a cosmonaut and a Politburo member.

My first Mensa meeting.

A lock turned and the door flung open. Zara and a guard entered the room and locked the door afterward. Faith rushed toward her, but stopped herself when she saw the woman's steel eyes and unyielding face.

Now Faith understood.

Zara had used her, betrayed her, attempted to kill her. She told herself the pain in her chest was from breathing the formaldehyde, but she knew better.

"It'll be easier for you if you'll cooperate with us, Doctor Whitney." Bogdanov looked away as she spoke.

"How can you do this to me?" Faith seethed.

"Who are your local accomplices?"

"You were the one who told me to go along with Schmidt or Kosyk or whatever his real name is. I'm here because of you, so I'd say you're my accomplice and you were working on behalf of the KGB, so I'd say the whole KGB is involved. You do work for the KGB, don't you? It was them you were working for when you tried to seduce me, wasn't it?"

"How did you plant the bomb on the airplane?"

"Are you out of your mind? I was *on* that plane. You did it, didn't you?"

"If I wanted to eliminate you, we wouldn't be talking. Who made the bomb?"

"Not me. I'd guess someone from your organization who didn't want me to make the delivery. You know, the delivery you were going to intercept and use to nail Kosyk and company? If you ask me, it seems not everyone at the KGB is on the same page with this one. Do you guys ever have staff meetings?"

"Turn around and put your hands against the wall."

"Maybe there's an empty wall here I'm not seeing. What's the deal with this place? You guys running out of space in Lubyanka all of a sudden?"

"Then place your hands on the desk and lean over."

"So you can fuck me some more?"

Bogdanov reached inside the breast pocket of Faith's leather jacket and removed two pens, a wad of dollars and rubles, a pack of Marlboro cigarettes and some matches. She flipped through the banknotes and threw them onto the guard's tray. She left the watch in Faith's pocket. "Why the cigarettes?"

"You know I'm a chain-smoker. Besides, they're a second currency around here," Faith said.

She clicked the top of the pen, but no point popped out. She dropped it onto the tray. Bogdanov's hand reached inside Faith's jacket. Bogdanov ran her hands over her chest, violating her. Faith jumped from pain and Bogdanov lightened her touch.

"I can't believe you're doing this to me," Faith said under her breath.

"Neither can I," Bogdanov whispered in English as she ran her hands down Faith's inner thighs. "Take your shoes off."

Bogdanov reached inside the shoe. She paused and made brief eye contact with Faith for the first time since entering the room. Faith knew she had found the C, but Bogdanov set the shoe down and searched the other one.

Bogdanov turned to the guard. "She's clean."

"I demand to see a doctor," Faith said.

"Trust me, you don't want to. We need you to tell us what you're planning. We have the plastic explosives you smuggled into the USSR."

"What plastic explosives?"

"The C-4 you gave to Lieutenant Alexandrov during your Bolshoi escapade."

"You know I don't deal in arms. I don't know anything about explosives."

"We have the bag and its contents and we've apprehended one of your co-conspirators. You'll confess, or someone you care about is going to get hurt." She turned toward the guard as she walked through the door. "Bring him in."

Bogdanov spun around on her heels and left the room. The lights went out.

Faith sat alone in the darkness, too angry and too terrified to cry. The Play-Doh would buy her time, but not her freedom, nor her life. She racked her brains, but at that moment, brains weren't much use to her.

Later the door opened and a body was shoved inside. Faith shuffled closer in the darkness, careful not to kick whoever it was. She heard a groan. "Frosty? It's okay. It's me. I'd hoped you got away." She knelt down.

He mumbled something. She pulled off his blindfold and noticed his hair was gone. Why would they ever shave his head? She ran her fingers over the wide forehead and the bald head. Then she felt a very familiar ear. *Summer.* She found the edge of the duct tape and ripped it from his mouth with a single jerk.

"Faith?"

She threw her arms around him and put her head against him, careful not to put pressure on her ribs. Tears flowed down her face.

"You okay?" he said.

"I'm pretty bunged up, but nothing that won't heal. They're going to kill us."

"Pull yourself together. We're gonna make it, honey."

"I know you're just saying that."

"Hell, yes. But you have to get it together and get my hands freed up before we can do anything."

"What are you doing here? Did you come after me?" She tugged at the tape around his wrists.

"Not exactly. Where the heck is here?"

"Moscow. Some old KGB lab's storage room."

"Holy moly." He wiggled his wrists, trying to get some slack into the tape handcuffs. "Moscow? I was afraid of that. They've kept me blindfolded, but I had a feeling we were flying east. Hell, I didn't need a feeling to know they were taking me to Russia. Where are Walters and Meriwether? I couldn't hear them on the plane, but I wasn't totally sure they weren't there."

"I have no idea who they are."

"The last I saw them, the East Germans had them," he said.

"I'm not sure what's going on, but something big. This isn't working. I can't get this stuff off." The tape stuck to itself. Her short fingernails picked at it.

"Don't suppose you've got anything sharp?"

"Hold on." Faith unscrewed a lid from one of the jars.

He sniffed loudly. "Jeez, someone dissecting cadavers around here?"

"You don't want to know." She smacked the jar lip against the heavy metal desk. Her finger explored the jagged edge. Sharp enough. Her foot raked stray shards under the desk. "Where are you? Talk to me."

"I'm not going anywhere. Over here. This way."

She inched over to him and sat on the floor beside him. "I'm going to do my best not to cut you, but I can't see a damn thing."

"Just take it slow, nice and slow."

She sawed through the tape a few frustrating millimeters at a time.

"How many of them are there?" Summer said. "Any idea what's outside the door?"

"At least two. Three or four guys brought me here, but I don't know if they're still around." She nicked herself with the makeshift knife. "I have no idea what's outside, but I'm pretty sure this isn't set up for prisoners. Summer, you need to know, I've got some C stuck in my shoes."

"A cap?"

"I had a blasting cap and time fuse in two pens, but she took them. She also took my matches."

The fluorescent lights buzzed, then glowed.

"They're coming." Faith stuffed the glass shard into her pocket and smashed the tape back to cover up her handiwork.

Summer looked around in the light. "What the heck is wrong with these people? Pickled brains?"

"They study brains of smart people to try to figure out the secrets of their success. Yuri Gagarin's over there. From rumors I've heard about his drinking and the truth behind the plane crash that killed him, he probably came prepickled."

Bogdanov walked in, carrying a white brick wrapped in clear plastic. The guard closed the door behind them and stood erect, his gun pointed at Summer's chest.

"I see you're making yourselves at home," Bogdanov said in English, startling Faith. "You're in the company of great minds." Her face fell, her mood shifting like a wind shear. She threw the brick to Faith, who caught it. "What's this?"

"Play-Doh. Personally, I prefer Silly Putty. I like to smash it on colored Sunday funnies and stretch—"

"I don't have time for foolishness. Where's the C-4?"

"I don't know what you're talking about."

"Guard, leave us alone for a few moments," Bogdanov said. "I think I might be able to be more persuasive without a witness."

"General Stukoi's orders were very clear. No one is to be alone with the prisoners."

Bogdanov snapped her head around toward Summer and raised her voice. "I'm talking about a CIA agent and a US Navy special forces commando who brought C-4 into the Soviet Union on a secret mission to assassinate General Secretary Gorbachev to stop his reforms and save the budgets of their Cold War–dependent agencies. You're here to save your military-industrial complex from the threat of peace and friendship with an open, democratic Soviet Union. I prepared your confessions. Sign at the bottom. It may even help you avert the death penalty." Bogdanov handed them the papers and two pens, both from the same Berlin travel agency.

Faith fingered the pen. It was the same one Bogdanov had confiscated earlier. She studied Zara's face, but it betrayed nothing. She skimmed the document. "This is dated May first. It's not May first yet, is it? And it's not a confession about an attempt on Gorbachev. It's a murder confession."

"Things will go much easier for you if you voluntarily confess. I only have you for another twenty minutes. I can't wait any longer. You have only twenty minutes. If you don't sign by then, I can't be responsible for what happens to you. Up until now, I've seen that you were treated well. Commander Summer's trained to hold up under torture, but Doctor Whitney isn't. Others can be more persuasive. Once you're outside this wall . . ." She made eye contact with Faith, then looked at the wall. "Once you're outside this wall on your way to Lubyanka, I can't help you. Trust me; you don't want to be in here in twenty minutes when they come for you."

"We're not going to sign. Forget it." Summer shook his head.

"I'll leave you alone for a few minutes to consider it. Would you like a cigarette while you're thinking?"

Bogdanov tapped the Marlboro pack until a cigarette tip came out. "Go ahead."

The guard objected in Russian.

She turned to him. "It can't hurt. What are they going to do? Put burn marks on Stalin's brain?"

The guard laughed.

Faith hesitated before she pulled the cigarette from the pack and put it in her mouth. Bogdanov tossed her the matchbox. Faith palmed two matches as she removed one for the light.

Summer leaned forward. "I'll take one, too."

Bogdanov put the cigarette in his mouth. Faith lit it for him and threw the matches to Bogdanov.

"You have less than twenty minutes. Think carefully about what I've said. Do the smart thing."

They left the room, but the lights didn't go out.

"She's the bitch who kidnapped me. I don't know what the deal is with her, but she made it pretty clear we'd better be out of here in twenty minutes."

Faith extinguished her cigarette and cut at the tape on Summer's wrists. "I'll have you out in a minute now that I can see what I'm doing."

"Don't worry about cutting me; just get my hands free. And get this cancer stick outta my mouth, but don't let it go out. We're going to need it."

"I got a couple of matches." Faith removed the cigarette and crushed it out on the floor. "The pens she left us have time fuse and a cap in them. And I swear she knew it."

"That KGB bitch is a slick devil. What kind of fuse did you get? How much?"

"About four inches."

"Four inches of time fuse will give us fifteen seconds or so."

"I don't know if it makes any difference, but it's Russian made."

"Then we've got a problem. I used Russian fuse in Somalia once. Burns like greased lightning."

"It's all I could get on short notice."

"You should've let me help you in Berlin. Guess we can use a cigarette as a timer if we have to."

Faith dug the glass shard into the tape, jerking it back and forth.

"You're doing this like a girl, Faith. I'm gonna pull my hands apart as far as possible—which isn't much. Now you're gonna poke it into the middle of the furnace tape. Don't worry about what you'll do to me long as you don't get an artery. Pull it as hard as you can toward yourself. Do it."

Faith plunged the crude knife into the tape and pulled back as hard as she could, rocking it so it sawed the tape. She tipped backward as the glass cut through the edge. The tape wasn't completely severed, but Summer was able to pull his hands apart. A few drops of blood smeared onto it. He stretched his shoulders through a range of motions as he stripped off the last pieces of tape. Faith excavated the C-4 from her shoes. It had become pliable from her body heat.

He unscrewed the pen and removed the short fuse. "I only had to walk up six steps, so I'm assuming we're at ground level. You start moving brains from the shelves and pile them up over there. There's a long crack in the mortar and I'm going for that weakness. The blast wave will go out toward the street, but that glass'll go everywhere. The only protection we'll have is that desk. I want it turned over. We'll hunker down behind it. Get to it."

Summer grabbed two jars, turned around and handed them to Faith with such force that she nearly lost her balance. The sweat from her palms instantly mingled with the thick dust, creating a grimy paste. She steadied the jars against her chest and set A. N. Tupolev in the corner and then wiped her hands on her slacks. She hurried back for L. P. Beria and T. D. Lysenko. She ferried the brains across the room, all the while dissociating her own mind from those she carried.

"Get a lid. I also need the tape. Hope it's got enough stick-um left." Summer pushed explosives into a crack. He rolled the rest into a ball, inserted the time fuse into the hollow end of the cap and crimped both together with his teeth.

Faith handed him a lid and the wad of tape.

"See what you can do with the tape. Pull enough pieces apart so I can use it to hold the lid against the wall."

"Can't you just stick the C to it?"

"Only in the movies."

She plucked at the tape wad. "This isn't going to work."

"Okay, we've gotta do something else. You go back to moving jars." He took the metal lid, placed it on the floor and stomped on one side of it. He wedged the flattened side between the shelf and the wall. Careful to keep the cap positioned correctly, he lodged the explosives between the wall and the lid. "Give me a cigarette and a match."

He struck the match against a brick, held the cigarette in his mouth and lit it, inhaling deeply. "I've gotta smoke this down a bit. We don't have enough time to wait for the whole thing to burn on its own time."

"Can't you just pinch off some of it?"

"Believe me, I need a smoke."

"Summer, do you smell that? It's not the cigarette. Look!" Faith pointed at smoke seeping through cracks in the door. "This place may be on fire."

"Dandy. Let's speed it up and get the desk into position."

Faith struggled to lift the heavy metal desk with her hurt shoulder and cracked ribs, but Summer picked up his end with only one arm. They flipped it on its side, the top facing the explosives.

"Get behind it. It's showtime." He dashed behind the desk. "It could take a minute or two. Don't think about looking up until after it's gone off. It's gonna be loud and messy, but fast. You might want your fingers in your ears. Just as soon as the sound stops, go out the hole. Go straight through it—don't look around and don't worry about the glass. Let's hope there's a hole there, because if something shifts, the wave might not go in the right direction. If it doesn't, see if the bricks are loose enough to smash 'em outward. If you can get out, just go. I'll catch up with you. If we can't get out that way, say a quick prayer and we're going out the way we came in. Stay right behind me."

Summer picked up the glass shard Faith had used to cut him free. He wound duct tape around the narrow part, creating a crude handle. Then he took the knife and split the time fuse a half-inch down the middle, exposing the burning compound inside. He stuck the head of a match into the slit. He wedged the burning cigarette on top of it, careful not to press too hard and extinguish it. Working as quickly as he dared, he taped the two halves of the fuse together with duct tape, securing the match and cigarette in place.

Faith held her breath as she watched Summer blow on the cigarette to make it burn faster. He dashed over to her, pushed her flatter against the floor and wrapped his body over hers. Her side hurt from the pressure, but the comfort of his body compensated for it. Summer clutched the makeshift knife tightly.

"What's that glass knife for?" Faith said.

"A contingency you're not gonna like. Anytime now, any—"

The doorknob turned. Summer sprang up, gripping the knife. He glided to the door and plastered himself against the wall. Smoke poured into the room. Adrenaline flooded Faith's body when she saw the guard step inside, his pistol drawn.

CHAPTER FORTY-TWO

LYSENKO RESEARCH FACILITY, MOSCOW
A FEW MINUTES EARLIER

Bogdanov left the temporary holding cell, the lingering formaldehyde smell sickening her. The second guard stood across the hall beside a glass display case crammed with a dusty assortment of books, scientific journals and plasticized human body parts. She already missed the German obsession with precision and order. She glanced at her watch. It was time.

"They require food and water. Go find something," Bogdanov said to the guard who had accompanied her with the prisoners.

"Colonel, there are no facilities here that have prison rations."

"Then get them something better. Go to the canteen and pick something up."

"Do you know where it is?"

"*Davai!*" the colonel shouted, then turned to the other jailer. "I have some things to take care of at headquarters. Make sure they don't escape while I'm away."

She walked through the musty corridor and down the main stairs. In the lobby she doubled back to a remote stairway and hurried into her temporary office.

She sat on the hard wooden desk chair, staring out the window. Every thirty seconds she glanced at her watch. She was pleased she had been able to arrange to take over a section of the second floor of the KGB's biological research facility for temporary detention. Lubyanka would've afforded her far too little privacy. Her reputation as a key player in the operation had given her enough clout to make such a bad choice in holding facilities and guard complements without anyone second-guessing her. Stukoi had actually believed it was a good idea to keep them at such an obscure location to prevent knowledge of their imprisonment from becoming widely known. After three minutes had passed, she rose from her seat and stuck a handful of old copies of *Pravda* under her arm. Anyone who saw her would assume she was on her way to the water closet with her own supply of makeshift toilet paper. No one would suspect what she was about to do.

Just as she was about to walk out the door, Kosyk pushed his way into her office with two KGB guards.

"What are you doing here?" Bogdanov said. "They're not supposed to be transferred for another ten minutes."

"I'm here now."

"This is a KGB operation. Why is the MfS involved?"

"To make sure it's done correctly. I want my prisoners now."

Bogdanov walked back over to her desk and scribbled something on a piece of paper. "Then you won't mind signing for them. Let's see. You received them at fourteen hundred twenty-six hours." She shoved the receipt across the desk to him, certain that the Prussian respect for bureaucratic procedure was on her side.

Kosyk removed a fountain pen from his jacket and signed.

"Wait here. I'll get the keys."

She hurried down the corridor and stopped in front of a door. She looked around to make certain no one was watching her. Using a piece of cloth to prevent fingerprints, she opened the door and slipped into the janitor's closet. She reached into a bag for a cigarette butt she'd lifted from Stukoi's ashtray that morning. She struck the match, lit the cigarette and held its glowing tip against the newspaper. She hoped Faith understood her message and would make swift use of the distraction. The newspaper smoldered. She puffed on it. *Burn, damn it. Burn.*

It had to look like a closet smoker had set the fire; initial suspicions of arson could expose her. When the newspaper burst into flames, she dropped it and the cigarette into a wastepaper basket and shoved it under a shelf of flammable cleaning fluids. She crept from the closet and shut the door. Black smoke poured through the cracks. Maybe she'd overdone it.

She returned to her office and handed Kosyk the keys to the makeshift holding cell. "Prisoners are all yours. Try not to lose them." Bogdanov then left the building, hoping Faith and the commander escaped before Kosyk got to them.

CHAPTER FORTY-THREE

LYSENKO RESEARCH FACILITY, MOSCOW
2:33 P.M.

"*Shto sluchil* . . . ?" The guard's words trailed off as Summer shoved the shard into his throat and twisted. Blood squirted onto Summer's arm as he pulled the glass through the tough tissue. The guard crumpled to the floor. Summer grabbed his gun, lunged behind the desk and wrapped his body over Faith.

Faith could feel Summer's heart pound. For a moment the smell of the guard's fresh blood overpowered the smoke of the smoldering fuse. Then the C-4 exploded. The deafening blast shook the room. A gust of air slapped her. Abruptly there was an eerie silence.

"Go, go, go, go, go." Summer leaped up, pulling Faith with him through the cloud of smoke and dust.

Pools of formaldehyde mingled with broken glass, chunks of human brains and other debris, forming a macabre swamp. The guard's blood swirled into the brew. Faith skidded, falling toward the floor. She held out her hand to catch herself and it smashed into a sliver of glass. Summer reached around her waist and caught her before the rest of her hit the ground.

A good portion of the wall was missing. She was grateful for the low-quality Soviet mortar and the high level of Summer's expertise. She stepped over the rubble and lowered herself to the sidewalk. Sirens wailed in the distance as people poured from the building. A shriveled babushka leaned on her broom of lashed twigs and watched.

"This is your town. You lead the way," Summer said.

"Hell, I don't know where we are."

"Then we're going this way." Summer broke into a sprint.

They reached the end of the tree-lined block. The drone of sirens was coming closer. They took a left and dashed onward. She looked around to get her orientation, but the four-story buildings could have been anywhere in downtown Moscow. They raced past a Gastronom grocery store with cans stacked in pyramids; it could have been any one of hundreds of such establishments in the city. The sirens screeched from directly ahead, but they were in the middle of a block, with nowhere to run.

Faith's heart pounded so hard she thought her body was shaking with its beat. She gasped for air and held her aching side. "You go on. I can't go much further. Let them get me. Save yourself."

"I don't leave team members behind—especially you. I'll carry you if I have to. Come on."

The sirens were almost upon them. She forced herself to continue, slowing with each step. A hundred meters ahead a driver closed the back door of a blue delivery truck.

"Punch it, Faith. Here's our ride."

She mustered every last bit of energy. About thirty feet away from the truck, she heard the engine start. Summer rolled up the cargo door and hopped in the back. Summer held out his hand for her and the truck started to move.

Just a little farther. Faster. Faster.

She grabbed at his hand and leaped just as a fire engine roared by. He grasped her by the wrist and yanked. Pain shot through her injured shoulder. Summer pulled her into the truck with the ease of a dog tossing a stuffed toy. The metal door protested with a loud squeak as he pulled it down, shutting out all light.

"Whew, this is one stinky country. You all right?" Summer said.

"I'm alive."

The truck hit a pothole and something slimy raked against the side of her face, knocking her off balance. Summer caught her, his fingers pressing into her sore ribs.

She scraped at the thick substance as she stifled a gag. She pulled a disintegrating Kleenex from her pocket and wiped away what she could. "This is vile."

Summer opened the door a crack for light. Decapitated pig carcasses swung like greasy pendulums from hooks on the roof.

"Oh, man. Couldn't you have picked a bakery truck?" Faith said.

The truck fell into another pothole and a carcass swung toward her, but Summer pushed her down against the floor. The draft from the movement blew over her neck.

"We've got to make our way through these piggies to hide from the driver before the next stop," Summer said.

Faith breathed through her blouse. "You're kidding. It's all I can do not to barf right now."

"Buck up, Faith."

"No, I'm drawing a line in the lard right here and now. When the truck stops, we jump out. We've gone far enough. If we get coated in lard, we're sure not going to blend in with the locals very easily, and every mutt in this city is going to be after us."

"We've got to get to the embassy. You know where it is?"

"That's the last place we want to go. Soviet militia and the KGB patrols it to keep everyone from running in and asking for asylum. You can bet they'll have our descriptions before we get there. Even if we could get in, I wouldn't expect a whole lot of help."

"I'm active-duty military. I was kidnapped by the KGB and brought here as part of some plot to kill Gorbachev and blame it on the US. Believe me, I'll get their attention."

"Even if we get in, there's not much they can do for us. You think the KGB would let them drive us out to Finland in an embassy car? I can guarantee it'd have a bad accident before it could get past the Moscow ring road. The Americans would probably put us up in the basement with those Russian Baptists who've camped there for years. You think you're frustrated now that you haven't made full commander? Imagine what a few years in an embassy basement with friends of Jesus will do for your career."

"I'm open to suggestions."

CHAPTER FORTY-FOUR

DZERZHINSKAIA METRO STATION, MOSCOW
3:15 P.M.

Bogdanov shoved through the crowds of Muscovites sneaking home early from work and wished deodorant supplies were a higher priority for the Party. Her nose was used to Germany. She slid a key into a door ostensibly restricted to metro personnel and entered an antechamber with a plainclothes KGB guard sitting at a metal desk that filled half the room. A colorful diagram of the metro was posted to his right and a painting of the metro station's namesake and the founder of the Soviet secret police to his left. Felix Dzerzhinsky's eyes always seemed a bit too glassy; she suspected miniature surveillance cameras were hidden inside as a fitting tribute to the brutal spymaster. Bogdanov flashed her KGB identification and stepped into the high-speed elevator to Lubyanka. Her stomach stayed on the ground floor while the West German–built elevator transported her nearly thirty stories to the surface.

She crept into her recently assigned office undetected and retrieved volumes three and four of the Faith Whitney file she had signed out from the central repository earlier in the day. Weeks before, as soon as she learned of Kosyk's interest in Whitney, she had familiarized herself with the contents.

From this analysis, she believed she could predict where Faith would turn for help.

Bogdanov flipped open the file to a report of Faith meeting with the well-connected antique collector Dr. Svetlana Nikolaevna Gorkovo. The files were stitched together at the top. She took a razor blade from her desk and excised the report, careful not to leave any marks on the page beneath it. She removed everything mentioning the doctor. When she finished, she folded the sheets and stuck them inside her inner jacket pocket. She didn't want any shredded documents in her office.

A phone rang. Stukoi demanded her immediate presence in his office. She returned the edited files to the documents repository and braced herself for his fury. The general screamed at her before she could close his office door. She stood at attention in front of his desk and waited for the tirade to extinguish itself.

"I'm sorry, sir; what caught on fire?" Bogdanov said.

"The fucking facility where you were keeping the Americans, you idiot."

"Did FedEx and Otter survive?"

"Not confirmed. Most of the guards abandoned their posts and ran out of the building. One guard stayed behind to get them out, but he hasn't been accounted for. The fire department is on the scene." Stukoi smashed his cigar into an ashtray. "How could you let this happen? They were in your charge, you fuckup."

"They weren't in my custody. Kosyk had already relieved me." Bogdanov held out a paper to Stukoi. "I even had him be a good German and sign for them. He might really be a Slav, but you can always count on him to act *Deutsch*."

"So the great Kosyk fucked up. That makes my day."

"Any known loss of lives?" Bogdanov said.

"Does it matter?"

Bogdanov tapped on a pack of Aeroflot cigarettes until one came out. "Even if the Americans died, we can put on a show of searching for them. We have enough surveillance photos to put together anything we want. A nationwide manhunt might work better for us than catching them immediately. We can always corner them in some building they set on fire with their remaining explosives. We produce their charred remains as evidence. Trotting them in front of a camera would've been nice, but they wouldn't have given us what we wanted, anyway."

"You cover your ass well, Bogdanov. Going by the time on that receipt, you had just handed them over to Kosyk right around the time of the fire."

"They were in his custody."

"How could he be so stupid as to sign a receipt for prisoners we don't want a paper trail on?"

Bogdanov nodded to Stukoi, indicating she wanted to use his lighter. He tossed it to her. "It's standard MfS procedure. He even stood there like he was waiting for me to pull out a stamp to make it official."

"What I don't understand is why the hell you would do it if you didn't already know they'd escaped."

"Maybe I wanted to make him feel at home. He's lost her before. I wanted to cover my ass, just in case."

"You fucked him and the prick deserves it. Good work. Always did say you have balls. I still don't like the fact that we lost them, but, hell, I like a good hunt as well as the next guy. We do have enough to pin it on them when we find them. And we will find them."

Bogdanov lit the cigarette. "They started the fire?"

"We don't know yet. There's a hole in the wall of the room where they were held. Something exploded there. It's a mess, but we found one body."

"There were chemicals inside. I don't know how volatile."

"We have one report from a babushka who was sweeping the street. She claims a man and a woman climbed out of the hole after an explosion and ran. We can't get a good description—bad eyesight."

"Any chance Gorbachev's people got word of the event, started the fire and helped them escape?" Bogdanov said.

"If his people knew, we wouldn't be here right now. Because of the old lady, I want to work on the assumption they're alive and on the run. We'll have to find them."

"As I see it, our hands are tied until tomorrow morning. We can't start a full search for them until after the deed. If we look for them now, it'll put Gorbachev's bodyguards on a higher state of alert, and we'll seem incompetent if police all over the union know we had foreknowledge but couldn't stop two American assassins," Bogdanov said.

"Agreed, but I'm going to have Popov's investigative unit see if they can quietly pick up their trail from the building. They can search known associates."

"Sir, I feel partially responsible for their loss, even if they were in

Kosyk's hands. I'd like to personally direct the investigation into known contacts."

"You're an excellent field operative abroad, but you've just proven you're worthless on home soil. You're perceived as too central to the operation to remove you at this point without too many questions, or I would. I don't want you touching it or anything else right now. You're expected at our final planning meeting tonight, so you'd better show up. Go home until then. Visit your father. I don't want to see your face around here. Dismissed." A phone rang and Stukoi lowered his ear to each one along the row.

Colonel Bogdanov walked from the office to see Stukoi's secretary, Pyatiletka, disappear out the main door. A note on her desk informed the general she had gone home early for her granddaughter's birthday. Thanks to her usual negligence, her computer terminal was still on. The colonel looked around the empty room and sat at the terminal. At the prompt she typed in KUSNV, then the password LATA33, and she was logged into the SOUD system on the mainframe. She quickly navigated through the hierarchy of menus and searched for records with both Faith Whitney and Svetlana Gorkovo. Fourteen hits. She pressed the delete button and an error message popped onto the amber screen. Only a high-level systems administrator could delete a file.

She logged off and raced to Faith.

CHAPTER FORTY-FIVE

MOSCOW
4:46 P.M.

Two hours after escaping from the brain trust, Faith knocked on Svetlana's door as hard as she dared. A loud bark came from the flat.

"Reagan, good dog," Faith said.

Svetlana's many eccentricities included talking to her dog in English, but Faith spoke in Russian so as not to give any hint of her nationality to any eavesdropping neighbors. The dog ignored her and barked louder. The more Faith pleaded in Russian, the more Reagan barked. He pawed at the door.

"Quiet!" Summer said. The dog fell silent. "She's not home or the dog would've had her here. Wait and I'll be back in a second." Summer went down the stairs, taking several steps at a time. In less than a minute he returned with a thin metal strip with a rivet lodged in one end. He fed the metal into the slit between the door and the frame just as a loud creak came from across the hall.

A shriveled face peeked through the crack. "What's happening? Who're you?"

"*Zdravstvuite,*" Faith greeted her. "I'm here with my husband to feed Reagan for Sveta, but forgot the key. Did she perhaps leave you a spare?"

"She said nothing to me about a trip. What's that smell?" The woman's accusing eyes darted between Faith and Summer.

"My apologies. I came from work and we had eleven bodies to embalm today. I don't understand why people always die in clusters. Cousin Ludmilla went into early labor and Sveta doesn't want to leave her alone." Faith turned toward Summer and gestured to the door. Her voice became harsh and she shouted at him in Russian. "Haven't you got that open yet? You forgot the key, so you go home and get it. And no drinking. Don't you dare come back here with alcohol on your breath."

Summer shrugged his broad shoulders and turned back to the door. The dog let out a deep bark. Faith hoped Reagan remembered her. Summer coaxed the metal strip into the lock and the door sprang open.

"Reagan!" Faith held her hands out to the dog, praying he didn't attack and blow her cover. The husky reared up on his back legs and frantically licked her face, slurping up the remaining lard. She petted the back of his thick neck and turned toward the woman. "Poor Reagan had no walk since yesterday. I'm afraid he left us a present. If you want, you can come over, visit with us and help clean up after him."

The woman let out a loud snort and slammed her door.

Summer grabbed Reagan's collar and wrestled him back into the apartment.

"I don't think she's going to be calling the police. We should be safe here for a little while," Faith said as she scratched the dog. "And thank you, Mr. Reagan, for getting that grease off my face."

The translucent blue eyes of the Siberian husky followed Summer as he paced around the central Moscow apartment crammed with antiques. St. George slew an assortment of lumpy iconic dragons while the Virgin Mary looked on with serene disapproval. The creak of the floor echoed from the high ceiling as he stepped across the worn oriental carpets. Reagan leaped up on an analyst's couch and curled up.

"What is this place? Are all Russian apartments like this?" Summer said as he looked around.

"Definitely not. You never find one person living in anything this spacious. She had political ties to Brezhnev through one of her husbands."

"I meant all of this crap. And this place smells like an old lady's face powder. I'm kind of glad the formaldehyde's still on me."

"I don't like this room, either. I never could get into classic Russian art. But to answer your question, this isn't normal—nothing about Svetlana is. Let's go clean up."

Faith patted the dining-room wall until she found the light switch. A kilim dominated one wall. Woven into the tapestry was the likeness of two Turkic women, their heads covered with bright yellow scarves. They wore matching baggy harem pants under blue and red flowered dresses and each one swung a sickle at wheat stalks.

"What a delight," Faith whispered as she touched it, admiring the weave. She stepped backward for a better view. "Oh, I want this. You can't imagine how rare it is."

"Faith, focus. This isn't the time to go shopping."

"We're safe for the time being. Give me just one moment of beauty." Faith studied the design. "I can't get the image of that dead guard's bloody neck out of my mind. You've done it before, haven't you?"

"I'm special forces. Sometimes my job means taking out the enemy. I've seen action in Grenada, Nicaragua and places no one's supposed to know I've ever been. I've only done it when absolutely necessary. You work the clean side of the Cold War, smuggling pretty rugs across borders. The Cold War's not all clean. It takes a lot to keep it from going hot. One of the ways both governments keep it from breaking out of control is by using guys like me and denying like hell they ever did it."

"I'm not sure that justifies it."

"Faith, we've been having this East-versus-West, hawk-and-dove debate since we were kids. Seems to me they just forced you onto my side."

"I don't take sides. I play the communist sympathizer with you, but that's just to hassle you, since you're such a dyed-in-the-wool American." Faith spoke without taking her gaze off the kilim.

"You were always the communist sympathizer, but never a communist. You're an American when you're around the Germans and they're bugging the shit out of you, but you're never a patriot. It's the same thing with relationships. You can't settle down. Things get serious, you're outta there."

"I was too young."

"You couldn't make up your mind about what you wanted, kind of like now. You can't take a stand on anything."

"I think that abortion in Tulsa counts."

"As a stand against your mama, but not for what you wanted. I haven't seen you make a choice about something since then. You sit on every fence you can find."

"Not fair." Faith choked back tears. "I've had enough today without this."

"I'm sorry. I don't mean to bicker with you. It's been a tough couple a days for both of us, and it's not over yet." He stood and put his arm around her waist. She pressed her head against him and closed her eyes.

"You know I love you," Faith said.

"I know." He stroked her hair. "But I don't know what that means."

"Neither do I."

Reagan raised his head and his ears perked. He trotted from the room toward the door.

"Must be Svetlana," Faith said. "You stay here so you don't scare her. I'll go."

"Faith, what's going on?" Svetlana said in Russian as she stepped over to Summer and took his right hand and turned it over. She pushed back the bloodied sleeve. Red muscle tissue was visible through a deep, six-inch-long laceration that zigzagged across his forearm. Blood seeped from the wound. She squinted as she examined the cut on his forehead.

"We need help," Faith said.

"I see that."

Faith switched to English: "This is Max Summer—the ex-fiancé I've told you about." Only when she introduced Summer to Svetlana did Faith notice how wrecked they both looked. Summer had a two-inch gash over his swollen left eye. The skin around it was various shades of dark purple. Stubble covered his head and face, but didn't quite conceal a long scratch on his left cheek. His clothes testified to his odyssey. His ripped shirt was coated in dirt and dried blood. Faith knew the blood wasn't only his.

Faith continued, "We just escaped from the KGB. We haven't done anything wrong—I'll explain later. I'm so sorry about breaking into your home, but you weren't here and I didn't know where else to go or whom else I could trust."

"I'll do what I can." Svetlana spoke English with a British accent. Svetlana turned to Summer. "Those wounds need to be cleaned up. Nothing urgent, but you need a couple layers of sutures. Faith, are you hurt?"

"The Stasi cracked some of my ribs a week ago. They're really sore, but mending."

"The Stasi? You two make friends everywhere you go. Faith, can you please grab my bag out of the hall closet? And, while you're there, fetch some old towels for you to sit on. You're both slightly soiled." Svetlana held Summer's arm and led him into the kitchen.

Faith set the old-fashioned doctor's bag down on the table and spread towels over two chairs. Svetlana opened a waxed-paper envelope, shook out two curved needles and set them on the packet. She snipped off a strip of gauze and cut away his shirtsleeve.

"Faith, keep the pressure on this while you take him over to the sink and rinse out the wound with running water and alcohol. Before you do that, put on some water to boil for tea and to sterilize the needle. I'll be back in a minute. Reagan, come along, dear." Svetlana disappeared into the bathroom. Her dog sat outside the door.

Faith opened a cabinet, squatted and stared at the hodgepodge. Pots, pans and skillets of every size, material and color were stacked on top of one another, but nothing matched. She chose a white enamel pot, but couldn't locate its lid. When she pushed the cabinet door shut, an avalanche roared inside the cabinet. She lit the gas stove.

Summer cut himself a fresh strip of gauze and pressed it against the wound. Red spots immediately appeared. "How sterile do you think all of this is?"

"I wouldn't worry. It's probably Reagan you'll be sharing needles with, so I'd say your biggest risk is distemper." Faith returned to the table. "This beats the average Soviet hospital. They're something you don't want to experience. I once heard a doctor here complain that American disposable needles broke after about a dozen uses."

Reagan rushed ahead of Svetlana toward the sound of the whistling teakettle. Svetlana turned the burner off and stepped into an adjacent room. She retrieved a stack of handle-less cups and a teapot, steadying the teapot against her chest as she closed the china-cabinet door.

Summer leaned over to Faith and whispered, "Do we really have to have a tea party? Can't we get on with this? We have to plan how to get out of here. I don't want to stay in one place too long."

"You're from the Ozarks. Act like it. We have to do some small talk before we ask for help. We're asking for big favors here, so play along. We're safe for now."

Svetlana set the cups in front of Faith. She recognized the tea set as Central Asian. She had seen countless Uzbek ones painted with the repeating white and indigo blue abstract in the shape of ripe cotton, but this set was extraordinary. Faith picked up a cup. A wreath of cotton blooms framed a painting of Lenin, but the Soviet hero's skin was darker than usual and his eyes were small slits. His facial hair was more reminiscent of Genghis Khan's Fu Manchu mustache than Lenin's pointy Vandyke. Arabic script was scrawled above the portrait. "Exquisite. Where's it from?"

"You tell me." Svetlana started to place her hand on Faith's lard-smudged shoulder, but leaned on the back of her chair instead. She turned toward Summer. "Of everyone I know, Faith has the most discriminating appreciation of these treasures."

"I can see how it takes someone very special to get into this stuff," Summer said. Reagan licked his pant leg.

"Reagan, where are your manners? Go to your rug. Now move along." She pointed to the corner.

Reagan held his tail low as he climbed onto a Muslim prayer rug woven with a portrait of Stalin. Summer raised an eyebrow.

Svetlana noticed his reaction to Stalin's image and said, "Don't get me wrong. I hate the communists like everyone else—after all, I am a Soviet citizen—but it was such an exciting time in the household arts."

Faith turned the cup in her hand. Dust coated the white interior. "Clearly Central Asia, most likely Uzbekistan. The Arab script dates it before the mid-twenties—Lenin after 1917. It could even be from one of the city-states after the communists took over, but before the USSR swallowed them. Bukhara? Samarkand?"

"Khiva is my educated guess. Most assuredly from the independent Khorezm Soviet People's Republic, circa 1923, before Lenin annexed it to the Motherland. I have the entire set, including the serving platter."

"I might be able to arrange for some chef's-quality All-Clad pans in exchange for these." Faith walked over to the sink and rinsed the cups. "You did get the Williams-Sonoma catalog I sent with Ian last month?"

"I loved it. I'll never understand why, as one of the world's most advanced countries, we can't produce decent cookware." Svetlana poured brewed tea into the antique teapot. "I've always wanted a set of the French Le Creuset pots—you know, the bright enameled ones."

"Hey, I don't mean to be rude here, but is this really the time to play Let's Make a Deal? As it stands right now, we can't get ourselves out of the country, let alone take some fancy cups out of it."

"There's always layaway." Faith smiled and turned toward Svetlana.

"Three-piece Le Creuset pot set for the complete tea ensemble. Deal?"

"Five-piece. Plus the five-quart stockpot."

"Three pieces including the stockpot."

"That will fetch you the set *sans* serving platter," Svetlana said.

"You can't break up a set like that and you know it. Okay, but only because I owe you for all of this. The five-piece set, including the stockpot."

"Agreed." Svetlana carried the silver teakettle to the table. She poured cold tea with her left hand and the hot water with her right, serving Summer first. She scooped red marmalade with a silver dessert spoon. Summer slid his hand over the cup to stop her, but was too late. Marmalade plopped onto his fingers.

Faith offered no resistance to the marmalade. She started to take a sip, but the cup burned her fingers, so she picked it up again by the rim. "We're in trouble, Sveta. Bad trouble."

"As bad as the time when you were detained in Omsk?"

"It was Tomsk, and that was nothing compared to this." Faith fished the sterile needles from the pot with a hemostat. She gave Svetlana a brief overview of their predicament while Svetlana threaded the needle.

Svetlana turned to Summer. "Do you require something for the pain? I don't have much, so I reserve it for those who really need it."

"Your dog might need it someday. I'll be fine."

"Would you like a shot of vodka to take the edge off?"

"Thank you, but, all things considered, I need to stay alert."

"Come on, tough guy. You're allowed." Faith found a bottle of vodka in the freezer and splashed some into his empty teacup. "Drink."

Summer downed it. "Okay, now's as good a time as any."

Sveta cut away jagged dead skin, then grasped one of the needles with a needle driver and plunged it deep into the gash.

"Dammit, girl!" Summer gritted his teeth. "From the looks of this place, I thought you were an antique dealer. I wouldn't have guessed you're a doctor."

"I'm chief of medical staff at the Moscow Zoo. Don't worry. I stitch up big animals all the time." Svetlana smiled, revealing a mouthful of tarnished silver crowns. She pierced a fat globule and Faith turned away.

"I was hoping you could pull off another one of your miracles and help us get out of here," Faith said.

"On such short notice, I can probably get you as far as East Germany," Svetlana said. "By the way, the ice cream was heavenly—better than the females of the non–working girl variety who ever got through that way."

Faith tilted her head and threw the last sip of tea into the back of her throat as if it were vodka. "I really hate the smell of fish, but heading to Finland via Estonia on a fishing co-op's boat might be easiest. Last I heard, the Finnish mobile-phone network bleeds over into part of Estonia, and the Soviets aren't jamming it. We might be able to get word out to someone."

"And how would we ever get a Finnish mobile phone?" Summer said.

"Mug a drunk Finnish tourist. They flock to Tallinn for cheap booze and they all seem to have those phones. Personally, I think they're a fad that will never catch on, but we might be able to call to the West with one. I don't suppose you could arrange a pickup with your guys?" Faith asked, pouring herself more tea.

Summer watched Svetlana sink the needle into his forearm, then pull the thread through. "The Gulf of Finland is a Soviet lake, shallow and littered with ears. Don't get me wrong. They could do it if they absolutely had to. The biggest problem would be getting Washington on board, and I don't think we have the time for that."

Reagan sprang from his bed with a bark and ran from the room, growling.

"He never does this," Svetlana said.

Summer took the needle from her.

"I'm not finished," Svetlana protested.

Rather than take time to tie or cut it off, he stuck the needle through his skin like a body piercing. He drew the gun that he had taken from the guard. "Give me two seconds, then get the lights out. Pull the fuses if you have to."

Reagan's bark echoed from the front room.

Then the barking stopped.

Mövenpick you brought two years ago. Now, I'm assuming you've got pa ports hidden somewhere in that container of frightening dinnerware 1 brought me."

"No, we need papers. And the GDR's no good. They know me."

Summer's voice was strained. "I thought you could get anyone and anything out of there. East Berlin's at least Berlin. Let's go there. I like your home-field advantage. There are even permanent American military missions there. American troop convoys pass through East Germany on their way to Berlin all the time."

"Getting out's not the problem. It's getting in." Faith swirled the tea in her glass, the fruit fragments circling in a tiny whirlpool. "We don't have time to get Hakan to make papers for us, and I've never found a reliable local source for documents here that wasn't hooked into the KGB."

"He's in Berlin. How would you ever get something from there?" Summer said.

"Clipper Class. I could have you a Big Mac here tomorrow afternoon from Rhein-Main if you wanted it, but that doesn't help us get out."

Svetlana tied off the first layer of sutures with a single hand.

"Given the circumstances," Faith continued, "the only option I see is to cross weak points in the border. I know one along the Turkish frontier, but it's grueling."

"That's NATO. I like it." Summer bit his lip from the pain.

"I've done it and I didn't like it. The mountain passes might still be closed by snow," Faith said.

Svetlana batted her eyes, flashing the heavy orange eye shadow that matched her bright lipstick. "I could get you into Iran through a sturgeon boat on the Caspian Sea."

"Caviar's tempting," Faith said. "But I can't handle the chador. Head-to-toe black is definitely not my thing. I couldn't bring myself to do it in Berlin where it's at least chic. Iran would also mean a high-mountain crossing of the Turkish border to get away from the Ayatollah. I don't like multiple borders."

"Agreed we go direct into a friendly."

"Too bad Gorbachev's trashed the economy and they can't afford to have the Finns do construction for them above the Arctic Circle anymore. When they were building projects like Kostamuksha and the Svetogorsk pulp plant, Mama loved to use commuting Finnish workers to smuggle us and her religious propaganda into the Soyuz. I'm sure we were the only

CHAPTER FORTY-SIX

MOSCOW
5:06 P.M.

"Freeze! Hands in the air." Summer pointed the gun at the intruder. Reagan growled, baring his canines.

"I'm here to help you," Bogdanov said in American English.

"Faith, check her for weapons. Don't stand too close, and whatever you do, don't block my shot."

"I have a shoulder holster with a gun and there's a knife strapped to my right leg." Zara clasped her fingers together, rested her hands on her head and turned toward Faith. "I didn't know they were going to kidnap you until after I returned to Moscow and discovered I'd been deceived. Only then did I find out you were walking into a show trial and execution. It was too late to warn you, but I wasn't going to let them do it to you, so I flew back to Berlin and brought Commander Summer here to help you. I didn't see any other way."

"I'm touched," Summer said. "What'd you do with Walters and Meriwether? Keep in mind the consequences if I don't believe your answer."

"I ordered them detained for border violations. They're guests of the GDR until this is resolved. I made it clear they're to be treated well."

"As we say in the South, mighty white of you." He scratched his forearm beside the wound. "Are you alone or working with someone?"

"Alone. I don't know who to trust. I came to help you and get you out of here before they realize where you are. I bought you some time by removing all references to Doctor Gorkovo from Faith's dossier, but I was working fast and could've missed something. I was unable to delete the computerized files."

"How did you know to find me here?" Faith said. "I know dozens of people in Moscow."

"Please, I'm your case officer and I've studied you."

"Where'd you pick up English along with the American accent?"

"Silicon Valley. I once earned a Stanford degree as part of my legend there."

Faith opened Zara's black leather jacket. The KGB-issue service pistol made it all so clear. How could she have ever been so naïve as to think she could have any kind of friendship with a KGB controller? She grasped the weapon with her fingertips and held it as if she were removing a rotten vegetable from her refrigerator. Summer took it from her, Sveta's needle still stuck into his forearm. She returned to Zara and continued frisking her, pausing occasionally when she remembered how it had felt to flirt with her only a few nights ago. Faith's anger surprised her. She didn't like it.

"I didn't have any way of waving you off. And I still have no idea who was behind the Pan Am bomb. My best guess is that someone found out something about the delivery and didn't know who to trust. They tried to stop it in their own crude fashion."

Faith patted her way down the right leg until she discovered the bulge of a knife. "So why did you do it to me?"

"I didn't. That's what I'm trying to tell you. There's a lot more going on here than some MfS renegades smuggling explosives to Moscow."

"Yeah, we figured out that much." She stepped back from Zara and held on to the knife. "The East Germans are planning some kind of terrorist attack or something to spur a crackdown and a return to more predictable days."

Zara motioned with her head toward Svetlana. "Can we trust her?"

"More than we can trust you," Faith said.

"Honecker does believe Gorbachev is endangering the system. The Germans were plotting to take him out and pin it on the Americans. Until I was recalled to Moscow, I thought this was limited to a Stasi operation. It's not.

The GDR leadership initiated it—not that it will matter to anyone but a historian. They approached me to recruit dissatisfied KGB factions to back them to make sure the right side stepped into the power vacuum."

"Why'd they believe you'd help?" Faith said.

"My father and I haven't fared well under Mr. Gorbachev. And I haven't hidden my conviction that he's bringing poverty and chaos to my country."

"If that's the case, why didn't you join in?" Summer said.

"Commander, I make the assumption you're a Republican, since you're in the military. If your president were a Democrat and you believed his policies hurt your country, would you then conspire to overthrow him?"

"Of course not."

"The KGB and Soviet Army have never stepped into our government. We're not a Third World dictatorship."

"I thought Andropov was KGB chief," Summer said.

"And Bush was CIA chief. What's your point?" Zara said.

Summer shrugged his shoulders.

Zara continued, "When my boss received my reports about the MfS plans, I'm speculating that he decided to either join forces with the Germans or use them in a plot he was already involved in. Either way, I was ordered to play along with them and make them think we were cooperating so we could catch them in the act after you delivered the C-4. I believed I was feeding them disinformation, but it was the truth."

"When's it going down?" Summer said.

"Tomorrow morning."

"We've got to get out of here fast," Faith said. "A hard-line putsch will shut this place down tighter than North Korea."

"That's not your biggest worry. This afternoon they've issued warnings to KGB operatives to be on the lookout for two American agents supporting Armenian terrorists. When Gorbachev's killed tomorrow, a full nationwide manhunt for you begins."

"We're screwed," Faith said. "No one's going to help us then. This isn't like the West, where we could go to some remote corner of the country, rent a flat and lie low for a couple of months."

Summer continued to point the gun at Zara. "The KGB won't stop hunting us at the border, will it? I remember something about Trotsky, Mexico City and an ice pick."

"Don't expect protection from your own government—it won't want anything to do with you. May I assume, Commander Summer, that you'll be declared a deserter and court-martialed? May I put my hands down? I'm not a threat. Remember, I was the one who helped you escape."

"Yeah, what was the think tank with all those brains all about? I know the KGB has to have better holding cells than that," Summer said.

"I've been trying to tell you; it's not an official KGB operation. So far as I know, only a handful of people are involved, but they're powerful." Zara explained her choice of a low-security KGB research lab. "And, Faith, you'll appreciate this. That's where they housed Lenin's corpse during the war to protect him from German bombing."

"How thoughtful of you," Faith said.

"I didn't take the C-4 when I saw it in your shoes and I returned everything you needed to break out and even started a fire as a diversion."

"I'm sure we set some mad scientist's research back decades." Faith turned to Summer. "What do you think?"

He lowered the weapon.

Svetlana grasped Summer's elbow. "Now that this is settled, I haven't finished with your arm." She and Reagan led him back into the kitchen, but Faith and Zara stayed behind.

"I'm so glad you're okay." Zara stepped toward Faith, but she moved away.

"So am I."

"I couldn't confirm it, but I believe your father is alive."

"I know." Faith turned and walked into the kitchen.

"Sveta, our captor here has hardly fed us. Do you have anything we could eat?" Faith said as she opened the refrigerator.

"I did what I could." Zara leaned against the sink, watching Svetlana push the needle through Summer's skin.

"All done." Svetlana knotted it and clipped the thread. "There's some cheese and sausage in the icebox for sandwiches, or I could make you some pork cutlets."

"Let's go with the sandwiches," Summer said. "I agree with the major here that we need to get a move on."

"It's Lieutenant Colonel."

"Kinda young for that, aren't you, comrade?"

"I was promoted to the rank years ago for my work in California."

Zara walked to the table. She picked up one of the antique cups, looked at it, then set it down.

"Hit a ceiling, huh?"

"You could say that," Zara said as she pulled out a chair.

"I know exactly how you feel. So what's your plan?"

"The future of my country is at stake. The problem is, I've been abroad and out of the loop, so I don't know who to trust. Help me stop the coup."

Faith rummaged through the refrigerator. "You're kidding, right?"

"That's another reason why I brought Commander Summer to Moscow. As a US Navy officer, I knew he wouldn't want to see the world return to the days of the old Cold War, and I mean a very cold, Cold War."

"Obviously you don't know the military, but you have my attention," Summer said.

"If they come to power, I can guarantee an invasion of Poland to stop Solidarity. The Party has gone too far in Hungary with their border liberalization and their market reforms, so I suspect we'll invade them, too. They were fierce fighters in fifty-six." She shook her head. "And fanatical totalitarians in command of our nuclear weapons won't make any of us sleep better at night. Remember Korea? Vietnam? Angola? And how many times have we nearly gone to war over Berlin? These men don't like West Berlin in the middle of the Warsaw Pact, as you call it. All they need to do is wait for a weak American president and they can take the city—finish the business Stalin left undone. Do I need to go on? I'm sure Doctor Whitney could assist me further."

"It probably wouldn't have hurt to mention the purges, gulags—"

"I was focusing on foreign policy, since our domestic policy rarely concerns your military. I know the people who'll take over and revenge is on their minds. Stalin has already shown the way. They'll hit hard before a resistance movement can develop, reestablish the gulag system. All of the journalists and entrepreneurs who thrived under glasnost will have knocks at the door in the middle of the night."

"I get your point." Summer spoke, shielding his full mouth with his right hand until he swallowed. "What are you thinking of doing?"

"We are not getting involved." Faith slammed the plate of food down onto the table.

"We are involved. If what she's saying is true, the next twenty-four hours are going to alter the course of world events, and I don't think it'll be for the better. If you don't see a way to escape after a coup, and you can't get us out fast enough before they start the all-out manhunt, then our best bet is to keep them from calling out the dogs on us."

"How can the three of us ever hope to stop part of the Red Army and KGB? I vote we run." Faith opened her sandwich and extracted a peppercorn from a slice of salami. "We can borrow Sveta's Lada, steal some plates. It's eight, ten hours to Tallinn. I have connections that could probably get us out on a fishing trawler."

"Come, now. It's not like you're going to a shipping agent and booking passage on a passenger liner. She also isn't telling you that you might have to literally jump ship in the Danish Straits." Svetlana dropped the used needles and hemostat into boiling water. "It's been done. But not many stevedores are willing to take the risk, and those who are usually turn out to be working for the KGB on the left. When I helped Faith get that sarcophagus out a few years ago, it took me a week in Estonia to find someone reliable to take it into international waters—and he's not available anymore." Svetlana's smile disappeared and she looked away.

Zara turned toward Faith and raised an eyebrow.

"It didn't have a body in it or anything," Faith said. "It was a couple thousand years old and it was a special order from a client who wanted to be buried in an ancestral coffin."

Summer turned to Faith. "Faith, it's getting riskier here by the minute. Let's hear the lady spy out and then make our decision. If her plan's not feasible, we're gonna run like hell and commandeer a boat if we have to. Think about what's at stake here. It might be time you decided to take a stand for what's right for once in your life."

"The conspirators are meeting in a dacha just outside of Moscow at nine tonight to coordinate final plans," Zara said.

"What kind of security are we talking about?"

"They won't want any uninvited guests, but they won't be prepared to fend off an attack. I would expect less than a half-dozen guards."

Summer popped the last bite of his sandwich into his mouth and reached for another. "I see you have exact mission specs. Why aren't they meeting on a base—somewhere more secure?"

"To not arouse suspicion. The GRU knows what happens at every military installation, and too many ranking KGB and Army officials in one place would make GRU worried. You don't want them worried. Unlike your Office of Naval Intelligence, the GRU has teeth."

"I know I'm not supposed to interrupt, but can't we just go to the GRU if they're pro-Gorbachev?" Faith said.

"They might be compromised," Zara said.

Summer washed the sandwich down with cold tea. "How were you thinking about taking them out?"

Zara gestured toward Faith. "My friend here was expected to bring with her some plastic explosives that I had planned on using to destroy the dacha. Thanks to her ingenuity, I only have something called Play-Doh."

"Hold on." Faith rose from her seat. "Sveta, can you come help me find something?"

"What are you doing?" Summer said.

"Taking a stand," Faith said as she left the room.

A few minutes later, Faith hoisted the cooler onto the table and removed a plate crudely decorated with blue and pink posies. "Compliments of Captain Ian's delivery service."

"Faith, I don't know what's with you, but we don't have time for any more wheeling and dealing. We've probably been here too long as it is." Summer picked up the plate and his fingers sunk into it slightly. He flashed Faith a grin. "I take that back. We might just be back in business."

"Couldn't fool you for a second," Faith said. "But then, it does get a little soft at room temperature. Dry ice kept it hard as a rock, though."

Zara picked up a plate and scratched off some paint. "I take it this is the C-4?"

"Yes, ma'am. Looks like we have enough to take out a dacha or two, depending on size and construction."

"Wooden, single-story and not very big. Maybe two hundred, two-twenty-five square meters. I can draw a rough floor plan."

"So where're the caps and time fuse?"

"We might have a small problem. I only had that one small strip of time fuse and one blasting cap. I wasn't exactly expecting to use the stuff. I did the Play-Doh routine to allow me to bargain for safe passage until I turned over the real thing." Faith handed Summer the Leatherman.

"That's going to be a problem, but I'm not sure we want to tackle it right now. I'm getting antsy we're staying here too long," Summer said as he shoved the multipurpose tool into his pocket.

"You're right." Zara got up from the table. "By now they should be questioning Faith's old friends and acquaintances, and Doctor Gorkovo's name might be mentioned. We need to remove every obvious sign that we were ever here. If nothing looks unusual, they won't stay. Don't worry about fingerprints, because it's not a crime scene and they're not interested in proving you were here. All they want to know is where you're going. Doctor Gorkovo, I suggest you leave town for a few days to avoid any unpleasantness."

Faith gathered the dishes from the table and repacked the cooler. "I'm either starting to get used to this formaldehyde or the smell's wearing off."

"You reek of vet school," Svetlana said.

"That could be a problem," Zara said.

"I'll throw some cabbage on to boil to mask the odor." Svetlana reached into the cabinet for a pot. "And I'll fetch you some clothes to change into before you leave."

"Sveta, you don't happen to have any fast-acting tranquilizers and one of those dart guns you use on big animals here?" Faith said.

"Faith, this ain't *Wild Kingdom*."

"Humor me. I have a thing against killing, and I want to be convinced it's the only option."

"It is," Zara said. "Tranquilizers take too long to work—plus, we're dealing with a group of people."

"So where are we going, comrade? Your place?" Summer said.

"Not advisable. I work for the KGB, so I have a flat in something like your base housing. But I do know one place no one would ever think to look for Faith. We'll regroup there and plan our assault."

CHAPTER FORTY-SEVEN

MOSCOW
6:41 P.M.

Zara's Zil sedan reminded Faith of a 1950s American gas-guzzler; if it had a pair of tail fins, it would have been an El Dorado—its ancestors certainly were. The spacious backseat gave Faith and Summer room to stay out of sight. Their bodies pressed tightly against each other and a tattered blanket concealed them from the casual viewer. Faith's face was so close to Summer's cheek that she couldn't tell if it was the wool blanket or the stubble from his day-old beard that was scratching her. She comforted herself that it was him and not the filthy blanket. He put his arm around her, and for a few seconds she was back in the Ozarks, secure in her high school sweetheart's strong arms, dreaming of the day she would escape the vicissitudes of her mother's fanaticism. She cuddled closer against him and wished she could change history.

"Kind of like old times, isn't it?" Summer said. "The only difference is that it's not your mama we're worried about catching us back here together, but the frickin' KGB."

"Frankly, I'm not sure if that's better or worse."

"Oh, come on, Faith. I could always handle Mama Whitney and you claim you can handle the KGB, so it's your turn."

"I grossly overestimated myself. We're fucked."

Zara turned off the engine. "Stay down until I tell you to get up. I'm parking in a courtyard. I'm going inside first."

"You know, there's a chance she's turning us over to the KGB right now," Summer whispered into Faith's ear.

"You're just trying to make me feel good by whispering sweet nothings, aren't you?"

"If she has, follow my lead. We won't resist if I don't see an opening. I don't want you to get hurt."

"And what about you?"

In a few minutes, the back door clicked open. Cool air rushed inside the stuffy car. Someone flipped back the blanket.

"Oh, my God," Faith said.

"Lordy, lordy, look at what the cat's dragged in."

"Mama Whitney," Summer said, springing away from Faith like a teenager caught in the act.

Faith pulled the blanket back over her head. "This isn't going to work."

"Come on, child. Don't get testy with me now. I don't like it, either, but we've got to get you hid."

"Let's go." Summer threw the blanket off them and pushed Faith up onto the car seat. "Now."

Faith slid across the vinyl and crawled from the car feet-first. Zara reached under Faith's arm and helped her to stand. For a moment, their eyes met. When Summer put his hand on her back to nudge her forward, Faith saw jealousy flash in Zara's eyes.

"Leave the keys in the front seat. Sasha will hide the car in the carport," Mama Whitney said.

"Grab the Coleman in the trunk," Summer said.

They rushed across the muddy courtyard into the orphanage. Cases of infant formula and diapers turned the hallway into a maze. Mama Whitney waddled around the stacks, leaning into each turn as if skiing a slalom course. A young woman in a white smock and cap stepped into the hallway. Mama Whitney shooed her away with a flick of the wrist. The woman jumped backwards and shut the door. Mama Whitney dug into the front pocket of her housedress and pulled out a string of skeleton keys. She opened an aging wooden door.

The spicy smell of mold rose from the basement. Mama Whitney pawed the wall in search of the light switch and then hurried down the steps.

Faith hesitated. She flashed back to the many spring storms when she had followed her mother down the stairs of the root cellar in search of shelter from tornadoes. As a small child, she had felt safe there as her mother comforted her with Bible stories. She grew older and the tales shifted from Noah's Ark and Jonah and the Whale to threats of fire and brimstone. By her teenage years, Faith chose to stay in the house alone and dare the wrath of the tornado. Since lightning bolts never struck the sinner, nor did the twisters ever blow down the house, maybe the tempest of the coup wouldn't find her, either, if she again didn't follow her mother.

Summer nudged her from behind and whispered, "It's not going to collapse. Go on."

She gritted her teeth and descended into her mother's basement. A lone bare lightbulb dangled on a frayed cord. Broken cribs, piles of donated clothes and stacks of wooden crates filled with baby bottles littered the area. A heap of unfinished projects nearly concealed a corner workbench. Mama Whitney plowed a path through the junk like Moses parting the Red Sea. The Israelites followed her into the wilderness.

Mama Whitney approached the workbench and reached for the floor, her arm flailing in the air. She stood back up, panting. "Summer, help me out, son. I can't bend over as well as I used to. You'll have to feel around. There's a panel in the floor that lifts up. When you get it up, reach in underneath on the bottom right-hand side and you'll find a round light switch. Flip it on. I think you children will understand that I can't go down there with you, but you'll be safe enough."

Faith turned sideways and inhaled to give him a few added inches of clearance as he slipped past her. Summer ran his fingertips along the floor until he found the outline of the panel. He picked it up, set it aside and stood. "Good to see you again, Mama Whitney." He leaned over and pecked her on the cheek. "I sure do appreciate your hospitality."

"Now, you gonna tell me what's going on? Is someone about to bust down the doors after you-all?"

"They're searching for us, but we don't believe they're on our trail," Zara said.

"What kind of trouble you in? You were always such a good boy, but being that you're with this Jezebel, I have all sorts of ideations. She always did get you into trouble."

Faith fought back years of anger. She opened her mouth to speak, but Zara leaned over to her and whispered into her ear.

"Ask her about your father."

Faith's confused reaction to Zara's warm breath distracted her from her ire.

Summer towered over Mama Whitney and placed his hand on her shoulder. "Now you two are going to have to bury the hatchet for a little while. It's a matter of national security. I know you've always been a God-fearing, patriotic American, so you're going to have to put your differences aside for the time being and give each other the benefit of the doubt for the good of the country."

"You're still in those special armed forces?"

"Yes, ma'am."

"Then it must be something real important if you're here behind the Iron Curtain."

"Yes, ma'am, and it hasn't gone too good, but with the help of these two ladies here and your hospitality—and the good Lord willing—we're going to get things straightened out. I'm not free to talk about it, so I hope you understand."

"You all stink to high heaven. There's an old shower down there. I'm pretty sure there's a dried-up bar of soap. I'll send someone down with shampoo, towels and the like. Can I get you anything else?"

"Mind if we help ourselves to some clothes and things laying around here? How about if you check on us in a half an hour after we've had a little time to regroup? I'm sure we'd all appreciate something to eat and drink then."

"I'll see what I can conjure up. Wish I'd a known you were coming, I would've whipped up some biscuits and gravy. They always were your favorite."

"Nobody makes redeye gravy like you do, Mama Whitney." Summer's eyes sparkled in the faint light.

Faith descended the ladder first. In contrast to the chaos of the upper basement, the dank secret room was orderly. Crates stenciled with the words INFANT FORMULA in both English and Russian were stacked along a wall beside a padlocked metal door. The heavy lock was new and shiny in contrast to the rest of the dingy room. Dust, mold and flakes of blue paint hugged the brick walls. A rusty showerhead was connected to overhead pipes and a drain was cut into the floor.

Faith palpated her sore ribs. "What the hell do we do now?"

Summer closed the wooden panel. "This is our war room. Time to plan out our op."

"Who do you think you are, bringing me here?" Faith said to Zara. "You must know tons of people in Moscow, and one of them has to have an empty garage or something."

"I don't know anyone I would trust with something this sensitive—not even my father. I've spent most of my life abroad. My contacts are in the KGB and diplomatic corps. And no one will ever expect you to turn to your mother for assistance."

"Present company included," Faith said.

"Amen to that, but she's not that bad and she is your mama." Summer pulled out a chair, turned it around and sat in it backwards at the table made from two sawhorses and an old wooden door.

"Maybe not that bad with you. You always could charm all of the Whitney women."

Zara's facial muscles tightened. "I'm sorry to interrupt, but we have a lot of work and not much time. First, I want an inventory of our resources, then a review of the target—"

"Hold on," Summer said. "I think the first thing we need is to agree on our command structure."

"Very well. I'm in command. As I was saying—"

"Not so fast, comrade. I command special operations all over the world and I blow things up for a living. You're a spook. You're used to sneaking around, kidnapping people—and I think you did a pretty crappy job at that."

"You're here, aren't you? And I didn't plan that one—my staff threw it together on short notice. Don't forget I'm a lieutenant colonel and you're a lieutenant commander. I outrank you."

"Just because the KGB has military ranks doesn't mean you've got equivalent preparation, particularly for this op. I'm a twin-pin—EOD and SEAL."

"And I was a Girl Scout," Faith said. "Why don't we vote on it?"

"No," Summer and Zara said in unison.

"Glad we're not fighting for democracy." Faith laughed, but Zara and Summer scowled.

"Without going into my extensive operations background," Zara said, "I do concede my work has been of a different nature, and I'll defer to your expertise for running this op, but only this op."

"Fair enough. Now, the first thing I want you to do is run this meeting. Carry on."

Faith rolled her eyes. "This is ridiculous. Let's get on with it."

"Faith, this is important. It might seem trivial to a civilian, but a clear command structure is vital to the success of any operation."

"Command structure? Come on, this is a pissing contest. There are three of us. We're hardly a SEAL or Spetsnaz team."

"Commander Summer has a point. You're going to have to trust both of us and go along."

"Whatever." Faith threw her arms into the air. "He's the captain, you're the platoon leader and I'm the troops. We're screwed."

"Let's review our resources," Zara said.

"Come on," Faith said. "We all know what we've got and it's not much—about ten pounds of C-4, the gun Summer took from the guard and whatever your pistol is. If I understand my recent explosives lessons correctly, we can't do much without time fuse and a blasting cap. Speaking purely as a nonprofessional, we're well equipped to knock off a Seven-Eleven."

"You're a good pupil, but you didn't make it to lesson two. There are ways to set off C without using a cap or fuse—if you absolutely have to. They're just not pretty. We have enough C to do anything we need, but we'll have to come up with an easily ignited explosive to detonate it. Give me a couple of minutes under anyone's kitchen sink and I can come up with a crude bomb. The issue's survivability. It's tough to jury-rig a slow-burning fuse to set off a high-velocity explosive."

Faith held up her hand as if stopping traffic. "Whoa. Survivability? Forget it if you don't think we're going to come out of this alive."

"Faith." Zara looked her in the eyes. "What we're about to do will save countless lives—maybe even prevent another war. We have to accept there could be casualties."

Faith turned her gaze to Summer. He nodded.

"I don't like it one bit," Faith said. "Casualties—as you so technically call one of us dying—are not acceptable."

"We can't take time to debate this. If you don't want to be a part of it, opt out now. The comrade here and I have a job to do," Summer said.

"Call me Zara." Zara turned from Summer to Faith and smiled. "You could always go upstairs and visit with your mother."

"That was low. Speaking of my dear mother, what the hell is she doing with a secret room she can't even squeeze her chubby self into? And why would anyone have to hide crates of infant formula?" Faith stood and walked over to the stacks of crates. "I might not be a professional spy or a SEAL, but I know the hallmark of a smuggler when I see it." Faith picked up the corner of a crate. "This infant formula is too light. Help me get this open."

Summer pulled the Leatherman from his pocket and slid a blade under a metal staple, digging into the wood. With a couple of twists, an end of the staple popped out. Within moments, he pried off the lid.

"I knew the orphanage was a front."

Faith studied the crate's contents. Black rubber was stretched over a round plastic case and fastened in place with a thin metal strip. Two knobs protruded outside the casing. A ring was attached to a pin inserted into the smaller knob.

Zara smiled. "Landmines. Problem solved, I take it."

"Yep." Summer picked up one of the mines and held it by its brown Bakelite case.

"An arms dealer," Faith said. "A Christian arms dealer. What a hypocrite. Can you tell where it's from? I've heard she's bringing in big sums of money and I wouldn't be surprised if she's shopping locally."

"I'll be darned." He turned it over and inspected the markings. "PMNs. Roosky. I haven't seen one of these puppies in years. This was the first mine I ever came across in the field."

"We have reports of some corrupt military selling them on the black market," Zara said.

"Even if she bought them here in Russia, what the heck is Mama Whitney doing with anti-personnel mines?" Summer said. "There are millions and millions of these little boogers in the world. They're cheap, easy to manufacture. If you want to get some of these to the West or to the Third World, you sure as heck don't have to go to the trouble of smuggling them out of the Soviet Union. Hell, the Russians give those things as door prizes to Third World guerilla movements that come begging to Moscow." He sat at the table and unscrewed the large knob on the side.

"She's probably not taking them out, so I'd say she's supporting an insurgency movement here," Zara said. "The Karabakh so-called self-defense army, maybe some groups in Chechnya, Dagestan. I'd also venture a guess they bring them in here through an underground tunnel behind that locked door. Given that this room is much warmer and damper than I'd expect, I'd say the tunnel is part of the hot-water system."

"Hot water system?" Summer said.

"Moscow uses a centralized system to pump hot water throughout the city," Zara said.

Faith looked at the reinforced steel door. "I totally forgot about it. In the summer they turn off the hot water for weeks at a time for entire sections of the city to clean the pipes. I remember freezing cold showers at Moscow State."

Summer removed the brown plastic knob, turned it and looked inside. He then rolled it across the tabletop to Faith. "Here's the detonator."

"Will it work as a blasting cap?"

"It could, but that would be the long way around, and we'd still have the problem of no time fuse or det cord. If I remember these suckers correctly, we can solve both problems and use the whole mine as a detonator and timer." He unscrewed the smaller knob and looked inside. "Just like I remembered. It's delay-armed. The mine's designed so that when you pull the pin, there's a fifteen to thirty minute delay until it's armed. That gives you some time to plant it and get away. That means you could actually step on it after pulling the pin but before it's armed and it won't go off."

Faith turned the knob as she inspected it. "I don't think we're going to get the chance to plant a field of landmines around the front door."

"It means we can trip the mine first by piling bricks or something on it, then pull the safety pin and it'll go off in fifteen to thirty minutes," Summer said.

Faith rolled the knob back across the table to Summer. "Give or take a few minutes?"

"The variation depends on the temp. If it's colder it'll take closer to thirty, warmer fifteen. You see, when you pull the pin, you release the striker, the spring-loaded firing pin. It presses against this steel wire, which eats through a lead strip. It takes a while to cut through it. When it does, the mine's armed and any pressure on the rubber plate on top will release the actuating plunger. Then the striker—"

"We understand. It blows up," Zara said, tapping her fingers on the table.

"There are a couple of steps before then, but you could sum it up like that."

"Then we do have the ability to set off the blast with adequate delay," Zara said.

"And I could cut the time in half by filing down the lead strip so the wire cuts through faster, say in seven to fifteen. Why don't I do that on a couple, just in case we decide to go that route?" Summer opened a blade on his Leatherman and whittled at the thin lead strip. "To finalize our inventory, the gun I took from your guard has a full magazine with eight rounds. What I wouldn't give for some night-vision equipment."

"I have at least fifty rounds of ammunition in the car and a second magazine. The magazine on the Makarov can be a bit tricky to remove. I suggest you practice, so you can reload quickly. I do have a small night-vision monocular and a small pair of regular binoculars in the glove compartment."

"That's convenient," Faith said.

"I keep them for night birding—owls."

"What kind of power are we talking about?" Summer said.

"I got them from a guy in the KGB Spetsnaz unit. They're not as good as what I have at home in Berlin, but they're our latest night-vision technology." Zara glanced at her watch. "We have to pick up our pace. The meeting is scheduled to begin in three hours. Unless someone knows of any additional resources, I propose we move on to the discussion of the target. The dacha's located on a stream in a birch forest about a half-hour north of the Moscow ring road. It takes another half-hour to get to the city limits from here, and that's without traffic."

"Any neighbors?" Summer said.

"They probably wouldn't be there this early in the season, not on a Sunday night. One is rather close, perhaps a hundred meters."

"What I wouldn't also give for some good overheads. We should get there as soon as we can and see if we can't borrow a dacha as a base. I'd like some time for recon."

"That was going to be my suggestion, but we're discussing the target now, not the plan," Zara said.

"You don't have to run this thing like it's some goddamn Communist Party meeting. We have to get a move on here," Summer said.

"But we do need structure to this operation, and I do believe you delegated that task to me after you took control."

"I don't know how you do it here in Russia, but when planning a mission, we Americans like the input of ideas."

"Give me a break, you two," Faith said. "This isn't the time for Soviet-American rivalry. Let's move on and tolerate each other's style differences." Faith understood the competition had far less to do with international than interpersonal politics.

"As I said, it's a two-story wooden dacha, no more than two hundred twenty-five square meters."

"So if my rough conversion is right, that's a bit over two thousand square feet. I take it we're not talking sixteen-inch support beams, but regular housing construction?"

"Standard Soviet housing construction, maybe fifty years old. Things were built much better under Stalin, but it's weathered, which says a lot with our winters."

"We have enough C-4 to give anyone inside a really bad day. We're going to need fifteen to twenty pounds of something to weigh down the mine. Do you know if there are any loose bricks around the house?"

"I've been at Stukoi's dacha perhaps three times in ten years, each time for mushroom hunts. There was always a lot of clutter, so I don't know what it's like now, but I'm certain you'll find something adequate." Zara forced a smile.

"We know anything about the meeting we're crashing?" Summer said.

"Not much, but it's going to be important for me to show up and get some kind of proof of the coup attempt. Without that, who's to believe why we blew up the place? I have a miniaturized camera and microphone I brought from Berlin that I can use to document it. We also need to find out how they're planning to get Gorbachev, since they didn't receive the C-4 delivery. We have to make sure that taking them out not only stops them from seizing power, but also saves the General Secretary."

"How many people? What kind of security?"

"With all due respect," Faith said, "we're going into the woods with a bunch of explosives, breaking into a cabin, spying on the neighbors and then winging it. I know you're both highly trained professionals used to teams with all kinds of high-tech gadgets, but you have to accept that you don't have your colleagues or your toys and, no matter how hard we try, we don't know jack about what we're really getting into until we get there." Faith stood and walked over to the crate of landmines. She reached inside and picked one up, surprised it was so light. "We've now entered the phase where my specialty pays off, and it's my turn to play leader. We're going to fan out and scavenge from these crates and that mess upstairs for anything we think might be remotely useful. We'll take turns on the shower. I thought I saw some gray coveralls in that pile of old clothes. Commander Summer, I suggest you turn your charms on my mother and see if you can get us some flashlights. A backpack would be really nice. You also better get her phone number and memorize it, just in case you make it out and we don't. I know your mission specs call for only a couple mines, but as the lead scavenger, I'm going to take a bunch, just in case. We might only need a couple, but you never know. Let's get a move on. The longer we've got on-site, the better the chance our half-assed plan might actually work."

A few minutes later, Faith scaled the ladder. The secret panel to the orphanage's basement lifted up just before Faith could push it open. She and her mother paused face-to-face and studied the changes in each other that the years of separation had carved. Faith caught a glimpse of something she hadn't seen or hadn't let herself see since she was a child. For a moment the woman before her wasn't a fundamentalist bigot, but a concerned mother, a mother worried about her child.

Faith looked away and slid back down the ladder to the hidden room. "Summer, I think you'd better go up first. You deal with her."

"You're a grown woman. Act like one. Get on up there."

Faith sighed. She climbed back up.

Mama Whitney held a plate of overstuffed sandwiches. "I don't know why on earth I was so tickled when you showed up. I nearly had to pinch myself to see if I was dreaming or if after all these years Jesus had finally forgiven me and brought my little girl back to me."

"Those two brought me here." Faith nodded down the trapdoor toward Summer and Zara. "If I'd known where they were taking me, we wouldn't be having this touching reunion."

"Child, I don't know whatever happened for the devil to cram so much hatred into you."

"My childhood pretty much covers it."

"Honey, I did the best I could in difficult times. Lord knows I've made mistakes. It sure wasn't easy raising a child alone back in those days, particularly with my Calling. When are you ever going to find it in your heart to forgive your mama?"

"That's a new angle. I didn't think your God had anything to do with forgiveness."

"I'll let that pass. I've been worried sick about you. A few weeks ago, a young lady who was the spitting image of you—not in looks, but in how she went around in the world—that dear soul was killed right in front of me and it started me rethinking a lot of things. Now I don't know what you're up to, but—"

"You dragged me all over creation acting like I was a ball and chain Jesus had strapped to your ankle to punish you for some unforgivable sin."

"I know you're caught up in something with with Yurij Kosyk. I don't know the whithers and wherefores, but I do know if he's involved, Lucifer himself isn't far behind. Either your life or your soul is in danger."

Faith stared agape. "How the hell do you know about Kosyk or Schmidt or whatever the SOB calls himself?"

Mama Whitney opened her mouth, then closed it. She moved her lips as if talking to herself, all the while shaking her head.

Zara climbed up the ladder behind Faith. "I'd love to let you two play this out in your own time, but we're on a tight schedule. Your mother met with General Kosyk in Berlin last week. And it was a rather protracted, personal meeting."

"With Kosyk? How personal?" Faith flashed a startled glance at Zara, then glared at her mother.

Mama Whitney looked away, but Faith saw the tears well up in her eyes.

"Mama, how could you—with *him*?"

"Honey, try to understand."

"You swore you'd never be with another man again after Daddy died."

Tears washed down her mother's face. "Lord, don't make me do this."

"Unless it's about Daddy, I don't want to know. I can't take any more of this today." Faith turned and rummaged through a box of clothes and held up a pair of coveralls. "Summer, I think these will fit you."

CHAPTER FORTY-EIGHT

EMBASSY OF THE GDR, MOSCOW
7:43 P.M.

Kosyk watched the second hand of his watch circle the dial. In a couple of hours, he would get even with Bogdanov. No one sets up Gregor Y. Kosyk. The bitch Bogdanov had manipulated events for him to take the fall for losing the Americans. The more he thought about it, the more it seemed she had known they were going to escape. She had probably even helped them. He would take care of Bogdanov soon enough.

Within twelve hours, the putsch would be in progress and the socialist world would be saved—only Kosyk didn't want the entire old order to be restored. The moribund GDR leadership had squelched his ambitions too many times, but not again, not this time. With a precisely timed phone call, he would set their plans in motion—a few hours prematurely. He picked up the heavy gray receiver and dialed the secure line to the head of the Ministry for State Security in Berlin.

"Mielke," the MfS chief answered.

"Your shopping list is complete, but your favorite shop closed earlier than expected. It reopens in the morning with new stock."

"You're absolutely certain it's closed?"

"Positively."

Mielke hung up on Gregor Kosyk for the last time.

Kosyk knew that Mielke was now relaying the news of Gorbachev's death to Honecker. Within hours, Honecker would order the air corridors to West Berlin sealed off. After the last West Berlin U-Bahn car crept under GDR territory around one the next morning, soldiers would open the long-sealed stations along the two routes crossing beneath their capital and soon afterward their soldiers would pour from West Berlin U-Bahn stations like rats fleeing the sewer. Kosyk wished he could witness the collapse of the Anti-Fascist Protection Wall as the GDR's military pushed into West Berlin. But even more than that, Kosyk wanted to see Honecker's and Mielke's faces when they realized they had no diversion of chaos in Moscow and no hope of Soviet backing. He wondered how long it would take for them to figure out they had unilaterally begun a war with the Americans.

CHAPTER FORTY-NINE

Whether you like it or not, history is on our side.
We will bury you.
—KHRUSHCHEV

NORTH OF MOSCOW
8:59 P.M.

On a dirt road a few kilometers from Stukoi's dacha, Faith steadied the flashlight while Zara and Summer reached into access panels in the Zil's trunk. Faith's thoughts were still with her mother. She knew it was childish to want her mother to be with no one but her father—even though he'd been gone for thirty years. She'd hardly admit it to herself and definitely not to Summer, but somewhere deep inside she believed that finding her father would make everything right with her family again. If only he'd been there when she was growing up to temper her mother's zeal. Now, when she was so close to finding him, her mother ruined everything by having an affair with another man—and not just any man: Kosyk, the Stasi general, the terrorist, the man who threatened to kill her. With a shudder of guilt, she hated her mother even more.

And then she wondered if Kosyk had forced her to sleep with him in exchange for information about her father.

Summer dropped a bulb into her hand. "Good thinking, Faith. We don't need brake lights to give us away." He gave her a single pat on the back, but she didn't like being one of the guys—not to Summer, not now.

Zara drove back onto the main dirt road and continued onward. In a few minutes, she slowed and turned off the headlights. Lights from the dacha flickered through the trees. They crept past it and into the neighboring driveway. The nearly full moon illuminated the rutted drive between the towering birches. Zara stopped the car in front of a collapsing shell of a burnt-out dacha.

"Great intel on our base camp," Summer said as he looked at the rubble. "Now I wish we would've gotten an earlier start."

Zara backed the car to conceal it as best as possible behind the cottage's remains. "I told you I haven't been here for a couple of years."

Summer smeared shoe polish on his face. "I don't like the moon phase one bit. It's far too bright for something like this. At least we found these dark coveralls."

Zara turned off the motor. "I'll go survey Stukoi's dacha and determine who's there."

"We agreed earlier that I'm in command of the op. I'll take the night scope and recon the area. You two wait here and be quiet. Comrade, you make sure Faith understands the importance of following orders."

Faith noticed Summer checking the Makarov magazine even though he had inspected it during the ride from the city. He had eight bullets and she hoped that was eight bullets too many and not too few.

The moonlight was too bright to risk dashing from tree to tree, so Summer crawled along the damp forest floor, picking up an unintended camouflage coating of mud, sticks and leaves. No one was walking patrol; security for the meeting didn't seem to be a priority. The closer he got to the dacha, the stronger the smell of burning wood. He paused to scan the area with the night scope. Expecting to see everything in shades of green, he was surprised to see tones of dark gray. Compared to the third-generation night-vision equipment he was accustomed to from the American military, the Red Army monocular was like looking through cheap sunglasses. What he wouldn't give for an infrared view of the target. At least the bright moonlight had an upside: It augmented the dated technology enough to help him make out three drivers leaning against one of a half-dozen parked cars. He'd have to get closer to be sure, but none seemed to be carrying visible firearms, though one clutched a bottle.

Drink up, buddy.

Summer moved close enough to see without the scope. Just then a car pulled into the drive and parked. He froze as he watched a short man with a goatee strut to the cabin. The man ignored the guards' greetings.

A woodpile was near an outbuilding some fifty feet behind the dacha and smoke curled above the wooden shack. No one seemed to be inside. The only voices in the still night air came from the dacha and the drivers. He sketched a precise mental map of the area and returned to the car.

Suddenly the car door opened, but before Faith could choke back an instinctive gasp, Zara's soft hand was across her mouth and Summer was scooting into the roomy backseat with them.

"Your comrades started a while ago without you. I heard a lot of laughing and some pretty bad singing, so I'd say they're a bit liquored up. They have to be nuts the eve of a coup, sitting in a cabin in the woods, drinking and singing about the Motherland."

"Welcome to Russia. Stalin used to hold all-night Politburo meetings at his dacha and made his greatest decisions inebriated. Do not underestimate us: We Russians are highly functional drunks."

"There was a building sort of like a smokehouse, but the smoke didn't smell like hickory," Summer said.

"The *banya* could be a problem," Zara said. "Someone might be getting ready to use it."

Summer knit his brow and made eye contact with Faith.

Faith whispered, "A Russian sauna where they steam themselves, beat each other with birch branches, then roll in the snow."

"Now that's a pretty picture."

"How many are we up against?" Zara said.

"I counted three guards. A stocky man marched in while I was—"

Faith interrupted. "What did he look like?"

"Stout, late-fifties, goatee—"

"Kosyk," the two women said simultaneously.

Faith continued, "Great. We're about to blow up the one person who knows about my father."

"I know the man well and we're doing the world a favor. There are other ways to find out what you need," Zara said.

"I thought all the documents are sealed," Faith said.

"Don't you think your mother knows?" Zara said.

Silence.

"Faith, hand me that paper and pencil so I can rough out a diagram of what we're looking at." Summer crawled under the blanket with a flashlight like a child reading under the bedcovers. A minute later he stuck his head out from under the blanket and whispered, "Okay, you two are going to have to join me under here for the briefing. I want you to see my map and I don't want any light leaking out and giving us away."

They gathered under the musty blanket and Summer spoke. "Three guys in some kind of military uniforms are standing here drinking. No visible weapons." He ran his finger along the crumpled paper, leaving a dusting of dried mud. "Two cars had antenna arrays. This last one blocked everybody in and this one here, too."

"A few generals in there. We have to take out the communications." Zara put her arm around Faith's lower back to steady herself in the awkward huddle. At first Faith pushed a little closer to her, but then shifted away.

"Noted. There was no sign of phone lines going into the house, only electricity."

"I thought Stukoi would have more pull than that," Zara said.

"The last two cars completely block in all of the others. The trees are too tight on each side for anyone to drive around them. Faith, you're going to take the mines and place them behind the back *tars* of the last two cars." His Ozark accent began to slip through even more strongly as Summer focused on the mission. "When they start to leave or chase after us if we slip up, they'll trigger the mines and the wrecks will pin in the rest of them. Comrade, any chance the cars are armored?"

"Only Gorbachev, Shevardnadze and a couple of others have them. Not these guys."

"Good. There's an entrance under the house here on the side facing us. I'll slip under there and set up the mine. There are a bunch of bricks laying around the foundation that I'll use to trigger it. They'll add a nice little anti-personnel aspect to the explosion. Now timing is going to be critical. Comrade, how long do you need to get what we're after inside?"

"They've been drinking, so it shouldn't be hard to get them talking. I have a long history of short appearances at social functions with Stukoi. Give me half an hour plus five minutes' margin."

"Remember, you can't let yourself get delayed. I'll set the mine for the cars nearest the guards, but Faith will do the two back ones later because I don't want someone leaving too early before the big show and setting them off prematurely. Comrade, move your car to the main road. Faith and I will meet up back here; then we'll catch up with you at the car." Summer turned off the flashlight and threw the blanket back. He dipped two fingers into the shoe polish and smeared it on Faith's cheek. "Sorry. I know how much you hate this."

"I'm developing an immunity to grime."

"Everyone understand what we're doing? Any last questions? Let's get our gear and be on our way."

"Whoa," Faith said. "What if something goes wrong?"

"Improvise and be glad your mama is on her knees for us." Summer snapped the lid on the polish and dropped it onto the floorboard. He opened the car door and hunched down behind it. Faith and Zara followed him.

Zara opened the trunk and handed Faith one of the rucksacks her mother had loaned them. "I never intended to bring you into anything like this. I'm so sorry."

Summer grabbed the pack stuffed with C-4 and two landmines and slung it over his shoulder. "It's now nine forty-three. Comrade, I'll give you a couple of minutes to park the car and talk to the guards. Be out of there by ten twenty-five at the absolute latest. I'll pull the pin then, and it'll go off within seven to fifteen minutes, give or take—and I can't emphasize enough how inexact this is. I did my best to whittle away half of the lead strip, but who knows exactly how long the mines will take to arm."

"Understood."

"I trust you have your little tape recorder and spy camera ready?" Summer said.

"Don't worry. We'll have our evidence. You're more likely than I am to run into a firefight, so you take the extra magazine," Zara whispered as she slid into the driver's seat.

"Thanks. One more thing," Summer said, crouching beside the car. "Make sure you leave the car unlocked and the keys under the driver's floor mat. Not that we plan on going anywhere without you, but just in case your timing's off." He winked at Zara.

Summer took Faith's hand as Zara drove away. "You doing okay, Faith? You up to this?"

"Wouldn't miss it for the world. It's been a long time since I've seen your fireworks." She looked at him from the corner of her eye and smiled.

They sat down on the ground behind the burnt-out dacha and waited. Summer didn't take his eyes off his watch. "So what do you think Mama Whitney was doing with that Stasi general?"

"I'm still trying to figure it out. It doesn't add up. Ever since I found out Daddy's alive, I've assumed he was captive in the Soviet Union, but it could be he's in Germany. I was thinking maybe Mama was forced to sleep with Kosyk as part of a deal to get Daddy released from an East German prison, maybe even Bautzen."

"I can't remember the last time I heard you empathize with your mother. At least some good's coming out of all of this." He nodded and looked up from his watch. "It's time. Stay put. I'll be back in five." He kissed her on the top of the head and disappeared into the darkness.

As the cool moisture seeped through her coveralls and underwear, she knew she had to summon the same fortitude as Summer, but she also knew him well enough to sense it wasn't real. He was scared and that unnerved her.

Her watch's minute hand had hardly moved since Summer left, though it felt like he had been gone too long. She pressed her eyes shut and strained to listen for Zara's voice, but only heard the laughter from the dacha and owl screeches from the woods. A breeze picked up and she opened her eyes. Nine fifty-two. *Where the hell is he?*

Summer suddenly slipped beside her. "Ready, honey?"

"You're not going to need the night-vision thing are you? Can you at least leave it with me? I'll go crazy here if I have to wait for you even longer next time. At least with it I could be a lookout for you after I'm done with my minefield."

"You might as well take it because it's not going to do me any good under the house. Just keep low." He unzipped a pocket, handed her the monocular and then looked into her eyes. "Faith, you know I love you, don't you?" He picked up the backpack and held open the strap for her.

Faith turned her back to him, put on the pack and paused. She swirled around and kissed him on the lips, smearing the shoe polish between their faces. She pulled away from him, unsure whether she dared tamper with the past, particularly at a time when it was being rewritten. "Be careful. I don't want anything happening to you."

"Same here. Remember to keep low and watch the time." He kissed her on the cheek and crept away toward the dacha.

CHAPTER FIFTY

In Germany you can't have a revolution because you would have to step on the lawns.

—STALIN

GENERAL STUKOI'S DACHA
A FEW MINUTES EARLIER, 9:28 P.M.

Even as Kosyk walked up the driveway of the dacha, he could hear drunken laughter. Tonight they should be reviewing plans and contingencies, checking and rechecking all that was so meticulously prepared, but he knew the drunkards hadn't even agreed yet which of them was going to run the country. He went inside. As expected, the Russians were swilling vodka and gorging themselves on caviar. Even Titov's protégé from the Berlin residency, Resnick, was sauced.

"Sit, sit." Stukoi poured Kosyk a glass and stuck it in his hand. "Drink with us."

"Tomorrow night, when we have something to celebrate." Kosyk shook his head and pushed the glass back to Stukoi, but he wouldn't take it.

"Tonight we have something to celebrate. We're on the eve of the future." Stukoi gulped vodka.

"I came to work, not to make merry. Is everything in place for tomorrow? Have you found FedEx and Otter?"

"Tomorrow will take care of itself. Enjoy yourself with your comrades tonight." Stukoi slapped him on the back, jarring him enough to splash his drink all over him.

"We have a problem with Honecker," Kosyk said, ignoring the indignation of the alcohol soaking into his clothes. "I just found out he's making a move on West Berlin tonight. I tried to talk them out of it, get them to delay until after the putsch."

General Zolotov waved his hand dismissively. "Let the Germans do whatever they do tonight. We clean up after them in the morning. You know what Stalin thought of you Germans."

"You can still stop him from blundering into war."

"You've done your duty. We'll remember it." Stukoi patted him on the back.

"You have to stop them tonight." Kosyk lit a cigarette. "Honecker can no longer be trusted."

"General Kosyk," Zolotov said, slurring his words. "We heard you. You're like a schoolboy tattling on your friends. I hated boys like you."

CHAPTER FIFTY-ONE

9:49 P.M.

Zara flicked on the tape recorder hidden in a brooch, fingered the miniature camera concealed as a cigarette packet and then turned the doorknob, but the door was stuck, swollen from the humidity of recent showers. She butted it open with her shoulder and caught herself before she stumbled into the room. Half-empty bottles were scattered on every surface and a smoky blue haze clouded the dozen men, most of whose faces she recognized; the KGB was well represented. She had expected the Soviet Army generals, but was surprised by the GRU's presence. She was more taken aback by the satisfied smile on Kosyk's face when he saw her. She recognized the sated look of revenge.

"Zara Antonovna," General Stukoi spoke with uncharacteristic familiarity. "Finally you join us."

"*Tovarishch* Bogdanov," General Zolotov said. "So you are the girl we have to thank for the restoration of order to our world. You make your father proud. You should have brought Anton Antonovich along. Someone get her a glass so we can drink to her."

"I can't take the glory. General Stukoi was the one who brought all of you together. And our German colleagues—"

"Our German comrades failed. Stukoi tells us they didn't deliver the American explosives and thanks to them we have to hunt down the smuggler and the commando," a KGB colonel said.

"As I explained," Kosyk said, "I was not the one who lost them." The irritation in Kosyk's voice was stronger than the smell of alcohol in the room, but his perfectly enunciated Russian gave no hint of intoxication.

Stukoi handed Bogdanov a used shot glass and poured vodka into it and onto the floor. "Tomorrow we find the Americans, but before that, we enjoy the May Day. The parade will be glorious and without the explosives we have no risk of damage to Lenin's tomb or any questions of why we weren't there with Gorbachev when the explosion occurred. A bullet's cleaner. It's better this way."

Zara took the glass. "So who has the honor in the morning of giving the sniper the final go-ahead?"

"Finished already," Stukoi said. "Everything is in motion. Zolotov can signal to abort if we need to, but that's not going to be necessary."

"A toast." General Zolotov raised his glass. "To Comrade Bogdanov, who helped bring the spark of revolution from Germany. Tomorrow, we Bolsheviks will once again rid the Motherland of the imperialists."

The toast dragged on in true Russian style, but Zara ignored it. Her disciplined mind forced herself to concentrate on the strategic situation. They were too late to save Gorbachev by only eliminating the conspirators. They would deal with the sniper in due course. She reviewed various contingencies and planned her responses. She kept coming back to Faith; the woman was a brilliant smuggler, but had no paramilitary training. If the guards discovered her, Stukoi and Kosyk would instantly understand that Bogdanov had helped the Americans, and her only option then would be to take out as many as she could with her eight rounds. Kosyk she would shoot first. He was sober, probably armed and he deserved it.

"To Comrade Bogdanov," everyone in the room repeated and downed the vodka.

Faith didn't see any point in writhing through the mud any longer than she had to, so she darted to a tree on the other side of the burnt-out dacha. From there she could see lights and the outlines of cars. She pulled out the night scope, but saw less than with her naked eyes. She dashed from tree to tree down the driveway of the abandoned cottage. When she had gone far enough, she lowered herself to the ground and crawled on all fours toward the target. She winced at the crackle of each leaf, sure it would give her away. The sound of the drivers unnerved her. When she was close enough to distinguish voices, she lowered herself to the ground. The coveralls were a wick for moisture and dampness touched her belly.

She heard a rustle in the leaves. She plastered herself as flat against the ground as she could. Footsteps came closer. If they found her now, it was over. They'd get Summer. Her fingers fanned out, searching for a rock. Her hands pressed into the soft mud, squeezing it under her fingernails. She struck a rock, but it was barely bigger than a crabapple. She clutched it, ready to do whatever it took. Leaves crunched beside her.

A deer emerged from the forest. She exhaled, startling the creature. It bounded into the night.

Her nerves tested, she inched onward until she came to a narrow clearing—the empty drive. She had overshot. She retreated a few yards back into the woods and paralleled the path until she spotted the last car. She crawled behind it and slipped off the backpack. The car blocked the moonlight, forcing her to work in the darkness. She ran her fingers along the top of the mine, making sure the rubber top faced upward, and then she lodged it behind the right tire, taking care not to place pressure on the rubber. She held her breath and yanked out the metal pin.

Moonlight seeped through the cracks between the decaying boards along the foundation of the house. The light was barely enough to help Summer navigate the lifetime accumulation of junk under the house. He plowed through broken sawhorses, scrap lumber and boxsprings as he cleared a path to the center of the structure. He set down the backpack with the explosives and crawled back to the opening, grabbing a dented metal bucket along the way. Like a wolf guarding its den, he emerged from the entrance on all fours.

Bricks were piled beside the house, awaiting some unfinished project. Tonight their wait was over. Summer placed them into the bucket, careful not to make any sound. He estimated he had a good twenty-five pounds' worth, giving him plenty of leeway.

On his way back under the house, he spotted a small propane tank. It was the perfect height to make a platform for the mine and it would add some punch to the blast. As he ferried the bricks to ground zero, he reminded himself he already had enough C-4 to turn the house into splinters.

As an EOD guy, he'd spent most of his career disarming explosives; the opportunity to blow up such a good target had come up far too seldom. He glanced at his watch and calculated he had ample time for temptation—if he worked fast.

He returned for the propane tank, pleased with how the job was shaping up and not admitting to himself the real reason he wanted it: If something went wrong, he'd shoot into the tank to detonate the charge instantly—even though he'd be too close.

He set the tank on the ground under the center of the building and rocked it to make sure it was on solid footing. On top of it he placed a wide board on which he positioned the mine. He unscrewed the detonator plug, just in case he had carved away too much from the lead delay strip and the mine armed instantly. Molding the C-4 around the mine, he left openings so he could pull the safety pin and screw back the detonator. He checked the time—twenty-two fifteen—and sat down and waited, gun in hand in case he had to do the unthinkable.

Zara excused herself to the kitchen in search of *zakuski* to munch on. She sensed Kosyk getting up as she walked by him.

He stalked her. "They told me the meeting didn't start until ten, but they were drunk off their asses when I got here."

"They told me nine."

"This is no way to prepare for a putsch. We should be reviewing contingencies, making certain we haven't overlooked anything."

"They don't make hard-liners like they used to," Zara said with a smile. "So, have we overlooked anything?"

"That's not the point. Typical Russian *Schlamperei*." Kosyk took out a cigarette and rolled it between his fingers. Tobacco fell from the ends. "And now we have to go with a sniper because you lost the C-4 I sent you."

"I lost nothing. It was never received, but it doesn't matter now. I've been visiting my father all afternoon and evening and I'm not up on the latest. Who won out on the sniper's position? Stukoi or Zolotov?" Zara fished for plan details as she pulled the top off a caviar tin. She spooned it into a dish.

"I'm not following their petty politics. The sniper's going to be on the top floor of GUM. It's a clean shot from the department store to the mausoleum. But that's tomorrow. Berlin worries me right now. I warned them, but the fools are too drunk to give a damn. Honecker's starting a war with the Americans as we speak."

"Have you been drinking, too?" Zara set down the spoon and pushed away the caviar. "What are you talking about?"

"I informed Mielke tonight everything's in place. The putsch is going down in the morning while Gorbachev reviews the May Day parade. It seems Honecker doesn't trust that the new Soviet leaders will give them what he really wants—West Berlin. He's sealing off the city tonight and annexing it. Before anyone realizes what's happening, the *Nationale Volksarmee* will liquidate the police, sever communications and seize government buildings. By morning the National People's Army will be sitting on the Americans' doorstep, daring them to start the next world war."

"That's insane. They know the Americans will defend the city."

"Reagan would've, but he's been gone for months. Honecker's counting on the confusion in Moscow to slow down their response. The Americans aren't going to want to start a war over Berlin with an unknown Soviet government—particularly if it wasn't involved in the action. The American finger isn't on the trigger anymore. They'll hesitate, debate. They'll be too late, maybe."

"It's the maybe that worries me. The Americans will fight for Berlin. That policy's never wavered. I can't believe no one in there would listen to you and stop it. The GRU could warn the Soviet Army units in Germany to stop them. Hell, any of them could get word through to the right people," Bogdanov said.

"Exactly. I thought they would do that immediately. They could clean house with Honecker tomorrow. A fitting epilogue. But you know what they said to me?"

"Cleaning house with Honecker—that's what it's all about for you, isn't it? They take out Honecker and his cronies, and you're the loyal German who dutifully reported their insubordination to your Soviet masters. You're putting yourself in line to run the GDR, aren't you?"

"I hadn't really thought about it."

"My ass. So is this about liberating your repressed Sorbian brothers, or is it just a power trip for you?"

"There are too many nationalists in this world. The Sorbs are respected, treated well in the GDR. They have money for their organizations, their little books and theaters."

"And so well treated that's why you haven't made it to the Central Committee?"

Kosyk reached into his sport coat. Just then Stukoi and Zolotov stumbled into the kitchen. Several others followed them.

"Come join us, little lady," Zolotov said. "We go to the *banya*."

He put his arm around Zara, puckered his puffy lips and lunged for her. She dodged. He toppled forward, grabbed at her and ripped the brooch from her jacket. It skidded across the floor. In an instant she grabbed his arm as if breaking his fall and bent his thumb backwards, but wasn't sure if he could feel any pain through the alcohol. "Watch your step. You could really get yourself hurt." She shoved him along and then reached down for the brooch.

But Kosyk already held it.

He flipped it over and handed it to her with a rare smile. "Please."

She thanked him and then turned to Stukoi, hoping she could use him to get away from Kosyk while keeping them above the explosion. "Why don't you wait to go to the *banya* until after I leave?"

"We added wood to the fire long ago. It should be perfect now. Come join us," Stukoi said.

"I don't think it's a good idea. I need to be going soon. My father isn't feeling too well and I get so little opportunity to see him."

The men wobbled out the back door.

Zara glanced at her watch. Explosion in ten minutes—plus or minus. She had to get out. And she had to do something about the men in the *banya*. "General Kosyk, it's been interesting as usual, but I have to excuse myself."

"You cannot go yet." He reached into his tweed sport coat and pulled out a gun.

It seemed like it had taken hours, but in less than twenty minutes Faith had crept to the cars, laid her landmines and returned to the burnt-out dacha to wait. She sat down in the familiar spot. The seconds dragged. *What was happening?* She knew it was too early for Summer to return, but she couldn't stand not knowing. She twisted a twig between her fingers until it snapped. There was no reason she couldn't wait on Summer closer to the dacha. With the night scope she could watch the entrance under the house and could be back at the rendezvous spot before him.

Still wearing the backpack with three leftover mines, she crawled toward the dacha. She perched behind a bush on a small rise from which she could view the entire area. She looked through the night-vision scope, but the resolution wasn't enough to make out much. Time slowed to a standstill. She waited, staring at the unchanging scene. The breeze shifted directions and she smelled smoke. Nothing was coming from the chimney of the dacha, but smoke curled from the *banya*.

Ten twenty-two—only three more minutes until he pulls the pin.

She raised the monocular to her right eye to watch for Summer. He should be pulling the pin and coming back within a minute. Then she saw movement. Four men staggered out the back door of the dacha. *Oh, shit.*

Faith shoved the scope back into her pocket, zipping it shut. She crawled on her belly toward the dacha, forcing herself to watch the obese men undress. Slowly they stripped off their suit jackets, dress shirts and trousers. One shoved his clothes at a peg on the side of the sauna, but they crumpled onto the ground. The men stumbled inside.

As soon as the last one shut the door, Faith crawled through a flowerbed and under the house.

It was time. Summer steadied the landmine with his right hand and pulled the pin. The metal striker whizzed out of the detonator plug hole, the tiny steel missile zooming through the air. Summer jumped back, sure he'd filled his pants. *Crap. Must've cut too far through the delay strip.*

Now the mine was useless.

He raced through the dark obstacle course of junk toward Faith and the extra mines.

Kosyk pointed the gun at the center of Zara's chest. His left eye twitched. "I assume you have an arsenal strapped to your body. Set them on the counter one at a time. You know the routine, any fast moves, any noise—"

She removed the Makarov semiautomatic from her ankle holster, holding the butt with two fingers. She spread her feet apart and held out her arms for a search.

He picked up her gun and stuck it in the back of his trousers. He patted her down with his left hand while the gun in his right pressed against her throat. He stopped at her pockets, removed the cigarette-pack camera and dropped it into his sport-coat pocket. "Marlboro. You won't need these."

Zara didn't want to call his attention to her concern with the time, so she didn't look at her own watch, but stole a glance at his. She knew that under her feet a spring-loaded metal pin was pushing against a steel wire, wearing away a thin lead strip between her and death. She guessed she had less than four minutes.

"You know, it never did make sense to me why you were the one who approached us with plans for the coup. Mielke has a close relationship with over half the KGB generals and considers the other half blood brothers. He knew exactly whom to trust and who hated Gorbachev. He even came to us directly a couple of years ago with a proposal we oust Honecker. If Honecker and Mielke decided to knock off Gorbachev—Mielke would've come straight to us."

"A rogue general is deniable—Mielke's not. I couldn't get the fools to understand that eliminating Gorbachev alone wasn't enough. They had to find a way to control the successor."

"You can't tell me Mielke didn't grasp that."

"He believed Gorbachev's support was weak and fractured. He had faith in his generation of Chekists and Soviet Army commanders and believed they'd seize power, maybe not immediately, but as soon as they thought the imperialists were behind the assassination. Mielke's getting old and losing his edge—they all are."

"Sad, in a way. He was probably the most ruthless, cunning bastard I ever met—present company excluded, of course."

"Of course." Kosyk smiled again.

"You know it makes no sense they'd make a play for West Berlin on the eve of a coup when there's the danger of Gorbachev getting involved, possibly changing his plans for the morning. Even if they're bold enough to invade the city on their own, they wouldn't do it before the chaos ensued in Moscow. I'm betting you set them up by signaling them that the murder had already happened. They're probably sitting in Berlin right now, listening to Radio Moscow, wondering why it isn't playing a dirge like it usually does in the interim between the death of a Kremlin leader and the official announcement." Zara knew the lead strip had become a little thinner. "You expected your Russian friends in there to contact their colleagues in Germany and stop Honecker, didn't you? You thought that would be enough for them to boot out Honecker and the whole bunch. After proving your loyalties to the new Soviet leaders, you'd be in line for a major role in the post-coup order, definitely Politburo, maybe chief of the MfS and quite likely the First Secretary." *Where was the explosion?*

"You flatter me." Kosyk's eye jerked to the left. "And you possess such an excellent grasp of politics; it is a shame to kill you."

Faith lunged through the hole under the house. The top of her head smacked into something hard, stunning her. She heard a muted grunt. Fingers reached around her throat.

"Summer." She choked.

"Jesus, Faith. You scared the shit out of me. I need another mine *now*. No time to explain."

"Four of them," Faith said, gasping for air, "just went into the sauna in the back."

"Shit. We've got another problem." He took the mine from her. "How many mines do you have left?"

"Just these two."

"Here's what we're going to do. I'm going to give you a couple pounds of C to pack around the mine. On your way out of here, you're going to find an old pile of bricks to your right. Shove half a dozen bricks into your backpack and book it to the steam house. Screw off the detonator plug and set it aside for a minute. That's the big one here." He took her hand and placed her fingers on a round knob. "Memorize how this feels and how it's different than the other one." He moved her cold fingers to the opposite side. "Next, you're going to mold the C around the mine, leaving holes for the plugs so you can pull the pin. Just smash it around. Doesn't have to be pretty. Now you're gonna pull the pin. Stay clear of the det plug hole just in case the little metal thingy comes flying out like it did on me. Screw the plug back into the mine, then stack the bricks on it and get the hell out of there. I'll meet you at the burnt-out building. Think you can do it, honey?"

"Yes, sir."

"Stay right here while I get you a slab of C." Summer retrieved some plastic explosive and handed it to Faith. "Now repeat what you're going to do."

Faith summarized his instructions, her speech fast and clipped from adrenaline.

"Good. Now one more thing. We have to coordinate so they go off as close to the same time as possible. Think you can do it in four minutes?"

"I can do it in three."

"It's twenty-two twenty-eight—uh, ten twenty-eight. Pull the pin at ten thirty-one."

"Summer, can't we speed up things by pulling both pins right now? They won't arm for a while and there's plenty of time to set them up."

"We could do that, but it might arm too fast and blow you up when you put the bricks on it. Get moving. Pull the pin when I told you."

"Summer, I'm in enough danger as it is." Faith screwed off the detonator plug and stuck it in her pocket. "A little more won't matter and we'll know if this one is another dud."

She pulled the pin.

"Better get yours out now before I get too much of a head start on you. See you at the ranch," Faith said. She squeezed out the entrance, took a quick right and shoved the bricks into her backpack, adding an extra one for good measure. She crawled into the woods. The bricks were much heavier than the light plastic landmines, but they didn't slow her down. She scooted to the back of the *banya* and dragged herself a few feet under the structure, leaving her legs protruding. She pulled the mine from the front pouch of the backpack, the steel wire now cutting through the lead delay strip. The sound of switches smacking against flesh came from inside the *banya*. She smashed the C around the mine and screwed on the detonator cap. She took a deep breath and she picked up a brick.

Dear God, please don't go off.

She lowered the brick onto the mine's rubber plate.

Kosyk shifted his aim from Zara's chest to her head. She listened for the charge. *Any second now.*

"Time we go for a little walk. As soon as you open the door, clasp your hands behind your neck. You're a professional, so I won't insult you with a reminder of all the things you can do to hasten your death."

Zara pushed open the door and considered slamming it back on him, but the rotting wooden frame was too flimsy. She walked down the steps with her hands behind her head, prepared to throw her body to the ground the second she heard the charge.

"Straight ahead. Past the *banya* to the riverbank."

If she could get a survivable distance from the explosion, she would have the element of surprise. She could overpower him, eliminate him and then deal with the splinter group in the *banya*. She listened for the pop of the charge, but only heard the sloshing of her feet in the mud and the voices from the *banya*.

She passed the *banya*. The moonlight glistened off the river less than fifty meters away. Constantly scanning the area for an opportunity, she spotted something. Legs stuck out from under the structure.

The commander?

Kosyk? Faith raised her head up and bumped it against the floor of the *banya*. She saw Zara walking at gunpoint. Summer was too far away to help, so she picked up the extra brick she'd stacked on the mine and wiggled out from under the building. She slithered along the ground toward the riverbank, pausing behind a bush to check her bearings and listen.

"So, you worked with the American even after you said you had no contact with her. Was she CIA? Are you doubling for the CIA and gathering tapes of conversations to use against me after I'm First Secretary?" Kosyk said.

"Your ambitions cloud your judgment. I'm not a traitor like you. I'm loyal to my country, my leader—and my family. You're not going to succeed. Gorbachev was alerted and Spetsnaz commandos are moving in any minute."

"I expected more from you. On your knees. Now."

"So you're going to make me suck your little cock first, you asshole?"

Kosyk shoved her down.

The brick cut into Faith's hand as she clutched it as tightly as she could. *Too far away.* With each crunch of a leaf, another drop of blood drained from her light head.

Kosyk prodded Zara with the butt of the gun. "Who are you working for? Why were you taping tonight's meeting?"

"Stukoi. He doesn't trust you. I think his exact words were 'double-crossing little prick.' He wanted me to gather the proof you were playing us off against the GDR leadership."

Only twenty feet. Faith moved closer. Then she heard the hammer click. Faith pulled her arm back, but stopped herself. *Too damn far. Keep him talking.*

"Explain one thing I couldn't figure out," Zara said. "Why did you attempt to recruit Faith at the MfS cabaret in front of all your colleagues? If you were going to succeed in pinning the blame on the Americans, MfS fingerprints couldn't be left anywhere. You're too good for such a blunder."

"What's the point of being the architect behind the most brilliant operation in intelligence history if no one even suspects it was your work?"

Faith steadied herself with the trunk of a birch as her foot sank into the mud of the riverbank ten feet from Kosyk. She looked at Zara and knew he was about to kill her, so she grasped the brick with both hands and held it over her head. She focused on the base of his skull and lunged forward, but slipped and only grazed the side of his head.

Kosyk spun around and fired at the same instant Zara lunged, spoiling his aim. Still, he kept the gun pointed at Faith. He smiled coldly. "Drop it." Kosyk motioned with the gun and spoke to Zara. "Over there, beside her."

Zara kept her hands visible as she inched toward Faith.

Faith turned to Zara for her lead, but glimpsed fear in her eyes. Faith knew it was over—at least for one of them, and Faith was the one facing the barrel of the gun. She trembled and the blood rushed from her head. She couldn't pass out now, not when she was so close to the truth. She forced a deep breath. Mustering all her self-control, she looked Kosyk in the eyes and said, "I know you're going to kill me. At least tell me what happened to my father. Where is he? What did you do to him?"

"You really don't know, do you?" He smirked and turned toward Zara. "You've figured it out, haven't you, Bogdanov?"

Faith jerked her head around toward Zara and then slowly turned back to him.

Kosyk spoke. "It was impossible for your father to stay with your mother. He always told her, 'We had no chance, but we—' "

" 'But we made ourselves one.' " A chill ran through her body as Faith recited the lines she had studied so often for comfort, for clues. She could see her father's bold strokes in his old-fashioned German handwriting. "How the hell do you know those words? They're from the only thing I've ever had that was written by my father." She searched his face for answers and she found them—in his wide cheekbones, in his high forehead and in the familiar way he cocked his head a little to the left. "You?"

"I offered you the opportunity to learn from me. You rejected it." His eye twitched.

"What did you do to my mother? Blackmail her? Rape her?"

"You were a love child. I was assigned an undercover mission to penetrate an imperialist front organization in Berlin-West that was a CIA springboard for subversive activities in the republic. My orders were to position myself as close as I could to the ringleader. I couldn't have gotten much closer." He laughed.

"You deceived her and used her."

"Never. I never used Maggie." He raised his voice. "I was always fond of Maggie, but she was a missionary and I was a career officer in the Ministry for State Security. Our love could never be."

"You can murder your own child in cold blood?"

"With regret. I'd planned on letting the Russians take care of you, but their usual sloppiness leaves me with little choice. Understand that tomorrow I'll be leader of communist Germany and I can't afford a capitalist bastard—no matter how lovely she is." He reached forward and stroked Faith's hair. "Before you die, forgive your mother. A Bible smuggler couldn't have the child of a godless communist any more than an MfS general could claim an American daughter. What happened wasn't Maggie's fault. You were a child of the Cold War." He paused. The moonlight caught his eyes and glistened on the tears that welled up inside them. "Join me."

"I can't." Faith choked on the words.

"Then turn around. Both of you. Now!"

"No. If you're going to murder your own daughter, you'll have to do it while looking me in the eye."

He paused for a few seconds as he studied her eyes and then he pulled back the hammer of the gun.

A white flash lit up the night and a fireball consumed the dacha. The concussion shook the ground. Kosyk jerked his head around in time for the second blast. At that moment Zara struck his arm, knocking the pistol to the ground. They scrambled for the weapon as flaming debris rained down around them. He grabbed the gun. Zara held on to his arm, struggling to keep him from pointing it at her, but he was stronger.

For the first time in her life, Faith wished her father dead. He was no longer the hero she imagined, but a scoundrel, a terrorist mastermind, a Stasi controller willing to sacrifice his own daughter to politics. He had betrayed her fantasy. He had betrayed her mother. He had betrayed her. Just as Kosyk started to pull the trigger, Faith smashed the brick into his skull.

Faith cradled the bloody brick while Zara fussed with the body. She had his nose, narrow, turned up a little at the end. The eyes definitely weren't hers, set back and with dark baggy circles under them.

Zara took the brick from her hands and tossed it into the river. Rings of ripples floated like ghosts across the still water. Faith watched them hit the bank and return in wave after wave to the center, crossing through one another over and over again until they were no more.

"He's unconscious but not dead, if you need to say something to him for your own sake. Brain hemorrhages can take a while, and they're not always fatal."

Faith dropped to her knees, clutched her father and sobbed. "We had no chance."

Where the hell is Faith? Summer looked at his watch for the hundredth time, although he had an excellent internal chronometer and was keenly aware of exactly how much time had elapsed. He'd listened as the shouts in Russian faded into moans, but didn't hear her. He should have gone to the car, but he couldn't leave her. He'd never forgive himself if something happened to her. Then he heard a rustle in the woods below his position, coming up from the river. He slid behind the burnt-out structure and waited for the target to emerge. *Please be her.*

Two figures stumbled through the woods, not even trying to conceal themselves. He aimed around the corner of the building. Flames lit up the night and he could make out the comrade leading Faith toward him. She stumbled as if injured. He rushed to her. "Where's she hurt?"

"She found her father."

Summer mouthed, "Kosyk?"

Zara nodded. "We have to get out of here. The drivers."

Summer stuck the gun in his pocket and picked Faith up, hoisting her over his shoulder. He was relived to feel her body against his and didn't want to ever let go.

They ran down the driveway toward the car. Three-quarters of the way down the path, a gun fired and they dropped to the ground.

"Get her to the car. I'll draw their fire and cover you," Zara said.

"Careful, comrade." Summer carried Faith toward the road.

"Go!" Zara crouched behind a tree, reached around and fired off two shots. The drivers returned fire. She hit the ground and crawled to the next tree. She looked around and could make out three figures in the shifting flames. One was headed into the woods to outflank her, so she fired at him and then saw him drop. She shot at the others and sprinted several meters, unloading her Makarov as she ran. She dived onto the ground. Automatic-weapons fire erupted. She slinked along the ground as quickly as she could with at least fifty meters until the road. Bullets sprayed a nearby tree, turning bark into pulp.

A gun resounded from the woods near the road. *The commander.* Someone screamed and the weapons fire stopped. She stood and ran toward the road. Like lightning branching across a night sky, pain suddenly radiated through her right arm, and then she heard the whizzing sound of the shot catch up with her. She spun around and emptied the magazine in the direction of the fire until a man let out an involuntary yelp of pain. Zara held her arm and ran, arriving at the Zil at the same time as Summer.

Automatic gunfire punctuated the night as she jumped into the passenger seat. "You drive. I'm hit."

Summer hit the gas. The tires spun, stuck in the soft mud. The engine roared, but it wasn't loud enough to hide the sound of the nearing Kalashnikov.

CHAPTER FIFTY-TWO

BERLIN AIR CORRIDOR
10:14 P.M. (12:14 A.M. MOSCOW TIME)

The 727 descended to nine thousand feet for the final crossing over East Germany to West Berlin. The day of milk hauls between West Berlin and West Germany had been long and uneventful, save for a bird strike in the late afternoon that threw them off schedule by nearly an hour. Frosty yawned as he scanned his console, all instruments reading within normal parameters. He knew his days were numbered as a Pan Am flight engineer. Flight engineers were slowly going extinct, thanks to declining profit margins and the genius of Boeing and Airbus designers. Modern jetliners had automated so many of the calculations that were the bread and butter of the flight engineer that even the latest models of the complex 747 had forgone their need. Sure, he was a pilot and could always become a first officer, but he was happiest as an engineer.

He patted the side of the engineer's station of the aging 727. *The old girl is built like a brick shithouse.* The boys at Boeing had so overengineered the '27 that he was sure she'd share the same fate as the DC-3. With occasional engine replacements, she'd be demoted from First World passenger service to hauling cargo around the Third World for a good half-century beyond her expected lifespan. The new Airbuses that were entering the Pan Am fleet with their joysticks and glass cockpit would never hold up like the 727. He shook his head at the irony of a disposable airplane disposing with his job. He never did make captain, but then he never did make history as he had dreamed when he first flew his dad's plane at eleven. Just when things were going right, life and women had a way of getting in the way. Maybe it was time to let go.

The kidnapping a few days before in Moscow haunted him. Faith might be dead now because of him. If he'd fought harder, he could've saved her. He shouldn't have listened to Ian; he should've gone ahead and reported her abduction to the embassy. He let Faith down. He wasn't useful for much nowadays. Maybe it was time to gracefully harden into the fossilized world of retirement. He looked at the worn photo of his chocolate Lab Clipper and smiled. Ever since he had rescued Clipper from the pound and Clipper had saved him from the loneliness of divorce, the dog's picture rode along on every flight, propped up on the engineer's station. *I'll be home soon, boy.*

The first officer was flying and Captain Henning was monitoring the radio. Frosty noticed his countenance suddenly drop. He grabbed his headset and listened in on the radio chatter.

"*Ich wiederhole*, Pan American, you are ordered to leave the sovereign airspace of the German Democratic Republic, heading two-two-five," the heavily accented voice crackled over the radio.

The afterburner of a MIG fighter flared in the distance. A few seconds later, it buzzed within meters of the American civilian craft.

"Jesus," Frosty said.

The captain's voice was steady, too steady. "Berlin Centre, Clipper six-six-one, we are experiencing substantial interference by unidentified craft."

Sweat beaded on Frosty's forehead. Of all the captains he could've been assigned, why did he have to get Captain Courageous?

"Say again, Clipper," the American air traffic controller said.

The MIG pilot interrupted, "Pan American, you are ordered to heading two-two-five at once. *Mach schnell.* You are violating airspace of the German Democratic Republic. Leave our airspace *sofort* or you will be considered hostile."

"Berlin Centre, Clipper six-six-one, we are being threatened by a MIG intercept. Probable Foxbat. Request heading two-two-five to return to West German airspace, best speed."

"Pan American, here is your final warning."

"Henning, fuck protocol. This guy is serious and not very patient. Get us the hell out of here. Now!"

The MIG buzzed them again at the same instant the captain took charge of the controls from the first officer and began to bank. The 727 shuddered and yawed to the right. Red lights on Frosty's monitors flashed like a pinball machine. A deafening bell drowned everything out, but years of training shoved fear aside. Frosty silenced the bell, and then confirmed the central power selector was set to the number-one engine. He called out the engine failure checklist from memory and the first officer acknowledged each item.

"Number-two engine thrust lever—closed; start lever—cut off; engine fire switch—pulled."

Frosty monitored the electrical load as he cut the power to the galley and shut off the fuel and hydraulics to the damaged engine. The fire-warning light for the number two was still illuminated. "She's still on fire. Discharging the bottle now." He hit the transfer switch.

The first officer followed the protocol while the captain struggled to control the machine as it dropped. And dropped.

Frosty's breathing stopped when he saw the number-three engine's low-oil-pressure light flicker and its generator trip off. Its EPR was going down faster than they were. The number two's fire-warning light burned steady as he counted down the seconds until the next extinguisher discharge. He feared he was going to make history after all. *Frosty McGuire, first casualty of WWIII.* No, he wasn't going to let the Red bastards win that easily. He prayed that the number one hadn't ingested any shrapnel as he discharged the extinguishers for both numbers two and three. Frosty McGuire was going down fighting.

CHAPTER FIFTY-THREE

NORTH OF MOSCOW
11:23 P.M.

The Kalashnikov fire came closer, but the tires of the Zil spun in place. The car slid sideways, splattering mud onto the windows. Summer eased up on the gas to creep out of the rut. It wouldn't move. "Son of a buck." Summer slapped the wheel. "I'll push. Think you can drive a little ways, comrade?"

"Yeah, but hurry. They'll be in range any moment," Zara said, her right hand applying pressure to the bullet wound.

Summer sprang from the car. At the sound of another round of fire, Faith let out an involuntary whimper. Mud sprayed Summer as he rocked the car, careful not to slip underneath it. Stepping on a large stone for traction, he shoved until he could feel the veins popping on his forehead.

Then the car moved.

He jumped into the driver's seat, nearly landing on Zara's lap. An engine started in the distance. Just as he was closing the car door, he saw a flash of light and a second later heard the report from Faith's mines. He then listened for the gas tank. Within seconds it lit up the forest. He threw the car into gear and stomped on the gas. The moon was bright enough that he could keep the headlights off. "You're going to have to direct me. I don't know where to go except away from here."

"Straight about twenty kilometers." Keeping her right arm stationary, Zara removed a cardboard box from under the passenger seat. She pulled out a package of gauze. Holding it between her teeth, she ripped it open. She slipped off the blazer, opened her blouse and pressed the gauze against the wound.

"How bad you hit, Zara?"

"Hurts like the devil, but doesn't feel like it got the bone. Bleeding's more than I'd like."

"You've been hit before?"

"Couple times. One grazed my scapula in Grenada during the invasion."

"Really? I took one there, too—in the butt."

"Hope you're not offended if I don't want to compare battle scars."

"So there definitely were Russian and not just Cuban advisers in Grenada." He glanced over to Zara. The white gauze was turning dark from blood.

"Not really. The Cubans can hardly build an outhouse without us, but they're not too bad with runways. I was based out of Havana at the time, doing some counterespionage work, and I was following up on reports of increased CIA activity when the invasion started. We suspected the CIA was establishing a station at the medical school."

"Faith, how we doing back there? Want to tell me what happened, sweetie?" He looked into the rearview mirror. She was stretched out, covered with the blanket.

"How do you live with yourself after you kill someone?" Faith said.

"You needed to have aimed lower, at the base of his skull. Where you got him, it would have taken much more force and probably multiple blows to kill him." Zara pressed on the wound. "You gave him a concussion, that's all."

"The thing is, I wanted to. I wanted him dead."

Silence.

"I want to see Mama now."

"Why?" Summer said.

"I just killed my father, so I want to sleep with my mother in some twisted Oedipus thing. What do you think?" Her voice cracked her façade. "I need her."

"The comrade's right that heads can take a real pounding. I'm sure he's alive. You try and get some sleep. We've got a bit of a drive and it's pretty much all over now." Summer crossed his fingers, pointing them toward Zara.

"I'm afraid it isn't. I was going to give you a couple of minutes of respite before I told you." Zara peeked under the bloody gauze pads, opened another pack and pressed one on top of the blood-soaked square.

"How's it look?"

"Bleeding's slowing. It's rather deep."

"I've got a good vet here in Moscow I can recommend."

"Don't worry about me. There are more important things. We're facing two separate situations. We stopped the coup back there, but not the assassination. The orders have already been issued and the assassin deployed to murder Gorbachev tomorrow morning during the May Day parade in Red Square."

"What kind of a dumb-ass outfit is that? You never give the green light until you're ready."

"Quite frankly, I doubt he would've been sober enough by morning to give the go-ahead. General Zolotov had arrangements to halt it if he had to, but he went up with the *banya*. Since they never received the C-4—"

"They did tonight."

"I stand corrected. Since they didn't receive the shipment as expected, they changed their plans to use a sniper from the top floor of GUM department store." Zara rifled through the first-aid supplies with her good arm.

"I sure hope that's the really bad news."

"Take a right here." Zara's face grimaced from pain. "It gets much worse. Honecker is making a move against West Berlin tonight."

"God almighty." Summer took a deep breath. "It's gonna be ironic if I end up getting vaporized by American nukes. Guess, in the end, it doesn't really matter who they come from."

"No, it doesn't. It really doesn't," the KGB officer said.

"Any idea of their exact plans?"

"Kosyk said they would seal off the city tonight, liquidate the West Berlin police, take over the government, cut off communications. By morning, he said the Allied bases would be cordoned off by the National People's Army. Faith, could you help me with this? I've reduced the bleeding to a trickle and I want to bandage it."

"Sounds like a textbook communist takeover." Faith sat up and took the gauze roll from Zara. Her voice grew stronger. "He forgot the part about installing a puppet government first so it can invite in the National People's Army and Red Army with a request for military assistance."

"The Soviet Army isn't involved. Honecker is acting alone." Zara opened yet another fresh square of gauze and piled it on top of the blood-soaked ones. "Help me get this blouse off and wrap my arm with the gauze strip."

Faith leaned over the seat and unbuttoned Zara's blouse, careful to keep her own mud-caked sleeve away from the wound. "Honecker's timing really doesn't make sense to me. They should have waited a few hours. The world would have been so stunned, they'd have a window to move and dig themselves in while the US administration was trying to figure out which faction was taking over in Moscow. The Americans would've been stymied asking themselves if the play for Berlin was a result of the coup or was the putsch to prevent the takeover." Faith pushed the blouse from Zara's right shoulder, holding it so she could pull the uninjured arm free. She paused for a moment with her hand cupping Zara's bare shoulder.

"Kosyk set them up. He signaled them that the assassination had already taken place tonight."

"Summer, I need your knife. I think I'd better cut this off. I'm afraid I'm going to hit the wound when I slip the sleeve over it," Faith said.

"I'm not that delicate. Go ahead and do your best not to bump it."

"Summer, the knife, please."

"Why would they believe him if the assassination hadn't been confirmed somehow by the news or something?" Summer dug in his pocket and held out the Leatherman.

Faith pulled out a blade. In a single motion, she sliced away the sleeve down to the elbow. Zara unbuttoned the cuff and threw the blouse onto the floorboard. She wore only a sleeveless white undershirt, now stained with specks of fresh blood.

"Kremlin politics are different from the White House. When a leader dies, they usually wait until the body smells before they announce it." Zara's strained voice betrayed her pain.

"Are there some painkillers in that first-aid shoebox?" Faith wrapped the gauze around Zara's arm. "Tell me if this is too tight."

"I don't like using drugs unless I really need them."

"If it's not something really strong that's going to make you loopy, go ahead and treat yourself," Summer said.

Zara shuffled through the box, removed a couple of pills from a cellophane packet and swallowed them dry. Summer turned onto a side road.

"What are you doing?" Zara said.

"Putting the brake lights back before we get pulled over for something stupid. It also helps to focus on a trivial task when you're pondering global destruction." He put the car in neutral and set the parking brake.

Faith opened the door, kicking off her shoes. She picked them up and beat them together to dislodge chunks of mud. "Actually, I think I'll take advantage of the rest stop to get these filthy coveralls off and to get the shoe polish off my face."

"My clothes are in a garment bag in the back. Please get them out along with a clean undershirt. We might need me in uniform."

Summer returned to the car wearing a faux leather coat Mama Whitney had found for him. He handed Faith a rag and her own jacket.

"Thanks." Faith rubbed the tattered T-shirt against her cheek, instantly turning the rag dark. "You know, Berlin is two hours behind Moscow, which makes it a little after nine-thirty there. I doubt they'd take any action until the middle of the night, since West Berlin is a party town. The good bars don't fill up until midnight and they close around four, though the streets start to really clear out by three. That's when I'd make my move and get troops in place before anyone realizes what's going on."

"Then there could still be time to do something," Summer said. "How do you think they'll do it? What comes first?"

"Sever communications," Zara said without hesitation. "The MfS—the Stasi—has access to the entire West Berlin phone system. It's no problem to shut it down. Also they'd sabotage the power stations." She pulled off the soiled undershirt, exposing her small breasts. Summer stole a glance. Zara pulled the clean garment over her head.

"Close the corridor," Faith added. "It drives the East Germans crazy that they don't have complete sovereignty over all air, land and sea routes through their territory. If you closed it first, the West would assume it's the beginning of another blockade, like in the forties."

"And they won't go through the Wall," Zara said. "At least at first."

"The U-Bahn." Faith leaned over, resting her arms on the front seat. "Two West Berlin subway lines go under the East connecting to points in the West."

"East to west sounds pretty direct to me. Why the heck would they build the thing under East Berlin, then back into West Berlin?" Summer said.

"It was built before the division, and it's not like Berlin was divided on a perfect north-south axis. When they put the Wall up, they boarded up the stations on those lines. You can see them when you ride those lines. They look like they haven't changed—or been cleaned for that matter—since sixty-one. I've actually seen guards there, sleeping on the benches with machine guns on their laps. Anyway, they can reopen the stations, commandeer U-Bahn cars and send in advance troops posing as civilians."

"How do you think the Americans would respond militarily?" Zara said.

"We won't give up Berlin," Summer said. "No way. Not even a Democrat in the White House would do that. I don't know the defense plans, but I think you know as well as I do they'll punch through the corridors, and they're not going to stay in a neat little convoy on the Autobahn. They'll fan out."

"As soon as the Americans stray from the established corridors, the Warsaw Treaty takes effect and the WTO states will respond." Zara retrieved fresh ammunition from the glove compartment.

"I've heard rumors the plans call for the use of tac nukes, and I'd expect it," Summer said.

"As in tactical nuclear weapons?" Faith said.

"Afraid so."

"If we can get word out to the Americans," Faith said, "they can at least put the Allies on alert and mobilize the West Berlin police. They're trained as paramilitaries for just such a possibility, since the West Germans aren't allowed to station troops in the city. They also have channels—military attachés and the like—to alert the Soviets to rein in their dogs. With Soviet opposition, the East Germans would stand down."

"You agree, comrade?"

"The East German regime cannot survive without our backing." Zara slid a fresh magazine into her gun.

"Then we have to figure out a way to warn them. Any ideas? I take it phone calls aren't an option—not even to the embassy?" Summer said, his voice tailing off as the first set of headlights appeared ahead of them. He put both hands on the wheel and scoped out the nearby terrain. The ditch looked shallow, but the car would never make it through the muddy field. Whatever happened, they would have to stay on the road. The car dimmed its lights and slowed down. Summer set the gun on his lap. After a few long moments, the car passed them, its taillights disappearing in the rearview mirror.

"My nerves are shot. I was sure that car was going to come after us," Faith said with a sigh.

"It's not a bad idea to stay alert," Summer said, returning the gun to the seat beside him.

Zara picked it up and exchanged magazines. "To answer your earlier question, we couldn't get a line to the West. You have to order the call well in advance, and I seriously doubt you would get one to the European Command or NATO or any military installation, for that matter. You could probably get through to the American embassy, but it would be monitored."

"I don't think that's much of an option," Faith said, "even if we got through to the political attaché, or, better yet, the economic liaison—isn't that usually the cover for the CIA station chief?"

"One or the other." Zara nodded.

"So even if we got through to someone who counts," Faith continued, "we'd have a hard time getting them to believe us. Let's say we made it over those hurdles. It'll go from there to the State Department; they'll deliberate over it for a while and if they deem it credible, they'll reluctantly pass it on to the CIA. After the CIA does its bureaucratic number, they'll go to either the White House or Defense Intelligence Agency, most likely the former. By the time the governmental bureaucracy gets through with the information, the East Germans will be in Bonn. The problem is getting it into the right channel. Frankly, I think our best bet is the media. The whole world monitors CNN. If we could get to their Moscow bureau—"

"We might be able to warn the Allies and even Gorbachev," Summer said. "Their offices can't be heavily guarded."

"They're not. They're in a building designated for foreign businesses with one or two guards posted there to keep Soviet citizens out and to monitor who's coming and going. Of course, the offices are under electronic surveillance, though I doubt anyone's listening at this hour. It's probably only taped and archived, but they might go live if the guard gets suspicious. We'll have to be fast. But one last detail: Why would anyone be at the CNN offices at this hour?"

"Depends on what time it is in Atlanta, I'd bet. What's the time difference to the East Coast?" Summer said.

"I think it's seven hours right now," Faith said. "Which makes it a little before five in the afternoon in the non-Soviet Georgia."

CHAPTER FIFTY-FOUR

INSIDE THE MOSCOW RING ROAD
12:07 A.M.

Faith had almost dozed off in the backseat when Zara directed Summer into an alley a couple of blocks away from the foreigners' compound housing the Moscow CNN bureau. Zara pulled on her blouse, slowly easing the fabric over the bandaged wound. She buttoned it and handed Summer the pistol with the silencer. "I'm not bad with my left hand, but I'm going to give this to you anyway. If the sentry gets suspicious, you know what to do. Since you won't understand the conversation, I'll lean back to signal you to take care of him."

"I'll understand the body language. Hey, where'd we pick up the new toy with the silencer?"

"Kosyk. But keep in mind it's a Czech-made CZ-52, so Makarov magazines won't fit it. We also picked up his shoulder holster." Zara handed Faith the Makarov Summer had used at the dacha. "And we now have enough to go around."

"No, thanks. I've done enough damage for one night," Faith said.

"Take it, Faith. You never know." Summer took the shoulder holster from Zara's lap. "You don't mind, do you? I can put it under my jacket, and I don't think it'd feel real good on you right now."

Summer stepped out of the car and circled it while Zara slid across the seat. Faith helped her into her uniform jacket. Zara drove to the compound and pulled up to the guardhouse.

"Good evening. Papers." The guard spit out the words, his breath reeking of alcohol.

"*Komitet.*" She held up her identification.

The guard closed his eyes and motioned with a nod for them to proceed.

The door of the building was open. They found no building directory, so they searched the halls until they came upon a white door on the third floor with the familiar red CNN logo. Summer reached for the latch, but it was locked. He knocked and they waited. Faith wiped a smear of shoe polish off Summer's face. He tried again and eyed the security lock, probably imported from the West.

"Can't we take it off?" Faith pointed to the hinges on the outside of the door.

"True Soviet workmanship," Zara said. "They're probably not allowed to change anything outside the unit."

Summer pulled the Leatherman from his pocket and selected the appropriate tool. In less than a minute, he removed the door and Faith helped him lower it to the floor. He unlocked it and hung it back.

Zara led the way into the empty CNN bureau, holding a flashlight. The office looked like it had been imported as a package from West Germany. The walls, chairs, desks, sofa and tables were clinical-white and spotless. Modern halogen lights sat on each desk. Everything was carefully arranged either parallel or perpendicular to the walls.

They searched the offices for the studio.

"No wonder they're not working late. Looks like they have too much time on their hands," Faith said, looking at a bookshelf with each section of books fastidiously arranged by size.

"We do put excessive restrictions on them so they don't go snooping around too much," Zara said.

"Found it. Here's the studio," Summer said.

They hurried to join him.

They all stepped inside and Faith closed the door behind them. She held up her arm, shielding her eyes from the sudden glare. An assortment of cameras and other electronic equipment was crammed into the limited space and cables crisscrossed the floor. A blue screen covered one wall, where Faith guessed that they projected shots of the Kremlin or other Russian scenes when they filed reports.

"Anyone have a clue how to do this?" Faith said as she studied the control console and flipped a switch, but nothing noticeable happened.

"I think we're over our heads. Comrade?"

"I'm sorry," Zara said as the three stared at one another.

"Well, fuck. Pardon my Russian," Summer said. "I saw a fax machine in one of those offices, and I can't imagine how they'd do business having to order a line for a fax hours in advance."

"They have special arrangements for overseas lines. I totally forgot since I don't work domestically. I'm not that up on things here."

"Well, hell, let's go make some phone calls," Summer said.

Faith commandeered the first office she came to, snatched up the phone and punched in the country code for Germany, then the West Berlin prefix.

"Anyone know the country code for the US?" Summer yelled down the hall.

"Dial eight, wait for the dial tone, then one-zero-one," Faith shouted as she hit the number for Hakan, not knowing whom else to call. The phone beeped and then a recorded message came on in German informing her that the circuits were down. She tried again, but got the same recording.

The takeover had begun.

Zara dialed her uncle's home phone, but no one answered after a dozen rings. A corporal finally answered his work phone.

"This is Lieutenant Colonel Zara Bogdanov. Let me speak with my uncle, General Ivanovski."

"The general's unavailable."

"Perhaps you didn't understand. I am Colonel Bogdanov with the *Komitet*, and it's imperative I speak with my uncle the general now. I don't care if he's asleep, drunk or screwing my aunt."

"He's having dinner with General Titov and ordered me not to disturb him. He'll have my hide if I interrupt him."

"He may, but the KGB can get your entire family—including the cousins you have never met."

The line clicked. She was on hold.

"Ivanovski."

"Uncle Yuri, it is I. I have an urgent message from Stukoi. Honecker has ordered the NVA to take over West Berlin tonight. They had planned on doing it tomorrow, but Kosyk double-crossed them and set them up. He's in custody. Stukoi is interrogating him right now. He wants you to stop the NVA and keep them from getting us into a war with the Americans before the deed in the morning."

"Idiot Honecker. Doesn't he understand that would mean—"

"I have no time. If you can keep the Germans in line, everything should go fine with our friend tomorrow. Can you do that?"

"We're not ready for war with the Americans," the general shouted into the phone with a drunken slur. "Not yet."

"This is Lieutenant Commander Summer. Get me Captain Moberly on the double." Summer opened a desk drawer and poked around inside.

"Can I tell him what it's regarding, commander?" a yeoman said.

"An imminent threat to national security. Get Moberly in the next five seconds or I'll personally see you're busted down to an E-1 and spend the rest of your tour painting the same goddamn bulkhead over and over again. Get to it!" The phone clicked and Summer found himself on hold, the closest thing to purgatory in this world. Within a minute, a voice came on the line.

"Moberly here. You'd better have a good one, Summer. My officers don't go AWOL on me."

"Sir, we'll deal with that later." The line crackled.

"Where the fuck are you?"

"This is going to sound crazy, but I was kidnapped and brought to Moscow, but that's not the problem right now. You've got to get word to the Joint Chiefs and the President that East German forces are mobilizing to take West Berlin tonight. They're going to cut off the corridor and probably invade through the subway."

"Moscow, my ass. That's a good one, Summer. Next you're going to tell me the Chinese are in Higgins boats, crossing the strait for Taiwan as we speak."

Faith walked into the room. "Lines are down to West Berlin."

"I just got word civilian communications with West Berlin have been severed. Listen to me. It's critical you tell them the Russians aren't behind it. They don't even know it's going on. We're trying to use back channels to notify them right now. The East Germans are acting on their own accord without Soviet knowledge or backing."

"How the hell can that happen? And how do you know about it?"

"Sir, I don't pretend to understand the politics, but I know it's going down right now. There's no time for details. Get them on alert. Cut through whatever red tape you have to—"

Faith interrupted. "Tell him to check on the last Pan Am or BA flight of the day and see if they've closed the air corridors. Make sure they understand it's not just a blockade."

"Sir, check on—"

"I heard it. Do you know what will happen if you're bullshitting me?"

"Do you know what will happen when the commies take Berlin? And that's not all, sir. Tomorrow morning they're going to assassinate—"

The line went dead.

CHAPTER FIFTY-FIVE

NAVAL ORDNANCE STATION, INDIAN HEAD, MARYLAND
5:28 P.M. EDT (12:28 A.M. MONDAY, MAY 1, MOSCOW TIME)

Who? Assassinate who? The base commander held the phone for a moment, listening to the dial tone in disbelief. Captain Moberly had known Max Summer for fifteen years and would have trusted him with his life. In fact, he had—more than once. He flipped through his Rolodex until he found the number of Colonel J. D. Drake. The Pentagon's joint services mandatory training seminar on environmental issues facing base commanders had been a colossal waste of time, but he did at least make some friends in other branches of the service through it. He punched in Drake's number and browbeat the corporal who answered the phone until he had Drake on the line.

The Navy captain cleared his throat. "J. D., this might sound a bit unusual, but I need to check something out with you before I make an ass of myself somewhere that counts."

"I'm busy right now. We have a situation here."

"Wait. Has anything unusual happened in the Berlin corridor to-night?"

"How the fuck do you know about that? I just found out two minutes ago. We think the goddamn Russians knocked down a Pan Am jet. Looks like they're throwing up another blockade. I knew that glasnost crap was to get us to let our guard down."

CHAPTER FIFTY-SIX

CNN BUREAU, MOSCOW
12:28 A.M., MONDAY, MAY 1—MAY DAY

"They cut the line. They're on to us," Summer shouted as he threw down the phone. He leaped from the desk chair, drawing his gun. He grabbed Faith's shoulder and spun her around, pointing her toward the door. She shined the flashlight ahead of them until Summer cupped his hand over it. "Turn that off."

Zara held her gun with her elbow bent, pointing it into the air. "Ready?" She flung the door open and aimed her service pistol down the hall while she shielded herself with the door. "All clear." She darted past the elevator to the stairwell. She took several steps at a time, but by the second floor she was breathing hard and holding her bullet wound.

"Need help?" Summer said.

"Take point."

Within a few seconds, Summer reached the door at the bottom of the stairs. He pushed the latch down. From the expression on his face, Faith understood someone was opening it from the other side. In a single movement, Summer stepped back, kicked the door open and fired into the surprised sentry's forehead. He crumpled to the floor, his weapon falling from his limp fingers.

Summer scooped up the gun and stepped over the body. Faith hesitated until Zara nudged her. She hugged the doorframe to scoot around him. They raced through the lobby. No sign of backups was visible through the double glass doors, so they ran from the building toward the car. Zara veered toward the guard shack.

"Pick me up on the way. I have to get his security log," Zara said.

Summer hopped into the car and drove to the gate.

Zara slumped against the guard shack, logbook in hand. Faith jumped from the car and helped her inside, where she collapsed into the seat. Tires screeched as Summer pulled through the gate. Sirens wailed in the distance.

"I need fluids and something to eat. It's bleeding again."

"Here. I lifted a Snickers from a desk drawer." Faith handed her the candy.

"Which way?" Summer said as the car roared down the empty street.

"Get off the main road. Turn left into this alley." Zara ripped open the bar and threw the wrapper onto the cluttered floorboard.

"Let's go back to the orphanage to regroup. I need to see my mother."

CHAPTER

FIFTY-SEVEN

NADEZHDA ORPHANAGE, MOSCOW
1:30 A.M.

"Lordy, lordy." Margaret shook her head when she saw the three of them; it wouldn't have surprised her if they had been in Hades, wrestling the devil himself for the Keys to the Kingdom. Faith and Summer were a fright, and the Russian girl was pressing bloody rags against her arm. Faith took a step toward her and then stopped herself. She tensed up. Margaret examined her face. She recognized the look in her little girl when her eyes were begging to express something she didn't know how to say. "Sweet pea, is there something you want to tell me?"

Faith nodded, tears filling her eyes. She took a deep breath and held it. "Forgive me," she said as she burst into tears and grabbed her mother in a desperate hug.

"Thank You, Jesus," Margaret whispered over and over again as she held her daughter for the first time in more than fifteen years.

"Mama, I understand now why you always acted the way you did toward me. I was a constant reminder of how you'd strayed—a curse from

God." Faith stopped crying and stepped away from her. "I know about Daddy."

"Honey, I was young. I didn't understand like I do now that you're God's greatest gift to me. I'm sorry."

"What's happened, happened."

"You should know we were engaged, or I thought we were. I was on my first mission abroad in Berlin—that was before the Wall went up. Yurij was a communist zealot, and he pretended to let me lead him to the Lord. He was so suave, so cosmopolitan; I fell for him like a lovestruck schoolgirl. When he found out you were on the way, he confessed he was married and working undercover for the Stasi. He broke my heart and I know I did his, too. Yurij's not the kind of man who would blow his cover even if his life depended on it, but he did for me. The hardest thing was that we had to play it out for several more weeks so the Stasi didn't find out he had up and told me. It would've ruined his career."

"Why did you ever do that?" Zara interrupted.

"I was afraid of him for both myself and my baby. Nothing comes between that man and his climb to the top. I woke up one morning and he was gone and a little note was on the pillow: 'We never had a chance, but we made ourselves one.' That man had the heart of a poet. I kept that note in my Bible for years until one day it disappeared."

"I took it, Mama, years ago. I'm sorry. I'd watched you read it and finger it and I knew it was from Daddy. I wanted something from him, some connection to him."

"I know you did, honey. I found it with your favorite maps and let you keep it."

"He tried to kill me, but I . . ." Faith choked on the words. "I killed Daddy."

"You're talking nonsense, child." Margaret turned her head toward Summer. He shrugged and glanced away. Margaret paused for a moment while she blinked back tears. "Then I'm sure he deserved it. He always did."

They showered, cleaned and dressed Zara's wound, then met Mama Whitney in the basement with her famous biscuits and redeye gravy. They slurped them down while highlighting the events that led up to Faith's action.

"We still have to figure out how we're going to get close to GUM in the morning to stop the assassination," Zara said.

"You can't get through because of the May Day parade. By now they've thrown up control points around the Kremlin, allowing only people with special invites to get by," Mama Whitney said.

"I could get through in uniform, but you two wouldn't."

"I know people here who'll sell me KGB uniforms," Faith said, her mouth still full.

"Your old contacts have been burned by now."

"I can get what you need, but I doubt I could rustle them up in time," Mama Whitney said.

"And even if we all made it past the checkpoints, we still have to break into GUM in front of thousands waiting for the parade." Zara studied Summer as he sopped up the last drops of gravy with a biscuit.

"Let's approach this like a smuggler." Faith wiped gravy from the corner of her mouth. "When all entrances are being watched—"

"You take goods in something so commonplace, no one would ever think twice or if they did, they wouldn't get what it really is," Mama Whitney said.

"Nice in theory, but they're closed tomorrow. No deliveries." Zara yawned.

"GUM has hot water, doesn't it?" Faith said.

"I'd assume." Zara set her plate on a stack of old shoes.

"Well, then," Faith said. "Maybe we need to think more from the rat's point of view."

4:49 A.M.

A miserable walk through a sweltering, damp tunnel of the Moscow hot-water system was almost a relief after the two hours of restless anxiety on the hard brick floor under the orphanage. The sweat and grime from the sultry tunnel hid all hints of their brief showers. The biscuits and redeye gravy were a dull memory; Faith could only taste dust. She shined the flashlight ahead of them, searching for the fittings and valves that served as landmarks on the crude map her mother had provided them. The main pipes were large enough Faith could easily have walked upright inside, but the dark tunnels had only enough room for them to go single-file beside the hot pipes. Her sides ached. At least she didn't have a chunk of lead lodged in her bicep or a gash in her forearm. She admired Zara and Summer for their silent endurance, but she secretly wished they would say something so she didn't have to keep her own complaints to herself, bottled up along with her fears. A cat-sized rat scurried in front of them and then lurked under the raised pipe.

"So, how are we doing, comrade navigator? I just hit fifteen hundred paces since the last turn." Summer stopped.

Zara held a flashlight above the drawing. "We should be coming up on some stairs anytime. When we find them, four hundred meters to go until we cross over."

They walked onward. Within a few minutes, Faith shined the light on a metal ladder. "Guess that's our stairway. Reset your count."

"We should notice two fittings close together where the smaller pipes branch out. Something called a flange," Zara said without referring to her map.

"A flange is just a collar at the end of a pipe where two mate," Summer said.

"As if we haven't seen a billion of those junctures already," Faith said.

"The ladder's at fifteen hundred fifty-three paces," Summer said with a rhythm that betrayed he was counting as he spoke. "We've been pretty consistent at running around ten percent over the specs. I say we'll find the juncture around four hundred forty paces from here."

They followed one another in silence until Faith's light hit another set of flanges. "Where's your count?"

"Just under four hundred."

"Then we're there." Faith shined the light on the joints.

"I don't think so," Summer said. "I'd put money on it the one we're looking for is a hundred meters up ahead. I'd really hate to pop up in Lenin's tomb or something."

"Actually, the mausoleum is pretty cool inside," Faith said. "They have the lights arranged so that Lenin lets off this bizarre glow. They've used too much wax and made him kind of shiny. I'll take you there if we get a chance after all this is over."

"I'll pass. I've had enough of you two taking me sightseeing in Moscow. I can tell you this: If you're thinking about going into the tourist industry, you'd better not quit your day jobs. No, sir." He laughed to himself. They filed along until they reached another junction in the pipes. "I'm at four thirty-six and we're a few steps away. I'd say we'd better get in the turn lane."

Patterns in the dirt, loose cement and handprints marked where maintenance workers had crawled under the pipe.

"It's definitely had more traffic than the other ones," Faith said.

"After you." Zara put her hand on Faith's back.

Faith squatted down and leaned over to get a peek at the other side. "You know, there's something that looks like rat crap down here." Faith flattened herself against the ground and squirmed underneath the scalding-hot surface, forcing herself to become one with the muck to minimize her risk of contact with the pipe. Pain stabbed her sides as she wiggled under it. She stood up, dusting herself off. "We've got another passage. Smaller, though. We'll have to hunch down to walk through it."

Zara let out an involuntary moan as she squeezed under the pipe. Faith helped her to her feet. "Shoulder okay?"

"About as well as can be expected when you rake a fresh wound over a rock. I'll be fine." Zara unfolded the crumpled map and took point, stooping to clear the low ceiling. "About twenty meters ahead, there should be a ladder and a thirty-centimeter pipe that feeds into the GUM complex. Hey, there's something else ahead." A half-dozen boxes blocked the path. Zara turned her light to the dark spot on the roof of the tunnel and found the shaft. "We have definitely found the right place. It appears someone is stealing from GUM and leaving the goods here to be picked up. Anyone interested in a new toilet seat?" Rusting metal rungs led straight up beside a pipe. Zara shined the light up the hole. "I can see about ten meters; then it looks like there's something blocking it."

Summer squeezed past Faith. He paused for a moment when they were face-to-face.

"I'll go first. Let me get it open and then you two can come up. No sense in making Zara hang on to the rungs any longer than necessary. We also don't know if they can hold weight for long," Summer said.

"I won't argue." Zara stepped aside for Summer.

Summer pulled himself up like a gymnast mounting a set of rings. Zara shined the light up the shaft as he climbed. A scraping noise echoed and loose pebbles tumbled down. Zara jerked her head to the side, but continued to hold the light.

"One side of a rung pulled out. You're going to have to be real careful."

Summer reached the top and pushed open a manhole cover. He climbed into the room, leaned back over the shaft and motioned for them.

"Let me help you up to the first rung. You shouldn't try to pull yourself up with your arm like that," Faith said.

"I've done worse. I'll be okay." Zara reached up for the rung with her left arm.

Faith wrapped her arms around Zara's upper thighs and boosted her up. She supported her until she could feel her weight transfer to the ladder. Faith borrowed boxes from the black marketeer and stacked them under the shaft. She climbed them until she could easily get on the ladder. She scrambled up, spreading her weight across three rungs at a time to minimize the risk of another pulling out. She made it to the top and sat on the floor of the boiler room to catch her breath. A tangle of pipes led off in different directions from a large tank, and the room was cluttered with buckets and mops. "How are we doing on time?"

"It's zero-five-fourteen. A couple of minutes later than we wanted, but within the margins. We should have plenty of time to set up a stakeout and wait for our sniper. Now, you're sure we're not going to set off any burglar alarms?"

"This is GUM, not Nordstrom's," Zara said. "I doubt if they even have alarms wired to the doors. No way will they have motion detectors."

They filed out into the hall. A foul stench assaulted them. Faith gagged. *Russian toilets.*

The first light of morning filtered down the stairs directly ahead of them. They climbed them to the top floor. Rays of sun now glistened on the arched skylights of the main arcade. Shops lined each side of the gallery, with a wide promenade separating them. The center was open to the ground floor with bridges linking the two sides.

"Any idea which gallery we're in?" Faith said.

"We're in the right place. The stores on that side should have back rooms overlooking Red Square. Gorbachev will be on the viewing stand atop Lenin's mausoleum—that way." Zara pointed to her right. "The sniper has to go through one of those stores to take his shot. We should set up our observation post in one of the shops across the gallery from them."

"Let's take the corner one. We can see everything from there and there's a bridge to the other side right beside it," Summer said.

They went over to their new observation post. Heavy red velvet drapes covered the shop window. The glass door was blocked off with similar curtains and no markings hinted at what was sold inside. Zara used the Leatherman to jimmy the lock quicker than most people could have opened it with the proper key.

Faith was totally unprepared for what she saw: stylish dresses adorning the mannequins. They could have been in Paris or London, but not Moscow, home of unisex underpants. She fingered a shawl—cashmere.

"I didn't think Russia had stores like this," Summer said. "What happened to lining up for a loaf of bread?"

"This must be a special shop only for the *nomenklatura*. We have a special shop at Lubyanka for KGB workers that stocks hard-to-get items, but I've never seen anything like this." Zara flipped through a rack. "And for rubles!"

"Okay, let's get organized. It's zero-five-thirty. The parade starts in two and a half hours. Now, I doubt our marksman arrives anytime within the next two hours, but you never know. He may be the obsessive-compulsive type that needs to come do his wacko rituals on-site before he can do the job, or he may be the one who likes to come in just in time for the mark, do the job and not hang around. Whatever the case, we have to be ready. We'll do thirty-minute shifts peeping through the curtains. I'll go first, then Zara, then Faith. Any questions?"

"Yeah. What are we going to do when he gets here?" Faith wrapped a cashmere shawl around her shoulders to keep warm.

"When it's time, I'll go over and take care of him. Zara will come along and cover me. Sorry, honey, but you'd be in the way and I don't want to put you at risk any more than I have to. You'll wait here."

Faith nodded as she spread out another shawl and lay down on the floor to rest.

Summer nudged Faith awake. "Okay, sleeping beauty. Time for your watch."

Faith opened her eyes wide and checked the time. "Hey, it's already eight thirty. What's going on?"

"We couldn't bring ourselves to wake you earlier. We pulled double duty for you," Summer whispered. "The parade began half an hour ago and no one's shown yet. We're starting to think we have bad intel and this is the wrong building."

"Psst." Zara motioned them over to the crack in the curtains. She held up two fingers.

A burly man with a crewcut slipped a key in the door of the shop directly across from them. He carried a brown case. A second sniper opened another shop two doors down. She carried the same style case.

"Looks like we'll have to split up after all. You take the lady marksman and I'll take the guy. I'm not being sexist here, but remember, women are always the worst. A lot of antiterrorist squads have standing orders to shoot the women first." Summer drew his gun from its holster and pushed up the safety. "Faith, you might have to cover us. Stay low and don't shoot us."

"That's some vote of confidence," Faith said.

"You have the Czech gun. Don't forget the safety and remember to cock the trigger before the first shot like I showed you," Summer said. He kissed Faith on the cheek. "Luck, everyone."

Faith clutched the clunky wood butt of the gun as she watched them dart across the bridge. Zara stopped with Summer at the first door. He placed his hand over the handle and shook his head. He pulled out the Leatherman, stuck a blade between the door and the frame and opened it. He handed the tool to Zara. Faith couldn't read lips, but knew he again wished her luck. Faith wished them both luck—good luck.

Summer crept into the shop, gun drawn. He swept the gun back and forth, although he was confident the sniper was in the back room, assembling his weapon. Praying he didn't step on a creaky board, he inched across the floor toward the long counter. A curtain hung in the doorway between the storefront and the back room. He pushed it aside with the barrel of the gun just enough to get a peek. Six tall windows covered the wall. For the first time he saw the domes of St. Basil's, the red bricks of the Kremlin fortress and the latest Scalpel missiles parading across Red Square, but his focus was on the man opening one of the windows. The assembled sniper rifle sat beside him. Summer didn't want to take him out now because a gunshot might compromise Zara before she was in place. She needed a couple extra minutes to get to the other store and open the lock. He watched as the man picked up the rifle. Summer pointed the Makarov at the sniper's head and waited for the resound of Zara's shot.

Zara wedged the blade between the frame and the door and popped it open, wondering why the stores even bothered with such poor locks. A safety on the tool prevented her from snapping the blade closed. Rather than waste precious seconds, she stuck it in her shoulder holster, still open. She slinked to the curtain separating the sales space from the storage room, wishing she had a god to whom she could pray for success. If they were too late, not only would Gorbachev die; they would be put to death. A fresh breeze alerted her that the sniper had already opened the window.

Faith watched the plate-glass windows of the shops for signs it was all over. Then she saw them. Two men were crossing the bridge toward the stores where the assassins were positioned. They didn't have any guns visible—

yet. *A cleanup crew. Assassins to eliminate the assassins. They'll kill Zara and Summer.*

Summer saw the sniper look at his watch and then raise the rifle to his shoulder. He heard gunshots, pulled the trigger and fired two shots into the sniper's brainstem. He hoped Zara had had similar success.

Zara pushed back the divider and saw the sniper in position, the barrel of the rifle barely sticking out the window. Dust sparkled in the ruby-red of the laser sight. The assassin's finger squeezed the trigger and Zara fired into her head, but at that moment she heard the spit of the silenced rifle. Smoke curled from the barrel and the spent case dropped to the floor. The woman had gotten off a shot. Zara prayed it wasn't a clean one as she hurried out the door.

As Faith rushed to the door, she flipped off the safety and pushed back the hammer. She cracked open the door, aimed the gun and pulled the trigger. Again. And again. The cleanup crew fired back, shattering the plate-glass window. Faith dived behind the doorframe and lowered herself to the floor.

Summer watched the assassin's body slump to the floor. Another gun discharged, but it wasn't from Zara's direction.

Oh, my God, Faith.

The sound of gunfire echoed from the arcade. Summer bolted to the door, kicked it and took aim at one of the gunmen. He emptied his weapon, drawing their fire away from Faith, and hit the ground. Bullets whizzed over him. He reached for the second magazine. It wasn't there. He glanced around for cover, but found none. He inched backwards to the shop. Just then gunfire rang out from down the promenade.

Faith crawled toward the storefront to look out to the promenade, clasping the gun as hard as she could. Broken glass slit her right palm. Blood dripped down her wrist. She peeked through the smelly curtain. Summer and Zara lay on the floor, bullets ricocheting around them. The gunmen crouched on the bridge, firing as they inched their way toward them.

Zara shot as she took cover, crouching behind a wide post in the promenade railing. Her gun was empty. She pulled the extra magazine from her pocket. A glass window behind her shattered.

Zara pushed the magazine release back until the empty magazine dropped. She held the loaded one in her left hand. Before she could shove it into the gun, pain seared her forearm and her hand released its grip on the magazine. It plummeted over the edge of the promenade, down three stories and splashed into the fountain below. Zara pointed her empty gun in the direction of the killers, all the while cursing the weakness of her left hand. She glanced at Summer. He signaled that he, too, had spent his ammo. Bullets pinged around them. They both had to cross at least five exposed meters before any hope of cover. She knew they couldn't make it. Then across the arcade she saw the velvet drapes of the dress shop move and the barrel of the CZ-52 poke through.

That instant, Faith leaped through the drapes of the shattered storefront. She spotted a head through the railing. She aimed the way Summer had taught her so long ago. She fired. Blood spattered on the dingy white rail. A bullet flew by her. She saw another clean shot and took it. Then silence.

Faith approached the bodies, her gun poised to fire at the slightest motion. Blood drizzled from a round dark hole in a man's neck. Fixed eyes stared toward the skylights. One hand touched his neck, while the other remained loosely wrapped around the gun.

"Clear!" Faith said as she kicked away their firearms.

Summer and Zara ran to her. Summer searched the bodies for weapons and felt for vital signs. He shook his head, looking up at Faith. "I'll be damned."

Zara picked up a gun with her left hand, her right hand applying pressure to her left forearm. "KGB issue. Why am I not surprised?"

Faith pulled Summer to his feet and squeezed him tightly. She kissed him as if the years hadn't come between them. She still held the gun at her side. Blood was smeared on the Bakelite handle.

"There's no time for celebration right now. We've got another problem." Zara took the gun and flipped on the safety. "And always assume a gun's loaded."

Summer pulled away from Faith.

"My sniper got off a shot the same time I hit her. I pray to whatever god will listen that I ruined her aim. Any moment now, some trigger-happy bodyguards will burst in and we definitely do not want to be standing here as easy targets. I think you know how these teams work. I suggest we get back into the dress shop and do our best to surrender."

They sprinted toward the store.

Summer turned on the lights and set his guns on the counter. "We don't want any shadows."

"If we succeed in surrendering, they'll be rough and split us up for questioning," Zara said.

"What do you mean, *if* we succeed?" Faith jerked her head around toward Zara.

"The assumption will be that we were the ones who murdered or attempted to murder Gorbachev."

They exchanged silent glances.

"Your arm okay?" Summer finally spoke.

"I'm getting used to bullet wounds. This one's rather superficial, but a bleeder." She pressed on it. "They'll be here any minute. Don't resist or insist on counsel or someone from your embassy or it'll get rough. Tell them exactly what happened, but leave out Mrs. Whitney's landmines. Leave her out all together if you can. They don't need to know. Say I got them from a Soviet Army contact and Mrs. Whitney only gave us shelter and clothes upstairs at the orphanage. I have my recordings and film I lifted from Kosyk from last night, but it'll take several hours to get them analyzed and to get an initial forensic analysis of this mess here, so don't expect a quick resolution."

"Lovely," Summer said.

A loud crash came from below. Boots smacked against the steps and heels clicked on the promenade.

"KGB. Don't shoot," Zara shouted in Russian. "Over here. Do not shoot! KGB." She held her KGB identification as high as she could with her left hand, still applying pressure with her right.

"*Vot!*" someone shouted. "*Von tam!*"

A dozen nervous KGB troops pointed their Kalashnikovs at them.

CHAPTER FIFTY-EIGHT

The main difference in the history of the world
if I had been shot rather than Kennedy is that
Onassis probably wouldn't have married Mrs. Khrushchev.
—KHRUSHCHEV

CNN CENTER, ATLANTA, GEORGIA
8:30 P.M. EDT

Bernard Shaw crossed off a sentence on his copy and looked into the camera. "We're back. For those of you who have joined us from Europe and the Mideast, recapping the top stories. The traditional May Day military parade in Moscow was disrupted today by a mad gunman. The Soviet news agency TASS reports that a recently discharged psychiatric patient fired a single shot toward the dignitary viewing stand atop the Lenin mausoleum before turning the gun on himself. General Secretary Gorbachev was evacuated as a precautionary measure. After a short suspension, the parade resumed without further incident.

"TASS also reported that several high-ranking KGB and Soviet Army officials were killed last night when a propane leak caused the explosion of a country home during an early May Day celebration. Western analysts pointed out that several of the deceased were known to have privately opposed Gorbachev's reforms. Ramsey Jackson of the Heritage Institute speculated that Gorbachev may be resorting to Stalinist tactics to eliminate potential enemies and consolidate his hold on power. Dr. Jackson added, 'I believe it's going to become evident over the next few months that Gorbachev's policies of glasnost and perestroika have been ruses to get the West to let its guard down.'

"In other news from the region, NTSB investigators on-site in Moscow have all but ruled out a bomb as the cause of Saturday's accident on Pan Am 1072 in which four flight attendants and three passengers were sucked from the aircraft. An NTSB spokesman stated, 'Everything we've seen appears to be consistent with metal fatigue.' The final report is not expected until the end of the year.

"Moving west, passengers on a Pan American flight to Berlin were surprised to find themselves landing in communist East Germany. A Pan Am plane made an emergency landing in Leipzig, East Germany, last night after a near miss with an East German fighter. Air traffic control systems and backups responsible for planes in the Berlin corridors went down for several hours, creating havoc in the skies. All other civilian flights were redirected back to West Germany or West Berlin without further incident, but sources tell us that several East German military aircraft weren't so fortunate. The air traffic control blackout resulted in several midair collisions during a routine National People's Army training exercise.

"In other news, the CNN Moscow bureau was broken into last night. Nothing was taken, but a Russian policeman was killed. Sources close to the police investigation speculated that rebels from southern Russia broke in with the intent to use broadcasting equipment to spread their message worldwide, but found themselves lacking the technical skills to operate it and fled."

CHAPTER FIFTY-NINE

Comrades, do not be concerned about all you hear about Glasnost and Perestroika and democracy in the coming years. They are primarily for outward consumption. There will be no significant internal changes in the Soviet Union, other than for cosmetic purposes.

—GORBACHEV

LUBYANKA (KGB HEADQUARTERS), MOSCOW
TUESDAY, MAY 2

Six. Five. Faith counted down the footsteps, moving toward where she lay exhausted on the urine-caked floor, trying to stretch out whatever rest she could get. *Four.* She pushed herself to her hands and knees. *Three.* She put her arms around the stool. *Two.* She pulled herself up and draped her body over the stool. *One.* The interrogator grabbed her hair and yanked her upright.

"If you cooperate with us like your friends, you'll have a nice bed. They told us everything, so we know you're lying. How long have you worked for the CIA?"

"Never. I cooperated with the KGB. Talk to Bogdanov."

"We had a long, satisfying conversation with the colonel." The interrogator cracked his knuckles. "Why did you kill the General Secretary?"

"I told you, we tried everything to stop it. Guess we were too late," Faith mumbled.

"When did you first meet Bogdanov?"

The lock turned and the metal door opened. A uniformed KGB officer and a neatly groomed man in a Western-style business suit walked into the room. With the flick of an arm, the officer signaled the interrogator to leave. Faith swallowed hard, but her mouth was dry and she only gulped air.

"Doctor Whitney, I'm Colonel Kusnetsov." He held out his manicured hand.

Faith flinched.

"You don't have to be afraid. And this is Viktor Petrov, special assistant to General Secretary Gorbachev. We're here to offer our sincerest apologies for any inconvenience. We've completed our initial forensics and you're no longer a suspect in the attempted assassination of the General Secretary."

"Attempted?" Faith opened her eyes and looked up at the colonel. "We did it? He's not dead?"

"We're in your debt."

Tears pooled up in her eyes. "Can you get me out of here?"

Petrov helped Faith to her feet. "We're taking you to clinic seventeen, a special restricted-access facility that you'll find more like a spa than a hospital. You'll receive medical attention and rest as our guest while some official matters are sorted out. In due course, we'll arrange contact with your embassy, since it seems you're without proper travel documents."

"Where are Summer and Zara?" Faith stood, wobbling.

"The commander is right now on his way to the clinic. Colonel Bogdanov is undergoing surgery to have bullets removed. You'll be able to see them both shortly."

"And Berlin? Moscow is still here, so I take it there was no war?"

"We came very close," Petrov said, his voice raspy from years of smoking. "I would say closer than we ever have, but your messages got through to the right people. General Ivanovski's troops prevented a full-scale invasion of West Berlin. The Americans understood we weren't behind it and quietly stopped the first wave of infiltrators. We'll officially deny this, but after all you did for us, you deserve to know. What made it clear to the Americans that we weren't invading West Berlin was when our MIG-29s cleared the skies of the GDR fighters. It was a regrettable loss of several fine Warsaw Treaty pilots, but it was the only way."

"I don't want to know, but I have to ask. At the dacha, did Kosyk make it?"

"We couldn't find him."

"We left him on the riverbank."

"The search was extensive, including the river itself. We have little doubt General Kosyk is alive."

Summer was surprised at the almost-VIP treatment, given the KGB's reputation. They slapped him around, but seemed careful not to break any bones. He was more worried about how Faith was holding up. He guessed he had been there nearly twenty-four hours when the interrogators were summoned away.

An Amazon ill at ease in her polyester businesswoman's suit and a man in a US Army uniform entered the room. A guard accompanied them and unlocked the handcuffs that were eating into Summer's flesh.

"I'm Colonel Holton Wilson, military attaché to the American embassy." The colonel spoke with a nondescript Midwestern accent. His skin was pasty white. "Chris Goldfarb is our deputy consul and legal eagle. We'd like to talk to you about what happened. We've heard the Russian version, but we want to get it from you straight. Chris will do everything she can to get you out of here and home as soon as possible."

An hour later, a squat nurse dressed in a white smock and hat that would have been more at home on a French chef escorted Faith into her lavish Soviet suite. The two rooms had furniture that would have made an American roadside motel proud. Although the plaid fabrics of the overstuffed love seat didn't match the swirls of the boxy sofa, the reds almost didn't clash. Clusters of tinted glass globes hung from the ceiling like a lost high school science project. Obligatory pictures of Lenin adorned the walls, reminding the guest who was really footing the bill.

"Put these on and Doctor Rukovsky will be with you soon." The nurse tossed a hospital gown and worn terry-cloth robe at Faith with the hallmark courtesy of the Soviet service industry.

"I don't need a doctor, just a shower, some sleep and Commander Summer." Faith dropped the clothes on the bed, grateful it was a regular double mattress and not a hospital bed with rails. She walked into the bathroom, hoping to lose the nurse, but she followed her.

The edge of the dry wall was a good half-inch shy of the corner. The rod of the shower curtain was higher on one side, but it did nicely parallel the slope in the bathroom tiles. The finest of Soviet toiletries were arranged on the bathroom vanity. Faith was happy for anything resembling a toothbrush.

"You're not allowed to have visitors, not even other patients."

"So Summer—Commander Summer—is here now?"

"You should be honored that Doctor Rukovsky is admitting you herself. The last time I remember the head of the clinic doing an intake exam was when we had Brezhnev's wife here and the chief was trying to get a new wing written into the next five-year plan." The nurse picked her nose and rubbed her hand on her smock. "We've never had an American here before. From the looks of you, you need a thorough workup. Those circles under your eyes tell me you need a vitamin B injection."

"Keep your needles away from me. Now if you don't mind . . ."

"Get undressed now. Put on the gown and I'll bring the doctor in to see you." The nurse stood in the bathroom doorway, gawking at Faith like a zookeeper observing a new arrival.

The pipes clanked when Faith turned on the shower. She pulled off her shirt, dropping it to the floor. "You can either leave me in peace or make yourself useful and scrub my back. If you decide to stay, make sure you wash your hands first."

Faith caught herself on the shower wall as she nearly collapsed from fatigue. She washed off the last patch of soap from her forearm and turned off the water. She wrapped herself in a towel, staggered to the bed and collapsed. Within moments of her head finding its way to the pillow, Dr. Rukovsky entered the room.

The gentle middle-aged woman examined Faith as quickly as she could and prescribed fluids, food and rest. She agreed the X-ray of her ribs could wait until after she had gotten some sleep. When Faith asked about Zara and Summer, she was ordered to rest—she could socialize later. The doctor instructed the nurse to dress the cut on her hand. By the time she finished cleaning the glass slivers from the cut, Faith was too wired to sleep.

When the nurse left the room, she waited long enough for her to return to her station and pulled on the gown and robe. She stood and the blood drained from her head. Light-headed or not, she was going to find Summer. She pushed down on the door latch. It was locked.

Faith stumbled back to the bed and flopped onto it in defeat. Her eyes drifted shut.

Something brushed against her cheek and she thought she was dreaming when she smelled Summer's familiar scent. He perched on the bed beside her. The beard that had grown over the past few days had been shaven away, and so had the stubble on his head. He was again as bald as Khrushchev, but much sexier.

"I lifted a couple medical instruments that made great lockpicks." He stroked her hair.

"You know I love how resourceful you are."

As she raised her head toward him, he slipped his fingers behind her neck, supporting her head until their lips met.

"God, I've missed you so much," Faith said. "I lo—"

The door flew open and the nurse charged inside. "What is going on here? Back to your room, now!" She pointed to the door.

Summer sprang away from Faith out of old habit.

Faith sat up in the bed and said in Russian, "Commander Summer is my fiancé and we're guests of Mr. Gorbachev, so I wouldn't like to be in your shoes when we tell him how you treated us. Leave!"

The nurse snorted, stomped away and slammed the door.

"Did you tell her what I think?"

Faith gazed into Summer's bloodshot green eyes. "I told her I was going to cheat history."

"You did not. What'd you say?" He smiled as his eyes followed along the lines of her face. "You know, you get more beautiful every time I look at you."

"I told her you were my fiancé." Her face relaxed into a soft smile. "And you know, I like the way I felt when I said that. It's been a long time, but then I am pretty damn tired, so I might be delirious and getting nostalgic."

"I know how you can keep saying it."

She drew him to her and kissed him. "Make love to me. It's been too long." Faith pulled him on top of her, but immediately wiggled out from under him because of the pain from her ribs.

They had slept almost a day when the nurse waddled into the room, clapping her hands. Summer jerked the sheets up to cover them. They watched the sudden flurry as four deliverymen followed the nurse, carrying garment bags and boxes. A young woman placed a mahogany jewelry case on the dresser while deliverymen filled the wardrobe. Faith thought she recognized one of the dresses from the GUM shop. The smell of fresh coffee and cooked eggs filled the suite as a woman dressed in a chef's jacket set the table in the adjoining room.

"Eat, clean yourselves up and get dressed. Someone is going to be here in three hours to pick you up, and I'm supposed to deliver you looking your best," the nurse said in Russian, her damning eyes glaring at them. "You know, this is never allowed here. I don't know what possessed the director to tolerate this."

"What's happening?" Faith sat up in bed, careful to pull the covers around her.

"Doctor Rukovsky is taking care of the pass herself, so I know you're not being discharged. You have appointments in our salon in an hour for hairstyling, manicures and facials."

Faith interpreted for Summer.

"Tell her the KGB gave me enough of a facial the other day and haircuts aren't much use to me."

The nurse let out a final huff and left. Summer rolled out of the bed and tracked down the coffee smell like an undercaffeinated bloodhound. He lifted the metal covers from a plate. "I think I'm going to need you to translate this, too."

Faith walked into the room, not bothering to tie the robe closed. She put her arms on his shoulders and kissed the top of his head. The fresh stubble tickled her lips. "What have we got? Scrambled eggs, blini, sausage and kasha. I'd say this is the kitchen's best stab at an American breakfast." She reached over his shoulder, grabbed a thin Russian pancake, rolled it up and took a bite.

"Sit down and join me. Aren't you starving?" Summer shoveled eggs into his mouth.

"Yeah, but I'm curious what they brought us."

"Clothes are clothes, and you've never cared a whole lot about them."

"No, but I want to know what they're planning for us." Faith opened the wardrobe, which was carved with the usual hammers and sickles, and she unzipped the vinyl garment bag. "Summer, I think you'll want to see this."

"Can't we have the fashion show after breakfast?"

Faith lifted open the lid of a hatbox, put the hat on her head and walked into the sitting room.

"Where the heck did they get that?" Summer pushed his chair back and followed Faith to the wardrobe. He pulled out a hanger with a white jacket.

"How the hell did they get ahold of one of my dress uniforms? They even got my medals right."

A few hours later, the driver opened the door of the Chaika limousine. Zara eased herself out, favoring her injured arm. She hugged Faith, their bodies pressing as tightly against each other as their respective injuries allowed. When they pushed apart, Faith kissed her forehead.

"We did it." Zara shook Summer's hand and kissed him on the cheeks.

"That's what I hear. It's been a pleasure to work with you, colonel." He slipped his hand behind her back and embraced her.

"The pleasure's been mine, commander."

"Glad the first joint Navy-KGB mission was a success, not that the Navy planned or had anything to do with it."

"Neither did the KGB." Zara smiled and motioned for them to climb into the limo.

"As a matter of fact, I'm not so sure about wearing my uniform here, but I guess it'll add credibility when we go to the embassy. That *is* where we're going now, isn't it?"

"I'm so sorry I got you into all this." Zara took Faith's hand and squeezed it.

"I was pulled into it before you got involved. I don't think I'd be alive without you."

"Faith, you need to know," Zara continued in Russian, "Berlin wasn't some honey-trap to solidify your relationship with the KGB. What I expressed was entirely personal and—"

"You don't need to explain yourself, but you should understand that kind of friendship isn't for me, not now."

Summer looked out the window, pretending not to listen to the two women, even though he really didn't understand the language.

"Let me finish." Zara switched to English. "You're a unique woman. I wish things could've been a little different, but I'm happy for you. As soon as I saw you two together, it was obvious to me you shared something very deep. I wish you much happiness."

"You already know?"

"Our walls have ears. And the charge nurse has a big mouth."

Faith hugged her, careful not to put pressure on her shoulder. "This awful experience reminded us both that no matter who's been in our lives, or whether we saw each other every day or once a year, we've been the most important person for each other. Right after he joined the Navy we were going to get married, but I could never quite settle on a date."

"Drives me crazy trying to pin this one down on anything." Summer tilted his head toward Faith. "I finally just gave up."

"If this whole ordeal has taught me anything, it's that you can't wait too long or history passes you by."

"So does this mean you're engaged again?"

Faith looked away from Summer. "I plan on staying here for a month or two and holding you to your word regarding the import-export business. We both suspect he's going to be tied up for a while in a long inquiry into what's happened here."

"My security clearance is probably blown to hell after this. Every time it's come up, I've hit snags because of Faith. To date I've squeaked by, and I've always been kind of amazed I did, but now I wouldn't be surprised if I end up having to resign my commission with an honorable discharge—seven years shy of retirement."

"I probably shouldn't say it, but there are other employment opportunities," Zara said.

"Thanks, but no thanks, comrade." Summer grinned.

"Only doing my job."

"There are tons of ordnance in the world just begging for an EOD guy to clean up. I've heard rumors the Navy's going to give back an island in Hawaii it's used for target practice forever, and some civilian contractor's gotta take that hardship post. So what are you going to do now, Zara?" Summer looked out the window as they drove through downtown Moscow.

"You only leave the KGB two ways: retirement or death. So I'll still be in the business, but definitely not in Berlin. I don't know if anyone's told you, but they decided this wasn't the time to remove Honecker."

"No way," Faith said.

"No one—including your people—wants speculation about how close we came to war over Berlin. They'll give it a few months, during which we basically run everything from behind the scenes. He won't be able to scratch his balls without a Soviet adviser approving it. We'll remove him this fall, when no one will link it to this week. Until he's gone and Kosyk's friends are purged from the MfS, Berlin isn't safe for me or Faith. For that matter, neither is Moscow until we're sure all the conspirators have been rounded up and Kosyk is found. Both of us have to disappear for a while. I'll see it through that you get set up in a storefront here, but you're going to have to wait. Personally, I'd love to be sent back to the San Francisco residency. I'd love to bird again at Point Reyes, and there's a club in the Castro I wouldn't mind going back to, but I'm afraid my affiliation with you two will cause our counterintelligence to view me as too big a risk to be deployed to the US again."

Summer watched as they drove past the red brick wall of the Kremlin, turned left onto Red Square and passed through the gate into the Kremlin compound. "I get the feeling we're not going to the embassy. So, is this going to be some kind of press conference?"

"They don't want the press involved," Zara said.

The driver stopped at a side entrance to a massive yellow building that Faith thought housed the Supreme Soviet. Viktor Petrov, special assistant to Gorbachev, greeted them at the door and escorted them into a wood-paneled elevator. Everyone else stared at the lit numbers while Faith admired a relief depicting a peasant woman bundling sheathes of grain.

"This way, please." Petrov held the elevator door open while everyone filed out into the hall. "Commander Summer, we realize you compromised yourself in regard to your government to save the life of Secretary Gorbachev and to de-escalate events in Berlin. Although we've put a press blackout in place, we are cooperating fully with the Americans so they understand your exact role in the matter. For your sake, we wouldn't want them to misconstrue things."

"And think I'm a spy. No, we wouldn't want that."

They followed Petrov into a banquet hall. A dozen Soviet generals and admirals were standing around, sipping cocktails and munching hors d'oeuvres, as were an American Army colonel and a handful of civilians. Everyone stopped talking and applauded when they entered the room.

Mama Whitney waddled over and hugged them. A distinguished gentleman waited for her to finish, then kissed Zara on both cheeks.

"I didn't think I'd ever be welcome back in these walls," he said in Russian.

Zara kissed the gentleman on the cheek. "I'd like all of you to meet my father, Anton Antonovich."

Before they all could finish shaking hands, Petrov interrupted. "You need to meet some people." He ushered the three away, then turned to the parents, shrugged his shoulders and said in Russian, "Protocol." He led them around the room, introducing them to an assortment of dignitaries, including the American Ambassador, the military attaché and someone from the political section.

The African-American colonel extended his hand to Faith. "I'm Colonel Holton Wilson, the American military attaché. Very pleased to meet you."

"*You're* Colonel Wilson?" Summer said.

"I was when I got up this morning." His teeth glistened. "Commander Summer, you sure got some folks' attention in Washington."

"This is going to sound strange," Summer said, "but is there another Military Attaché posted to the embassy—another Colonel Wilson, a white guy? I think I know the answer to this one, too, but is there a lawyer, a husky woman named Chris Goldfarb?"

"What's this all about?" Wilson said.

"These two claiming to be from the embassy stopped the KGB's interrogation and met with me for a good hour and a half yesterday morning."

Faith and Zara made eye contact and smiled.

"The embassy's been trying to find you ever since your call to Indian Head. This morning when we were invited to this reception was the first we knew of your whereabouts." Wilson snagged an hors d'oeuvre from a waiter.

"Looks like you were false-flagged, honey." Faith patted him on the arm.

Summer shot a glance at Zara. She nodded her confirmation. "At least you don't have to rough people up that way." Zara took a sip of white wine. "I've heard stories from some old-timers of how we had a whole team in Berlin right after the war who'd pose as American Army officers. They'd approach Soviet citizens who they thought were at high risk for defection. They'd convince them to go over to the Americans, pick them up in a fake American staff car and pretend to drive them to a safe house in West Berlin, but they never left the East. They'd debrief the poor bastards and ship them off to the gulags—if they were lucky."

Petrov ushered Faith, Summer and Zara to seats directly behind a podium. "If I could have your attention, please," Petrov announced in both English and Russian, but before he could finish, General Secretary Gorbachev strolled up behind him.

Gorbachev lowered the mike and it screeched loudly. He jumped back in an exaggerated gesture and turned it off. "Andrei Sergeyevich, you hear me back there?" A silver-haired officer nodded. Gorbachev continued, "I always know that if the admiral hears me, everyone can, so I won't use this thing." Everyone in the room laughed; a few delayed chuckles betrayed the non-Russian speakers who were relying upon the interpreter standing to his right. "Today we're honoring three individuals who placed concerns of our country and world peace above their own. For this, my country is grateful. And for saving my life, I am personally indebted." Gorbachev flashed a smile and launched into a long discourse on the importance of Soviet-American cooperation to world peace and regional stability in Central Europe.

Faith tuned him out and focused on Summer. She surprised herself at how happy she felt as she daydreamed of a vacation together on the shores of Siberia's Lake Baikal. When a man approached Gorbachev carrying several small cases, Faith started listening again.

"Although the world cannot know what these three individuals did for the preservation of peace, I would like to recognize them today on behalf of the people of the USSR. Lieutenant Colonel Zara Antonovna Bogdanov, I am promoting you today to full colonel, with all the rights and privileges of that rank. Congratulations." Gorbachev clapped and the crowd followed his lead. The aide opened the first small box. The Soviet leader held up a red ribbon with a gold star dangling from it. A raised hammer and sickle decorated the center of the star. "Colonel Bogdanov, Lieutenant Commander Maxwell Summer and Professor Faith Whitney, in recognition of your courage and your heroic actions, I am pleased to bestow upon you our highest title, Hero of the Soviet Union."

Faith stood and tugged at Summer. "Get up."

"I don't know if I can accept this. I'm an American."

"Don't blow it for me. Do you know how hard these are to get hold of?" Faith whispered as she pulled him up from his chair.

Gorbachev shook their hands and pinned the awards on their chests. Summer's hung beside his Purple Heart. Gorbachev held up another medal attached to a red ribbon bordered with gold stripes; gold bands of wheat framed a platinum bust of Lenin above a small red enameled hammer and sickle.

"That better not be what I think it is," Summer whispered to Faith.

"Not as hard to get, but right up there. Eight hundred bucks on the black market. We'll have to sneak them out before this is over because the Sovs will take them from us for safekeeping."

"I can't have a cameo of that Bolshevik stuck to me."

"And I present, to these Heroes of the Soviet Union, the Order of Lenin for their actions strengthening peace between peoples. Congratulations."

Faith followed Zara's lead and thanked the General Secretary without trying to make a speech. She held her breath as Gorbachev pinned the Order of Lenin on Summer's dress white US Navy uniform.

Summer opened his mouth.

Summer, no.

He hesitated, then said, "I appreciate the gesture of goodwill, Mr. General Secretary. As you know, I was not acting on behalf of my government, but as an individual thrown into extraordinary circumstances. As an officer of the US Navy, I'm not sure I can accept an honor from your government like this. Don't get me wrong, but my understanding is the only American military you ever hand these things out to are spies. We all know I'm definitely not one of those."

Gorbachev stared at the floor as he listened to the translation, and then he looked up. "I shared your concern when I first discussed it with my staff, but they tell me we've awarded our highest military honor, the Order of Victory, to your General Eisenhower. You're in the company of your presidents, Commander Summer."

After the ceremony broke up, the assortment of military brass and high-ranking Communist Party members again shook hands with the honorees, but Zara's father and Faith's mother were too enthralled with each other to pay attention. Afterward the US military attaché and the Ambassador strolled up to them.

"Lenin looks real pretty on you, commander," the military attaché said with a chuckle.

"How in the heck am I ever going to explain this one to my CO?" Summer glared at Lenin resting on his chest.

"Don't worry; I'll take it off your hands as soon as we get it out of the country." Faith kissed him on the cheek. "And that Hero of the Soviet Union status will get you all kinds of perks here—free public transportation, a free yearly visit to a sanitarium, one free first-class domestic round trip on Aeroflot each year—"

"Don't forget priority on the housing waiting list and an extra fifteen square meters of living space," Zara said.

"And speaking of getting out of the country," Faith said as Summer handed her a flute of Crimean champagne, "is the embassy going to help us get our passports? I don't know how much of the story you know, but I seem to have lost my passport in the shuffle and Summer was kidnapped and brought here without any documents."

"In due time we'll get them to you. It's a long process to verify your identities and your stories," Colonel Wilson said.

"With all due respect, sir, that's bullshit. I don't think you have any doubts who we are," Summer said.

"I'll begin the debriefing with Commander Summer this afternoon. Someone else will be speaking with you, Doctor Whitney. Other folks are flying in from Washington to talk with you both, meet with Soviet officials and go over the evidence they've shared with us. I suspect we can have this wrapped up on this end within a week or so, and then you'll have some meetings stateside."

"Sir, I have a date this afternoon that I've been waiting over a decade for," Summer said.

"Then a few more days won't matter. We're going to have to keep you two separated until we've finished talking to you."

Zara hurried to swallow a canapé. "Colonel Wilson, I regret to inform you Doctor Whitney and Commander Summer were both injured performing their heroic actions and are currently patients at one of our top medical clinics." Zara pulled a document from her inside jacket pocket and flashed it to the embassy officials. "Their doctor agreed to allow them only three hours away from the clinic, and she agreed to this only after Gorbachev himself persuaded her to go against her own medical judgment. As soon as they're fit to be released, we will deliver them to your embassy. Good day, gentlemen. It was a pleasure." Zara led Faith and Summer away.

"What about Mama Whitney and your dad?" Summer glanced back at them. They were laughing together as if they had known each other a lifetime.

"Let's leave them to themselves. My father hasn't flirted like that with a woman since my mother died."

"You're certain she's dead?" Faith said.

"Faith!" Summer elbowed her.

As they hurried to the elevator, Faith turned to Summer and said, "You know,

I was thinking about that date this afternoon. We're already dressed for the occasion, and I'm sure, with a little baksheesh, we can work our way into the schedule at the People's Wedding Palace." Faith gestured wildly with her hands. "They're set up using communist iconography in place of religious symbols. Red satin, busts of Lenin everywhere—better than Vegas."

"You're crazy." Summer punched the button for the elevator.

"And that's why you love me. I could never warm up to a church wedding, but I could really get into this. The Sovs have these great traditions, like the bride in her wedding gown laying roses at the tomb of the Unknown Soldier and Lenin's—"

"You want me to get married in front of a statue of Lenin? I'd never be able to show anyone my wedding pictures. I know you can't be serious."

"It's not any weirder than in front of a statue of a bleeding martyr on a cross."

"She's got a point," Zara said as they walked into the elevator. "I'd be honored to be a witness if you did it here."

"Summer, if we do it here today under the eyes of Lenin, I'll even ask my mother to officiate. She's ordained in Arkansas."

Just before the door closed, a hand reached inside and stopped them. Gorbachev joined them in the elevator. He nodded to them and then stared at the lit floor numbers.

Summer lowered his voice. "Mama Whitney in a communist chapel? Now I'm sure you're pulling my leg."

"Careful, Summer, or history will pass you by again." Faith backed up, giving Gorbachev a few more respectful inches of space.

"You know, the thing about history is sometimes it goes too damn fast for some of us to keep up," Summer whispered, barely moving his lips.

"Then can I at least interest you in a visit to Lenin's mausoleum? Time creeps in there. As Heroes of the Soviet Union, we can jump to the front of the line." Faith motioned to Summer's new decorations.

The General Secretary eyed the medals and smiled.

Summer then put his arm around her.

"Not now." Faith blushed.

Gorbachev winked at Summer.

"I don't care if he is a world leader." He pulled Faith close and kissed her. "You've got a deal."

EPILOGUE

Go on, get out.
Last words are for fools who haven't said enough.
—KARL MARX